"The man who gives voice to injustice will never go unnoticed, nor shall avenging justice pass him by."

The book of Wisdom

The Resurgence:

Chronicles of the Shadow Chaser

Randal J. Belaire

The Resurgence: Chronicles of the Shadow Chaser
By Randal J. Belaire
First Published 2010
ISBN 978-0-9865363-0-4
Copyright © 2005 Canadian copyright registration number 1027158
Copyright © 1995 Standard copyright.

Come visit the world of the Shadow Chaser on the internet at:
www.theshadowchaser.com

Acknowledgments

No Author Stands Alone

Thank you God for giving me the gift to tell a story and the imagination to travel to another world. To my mom, Lillian, my strength and my spirit. To my dad, Hector, who was taken away before his time, I know you are watching from heaven. To my family, my brother, Ron, my sister-in-law, Kathleen, my nephews, Mark and Ron Jr., and my nieces, Joanne and Kathy. To my cousin, Rene Lecompte, thank you for listening to my story ideas. To my friends who stood by me, they were always there when I needed them, in the good times and the bad. Special thanks to my two best friends, Mike Gennings and Derek Van-Hoof.

To the teachers who influenced me the most. Joseph Beaulieu and Mark Furlong. For they were the torches that lit up the dark road of reality—for that I thank you.

To my team, marketing adviser and copy editor, Wayne Carrie, web development, Gregg Thomas, editor, Ernst Ambler, and Ron Belaire Jr., inker. Without your help, the story would not have been possible. You guys are the best.

Thank you to owners, Nicholas and Xenia Kastanias and the staff of Fresco Café & Grill for allowing me to spend countless hours drinking java and bringing the Shadow Chaser alive with my laptop. Also, for allowing me to sell the novel at your establishment; you have all made me feel like part of the family.

Finally, to my readers. Thank you all for taking a leap of faith with me as you enter the world of the Shadow Chaser. For a story is nothing without the reader.

Special Thank You Page

I wish to thank all the over 1,600 members of my Facebook fan group, "The Shadow Chaser: Enter the Shadow Crypt." The following names are from my members who have replied to the special thank thread and who have supported me along the way. Members are welcome to check this link: www.theshadowchaser.com/members. Thank you all, my friends.

Michael Netzer; the late Dave Simons; Danny-Dog Kelly; Michael Perkey; Sandy Schroeder Bucholtz; Chantal Eggert Smith; Jody Peloquin; Jade Arcade; Jay Piscopo; Larry Swearingen; Michael D Hamersky; Tyrell Tinnin; Ryan Deschambault; Riel Langlois; Jacqui More; Giovanni Medina; Amy Lord; Jenffer A Jay; Cheryl Antonio; Nicole Falk; Lori Louise Collicott; Avery Collicott; Dorothy Gitman; Ambar Nair; AJ Murphy; Dana Ledford Arcade; Alexander Arcade; Ed Brown; Veselin Brajović; Jeremy Bell; Dan Barnes; Clint Csori; Jeffrey Peter Hauck; Genevieve Andrews-Kelly; Kimberly Dunn-Blais; Scott Wlock; Tammie Lamothe; Manny DeJesus; John "The Shadow Chaser" Stein; Raymond Jacob; Deborah Voigt; A.P. Fuchs; Xylon Otterburn; Steve Bartlett; Nolan Kinshella; Tammy Perry; Kei White; Pempho Louise Kabinda; Monique Laverdure Plummer; Mark A. Saxton; Bruce Durham; Mariska Hadienns; Rigs Jimenez; Rachel Robbins; Cody Wood; Michael A Gordon; Jim Mohan; Ronaldo Demersio; Monique Jodouin; Cat Gough; Jerry Laverdure; Justin Jude Carmona; Erik W Hendrix; Ashley Simpson; Erin Mac Dougall; Maf Comics; Tom Perna; Chris Marcellus; Jamie Mahoney McMann; Julie Burnett MacLean; Robert Jaz; Michelle Kuhrazee; Sean Koury; Patti Lynn Payne; Todd Banks; Roger F. Castro; Jean Lepage; John Smith; Travers Cleeman; Myra Barnhart; Sophie Lacoste; Pannel Vaughn; Denise Gilmore; Robert Scaife; Nickolas Ste-Croix; Mary Wilson; Susan Renee Maltby; Tracy Nancekivell; Amber Churchill; Amanda Popkie; Debra Delorme; Billie Rae Bates; Corey Eggert; Ken Carnahan; Angel Maria Martínez; Mark Chagdes; Jason White; Michael Wood; Dan Omega; Roderick Mackinnon; Lee Racca Bird; Steven Thadeus; Mike Lawson; Brayden Hauraney; Michelle Lee Jeanneret; Kevin Lee; María Isabel Flores; Lisa Hager-Duncan; Frank Jerry; Diane Balqish Nur; Heath Desjarlais; Art Boulton; Scott Dutton; Ron Lauzon; Sam Welch; Diane Ozerow; Jenna Cyr; Tony Bohemier; Frank Schildiner; Nasrullah Anwar; Doc Boucher; Gary Fellman; Glynis Coutsides; Shirley Martin; Trina Johnson; Sarah L. Gerhardt; Bonnie Toews; Tera Maguire; Tiina Birgitta Räisänen; Dave Mintun; David Price; John Ottinger III; Lynda D'argensio; Rachel Bisson; Sergio Clavijo; Benjamin Widdowson; Jerry Butler; Kevin Agot; Adam Dechanel; Dennis Johnson; Scoot Away; Duane Johnson; Monique Poulin; Patricia V Stoyles; Doug Devries; Mark-Anthony Cardenas; Agimat Comics; Olubusayo Akano; Javier Sama Acevedo; Paula LaPierre; Phil Latter; Elisabeth Fry; John Donahue; Cory Van Hoof; Gail Kelly; Zak Kinsella; Jackie Robar; Chris Perridas; Lynn Arscott;

Jon Holland; Cheryle Meador Wilson; Mike Vaillancourt; David Rodriguez; Bill Code; Kirk Harris; Elleanor Donna Tricia; Derek Cranmer; Luis Rafael Martinez; James Kenneth Woodward; Alexander Adams; Napat Phromphruk; Samantha Moss; Cindy Dion; McKinzie S. Heart; Clayton Murwin-The Hero Maker"; Jw Schnarr; Marisa Dawson; Jordan Dunn; Caroline Prior; Michelle Cox Adler; Kelsey Pitchenese; Tc Ford; Maddy Harmer; Jeffrey Allan Boman; Joseph J. O'Donnell; Brenda Agard of I Poetry TV; Dexter Wee; Nathan Weber; Kristoffer J. Lapointe; Stacey Groulx; Jamie Alverez; Randy Grover; Rich Gould; Eduardo Lugaro; Matthew Kennedy O'Toole; Preston Shuttlesworth; Natasha Laramee; Mark Poe; Ulysse Bouchard; Aline Bouchard; Chris Aldo; Corey Eggert; Brenda Laporte; Murielle Brochu; Rudy Vasquez; Michael Garriques; Karen Ranger; Eric Vogin; Kenway Afam Oforeh; Clive Kay; Stephanie Pernell Morris; Christina Wilbur; Tina Klein; Baden James Mellonie; Christa Ingrid; Sandy McIntire; Steven Wilcox; ComicZone Az; Kylie Utz; Calvin Daniels; Ken Anthony II; Doug Shackleton; Dean Buchfink; Gerald Hall; Roger Rautio CEO The Comic Book Hall of Fame; Jester Press Comics; Shelly Loback-Moncion; Jeff Richardson; Cheryl Shoals; Shadow Welch; Max Radico; Anastasia Cassella-Young; sir'Valentino Tino; Chris Lee; Vicky Healy VanMassenhoven; David Zuzelo; Damiano Manduca; James Babarinde; Maureen Mirault; Bev Bieber ; Judy Raymond; Bearded Skull Comics; Manon Pleau Hearty; Brad Hearty; James Michael Czenk; Nichole Weir; Joe Nicolazzo; Alexandre Roberto Chieffi Marengo; Zedekiah Zèðèkìäh Oenga; Michel Smithers; Bubba Beasley; Gilbert Ferretula Murillo; Mike Dubisch; Deb Pike; Bennett Pisek; Dawn Innes; John Shires; Mike Spicer; Darrell Goza; Nonstoptoys; Imre Pinczi; Ashley Schulz; James Michael Czenk; Lynn Neadow; Jason Morgan; Kenneth Jacobs; Jimmie Vinson; Ivano Daccò Andromeda; Tess Blaedow; Zuzana Stovicek; Devon Camel; Mason Krug; Craig Anderson; Renato Iattoni; Frank Simonian; Ricky Blais; Paula Turner; David E. Roy; Shae Larocque; Dawn Laurie Wilson Durant; John McCormick; Patrick Charette of Charettes-ArtGallery; Adrian Putrawan; Ryan Gaumer; Angel Sirois; Laurie Juspeczyk; Line Giguere; Christopher Durant; Marc Rheaume; Aron Larocque; Dennis Lauzon; Jason McLeod; Amy Shultz; Rhiannon Blaedow; Merryn Blaedow; Dylan Laverdure; JMark Sappenfield.

Thank you all!

Chapter 1

Chicago, Illinois. USA. October 30, 1987:

" You have ten hours to bring me five million dollars, or your little boy is dead," the voice on the phone said. Tomas Collins hung up while the police looked on.

Collins asked, "Did you get it?" He tried to swallow, but his throat was dryer than the desert.

"No, we just missed it," the policeman said. "But we'll be here when they call back."

"It's Stavros," Collins shouted. "He wants my company, and I won't give it to him. So, he has kidnapped my son—and he's going to kill him!"

"Tom, please. The FBI has had great success with kidnapping cases," the man in a navy blue three-piece suit said.

"He's right, Mr. Collins, we are the best at what we do," the agent replied. "Could you please explain your connection with Antonio Stavros?"

"A few months ago, Stavros came to my office and wanted to buy forty-nine per cent of my equity in the business. He offered me fifty million dollars. I felt I had to turn him down because of his reputation and connections with organized crime. His face is all over the news."

"Did he threaten you or your family at that time?"

"No, not at first, but weeks later, I received some strange phone calls, and experienced some odd encounters on the street. Last week, I was almost driven off the road."

"Could you tell us more about your business?"

"Collins Hope is a financial aid institution," Collins replied. "We help low-income families with loans to help them with mortgages and other bills."

1

"I can see why Stavros would want to put his claws in a business like yours. He could control the loans and make a profit as well as having a front to move into the East Side of Chicago," the agent said.

"But he didn't actually threaten you, Tom. You can't just say that he is responsible for Patrick's kidnapping," his friend said.

"Earl, you know what he's capable of doing. Stavros is a powerful man. Agent Flynn, can you absolutely guarantee my son's safety? Can you look me in the eye and guarantee you will bring my son home?" Before Agent Flynn could reply, a frantic woman entered the room. Tears streamed down her cheeks and fear consumed every inch of her body.

She collapsed in his arms and asked, "Tom, is it true they have him?"

Collins cradled his fragile wife. "Diana, we'll get him back."

The phone rang.

The police took their positions and waited for Flynn's instructions.

"Let's get it right this time, people," Flynn said, and nodded at Collins to answer it.

"Hello."

"I want you to put the money in a Swiss account. The account number is 674239-12. There's been a change of plans," the rugged voice said. "We want half of the money in half the time, or the little brat is dead."

"I will do whatever you want," Collins said, "but please let me talk to my son." Silence and a sense of dread enveloped the room; then he heard the voice of a frightened five-year-old boy.

"Mommy, Daddy! I want to go home." The voice of their little boy quivered. Collins felt the icy touch of fear within his son. A frustrated Collins tried in vain to reassure his child with the warmth of his voice.

"Daddy is here, son. Everything is going to be okay." But before the child could utter another word, the kidnapper took the phone away.

"Well, wasn't that touching, but you better have the money in five hours, or the next time you want to talk to your boy it will be through Jesus."

"You'll have the money, I promise." The dial tone ended the call.

"Patrick," his wife yelled at the top of her lungs.

"Everything will be all right, Diana. We'll pay them what they want, and then we'll get Patrick back home." Collins clutched onto his wife with all the affection he could offer in this time of horror.

"Did we get it this time?" Flynn asked.

"Stand by, sir," the agent replied, checking his equipment.

Uncertain of the child's future, Flynn said, "Alright, men, we'll monitor this house and the phone lines in case they call back."

"Sir, we have them," the agent proclaimed.

"Where are they?"

"According to the scanner, they are about three miles south by the old, abandoned theatre on Racine Street."

"Let's get going. We'll notify you when we get there, Mr. Collins," Flynn said, but before he could leave, Collins grabbed his left arm.

"Again, Agent Flynn, I ask you. Can you promise me that you will bring back our son to us?" Tears ran down his face.

Flynn replied, "Nobody can make that promise, sir." Flynn turned towards the door and left to deal with the unexpected.

Unknown to both, the Collins's and the FBI, someone else was eavesdropping on the various conversations within the house and the telephone calls from the abductors. Approximately thirty yards away from the Collins family home, a parked van with Ontario plates appeared abandoned. But inside sat a man surrounded by equipment that he installed for electronic surveillance. Arthur Brown knew what Tomas and Diana Collins were feeling—having himself suffered from the pain of losing a loved one. Ten years ago, a serial rapist and his gang had killed his wife, Claire. The system failed him and freed the perpetrators.

We, the jury, find the defendants not guilty by reason of insanity.

The words of the jury foremen haunted his life to this day. At that moment, Brown swore the guilty would be held responsible for hurting the innocent. He spent the next five years training both his physical frame and mental psyche to prepare himself for the war in which he was about to enlist—the war on injustice. Brown, a man in his mid-thirties, but he was already one of the most prolific inventors of his generation. He used his knowledge to a tremendous advantage. A genius, thirty years ahead of his time, Brown had created numerous weapons and a combat suit he used against the scum of society. The black suit consists of high-tech fabric overall garment that covered his entire body, a long cloak, and a black fedora, which he used as an advanced type of boomerang. He even installed red lights in his cowl to make it appear he had red eyes, an illusion to fool the enemy. Also, he equipped the cowl with an equalizer to mask his true voice and create the impression that the enemy would be fighting a spectre instead of a man. Brown pursued criminals the law had determined to be 'Untouchable' either because of a lack of evidence or because of loopholes in the justice system. While fighting his war against evil, an expensive proposition, his resources dwindled. Allocating more time to the war at the detriment to his professional endeavours began to take a toll on his finances. But for now, the boy's life became his main priority. Brown traced the call with one of his newest inventions.

According to this, the party is being held at the harbour docks about four miles north of here. Stavros's men have the FBI believing they are further down south. It appears they have prepared for every contingency. Except for me. Brown thought while he stared at the computer screen.

"Stavros is up to his old tricks again. Well, it looks like it is time to balance the scales of justice for him and his associates." Brown closed his surveillance equipment.

3

The phone rang.

Brown grabbed the receiver of his car phone.

"Doctor Arthur Brown here."

"Art, it's Alex. I heard you were coming to Chicago on a business trip," the voice said.

"Alex, it is good to hear from you. Listen, you have caught me at a bad time. I am in a meeting. May I call you back?"

"Sure, Art. I just wanted to let you know we have a suite at the same hotel where you are staying, and I was wondering if we could get together tonight. Virginia wants to see you."

"Sounds great, Alex. I am in room 205. My meeting will not take long. I'll call you when I get a chance."

Taylor replied, "Excellent. I'll see you then." And Brown hung up. The business community considered Brown's best friend, Alexander Taylor, one of the up-and-coming stars in the business world. He had equity stakes in a number of companies most notably oil, mining, computers, and now he started to venture into the new biotechnology frontier. Taylor lived the life Brown could only dream of having. Rich as a small country, and married to a beautiful woman; indeed fortune smiled on Taylor. Even though he had earned his fortune the honest way, Brown felt a little envious of his friend's perfect life. However, Brown had no time to sink into self-pity.

"I only have four hours to save this child—or he's dead." Brown started to put on his combat suit.

"Arthur Brown has done all he can for the Collins family. Now, it's time for justice to come in and do its job." Brown pulled the mask over his face and activated the voice equalizer.

"Now, enter the Shadow Chaser," he said as he headed for battle.

Chapter 2

A stoic Antonio Stavros sat in his office and waited to hear from his bookkeeper. Cocky and arrogant, Stavros knew the authorities would not locate him in this old, abandoned warehouse located by the harbour close to Lake Michigan. The police considered Stavros the reigning king of the underworld. With the voice of a stern businessman, the looks of a Latino lover, and the temper of a pit bull, Stavros fought his way to the top in order to achieve this power. His recent activities included the murder of his mentor and boss, Big Daddy Marino. Upon his death, Stavros took over the Scorpio Syndicate. That alone demonstrated his true ambitions and brought fear among the other families. Stavros always got what he wanted, so when Tomas Collins took a stand against him—he had to pay. The price for his opposition would be the death of his son Patrick. Even if Collins delivered the ransom on time, the boy had to die. Stavros grabbed his phone and dialed one of his associates.

"Hello, Juan. Has our transaction been completed yet?"

"No, sir. However, our client has three hours left to complete the first half of his financial obligations. We will notify you the moment the transaction is complete, sir."

"Excellent. Until then, Juan." And he ended the call. Stavros always used business terms to carry out orders, just in case someone bugged his phone. In doing so, Stavros prevented the police from using any wiretap evidence against him. A man who looked like he belonged to the Capone gang entered his office.

"Mr. Stavros, the area is secured. I got Louis and Victor checking the port. We are ready to take out the little tyke when you want, sir."

"Get Clyde here. When the time comes, I will give him the order to waste the bambino," Stavros said. The goon complied with his order. Minutes later, another goon walked in the room.

"You sent for me, sir?"

"Clyde, has the kid finished his meal yet?" Stavros asked.

"Yes, he's done, Mr. Stavros," Clyde replied. "He's a good kid. He beat me in checkers."

"That doesn't surprise me, Clyde," Stavros said with an annoyed look on his face. "Once I get the call that the money is in my account—kill him."

"Kill him, sir?"

"Yes, kill him. What? Is there a damn echo in here?"

"No, sir. But he's just a kid." Clyde felt sympathy for the child. "We're goin' to get what we want. Why does the kid have to die, too?"

"You don't want to kill the kid?"

"No, sir. I don't."

"I understand, Clyde. I'll tell you what. You just go back there and get the kid ready, and we'll let him go—after we get the money of course." Stavros smiled.

"Thank you, sir."

"Now run along, Clyde," Stavros said. Clyde got up to leave the office, but Stavros had something else in mind. Stavros pulled the trigger and again. The bullets pierced Clyde's spine. The thug's body thumped onto the concrete floor.

Stavros said, "Never question my orders again, Clyde." And he walked towards the body and fired more shots into his former lackey. Three of his men ran towards the office.

"What's wrong, boss?" one of them asked as they spotted Clyde's dead body drowning in his own blood.

Stavros replied, "Oh, Clyde just gave me his resignation. Bobby, take him out of my sight. The rest of you, stay alert," Bobby remained with Stavros while the others continued with their duties.

"Where do you want me to put him, boss?"

"Put him with the boy. Let the little brat see what awaits him." Stavros smiled.

"Yes, boss," Bobby said before he dragged Clyde's body out of the office.

About three hours had passed, and still there was no answer—until now.

Brrrinnng!

"Hello," Stavros greeted. "Yes, Juan. Excellent, we'll meet shortly." Stavros hung the receiver in its place to end the conversation.

"Was that Juan, boss?"

"Yes, it was. Bobby, you know what to do."

"Quick and easy or slow and painful?"

"Oh, slow and painful, please," Stavros said. "Once you are done, come back here. I want us all to leave together." Bobby acknowledged his boss with a quick psychotic grin and left the office. He walked to the other side of the musty old warehouse before he arrived at the room. He opened the door and noticed the little boy beside Clyde's dead body.

Crying, the boy asked, "Can I go home now?"

Bobby took out his blades and grinned. "Yeah, kid, it's all over."

A voice came from the shadows. ***"You are right, scum. It is over for your kind. The ghost of justice is here to cleanse this dark room."***

A pair of red eyes stared at him in the darkness. "Who are you?" he shouted. "D--d--don't come any closer, or I'll gut ya." But the eyes moved closer.

"Your reign of terror is over, scum," the cold voice of death exclaimed.

"Stay away from me!" Bobby felt his heart racing, and his fear started to smother him.

"Are you going to talk or fight, scum?" The voice became even more frightening. Bobby tried to slash the shadowed stranger, but failed.

"My turn now!" The stranger grabbed the goon's left arm and broke it. His arm snapped like a twig and in three different places.

"My arm," he screamed in pain, but the stranger continued the attack.

Stavros was about to leave when he noticed that Bobby failed to report with his men.

"I know that psycho loves his work, but it has been over twenty minutes. Louis, go see what's taking him so long."

"Yes, boss." Louis headed for the room where they confined the boy. Along the way, he caught a whiff of the damp air around him, and it irritated his nostrils. When he arrived at the door, Louis opened it and expected to smell fresh blood. But when he stepped inside, he could not detect any odour of death.

"Hey, Bobby," he said. "Where the hell are ya?" With the exception of Clyde's dead body, Louis found himself alone in the deserted room.

"Over here," the voice shouted at him, and Bobby's body flew right on top of him. Louis groaned as the body connected with his chest. A few seconds later, Louis rose from the ground and checked his partner out.

He glanced at the mangled condition of his associate's body and asked, "Bobby, are you all right?"

"His conscience was getting to him. Now, it is your turn," the stranger said.

Louis shouted, "Oh God, it's the Devil." And he spotted the red eyes appear out of nowhere.

"Time's up." The stranger gave him a roundhouse kick before he could grab his handgun. The boot connected with a bone-jarring smack to the goon's face, and the thug fell like a stone onto the floor.

He shouted, "I'm getting the hell outta here." And he sprung from the floor and ran towards Stavros. Louis screamed in terror. "Boss. Boss. The Devil's got Bobby."

"What the hell are you talking about? What devil?" Stavros asked.

The voice said, *"He means me, Stavros."* The red eyes appeared to the last few of the syndicate.

"How the hell did you find me?" Stavros screamed.

"The stench of evil can be smelled everywhere. And you reek, murderer."

"That's no devil. He's the freak I was telling you about. He's been after me for months now, but tonight we kill him."

"Who the hell is he, boss?" Louis asked.

Stavros took out his weapon and replied, "They call him the Shadow Chaser."

Chapter 3

*S*tavros and his men had their guns pointing at the Shadow Chaser. The odds were not in his favour, but he did not care.

Stavros ordered, "Take him down, boys." His men began to discharge their guns. Their weapons fired like lighting for about a full minute before they stopped. The last of the shells rained down around them.

"He must be in those crates. Go fish him out, Mario," Stavros said. The thugs headed towards the damaged crates.

"He's not here, boss."

"Bullshit! He was just there," Stavros said when they noticed a cloud of smoke appear to the west of them.

"You can do better than that, scum. I saw your attack coming for days," Shadow Chaser said. The goon squad prepared to fire at him, but Stavros grabbed onto one of his men's shotgun.

"No, you morons. He's right on top of those gasoline barrels. If you miss him, you blow this place to kingdom come."

"You should listen to your boss, scum."

Louis kept his aim on the Shadow Chaser and said, "You can't stay up there forever, you gruesome son of a bitch!"

Shadow Chaser replied, *"Forever is all I have left. Now, it's time to level the playing field."* He snapped his fingers, and all the lights in the old warehouse extinguished in an instant.

"How the hell did he do that?" one of the goons demanded.

"I tell you, boss, this guy is the Devil. Who else could do that?" Louis pondered.

"He's not the Devil. He's just some creep in a fancy costume living out some childhood dream. Look sharp and watch where you are firing," Stavros warned his men. "One missed shot, and this place becomes a flare for all of Chicago to see." Stavros and his men skulked around the unlit building.

9

"Scum can run and hide, but justice will find you and show you no mercy." The voice of the Shadow Chaser surrounded the room. It was not difficult for him to extinguish the lights. Prior to the offensive, he configured a shutdown switch with one of his gadgets while the goons guarded the child. When he snapped his fingers with his left hand, he activated the miniature remote control with his right hand, creating the appearance that he could turn the lights off and on with just a thought. Miniature speakers installed throughout the room amplified his voice, creating a sense of omniscience throughout the theatre of engagement. Shadow Chaser knew it would intimidate Stavros's goons, but he knew Stavros wouldn't fall for his illusions. The psychological gamesmanship gave him an advantage against all of those guns aiming for him.

I count five guns—if I don't count Stavros. I see two of them have split up and are near the back exit. Now, is my time to attack. Shadow Chaser thought and looked through a pair of infrared binoculars. With this fancy gadget, he analyzed the entire room and prepared his strategy. He had the kid hidden in a closet in the same room where he found him. With no one near the room, the child remained safe—for now.

Louis and Mario scouted the back exit. Mildew covered the walls of the old structure and gave off the scent of isolation and abandonment. Both men had their weapons loaded and ready for the kill.

"I hope he comes here," Mario said. "We'll give him a reason for wearin' a mask!" But Louis did not share his friend's enthusiasm.

"I still think it's the Devil, man." Louis strained his eyes as he tried to see in the dark.

"You think everybody is the Devil. Your wife, kids, in-laws, and that little dame you had in the room last night." Mario smirked.

"An intoxicating danger, man." Louis laughed. "Say, why is he after the boss?"

"The way I hear it, the boss got away with killin' an undercover cop. The boss framed him as a dirty cop workin' for the Cabera family. The fuzz believed old man Cabera ordered the hit on the pig, so case closed, right?" Mario whispered. "Wrong. After that, the boss starts gettin' some strange letters and photos about his empire. And warned the boss about his crimes. Really freakin' weird."

"What do you mean weird, Mario?" Louis probed. He started to feel a little uncomfortable with his current situation.

"He was usin' some quotes from the Bible about justice and vengeance. Stuff about the reckonin'."

"The Bible! I told you the guy is the Devil!"

"Will you stop that devil crap!" Mario clapped his hand over Louis's mouth. "Do you want to let all of Chicago know we're here? Besides, do you want me to tell the rest of it?"

"Okay, man. So, what happened next?" Louis asked, and looked around the dark area.

"Well, about a month ago, the boss had a big shipment of heroin comin' in from Afghanistan. It was foolproof, but that's when the chaser guy came into the picture. You know how much the boss likes to have hidden cameras all over the place."

"Yeah, he calls it a good investment for an untrusting world."

"Well, the shipment was going good until the freak broke into the boss's office and took all of the dealers out, includin' our men."

"All of them dead?"

"None were killed—until the boss got to them of course. But he had knocked them around so much they wished they were dead. It took the freak about fifteen seconds, if that. Then he looked straight into the hidden camera and told the boss the Shadow Chaser was the one who would destroy him; the freak also said the boss's days were numbered."

"Then what?"

"Then this Shadow Chaser opened the boss's filing cabinet and took out all of the information he had on the cop, includin' the evidence that would clear the cop's name. He did this, so the boss could see everythin' on tape. Then he called the cops and told them about the drug deal."

"No wonder the boss wants this guy dead."

"It gets better. He then left about half of the shipment and a quarter of a million dollars behind for the cops to nail the guys he took down. When the sirens appeared, he ran with the rest of the money, the shipment, and the file."

"So, he kept it?"

"No, man. When our guys were at court, the DA got a parcel that contained the rest of the shipment, the money, the file, and a videotape," Mario said.

"But how did he get the tape?"

"It wasn't the boss's tape. He taped the event as it went on."

"You mean he had the whole bust planned?"

"Yeah, with the file, he cleared the cop's name. With his tape, he sent our boys to jail. But somehow, he contained the rest of the evidence the cops had, just in case the boss had any plans to bribe someone to make it disappear. And believe me the boss tried to get it back. This guy is a real pro."

"But the boss didn't get charged?"

"The guys said they acted alone and broke into his office to do the deal. The boss had a good alibi at the time of the crime. As for the file, one of our guys said they were gonna frame the boss by plantin' the file in his office."

"But you said the boss killed them. Didn't you?"

"The boss couldn't trust them, so he had them put on ice in jail."

"So, did the boss go after the freak?"

"When he arrived to his home after the trial, the boss got a phone call from the jerk. The voice told him the Shadow Chaser wouldn't rest until he stopped the boss. The boss had fake meetings with his lieutenants just in case this Shadow Chaser was gonna bug his discussions. Everybody in the family believed the boss was goin' to Florida. In the meantime, he hired some of the best hitters in the country to kill the freak. He mentioned that he would make an arms deal in Orlando. He gave the name of the building, the time, and the day."

"So, the man would take the bait, and the hitters would finish him off when he arrived."

"That was the idea, but it didn't work out the way the boss had planned it. The freak never showed up. We didn't hear zip from this guy for months. We thought someone killed the freak, or he got scared and quit. He was no longer chasin' the boss. Besides, the boss had a gang war to win, and he didn't have the time to play cat and mouse with a costumed idiot. So, he just went on with business as usual," Mario said.

"Until now."

"Yeah, until now," Mario replied. The words had just left his mouth when they heard a *crack* about five feet in front of them.

Louis asked, his voice on edge. "What was that?" He shook in his three-hundred-dollar shoes. The thug remained convinced that this stranger was the prince of darkness.

"I am gonna check it out. Wait here, Louis." Mario grabbed his shotgun and tightened his grip on it.

"You're not gonna leave me here alone, man." Louis started to feel his blood pressure rising. "The Devil is out there."

"What did I tell you, stupid? He's not the Devil. If he were the Devil, he would make me disappear before I had the chance to scream." Mario laughed. "Now stay here, I'll be right back." And then he stepped into the darkness.

Shadow Chaser listened to their conversation and remembered what happened on the night of the drug deal. He also recalled the false information he received from the bug during that meeting.

Stavros almost had me fooled with his scheme. It's a good thing I knew those hit men were waiting for me, or it could've gotten ugly—real ugly. Shadow Chaser thought as he observed Mario walking in his direction.

"Excellent. Now, is the time to take the offence." Shadow Chaser dove from the boxes to the ground. With panther-like reflexes, he positioned himself without Mario even hearing him, or knowing the better. Mario stood three yards away from a trap—unaware that the dark stranger awaited his next move.

Mario pointed his shotgun, aimed it all around him, and shouted, "Come out, come out wherever you are."

"As you wish." Shadow Chaser grabbed Mario from behind and took him out with a sleeper hold. Seconds later, he cuffed the goon with his manacles. Before he left the scene, the dark hero took off Mario's shoes and gagged him with his own pair of socks.

"I hope you wash them frequently," Shadow Chaser said. The mask he wore covered his smile.

Louis became more anxious by the minute. Mario had been gone for about ten minutes, and he should have returned by now. Sweat dripped from the tip of his nose, his body reeking of perspiration. His heart pounded faster. Faster. In the end, he snapped the silence with the tension of his own anxiety.

"Mario, where the hell are you? Come on, man." He trembled. "Stop this crap right now. I'm serious!" His speech pattern shifted from scared to terrified.

"Mmmff!" The noise came from the area where Mario went.

Louis asked, "Mario, is that you?" Reluctant to continue, but his fear of failing Stavros outweighed his horror of the dark stranger. Louis shuffled towards the sound.

"Mario, where are you?" Louis probed again. "Where are you?" Louis turned around and saw a pair of red eyes staring back at him. Shadow Chaser's left boot connected with Louis's right hand. The thunderous blow sent the goon's gun tumbling to the ground. The darkness made it impossible for Louis to find his lone insurance marker. The red eyes closed in, and the figure began to speak.

"Time to join your friend." Shadow Chaser held onto a gun with a silencer attached.

"No. Don't kill me, man," Louis shouted, but the dark vigilante fired his weapon. A dart whistled towards him like a thin, fast wind through a crack. Seconds passed; then Louis fell to his knees.

Louis looked at the dart in his chest and said, "You drugged me, man."

Shadow Chaser replied, *"I wouldn't waste bullets on you, scum. I'm on a tight budget."* Louis fell unconscious from the sleep-inducing drug.

"Two down, three to go." Shadow Chaser left the thug and continued his crusade.

Stavros and the rest of his men were around the area when they heard a scream.

"That sounded like Louis," one goon said.

Another goon approached Stavros and said, "I got the flashlight from your office like you asked, boss."

"Give it to me. Now follow my lead." The goons followed him. As they got closer to the back exit, they heard a strange muffled sound.

"Mmmmf! Mmmf!" The noise grew louder.

"It's coming from over there," Stavros said while he shined the flashlight to the right. The goons followed the sound. One of them scouting the area almost tripped over a body.

The goon said, "Boss, it's Mario!" Stavros and the others ran towards him.

"What happened here, Mario?" Stavros demanded, and yanked the socks out of his henchman's mouth.

"It was the Shadow Chaser. He got me, and I think he got Louis, too," Mario said. The glare from the flashlight began to annoy his eyes.

"Boss, I found Louis here. He's fast asleep," the other goon said.

"Are you trying to say that two of the top hitters in the syndicate got slapped around by some freak in a Halloween costume," Stavros said with anger in his voice.

"He got us by surprise, boss," Mario said while the other goon tended to Louis.

"It looks like he shot Louis with some sort of tranquilizer, boss," the goon said.

Stavros took out his gun and said, "Well, he's not gonna feel this then—will he." Stavros aimed it at Louis's head and fired.

Bramm! Bramm! Bramm!

The bullets pierced through Louis's skull like a sewing needle through fabric. The rest of the men felt first disgust towards their employer; then a sense of anxiety, no one dared to debate the issue. Aware that the penalty for failure was death, the men remained silent. Mario watched the blood spilling to the ground and feared he would soon be next.

"Boss, it wasn't my fault. I tried to stop him," Mario sobbed. "I honestly tried to stop him."

"Mario, please. I hate to see a grown man cry. I know you tried, but don't take it so hard," Stavros said. "I have nothing against you, so I'm not going to kill you." Then he untied Mario.

"You're not?" Mario said, controlled by fear.

"No, I have too much respect for you. You're like a son to me."

"Thanks, boss," Mario said.

"I don't have the heart to shoot you." Stavros looked at the third goon and said. "Jack, would you do the honours?"

"Yes, Mr. Stavros." Jack aimed his machine gun at Mario.

"No, please. I'll do anythin'," Mario yelled.

"You had your chance. Waste him," Stavros shouted. The goon fired upon his former colleague.

"Nooo," Mario screamed, but they ignored his cry. Each round exploded like a cannon. When the smoke from the shots dissipated, they witnessed Mario's lifeless, bloodstained body.

"Anybody else going to fail me now?" Stavros asked.

"No, boss. That Shadow Chaser guy is as good as dead," they vowed.

"Good. Now, let's get back to work. You three search the area; I will meet up with you later."

"What are you gonna do, boss?" Jack said.

Stavros whispered, "I got a surprise for our friend." And he left the area.

In the shadows, the dark vigilante had just witnessed the death of two of Stavros's men. He did not care if the criminals would kill each other off. But Antonio Stavros did not play by the rules—even by the mob's standards. Stavros needed no reason to kill. Shadow Chaser knew he had to stop Stavros, now more than ever—even if it meant dying in the attempt.

Their deaths were ruthless, even for their kind. Even I never thought Stavros would have gone over the edge as he did a few minutes ago. Shadow Chaser thought. *I have to get the child out of here. So, the only way you're going to do that, Art, is to finish this now.* Shadow Chaser noticed the last of the men walking around the area and looking for blood.

"Let's see if they are ready for this." Shadow Chaser plunged from the crate and drove two of the three goons to the ground.

Two heads cracked against each other, then the surface of the floor, rendering them unconscious.

"Shadow Chaser," Jack screamed. The dark spectre with the red eyes turned and stared straight at him, as if it were judgment day.

"It's over, scum." Shadow Chaser bounced back to his feet and waited for Jack's next move.

Jack took out his gun and said, "I'm not letting you take me!"

"The life of crime has already taken away your soul. Don't let it take your life as well," Shadow Chaser said. However, Jack would not listen.

"Screw you, freak." Jack fired his handgun. Several bursts of fire came from the barrel as bullets sliced through the darkness. Shadow Chaser shifted from side to side, evading the projectiles, and once again, he disappeared in the same way he appeared—in a shroud of mystery.

"Where did you go?" Before he could say another word, Jack felt somebody tapping his left shoulder.

Shadow Chaser replied, **"Over here."** And struck the goon on the jaw. Jack moaned and staggered before colliding with some crates. The broken boxes crumbled like a house of cards underneath his weight.

It's a good thing I had my grappling launcher, or I would not have been able to avoid harm's way and take that fool by surprise. Shadow Chaser thought about the bullets meant for him. The darkness allowed him to make Jack believe he had just vanished into thin air. The echo of the crash faded, and dust began to clear from the area. Shadow Chaser made note of his surroundings one last time before going for the prize.

"Now, for the child. With those guns out of the way, I could get the boy out of here and come back for Stavros." Shadow Chaser ambled towards the room.

Patrick feared for his life and hid in the dark, damp closet. He missed his parents, and he wanted to be with them. He remained in the closet, hushed, just as the man with the red eyes instructed him. Fifteen minutes ago, he was crying for his mommy when he spotted somebody entering the room. The stranger with the red eyes looked scary to the child.

I am not here to hurt you, Patrick. I'm here to take you to your mommy and daddy. A man is coming in the room. Don't tell him I'm here. Patrick remembered the words of the dark man. *Stay in the closet until I come back, kid. I have to take care of the bad men.* He continued to relive the incident and waited inside the closet for the man to return. Patrick heard the door open in the room. Footsteps approached louder and nearer by the second.

As the door opened, he shouted, "Mommy. Daddy."

"Not yet, Patrick, but soon," Shadow Chaser said. With the child cradled in his arms, Shadow Chaser headed towards the door.

"You came back, Mr. Red Eyes."

"How about calling me Shadow Chaser, kid."

"Why do you look so scary?"

"It's to scare the bad guys."

"Stupid bad guys." The boy giggled.

"Yeah, stupid bad guys." Shadow Chaser smirked along with the young child, but the levity became short-lived. A dozen halogens illuminated the room.

"Damn it, the lights are back. How the hell did that happened?" Shadow Chaser pondered when a thought came to his mind.

"He has a backup generator. That son of a bitch," Shadow Chaser said. The boy stared at his saviour.

"That's a bad word, Shadow Chaser. You should not use bad words—it makes baby Jesus cry," Patrick scolded the dark guardian.

Shadow Chaser replied, *"You're right, kid. Sorry."* Shadow Chaser realized how well the Collins's had raised their boy.

"That's okay. But you can't have any dessert when you bring me back home, okay."

"Okay." Shadow Chaser nodded, and they left the room.

Bramm! Bramm! Bramm! Bramm!

He heard the shots, but could not see the shooter nor where the bullets came from. He had no time to hesitate.

"Hang on, kid." Shadow Chaser attempted to evade the bullets. Any other time Shadow Chaser would have been able to navigate with great ease. However, he had a child clinging to him, a child whose safety became

16

paramount. Shadow Chaser vowed that the bullets would not hit his little body. The ghost of justice dodged the first three bullets, but the fourth penetrated his left leg.

Shadow Chaser groaned and collapsed into the crates. However, he made sure he would take the blunt of the collision instead of the child.

"Are you okay?" the boy asked.

Shadow Chaser examined his leg and said, ***"I'm shot, kid. Run and hide in that crate over there."*** Gunpowder and burned flesh perfumed the wound.

"The bad man is coming. I can't leave you here."

"Don't worry about me, kid." Shadow Chaser pushed him towards the crate. ***"Go!"*** The boy started to run while Shadow Chaser tried to rise from the bloodstained floor.

"Armour piercing bullet. Penetrated the body armour and an artery; I have to tighten the wound—or I'm dead." Shadow Chaser took off his combat belt and tied it around the wound.

"That should slow down the bleeding," he said. But before he could get to his feet, he felt a mysterious boot to the back, creating an additional sharp pain. His face caressed the floor.

Stavros towered the injured vigilante and boasted, "You don't look so tough now, hero. And you bleed just like the rest of us."

Shadow Chaser replied, "We will just see how tough I am, killer." He used his other leg to trip his adversary. The move gave him a little more time to stand. However, Stavros had the advantage.

"I see you're a good fighter, Shadow Chaser," Stavros said. "But let's see how you do against me." Stavros demonstrated his mastery in the martial arts. Shadow Chaser tried to evade to the best of his ability. If not for the lodged bullet in his leg, he would be able to demonstrate the skills a Shadow Art master had to offer. However, life, as Shadow Chaser knew, was not always easy or fair. The fight continued for several minutes until Stavros took the advantage.

I'm hurting bad. I lost the feeling in my leg. I am starting to lose my focus. His punches aren't helping either. Shadow Chaser thought, for the loss of blood had drained most of the life right out of him.

"Where's your courage now, freak," Stavros said, and begun to deliver blow after near lethal blow to the helpless Shadow Chaser.

"It's all over," Shadow Chaser said, and fell hard onto the ground. Stavros strode towards his defeated opponent and laughed.

"I would like to see who is behind that mask and kill you. However, I want to waste the brat first, so you could hear the sound of the gun that will kill him. After, I will bring the kid's dead body to show you," Stavros said. "Then I'll kill you; so your blood will mingle with his." Stavros left to resume his search for the boy. After many minutes of deliriousness, Shadow Chaser started to regain consciousness. With no feeling in his leg, he feared he might lose it. He knew his life would end like this; taken out by the scum he vowed to battle. He knew someday he would die at the hands of a powerful enemy or some lucky thug. He took the risk and accepted the consequences of his actions. But he regretted he could not save the young child from the mob boss. Stavros will kill him for no reason at all.

I failed to save him as I failed to save my beloved Claire. Shadow Chaser found it difficult to breathe. While he lay there thinking about his failures, Shadow Chaser thought about his wife. He knew how much she cherished life. From that thought, a new drive appeared in both the Shadow Chaser and Arthur Brown.

"Claire didn't quit. Even when those monsters had her, she fought them until the end. I mustn't quit now," he said to himself. Shadow Chaser clutched the closest crate and pulled himself up from the ground.

"Hold on, Patrick. I'm coming." With the valour of a soldier, Shadow Chaser carried on with the fight.

Chapter 4

Stavros skulked through the warehouse and searched for the boy. Using his hatred as a compass, his eyes scanned the perimeter. He expected that Tomas Collins and the Shadow Chaser would succumb in this conflict. The boy would be his next victim.

"My sole regret is that I won't be there to see Collins's face when he gets his boy back in tiny pieces. As for the freak, I will miss the pursuit he provided. He was a good challenger, but Antonio Stavros always wins the war." Stavros laughed when he heard a sound coming from the barrels carrying gasoline.

Stavros sang, "Oh, Patrick. I want to talk to you." The little boy panicked.

"Get away from me, bad guy," the boy yelled, and started to run.

"Got you, you little punk." Stavros grabbed the child.

"Let me go, you big bully!"

Stavros replied, "As you wish." And he threw the child on the crate. Patrick's tiny frame collided with a steel barrel. The impact caused the top of the barrel to open, and the huge drum tipped to the side, flooding the floor with the flammable chemical. The steel cover made a huge clanging sound and bounced until it rolled to a rest.

"Stop hurting me, you big meanie!" the boy said. "I'm going to get my daddy after you!" The tears blurred his vision.

"Your dad is the one who got you in this mess in the first place, you little bastard." Stavros aimed his gun towards Patrick.

"You just said a bad word. You're in trouble now." The boy stuck to his beliefs.

Stavros mocked the child's fear and pain. "I don't care." And with his finger massaging the trigger, he watched the tears fell from the child's eyes.

"The kid is right, scum. You should not use bad words—it makes baby Jesus cry," a voice yelled from behind the mobster. Stavros turned around and cursed out the name of his greatest enemy.

"Shadow Chaser. Why don't you know when to die?" Stavros screamed like a demon drenched in holy water; his attention shifted to the injured hero. *"Because if I would die, then you would win; and I am never going to give you that satisfaction,"* Shadow Chaser proclaimed.

"We shall see, freak." Stavros aimed his gun and prepared to fire. Shadow Chaser felt like a mouse in a maze. Trapped with no other defensive option— but one. Taking off his hat, he threw it at Stavros's weapon. With the steel trim around the tip of the hat, his fedora doubled as a powerful weapon. If thrown right, it could break or slice through a bone. The hero hoped his reflexes were superior to Stavros's aim. The fedora flew like a turbo-charged frisbee and connected with the gun, altering the aim sufficiently.

"Son of a bitch," Stavros squealed; the pain rushed to his head. His finger twitched, and a loud *bang* followed.

The bullet from the gun grazed the puddle on the floor and ignited an inferno. The flames coiled around the crates with barrels exploding, and debris flying to the roof. The hungry blaze consumed most of the oxygen in the room, and tar-black smoke spread throughout the warehouse. The aromas of burned wood and charred steel filled the area. The dark vigilante knew the smoke would soon travel into the child's lungs.

"Come on, Patrick. We are getting out of here." Shadow Chaser grabbed the child.

"Where can we go?" he sobbed.

"Up!" Shadow Chaser took out his grappling launcher and fired it for the top window. The hook smashed through the window and fastened itself to a steady roof beam. Shattered glass fell like rain, and Shadow Chaser covered the child from its razor-sharp shards. When it cleared, Shadow Chaser motioned to the child.

"You ready?"

"Yes."

"Let's do it." Shadow Chaser attempted to activate the launcher.

Stavros hollered, "No you don't." And then he grabbed the Shadow Chaser's injured leg, and they began to elevate towards the top. Flames fired ten feet above the ground. The child's chances of survival dwindled by the second. Shadow Chaser knew he had to put a permanent end to this war.

Shadow Chaser said, *"To God I send you, killer. May he be more merciful than I."* The ghost of justice kicked him with his good leg.

"Nooo," Stavros yelled as he fell to flames below. The pair continued to propel towards the roof. Once they were outside, Shadow Chaser realized that, for the first time in his career, he had taken a human life. But for now, he had to put aside his conscience and focus his efforts on an immediate escape. He scrambled to the edge and deployed a belay device to lower them to the ground. When his feet landed, Shadow Chaser felt pain shooting through his leg, but struggled to continue.

"Get in the van," Shadow Chaser said, and the boy complied. Seconds later, he started the engine and left the harbour. The van drove away into the darkness while the building exploded behind them, leaving nothing but flames and buried, tortuous memories. Louder than an angry volcano, the powerful boom echoed over the city. Sirens blended in with the percussion of the explosions and the crackling of the fire. Ashes from the debris fell like white snow and sprinkled over the harbour.

Once they arrived at the Collins residence, Shadow Chaser looked upon the boy one last time.
"You're home, Patrick."
"Are you coming with me?"
"No, I can't, kid. Just promise me you will always help someone in need. You think you can do that?"
"You bet. Bye, Shadow Chaser. Thank you for bringing me back to my mommy and my daddy," Patrick said, holding out his arms.
"Anytime, kid." Shadow Chaser hugged the child for a brief moment. *"Now, get out of here."* The dark hero opened the passenger door. The young boy waved at him and toddled towards his front door.

Tomas and Diana Collins sat on their sofa and held each other while they waited for some sort of news. They heard a rap on the door like angry drum. Collins rose and answered.
"Agent Flynn. Where is our son?"
Flynn hesitated at first, but said, "He fooled us, sir." He looked at Collins and added with false confidence. "But we will continue the search."
"What you're trying to say is that my son is still out there?" Collins said.
"Yes, but don't give up on us yet, sir," Flynn said. The phone rang. "Answer it. We will get things moving from here." Flynn monitored the police bug.
"Hello."
"Mr. Collins, this is the Shadow Chaser. Your son is safe, your money has been returned to you, and Antonio Stavros will never bother you again."
"Who is this? Where is my son?"
Shadow Chaser replied, *"Open the door, sir."* Agent Flynn took the phone from Collins.
He roared, "You again. You have no right to meddle in our business." Flynn heard the phone click, and the line went dead. During that time, Tomas and Diana Collins moved towards the door. Both of them feared the call could have been someone's sick joke, yet they had to open it.
"Mommy, Daddy," Patrick screamed and hugged his parents.
"Patrick," Diana shrieked like a banshee. The tears mixed with her makeup and moistened her son's cheek.

Collins kissed the top of his head and cried, "My son!"

"I am okay, Mommy, Daddy. Shadow Chaser saved me," Patrick said when Flynn entered the conversation.

"Where is the bad guy that took you away?"

"He's in the fire. He made Shadow Chaser mad," Patrick said. Flynn grabbed his police radio to see if he could confirm the boy's story.

"Are there any reports of fire near town?" he asked.

"Funny you should mention that, sir. One of the warehouses at the harbour blew up. They were storing gasoline, and the place went up like a rocket," the voice said.

"Check the area. There may be some bodies inside. Flynn out." Flynn dashed for the front door.

"What are you planning to do?" Collins asked.

"I've been after this vigilante for a long time, and I'm going after him. I know he saved your son, but he broke the law. I have to go now, I'll be back later," Flynn said, and then he left the house. Collins looked at his wife and child. They were a family again all because of a vigilante who cared.

"I hope you never find him, Agent Flynn."

Taking off his mask, Arthur Brown realized he needed immediate medical attention before he bled to death. He knew the police would have an APB out on him, so he called the one man he could trust, his friend Alexander Taylor. Brown, in his costume, used his car phone and hoped he could reach his friend.

"Hello, Virginia. It's Art. Would Alex be in?" Brown asked while he tried to stay alert.

"Art, you sound terrible. Are you all right?"

"I'm fine. I just need to talk to Alex."

"Just a moment," she said, and gave her husband the receiver.

"Hey, Art. Are you ready for dinner?"

"Alex, I'm hurt…bad. I have…to get to…the hospital." Brown felt dizzy and weak.

"Where are you?"

"I'll be at the… hotel in three…minutes."

"I'll wait for you at the front," Taylor said before he hung up.

"What was that all about, dear?" Virginia said.

"I just have to meet Art. He wants to show off a new invention, this shouldn't take long." Taylor smiled at his wife and left the room. He trekked towards the front exit and waited for his friend to arrive. Just as he approached the exit of the hotel, Brown's dark van appeared. Alex hopped in and found his friend bleeding from his left leg.

"Hey, buddy," Brown said. Taylor helped Brown remove his combat suit.

"Put your clothes on," Taylor said, handing Brown his regular clothes.

"Thanks for…coming, Alex."

"Why are you risking yourself out there, Art? There is no profit to be made in this venture." Taylor took the wheel, started the engine, and drove to a private hospital, which he had made numerous donations to in the past.

Brown replied in agony. "Don't fight with me today, Alex. I don't expect you to understand." Taylor knew Arthur Brown bore the identity of the Shadow Chaser; but he did not believe in fighting a hopeless cause.

"Alright, just save your strength," Taylor said, but before he could blink, Brown fell into unconsciousness.

Taylor yelled, "Art. Art. Hold on. We will be there shortly." Taylor floored the pedal, and the van accelerated towards the hospital.

A few hours had passed since the hospital admitted Arthur Brown for the bullet wound to his leg; but the staff had no report to offer. Alexander Taylor lingered in the private waiting room for any news on the welfare of his friend. He anxiously awaited the doctor's arrival, but he remained patient. The sterile-scented hospital could not remove the odour of fire emanating from Taylor jacket. He carried his semi-conscious friend to the emergency doors, and then the ER team took Brown away. Taylor never heard a peep since. After glancing through the same periodical for a third time, Taylor noticed the doctor walking towards him.

"Mr. Taylor, your friend will survive."

"Thank you, doctor."

"I do have some bad news, however. Because of the severe damage to his leg, I'm afraid Mr. Brown will need the help of a cane for the rest of his days. I wish we could have done more."

"As long as he lives, doctor. That's good enough for me. But one more thing, doctor. I talked to your administrator and requested that this be kept confidential," Taylor said. "If any information regarding this event is disclosed, donations from my foundation could be affected, and that would be most unfortunate."

"I assure you, sir," the doctor said, "it will remain confidential."

"Thank you, doctor. May I see my friend?"

"Of course. Three doors down to your left," he said. Taylor nodded at the doctor and walked into Brown's room. His friend allayed motionless in the bed and gazed at his wounded leg.

"Hi, Art. How are you holding out?"

"I'm fine, for a cripple. The doctor gave me the word."

"I'm sorry, buddy."

"Don't be, Alex. You saved my life, but if you will excuse me, I think I need some shut-eye."

"Sure. I'll talk to you later," Taylor said before he left the room. Brown lifted the bleach-scented sheet and looked at his leg. He remembered Antonio

Stavros's death cry when he had shaken the mob boss loose from his leg and delivered him to the inferno below. Brown will never forget the look on Stavros's face as he plummeted to his death.

"Antonio Stavros is dead—and so is the Shadow Chaser," he said. "A fitting end to both our kind." Brown closed his eyes and fell asleep.

Chapter 5

Windsor, Ontario. Canada. October 30, 1997:

Arthur Brown sat like a hermit on a barstool in a local pub, alone with his thoughts, and ignored by the patrons surrounding him. Clouded by the aroma of whisky, and reeking with the stench of regret, Brown held the glass in his right hand and gripped his cane with his left. On the tenth anniversary of his final battle as the Shadow Chaser, Brown cradled his glass, nursing the relationship with his best friend of the last five years. The battle that ended his career also ended his capacity to walk with a normal gait. A man who at one time required a mask to facilitate his need for vengeance and justice; now found himself needing to consume a bottle of hard liquor to help him forget about the unfulfilled promise he once made to his wife Claire. Arthur Brown had aged ten years, but the alcohol abuse made him look twenty years older. The punishment he received from the bottle was far worse than any physical impairment he received as the Shadow Chaser. Brown no longer cared about anybody or himself.

I'm through! Finished! He wanted to give up and die. Die, like the scum he believed himself to be.

"There is no cause left to believe in. War is among us; crime has gone up; and innocence is traded in dark rooms for profit. The time of reckoning no longer applies in a world without hope or without someone to admire. If heroes no longer exist, then why should I?" Brown grabbed his shot and swallowed the whisky without remorse. The alcohol slipped down his throat like a slow-burning, comforting fire.

"You want another shot?" the bartender asked. Brown looked at him with a puzzled expression.

"Another shot?"

"Yeah, do you want more booze or what?"

"Yeah, sure. Fill it up."

"Hey, mac. What did you think I said?"

"It was nothing…nothing at all," Brown said, but he thought about fighting for the cause one last time.

But how the hell am I going to do that? Brown thought. His financial predicament required that he forfeit his invention patents to repay his creditors. The recession had contributed to a mounting debt, forcing his company into bankruptcy five years earlier. His physical abilities were average, but his leg cursed him to a life of self-destruction and self-pity.

Hey, look at the cripple. We can crawl and still get away from the freak. Maybe, I could change my name to Peg Leg, the seeker of gimp's justice. He thought as he drank another shot of whisky. Brown knew he could never be the man he once understood himself to be, but believed he could resurrect the Shadow Chaser. While he thought about the possibility, the bartender turned on the television.

"This week on *The Eye of the People*, it has been ten years since North America has heard from the part myth, part folk-hero who helped victims get justice. Today's focus: The Shadow Chaser—reality or myth? For today's panel of experts, we have the head of the Vigilante Crime Unit of the FBI, Agent Jackson Flynn, Toronto Gazette reporter, Mike Smith, criminologist with The University of Chicago, Martin Godley, and businessman and philanthropist, Tomas Collins, who says he owes his son's life to the Shadow Chaser." Brown sat on his barstool and listened intently to the program.

"Thank you for being here today, gentlemen," the host said. His guests acknowledged the welcome. "Agent Flynn, you were in charge of following the Shadow Chaser's exploits?"

"That is correct, Mr. Gerald," Flynn said. "The bureau assigned me to the task force a short time after that vigilante made his first appearance in 1977. However, we have reports that spotted him all around the United States, Canada, and even in Mexico. We had the cooperation of both the Canadian and Mexican authorities. He was—and still is wanted in the U.S., Canada, and Mexico."

"Mr. Smith, you were assigned to cover the Shadow Chaser?"

"My editor gave me the story about a drug bust in Montreal back in 1978. When I arrived, all I heard were stories about this Shadow Chaser guy who came out of nowhere and took out a gang in a matter of seconds," Smith said. "I thought if I just keep my mouth shut, I may come out with a great story. Some time after that, rumours appeared about another Chaser sighting, this time in New York City. A hostage situation had taken place at the Empire State Building. Two Iranian terrorists demanded that their imprisoned leaders be released by the Justice Department, or they would kill everyone in the room. I should remember because I one of the hostages."

"Then what happened?"

"The official report stated the lights went out for a few minutes, and when the police stormed inside, the two suspects were found on the floor unarmed and cuffed. However, I know the truth. The lights did go out, and then a pair of red eyes appeared out of nowhere," Smith said. "In a matter of seconds, those clowns were kissing the floor." Tired of what he was hearing, Flynn opened his mouth.

"You hear this? That's the kind of misrepresentation I am trying to disprove. This guy is neither a spirit nor a hero. He's a person who has no respect for the law or society. He's as dirty as the scum he claims to hate," he replied. "If he stood for justice, he would have allowed us to do our job and manage our own affairs. As for the cloud of smoke and the red eyes, it's all a scam. That's why they don't go on the reports. People believe what they want to believe."

"Are you calling me a liar, sir?" Smith asked.

"I am not making accusations, but you could have been drugged by him. Then again, you're a reporter, and it's not the first time the press has massaged the truth to improve readership."

"Why do you want this guy so bad, Agent Flynn? Is it because you are committed to your job, or is it because he made you look like a fool so many times in your career? But then again, was he the one who rescued your butt out of the fire when you failed to save the Collins child from one Antonio Stavros?" Smith fired back. Angry over the reporter's comment, Flynn stood from his chair.

"How dare you attempt to compromise my reputation, you canoe-making son of a..." Flynn said, but the host interrupted him.

"Please, gentlemen. Could we conduct ourselves like adults here," The host requested, and after a few grunts, the storm calmed. Seconds later, the discussion resumed.

"Mr. Godley, what would make a man do these kinds of things?"

"It's hard to point out the actual reason, Mr. Gerald. It could have been because the person was abused by a parent, an injustice was done to this person, or the death of a loved one. Those are but a few breaking points that may bring a person to the point of instability. However, in the case of this Shadow Chaser, his identity represents the victim. This person was so far into this character that the rules of right and wrong may no longer apply. The person hides behind a mask as executioners did in the past to represent society."

"Do you believe this person needs medical attention?"

"Definitely, Mr. Gerald," Godley replied. "This person needs help, or it could be catastrophic. However, he may already be in a mental institution since we haven't heard a thing about him since 1987."

"Mr. Collins, your son was kidnapped in 1987. Could you tell us about it?"

"It was terrible, Mr. Gerald. Our son was five years old when Stavros took him away from us. They wanted five million dollars, or they would kill our son. Agent Flynn was there with the FBI, but it wasn't them who saved him. It was the Shadow Chaser." Collins looked at Flynn. "We were all about to give up hope when I received a phone call from a man saying everything was okay. He told me to go to the front door and our son would be there. When Diana and I opened the door, Patrick stood there with open arms. So, I don't care what anybody says about him. I owe the Shadow Chaser my son's life."

"Besides your son's return, things started to improve for your family, did it not, sir?"

"It was all over the news that I refused to let the mob move in on my business, so within hours of Patrick's rescue, I received calls from investors wanting to invest in a company that appreciated high moral standards. Our profits and clients doubled. But the most important thing is that our son taught us a lesson that day."

"What would that lesson be, Mr. Collins?"

"Our son told us we have to help people who need our help. He promised the Shadow Chaser he would do his best. We cannot go out and do Agent Flynn's job as the Shadow Chaser did, but we could do the next best thing. We donated money to the community. This is our way to thank the Shadow Chaser for all of his help."

Determined to have the last word, Flynn added, "Mr. Collins, it's great that you are helping the community, but there are a few facts you failed to mention. For one, Antonio Stavros was not proven to be the one who took your child. He went missing on the same night. At the same location your son claimed he was taken captive, a fire broke out there killing everybody inside, and we couldn't identify the bodies. So, maybe the Shadow Chaser caused it. According to the Stavros family, Shadow Chaser killed Mr. Stavros. I don't find this hard to believe because he thinks he is above the law. Also, how can you be sure he didn't stage this kidnapping from the beginning? Then make it look like he rescued your child," Agent Flynn said. "I tell you right now, I will not rest until I find out what happened to the Shadow Chaser. If he's dead, let him stay dead. But if he's still out there, I will find him and bring him to justice."

"That should be fun. Another circus trial brought to you by the American judicial system." Smith grinned.

Agent Flynn pointed his finger at the journalist and said, "You should just stick to writing tabloid pulp, Canuck!"

"That's all the time we have for today. I am Gord Gerald leaving you with the history of the Shadow Chaser next on KRJB Chicago," the host said just before the bartender turned off the television. Despite his drunken condition, Brown wanted to see more of his life story. But with the flick of a switch, the program, like his career, faded into darkness.

"Why did you turn it off? I was watching that," Brown shouted. He took another shot from the glass and gave the bartender a dead stare.

"It's eleven p.m., time for the wet T-Shirt bikini contest, bud. Trust me, when you see these racks, you won't give a hoot about some mask-wearing weirdo," the bartender said.

"I don't give a damn about those hussies. I want to watch that show," Brown shouted, the whisky speaking on his behalf.

"You don't like it, friend, then get the hell out."

"I pay you good money to get drunk, so I'm going to watch whatever I want," he said. With a slight nod, the bartender called his bouncers towards Brown.

"This gentleman will be leaving the establishment," the bartender said. But as Brown rose from the stool, he noticed the cane.

"Be easy on him, boys. He's a peg-leg, and the last thing I need is a cripple suing me," the bartender said. The bouncers nodded at their boss and tried to grab Brown.

"Come on, gimp. We don't wanna hurt you," one of the bouncers said.

"You sons of bitches. Even with this leg, I could still take you two clowns out." With those last words, Brown prepared to fight.

"Have it your way, gimp," the other bouncer said. Even in his current state, Brown, a Shadow Art master, could still fight with the best of them.

That's it, stupid, use your weight against me. Brown thought as the bouncer charged him. Brown's cane connected with the bouncer's jaw. The patrons heard the jawbone crack like a walnut. The huge man fell onto his back, breaking a table on his way to the floor.

"You want some, too—steroid freak," Brown said, and the other bouncer accepted the challenge. One minute later, the second bouncer laid on the ground next to the first one.

"You're all fools. Don't you know whom you are dealing with? I am the Shadow Chaser," Brown yelled through his alcohol-induced haze. "If it weren't for this damn leg, I would have crushed your skulls."

"There's the Shadow Chaser!" People hollered and jeered at him in the bar because of his claim.

Angered over their amusement at his expense, Brown cried out. "Stop laughing at me, or you're all going to feel my wrath." What he would say or do no longer mattered to him.

He slurred, "Behold, scum." Brown took his cane and smashed the glasses on the bar. "If I can't watch TV, nobody can." Brown grabbed his empty shot glass that survived his assault and threw it towards the television, smashing the screen. Brown expressed a sinister smile. The crash of the shattered glass distracted Brown long enough for the bartender to sneak up behind him. He swung his bat like a club, and it connected with Brown's shoulder like a hard-pitch fastball.

"Ughhh!" Brown moaned, and he fell onto the ground.

"And I'm John Wayne, gimpy. Hold him, boys, I'm calling the cops," the bartender said. He walked around the broken glass and pieces of wood before he made the call. The bouncers held onto his unconscious body and waited for the police to arrive.

29

Chapter 6

Detroit, Michigan. USA. Two hours later:

*A*lexander Taylor was hosting an evening in his town house for his clients and investors. But Taylor's town house looked more like a castle. The successful businessman had the resources to live a life of luxury and riches. At forty-seven years of age, he already owned a majority stake in a Fortune 500 company; he stood among the kings of the financial world. His wife of twenty-seven years looked no older than thirty. His daughter Margaret, a pretty five-year-old girl who walked like a princess in a fairy tale story. Taylor had it made, but he never forgot about his friend Art. It seemed funny how both men could be good at heart, and yet have two such disparate lives. While Arthur Brown was on the elevator going down, Taylor ascended to the penthouse. Taylor couldn't fathom why his friend risked his life helping people he didn't even know. He could not comprehend the desperate desire for vengeance or the need to find absolution for one's own guilt. Of course, he empathized with the victims of crime, but playing a physical role in crime prevention was a waste of time and valuable resources. With no opportunity for profit or gain, he wanted no part of Brown's high-risk venture. He made his choices, and so did Brown. Today, he held his champagne glass high in the air while Brown laid his head low in the dust.

"Art, you could have had this, too. Why didn't you just leave the past in the past," Taylor said to himself. His wife walked towards him and coiled her arm around his shoulders.

She looked at her strong-minded husband and smiled. "Dear, they are expecting you."

"Yes, dear," Taylor said. But she noticed a change in his voice.

"You still thinking about Arthur?" she asked while they strolled towards his guests.

"It's has been five years since we spoke to each other. I wanted him to work for me, Virginia. With his skills, we could have ruled the market together. He's my friend, but I couldn't accept his way of life."

"You don't talk much about Art's life to me. Why is that?"

Taylor wanted to tell her, but she was unaware of Brown's alter ego, and he felt compelled to maintain his vow of secrecy.

"He was never the same since those monsters killed Claire," Taylor said. "It seemed he became more anti-social and closed his emotions to the world."

"You knew that for a long time. But why haven't you both reconciled your differences," Virginia said. "Five years is a long time to hold a grudge."

"I have tried four times, but Art is a man who holds a grudge," Taylor said, knowing from experience.

"Luv, talk to him, tell him you're his friend," Virginia said. "Why don't you go along with his business proposition?"

"I will not jeopardize everything I worked hard on for his dream, dear. I owe you and Margaret, not Arthur Brown and his wild ambitions. I offered him a position and a chance at true power and respect. It's not my fault he turned it down and got mad."

However, Taylor knew the true reason of the falling out. When Brown lost his business, Taylor offered him a position at Taylor Enterprises, but Brown had another idea. Brown wanted Taylor to use his resources to create a solution against crime. He called it, "Operation: Resurgence." Brown would find and train a new Shadow Chaser, and Taylor would supply the Shadow Chaser with weapons and equipment to eliminate not just the crime in North America, but all over the world. Brown proposed that Taylor keep a quarter of the money from criminals and dump it back into the program. Use their own money to stop them. However, Taylor did not see a profit in that, so he refused to go along with his friend's proposal. A huge moral and ethical debate heated up between them, provoking a disastrous clash. Brown stormed out of Taylor's Toronto home and vowed never to return. Taylor never took his friend at his word, until now.

"Dear, this is Mr. Preston. He's with the Anderson Group," Virginia said, bringing Taylor out of his thoughts and back to reality.

Taylor shook the gentleman's hand and said, "Mr. Preston, I'm glad you could make it."

"The honour is mine. I wouldn't have missed the opportunity to dance with your wife even if it is Devil's Night." The man laughed.

"Don't be concerned about those ruffians, sir. The police can take care of them. Society tried, but they did not want to change, so it is up to our legal system to do its always-superb job in apprehending those outcasts of society. Besides, we are here to enjoy ourselves," Taylor said. "My dear, would you show Mr. Preston around to our guests?"

"Certainly, dear." Virginia grabbed Preston's left arm. "Mr. Preston, would you follow me, please."

"Mrs. Taylor, I would follow you to the ends of the earth," Mr. Preston said, and they joined the party. He made a positive impression with Preston, and that pleased Taylor, for he wanted Taylor Enterprises to merge with the Anderson Group for a year now. He believed this event would guarantee the deal.

Everything is going according to plan. Taylor thought. After taking a quick sip of champagne, he greeted his other guests.

"Alex, superb party. Where is the wife?" a distinguish man asked.

"Marcus. It's good you made it tonight. As for my wife, she is entertaining Mr. Preston."

"The Mr. Preston. The Anderson Group's Mr. Preston?"

"That's the one. I will be seeing him in my office tomorrow, and if it works out, we will close the Anderson Group merger."

"Wonderful news, Alex," Marcus said. "Taylor Enterprises will be virtually unstoppable in the global market. You did great, Alex. You've worked hard to get where you are today."

"Thank you, Marcus. It was a team effort. I couldn't have done it all by myself."

"Sure you would have, but it would have taken you a little longer." Marcus smiled.

"How long may I ask?" Taylor returned the grin.

"Fifty instead of forty-seven. After all, you do have me as your vice-president," Marcus said, then both men laughed. While the party went on, Mr. Preston stopped the festivities with an abrupt a-hem and tapped on his glass with his spoon. Mr. Preston had the prestige of a world leader, and the guests turned their attention towards him.

"I would like to thank the Taylors on a magnificent party. Please take a bow," Mr. Preston said. The people applauded with delight.

"The party is only as good as the guests that come," Taylor replied. "Thank you so very much for attending."

"Yes, we are glad that all of you were able to make it," Virginia said. Mr. Preston smiled at the beautiful lady for brief moment before he continued with his speech.

"I was waiting for tomorrow to say this to Mr. Taylor, but no matter. My company will agree to a friendly merger with Taylor Enterprises. At long last, we have a foothold in the market, and the time to join forces is now," Mr. Preston said, lifting his glass in the air. "Mr. Taylor, my company is yours to navigate into the future."

I have done it. Taylor thought as he joined Mr. Preston.

"Today we live in a new world. Business is expanding every day, and we have to be there to supply the needs of that world," Taylor said. "This partnership will guarantee the pledge that Taylor Enterprises has made to the global consumer. The future is now." And then he raised Preston's left hand as a sign of victory.

"Bravo." The guests applauded the news with great enthusiasm.

"I must say it wasn't your company's record that persuaded me, Mr. Taylor," Mr. Preston said.

"No? What did persuade you, sir?"

"Your wife," Preston said, and then laughter filled the room. "She's a wonderful dancer."

"That's why I married her."

"Mrs. Taylor, would you do me the honour of another dance?" Mr. Preston asked.

"I would love to," she replied. She followed him to the dance floor, and they waltzed. Others followed their suit. Taylor stepped towards the hallway when his butler came down the stairs.

"Excuse me, sir," the butler said. "You have a telephone call. They said it's important."

"Did they identify themselves?"

"Yes, sir. They claimed to be the Windsor Police Department."

"Windsor, as in Windsor, Ontario—Canada?"

"That is correct, sir."

"I will take it in my study." Taylor walked the corridor until he stood in front of a large English Oak door. Entering his study, he grabbed the phone and hoped to get a few answers.

"Hello, this is Alexander Taylor. Whom am I speaking to?"

"Mr. Taylor, I am Constable Joseph Chang of the Windsor Police Department. We have a drunken person in our cell claiming to know you. We wouldn't have believed him, but he gave us this number. He said we could reach you at your town house in Detroit."

"Who the hell do I know in Windsor?" Taylor asked. "Is this some sort of prank? If it is, I am not laughing."

"I can assure you, sir. This is not a prank. His name is Arthur Brown. He said to call you, so you would get him out of here."

"Is that what he said?"

"Well, he was a little more profane with his words, sir. Shall I tell him you're not coming?"

Taylor knew if he would turn his back on Brown this time, there would be no second chance to save his friendship.

"You tell him to hang tight. I will be there soon. Goodbye." Taylor said before he ended the conversation. He walked towards his butler and nodded.

"Is there something I could do for you, sir?"

"Yes, tell my wife I had to go to Windsor and see Art. She will understand," Taylor said. "In the meantime, see that everything continues to go smoothly."

The butler replied, "Understood, sir." Taylor left his house and entered the limo that waited for him at the front driveway. Taylor instructed the driver, and the limo drove away from the mansion.

An hour after the arrest, Arthur Brown sat in his cell. The alcohol had worn off, and his calm temperament had returned. The stench of the jail reminded him of his own failures and choices. Brown started to rub his eyes when his one-time friend walked towards him.

"Is this your friend, sir?" the guard asked.

"Yes, he is. How much is his bond?" Taylor queried.

"Five hundred dollars, but the owner of the bar wants to charge him for the damages."

"How much?"

"Close to five thousand dollars."

"Is the owner of the bar here?"

"Yes, he's giving a statement to the sergeant."

"Tell him I will give him thirty thousand dollars if he doesn't pursue the matter any further," Taylor said.

"Very well. I'll be back in about five minutes," the guard said. Taylor looked upon his semi-sobered friend.

"Doc, you look good," Taylor said with an added touch of sarcasm.

"Listen, Taylor. I don't need you to give me a lecture. Are you going to help me or not? If you are, I will pay you back. If not, then get the hell out of here," Brown said.

"Can we please get off this subject, Art," Taylor said. "I'm here to help you, but you have to help yourself."

"If you want me to tell you that I was wrong, and you were right, fine then. I was wrong, and you were right," Brown said. "You are always right, Alex. You are the best of the best."

"You are just as good as I am, if not better. You just have your priorities mixed up, that's all."

"If you're talking about my plans on helping the innocent, Alex, don't worry your rich head. I am through with helping people. The innocent are no longer my responsibility," Brown replied. "The Shadow Chaser has been dead for ten years, and dead he will remain."

"If you accept that, then come back with me to Detroit. I have plans for you." Brown rose from the bed and probed, "What kind of plans?"

"We just merged with the Anderson Group, and I want you to work for me as the head of the technology and science departments for Taylor Enterprises. You are the one inventor I know who can create a fusion bomb out of bubble gum wrappings. I need you more than ever."

"I am broke, unemployed, homeless, lifeless, and I am a genius. I guess I would be a fool not to accept."

"I think so, Doc. So, come on, what do you say?"

"Well, I have nothing else to do. Okay, I accept. On one condition."

"Name it."

"I don't have to deal with those idiots in three-piece-suits telling me how to do my job."

"Agreed," Taylor said. The guard walked towards the cell.

"Well, did the owner agree with my proposal?"

"Once he heard what you offered, he decided to take the money."

"Excellent. Now release this man," Taylor said, and the guard complied. The cell door opened with a grinding clang.

The guard said, "Would you follow me." Brown and Taylor stepped towards the main desk. After signing a few legal documents, Taylor paid the bond and the owner of the bar.

"Here's your money, sir." Taylor handed him a cheque.

"Thank you, Mr. Taylor," the owner said, and looked at Brown. "As for you, stay out of my bar and don't come back. I will not have you assaulting my staff and frightening my customers again.

"I do apologize for my attitude, sir. As for your bouncers, they are in need of training. If a drunken cripple could overpower them so easily—anybody can." Brown smiled, and they left the station.

"I think I would have paid money to see that." Taylor smiled while they walked towards his limousine.

"I can't even remember what happened. Damn it, I was so plastered. I'll never drink another drop, I'm done with it," Brown said.

"Where to next, sir?" the chauffeur queried.

"Take us back home, Jefferson," Taylor said.

The driver opened the door for them and replied, "Very good, sir."

"You know something, Alex?"

"What's that, Doc?"

"Even though you helped me here tonight, I still don't like you." Brown smiled with a quiet happiness. Like a seamstress mending a torn garment, both men healed the wound in their friendship.

"I don't like you either, but I need your skill to make me some money." Taylor returned the smile.

"Oh, shut up." Brown smirked. Both men looked at each other and laughed before they entered the limo. Seconds later, the limo left the station's parking lot, heading back to the United States, and a second chance at life for Arthur Brown.

Chapter 7

Toronto, Ontario. Canada. July 21, 2006:

*T*aylor Enterprises grew—as Alexander Taylor foretold. With the help of his friend, Dr. Arthur Brown, the company's inventions skyrocketed, making them one of the biggest high-tech companies in the world. Healed from his mental breakdown, Brown resumed his training in the Shadow Art and returned to the level of physical conditioning he had maintained when he wore the hat and cloak. But he continued to walk with his cane. Taylor was beginning to look his age—the price of success. Today, the company was preparing for a crucial meeting with military, political, and medical personnel. The outcome of this meeting could determine the difference between sustainability and profitability. Taylor remained in Detroit, but Brown returned to Canada a few years after he joined his friend. Brown took the new role of department supervisor of the new technology wing of Taylor Enterprises Canada. For Brown it gave him the chance to come back home. Brown sat with his colleagues and opened the meeting.

"Good morning, everyone. I just wanted to have a word with you all before Mr. Taylor arrived."

"Good morning, Dr. Brown," they replied in the same voice.

"We are scheduled to meet the Canadian Medical Association today to discuss Dr. Simms's research on human evolution. Most of his work, I believe, is in the preliminary stages."

Brown looked at his agenda when one of his colleagues asked, "Is it true the Canadian and American militaries are here as well for this meeting?"

"Well, you never know," Brown replied. "It's true that a U.S. delegation will be here today with the Canadian ministers of health and national defence. But they are here for our military projects." Before Brown could continue his briefing, Alexander Taylor entered the room.

"Good morning, gentlemen," Taylor said while they stood.

"Good morning, Mr. Taylor," they replied.

"I hope I was not disturbing anything," Taylor said.

"Of course you did," Brown said with a smile, "but since you pay our salaries, no one is going to complain." After a moment of laughter, the meeting continued.

"As I was saying, Dr. Simms here will give you all some brief notes of his findings, so we don't look all shocked when we meet with our potential clientele," Brown said.

"Are we still working on the exotic diseases file?" one of the members asked.

"Yes, we are," Brown replied. "Then after that, we will update the defence minister and his delegation on our new thermo suits." Brown sat and allowed Taylor to take the floor.

"Before we go in there, I just want to thank you all for making this division the most successful of all of my divisions at Taylor Enterprises. I promise to reward each and every one of you. Thank you," Taylor said.

"Thank you, Alex. As for the rest of you, we will meet at the conference room in thirty minutes," Brown said. "Until then, gentlemen." The team members stood and left the room. Taylor and Brown stayed behind to catch up on a few things.

Taylor shook his hand and said, "How are you, Art."

"I'm fine, Alex. How are Virginia and Margaret doing?"

"They are doing great. They are off visiting the CN Tower."

"So, how are things going in Detroit?"

"Just great, you should have stayed there with us, Art."

"You kidding, this is where I belong. I missed home. Besides, we are getting things done here."

"How's your leg holding out, my friend?"

"It has its good days and its bad days. Ever since I returned to my disciplines, it seems to have gotten stronger."

"I've noticed. I also see that this Dr. Simms is on the verge of something amazing."

"More like frightening," Brown said, scratching his beard, "I don't know if we are doing the right thing, Alex." Taylor looked at Brown and wanted to know more about his friend's concern.

"What's troubling you, Art?"

"You will see in the meeting, Alex. By the way, I guess you wanted to know about the delay for those thermo suits."

"I knew you must have a good reason."

"The prototype is finished, but I am currently working on a different type of project."

Taylor glanced at the notes and said, "I wasn't aware that we had another project on the burner."

"You won't find it there. Besides, it wasn't sanctioned by you or the company," Brown said.

"You holding out on us, my friend. I didn't notice your department being over budget," Taylor said.

"That's because I used my own funds to create it." Brown smiled.

"I would have funded the project, Art. You know that."

"I know, Alex. But I couldn't let anyone find out about it."

"That top secret, eh," Taylor said.

"I knew you would start talking Canadian someday," Brown said. "But seriously, it is. If this project is successful, you will see the evolution of combat intelligence that's at least twenty to thirty years ahead of its time."

"You have something visual, a drawing, I can take a look at?"

"You, bet. I can show it to you before the meeting if you want."

"Well, what are we standing around for? Let's go," Taylor said with enthusiasm. Brown led him to his personal lab, and after a few left turns in the hallway, they arrived at the main door. When they entered the tech lab, Taylor noticed a large computer mainframe and a human-sized vault next to it.

"What's this?" Taylor probed.

"This is my super computer NIGHT. The most advanced computer system on the planet. Bill Gates doesn't even have one like this." Brown grinned and activated the computer.

"NIGHT?" Taylor pondered.

"Nano-cybernetic Intelligence Global Hybrid Technology. But you could call him NIGHT; he likes his name," Brown replied.

"So, he likes his name. Well, I am glad to see the both of you get along so well," Taylor said in a snide tone. "What's its purpose?"

"The ultimate surveillance tool and a hook up for this." Brown opened the vault and exposed the contents of the vault.

"That looks like..." Taylor said, but Brown beat him to the punch.

"Like one of my Shadow Chaser suits, but it is more advanced," Brown said. "This suit is made from a layer of computer circuitry. Then between the fabrics, a layer of nanotechnological circuitry activates the features within the suit."

"What kind of features?"

"Everything from gadgets, communications technology, five types of enhanced perception technologies, and strength optimization devices. The nanite-based body armour is so effective it absorbs a shotgun blast at close range leaving you with a bruise. It is also equipped with a robust electromagnetic field to alter the course of bullets. It works on the same basis as the magnetic powered trains in Japan and China.

"Art, most bullets are made of lead, and magnets do not work well with lead," Taylor said.

"True, lead is not ferromagnetic, it's diamagnetic. Diamagnetic and paramagnetic materials have a feeble magnetic interaction. So, you are right, it would not work. However, thanks to my nanite technology, I came up with a way to repel diamagnetic objects such as lead. By amplifying the field to work like Diamagnetic Levitation, I could repel certain types of diamagnetic metals."

"Diamagnetic Levitation?"

"Diamagnetic Levitation happens when a diamagnetic material is in close range to a material that generates a magnetic field. The diamagnetic material will repel the object, creating the magnetic field. For example, science has proven that if you place a small frog into a strong static electromagnetic field, the frog, which is made of mostly water, acts as a weak diamagnet. Thus, the frog levitates in a magnetic field," Brown explained. "In this case, the nanites strengthen the field and produce the effect. So, it creates a lead magnet."

"That is incredible."

"It's years ahead of its time. Unfortunately, I haven't figured out a way to repel other materials such as wood or plastic."

"You never cease to amaze me, Doc."

"Thanks, boss. As for the suit, I also added some of the goodies that the Mark I was comprised of."

"The Mark I?" Taylor asked

"I dubbed my original suit the Mark I. This baby is the Mark II," Brown said. Taylor assumed the worst.

"You are not thinking of doing this Shadow Chaser nonsense again?"

"No, of course not, but imagine this suit as the battle gear of today's soldier. We can sell this to any democratic government." Brown held out on his friend. Brown hid his intention of using this suit to resurrect the Shadow Chaser, but he did not want to forge another wall between him and his friend.

Taylor looked at the schematics and said, "This thing has everything from X-ray vision to a thermo-climate control system."

"With this suit, Alex, you don't need an army—you are the army."

"I see why you wanted to keep this thing a secret. I assume you will not be demonstrating your creation to the delegation today?" Taylor queried.

"No, I still need to do some testing first," Brown replied.

"Then I will add a few more dollars to your private fund to continue your work. This could make this company the strongest in the world."

"I owe you for what you and your family did for me, Alex. It's the least I could do."

"Hey, you are my friend. I don't need anything else in return." Taylor glanced at his watch. "I think we better get to the meeting."

"I'm right behind you, Alex." Brown locked the vault and deactivated the computer. Minutes later, they left the lab and headed for the meeting.

Dr. Winston Simms was working on the final touches when the other members of his department entered the conference room.

"Is there anything we can do to help, Dr. Simms?" one of his colleagues asked.

"No, I'm all ready. Thank you," he replied. Simms spent years working on a theory to accelerate the evolution of the human race. After years of numerous tests and millions spend for research, he believed he had come up with the genetic markers. Within a few minutes, the delegation and the members of Canada's elite medical profession entered the room.

"Welcome, ladies and gentlemen of the CMA, Health Minister Hartman, Defence Minister Gould, and his delegation," Simms said. "We will begin once Mr. Taylor and Dr. Brown arrive." As the introductions were completed, Taylor and Brown walked in.

"Good morning, ladies and gentlemen. Please forgive the delay," Taylor said. "Dr. Brown was getting the updates on the new thermo suits."

"I see we are all here for the presentation. It's your show, Dr. Simms," Brown said before he sat with the rest of attendance.

"Thank you, Dr. Brown. Evolution, the ultimate act of the divine. According to the Bible, it took God six days to create the universe. As the world evolved, the human race gradually became the dominant force on this planet. But that occurred after millions of years of evolving to that state. Darwin had it right all along, but not even he knew at what point this process could take us. When will the evolutionary process become a significant factor? I believe the time is now."

"You have proof of this new evolutionary process?" Hartman asked.

"Minister, the last time we evolved was thousands of years ago; except for minor tweaks resulting from better nutrition. Now, I believe I have found a way to speed up the process," Simms said.

"Is this possible?" one of the gentlemen in a military uniform asked.

"I believe it is. I can show you the findings, sir." Simms smiled and passed out his notes on the subject. After doing so, he took a white sheet that covered a rectangular object and unveiled a rodent in a cage. Taylor looked at Brown, hoping he could help clear some of this info for him.

"What is going to happen with the mouse?"

"If it's what I think, watch and see." Simms took a scalpel and a syringe out of his case and opened the cage.

He activated the monitoring screen and said, "As you can see, I previously injected the mouse with a dye, so you can see exactly how this mouse will evolve into the next step of its evolutionary process." Simms took the syringe and injected the rodent with the serum.

"What did you inject the mouse with?" Gould asked.

Simms took the scalpel and replied, "The equation to the laws of evolution."

"What are you going to do with that?"

"This." Simms started to cut the rodent open. Appalled by the brutality to the mouse, most of the members refused to watch. One of them said to Simms. "That's enough, Dr. Simms."

"Please, wait. You can see the wound on the rodent. Now, look closely at him," Simms pleaded. At that moment, they noticed a change in the mouse.

"My God, the wounds are healing. They are healing instantly," the attendee said, his tone expressed his astonishment.

"Look at the monitor, the mouse is reproducing his own blood cells to compensate for the blood it lost," Taylor said with amazement in his voice. Simms took the second rodent from a different cage and prepared for the second test.

"My next subject was born with a missing leg; as you can all see." After observing the rodent, the members nodded in agreement with Simms.

"Now, I will inject this species with the same equation I injected the first subject with. I want you to observe these findings," Simms explained while he injected the rodent. Within a few minutes, the impossible became the possible.

"I can't believe it, the mouse is growing a new leg," someone said, looking at the event unfolded right before their eyes. Taylor looked at Brown with enthusiasm about this new discovery.

Taylor looked at his friend and probed, "Art, you know what this means?"

"Yes, I do," Brown said, but kept his true thoughts to himself. *We are playing God.*

"Ladies and gentlemen, we live in an age that cloning and DNA mapping are a reality. Now, I bring you the equation that will bring all the answers to the mysteries of life. This is my equation I offer to the world. It's called the Darwin Vaccine," Simms said.

"Has it been tested on a human subject?"

"No, we have just finished Phase One. Phase Two, a larger animal subject and human cells will be tested, hopefully within a year."

"I would approve of this, but first I would like to see further testing. Also, I must inform the prime minister. However, in the meantime, if you are looking for a contract or a grant, I'm sure we could come to an agreement," Hartman said.

"I agree with Minister Hartman," Gould replied.

"Dr. Simms, we would like to invite you and your colleagues to the Canadian Medical Association's meeting in September to discuss your vaccine," one member said.

"I would be delighted to, doctor," Simms said when another military personnel of the delegation spoke out.

"I'm General Storm, U.S. Army. I have a question, doctor. Will your discoveries will be shared worldwide?"

"Yes, general, I'm heading to New York for the UN's science meetings. I intend, or should I say, Taylor Enterprises intends to share this with the world.

We have the chance to defeat disease, aging, and maybe even death," Simms said. Brown raised his hand.

"Yes, Dr. Brown."

"Thank you, Dr. Simms. As head of the department, I just want to inform everyone that we will perform our due diligence before we begin testing this Darwin Vaccine on human subjects. According to Dr. Simms's research, we still can't ascertain what the actual effects would be on humans or whether or not we can expect any side effects."

"Dr. Brown, it sounds like you don't trust Dr. Simms's work," General Storm said.

"It's not Dr. Simms I don't trust, sir. It is society. Dr. Simms has opened the door to a new and dangerous world. We must study it before go out and jump the Grand Canyon—and survive. But if this is successful, we will definitely know who will be 'Biography's Person of the Third Millennium'." Brown smiled, and the members applauded.

"Are there any more questions?" Simms asked.

"It appears you have answered all of our questions for now, doctor. Mr. Taylor it looks like you have done it again," Hartman said.

"The credit goes to my team, minister. I'm just footing the bill."

"If this works, we will be giving you unlimited resources. Congratulations to you all," Gould said.

"We look forward to meeting you at our assembly in September, Dr. Simms," the member said.

"And in New York in six weeks," Storm said.

Simms replied, "Until then, gentlemen." And the meeting came to an end.

"Thank you all for coming," Taylor said. The delegation left the conference room. "Congratulations, Dr. Simms." Taylor shook his hand. "Impressive work"

"Thank you, Mr. Taylor." Simms smiled.

"Well, I have to run. We're still on for tonight, Art?" Taylor asked.

"For sure. I look forward to seeing Genie and Margaret tonight."

"See you later. Once again, Dr. Simms, excellent work."

"Thank you, sir," Simms said. Taylor nodded at the scientists and left the conference room. Simms wanted to hear Brown's opinion on the presentation. He knew Brown stood against genetic manipulation in the past, but he hoped this presentation would convert him into a believer.

"So, what did you think, Art?"

"Mary Shelly would be proud." Brown smiled.

"Come on, Art. You have to admit this has so much potential for good."

"It does, but I'm a scientist. I always look at the other possibilities."

"What scares you so much about this project?"

"The human race. We tend to make big mistakes, and we fail to learn from history."

"Are you saying you will not support my work?"

"Not at all. You made the impossible happen. I just hope we are ready for it."

"Have a little faith in your fellow man, Art," Simms said, but he noticed a look he had never seen in Arthur Brown before.

"I gave up believing in man a long time ago, my friend," Brown said, his thoughts brought him back to another time and place.

"What do you believe in, Art?"

"God."

"May I ask why?"

"What do you mean?"

"You are willing to believe in God, but not in man, why?"

"Because, my brilliant friend, my wife is not in this world anymore, and I refuse to believe she is gone for good, so she has to be with God. Therefore, he exists."

"That's not a logical answer."

"No, but it is my truth." Simms did not have anything else to say on the subject at hand. Looking at his watch, he tried to find a way out.

"Look at the time. I have to go and meet the wife for lunch," Simms said.

Brown tapped him on the right shoulder and said, "Alright then, I'll see you later, doctor. Good work today, you'll go far."

"I had a good teacher," Simms said, and then he left the room. Brown sat with serenity and revisited his past. Remembering what it felt like being with the woman who made him feel lucky to be alive, Claire was indeed the flower in his garden. But now with her gone, all that remained in his garden was barren soil and rock. The cell phone ring brought him back to reality. The Mozart ringtone repeated until he pressed the talk button.

"Dr. Brown speaking."

"Art, it's Alex."

"Alex, what's up?"

"I was supposed to meet Virginia and Margaret for lunch, but I have another deal to take care of first. Could you give them the message for me?"

"Are they coming here?"

"Yeah, they should be there in about sixty minutes."

"Well, I'm going swimming in the pool, but I can let them know."

"I will leave a message with my executive assistant to tell them you will be at the pool, so they can meet you there. Thanks, I owe you one."

"It's not the first time, bud. Is this other meeting so important that you need to miss them?"

"It is, Doc. It could increase the value of the firm substantially if this meeting is successful."

"You just came from a meeting that will make you the richest person on the planet, and you are trying to top that."

"You are such the comedian, Art. Anyway I have to go, thanks."

Brown replied, "No problem." And he snapped his phone shut and left for the pool.

Chapter 8

Virginia Taylor and her daughter, Margaret, entered Taylor Enterprises Canada, hoping they could at last spend time with the most important man in their lives. As Taylor's empire grew, they have seen less and less of him. All those business trips were taking a toll on their family life and marriage. The mistress that stood between Taylor and his family was Taylor Enterprises. His company consumed their best years and the memories that could have come with them. Alex promised them he would relent a bit, but Virginia knew something new would always present itself and stand in their way. While they walked towards the elevator, Margaret hoped her parents would be able to patch things up.

"I wonder what Father has planned for the day?" she inquired while she fixed her hair.

"I'm sure it will be interesting, dear," Virginia replied. "Why are you fixing your hair? There are no teenage guys in this building."

"Oh, Mother," she replied as they entered the elevator.

"Sorry, dear. I couldn't resist," Virginia said, and pressed the button. The elevator ascended to the top floor.

Margaret glanced at her mother and mocked, "How can I meet any guys when I'm in an all-girl private school?

"That's the idea, dear." Virginia smiled, and the elevator opened its doors.

She replied, "Cute, Mother, cute." After vacating the elevator, they stood in front of Taylor's office. Taylor's executive assistant greeted them upon their arrival.

"Mrs. Taylor, it is good to see you."

"Hi, Wanda. We're here to see Alex," Virginia said.

"Mr. Taylor is not in his office, but I have a message from him for you to go the bottom floor. It's the private swimming pool." Mrs. Dennison gave Virginia the message.

"Cool, we get a chance to try out the pool," Margaret said. "Mrs. Dennison, any cute guys in the private room?"

"Well, the lifeguard, maybe." Mrs. Dennison smiled.

"Margaret, we are here to see your father. Remember him?"

"I know, I was just asking."

"Is there anything else I can do for you, Mrs. Taylor?"

"No, thank you, Wanda. Take care."

"You as well, Mrs. Taylor. Bye, Margaret."

"Bye, Mrs. Dennison." And they headed for the elevator again.

Arthur Brown had just finished an enduring hour of lap swimming when he decided to do his cool down period in the pool. He told the on-duty lifeguard to take his lunch break. Brown hated an audience, and with his training, he refused to have a brat supervise him in the pool. Brown closed his eyes and started to meditate. The calm water eased his emotions; Brown, alone in the room, found harmony and peace. While he meditated, he cleansed his thoughts from his mind and allowed his consciousness to become one with his soul. He remembered his wife's life and her death; then the promise he made at her grave. The four years he spent in Japan learning the art of the samurai, the shaolin, and the ninja as well as the Shadow Art. The creation of his suit and weaponry, and the long hours and the sacrifices he made. Then his thoughts shifted to the ten years he spent being the Shadow Chaser. The chance he had for a new love, but the call of vengeance ruined that for him as well. The memories shifted to his last mission, the abduction of Patrick Collins. The armour piercing bullet shredding his skin, arteries, and muscles like paper. The face of Antonio Stavros, the man he killed, and the thoughts of breaking his solemn vow.

"Never adapt to the ways of evil, or you will become no better than the evil you sought to destroy." The words of his teacher, Makoto Tanaka, kept on repeating in the cycle of his thought. He took the life of a human being so another one may live. However, the haunting memory will blacken his soul for a time to come.

Forgive me, Claire, for dishonouring your memory. Forgive me, master, for disobeying your teachings. Brown heard the door open. His trance faded as his consciousness returned to the present; his body feeling the cool sensation of the chlorine-scented water in the pool.

"Hey, stranger," a familiar voice said from the deck.

"Hey, Genie. I'll be right out," Brown said, and approached the steps of the pool. Brown ambled out and grabbed the robe he had left on the towel rack.

"Hi, Uncle Art," Margaret said, and turned her head towards the lifeguard station.

"How are you, Genie?" Brown grabbed her hand. "I'd hug, but I don't want to get you wet."

Virginia replied before she hugged him. "I'll take that chance."

"What are you looking for, Margaret?" Brown asked.

"I was just wondering if the lifeguard was here."

"I know I'm not as young as I used to be, but I don't think I need any help." Brown smiled.

"I know, Uncle. I just wanted to see what he looked like."

"Well, I sent him away, but I'm having lunch on the deck. Would you care to join me?" Brown queried. "He should be back any minute."

Margaret wanted to see the lifeguard, but Virginia had other plans.

"To be honest with you, Wanda told me to come down here to find Alex. Do you know where he is?" Brown scratched his head and tried to find the right answer.

"Well, Genie, it's like this. He called me on my way here and asked me if I could tell you he couldn't make it. He was detained."

"I knew it, Mom. He's bailed out again," Margaret said with bitterness in her voice.

"I'm sorry, dear. But I'm sure it was important," she replied, but hid her displeasure.

"Hold on. Since you are here, why don't you join me for lunch? Margaret, there are bathing suits of all sizes in the locker room. Why don't you go for a swim? The lifeguard will be here in a little while. Come on, what do you say?" Brown suggested. He hoped to use this opportunity to talk to Virginia for his friend's sake.

"Mom, this may be my last chance to have some fun. Please. Please, Mom."

"Alright then. We'll do it."

"Thanks, Mom," she replied when the lifeguard came in.

"Sorry, Dr. Brown. I thought you were gone."

"Don't worry about it, Paul. I'm having lunch with my friends," Brown said, then glanced at Margaret.

Margaret stared at the athletic blond walking towards the lifeguard station and said, "He's gorgeous."

"I take it you're going for a swim?" Brown smiled.

"Way! See you later, folks," she said. Margaret turned around and walked to the locker room.

"You can join her for a swim while I call the waiter," Brown said.

"I don't dare go in the pool with her. She'll never forgive me." Virginia smiled.

Brown replied, "I know what you mean." Brown paced towards the table, raised the receiver, and pressed the service line. "Hi, may I have three menus brought to the pool deck. Thank you."

"So, how are you doing, Art?" she asked.

"I'm doing well. For the first time in a long time, I feel I have a life again."

"I'm surprised about how you look."

"What do you mean?"

"Just nine years ago, you were knocking on death's door, and now look at yourself. You are in better shape than most people in their twenties. If it weren't for your car accident; you would be running the marathon," she said. Brown knew she did not know the true cause to his injury.

"Well, I'm just lucky you and Alex were there for me."

"I just wish we can be there for each other," she said with sadness.

Brown held onto her right hand and asked, "Are you two doing okay?"

"We're fine. We have wealth beyond our dreams, comfort, and prosperity," she replied, but then a tear rolled down her cheek.

"Except him to share it with you."

"I love him, Art. I know he loves me and Margaret—but he's always gone. You know he missed his daughter's first steps, birthdays, and even our anniversary," she replied when the waiter arrived with the menus.

"There you go, sir and madam."

"Thank you," Brown said and looked at the menu. A few minutes later, Brown made the selections. "Do you trust me?"

"I think I do," she replied with a puzzled look on her face.

"Make it three iced teas and three house specials," he said to the waiter.

"Of course, sir," the waiter replied before he left the room.

"Iced teas?"

"I haven't touched alcohol in nine years. Pollutes the senses."

"I see." She smiled.

"I could change your drink if you like?"

"No, that will be fine." Brown knew he had to find a way to help both of his friends before this situation got worse.

"Getting back to the matter at hand; I want you to know that he does care about you both. You are his whole life, and he always talks about you. Makes me kind of jealous to tell you the truth." Brown smiled.

Virginia returned the smile. "Oh, behave, but you are a sweetheart, Doc."

"Do you want me to talk to him tonight?" Brown asked.

"No, I don't want him to know I'm talking to you about this."

"I have some vacation time coming. Maybe I can go to Detroit and talk to him there alone."

"That would be a good idea. Besides, you are always welcome, Art," she said as the waiter came back with the order.

"Bonne appétit."

"Thank you," They both replied to the waiter before he left the room.

Virginia looked at her daughter talking to lifeguard and said, "Margaret, your meal is here."

"I'm not hungry, Mother." She decided to stay and chat with the lifeguard.

"How old is he anyway?" Virginia asked.

"I think he's seventeen or eighteen."

"Thanks a lot. Now, she will never want to leave." She smiled.

"All a part of the service." Brown grinned, then looked at his meal. "I don't know about you, but I'm starved."

"Me too," she replied, and they began to eat.

Thirty minutes later, the plates were empty, except for Margaret's. She continued talking to the lifeguard while Virginia and Brown engaged in a discussion of their own, sharing memories of earlier, happier years for them both. As well as talking about the present and the future. Virginia, while pleased to have had this time with her friend, wished her husband could have joined them as well.

Brown spotted the guardian angel made out of gold and said, "I see you are still wearing the pendant I gave you."

"I never part with it. Margaret wears hers all the time. And Alex turned his into a tie pin," she said.

"This is nice, just relaxing here and spending time with the both of you."

"I wish Alex were here right now. He missed out on a great time."

"I agree. It's been a long time since we were all together."

"Look at her, Art. She is still talking to him. This is the first time I've seen her happy in a long time."

"She is a great kid, and she is like the daughter I never had."

Virginia looked at Brown and smiled. "You would have made one hell of a father, Art."

"Thanks." Brown grinned with a touch of sadness.

The phone rang.

"Dr. Brown, here. Hey, Alex. Yes, she is right here. It's for you." Brown handed her the phone.

"Hi, hun. I see. No, no—I understand. No, that's okay. I will tell him. I will see you in fifteen minutes. Love you, too," she said before she passed the phone to Brown.

"Hello," Brown said, hoping to get a word in, but Taylor had already hung up.

"He's gone. We have to go back to Detroit; another major deal. He's sorry he had to cancel our evening. Same old, same old," she said while she stood.

"I'm sorry, Genie. I will be visiting you before long," Brown said, and rose from his seat.

"Margaret, let's go. Your father is picking us up."

"Okay, Mom," she said, then looked at the young lifeguard. "Bye, Paul."

The lifeguard gave her a piece of paper and said, "Bye, Margaret."

"What did he give her?" Virginia queried.

"Maybe a phone number," Brown replied.

"Thanks a lot." She did not hide her sarcasm.

"My pleasure." Brown returned her playfulness as Margaret walked towards them.

"New friend?" Brown asked.

"Maybe," Margaret replied. The teen tried to confine her excitement.

"Better get dressed, dear," Virginia said.

"Okay." Margaret walked towards the locker room and glanced at the lifeguard.

"Thanks for turning this day from a disaster to a pleasant one," Virginia said, and hugged Brown.

"It was my pleasure, Genie. Good to see you both again."

"Coming to our rescue like some masked avenger. But I bet you been told that a few times already," she said.

"Lady, you don't know the half of it." Brown smirked. After a quick change, Margaret left the locker room to join her mother.

Brown hugged her and said, "Take care, sweetheart."

"Thanks for the dish, Uncle Art."

"You didn't even touch your meal."

"I wasn't talking about the food, Uncle."

"You better watch your daughter, she's growing up."

Virginia replied, "I will, take care, Art." And left the room.

"Bye, Uncle Art," Margaret said, and winked at the lifeguard.

He replied, "Bye, dear." Alone in the room, Brown turned his head towards the lifeguard and looked at the teen. *I have my eye on you, kid.* He thought.

The phone rang again.

"Brown, here."

"Hey, is the family ready?" Taylor asked.

"Yep, they just left. How did your meeting go?"

"Excellent, they took the thermo suits."

"You cancelled the day—for that?"

"Not just that, the US military wants to look into a deal to upgrade their defence computers. That's why I have to go back to Detroit."

"I see. Listen, I'm thinking of taking some vacation time in the next couple of weeks, maybe we should get together and talk about a few things."

"Sure, Art, sounds great. But I have some more contracts to work out, but you go ahead take a vacation, and whenever I have some free time, take another one and come here. Sounds like a plan?"

"Yeah sure, maybe I can talk to you for a few minutes, it's important."

"Something wrong at work?"

"No, nothing at work, I just want to talk."

"The wife and Margaret are coming out now, I have to go. I will call you tonight. Okay."

"Sure, Alex."

"Great. I have my broker on the other line. I just bought thirty-five per cent of the Centurion Security Agency. I will talk to you later. Thanks for staying with Margaret and Virginia."

"It was my pleasure, take care, Alex," Brown said before he lowered the receiver into its cradle. *My poor friend, you are gaining profit, but you are losing your family—and your life.* Brown thought to himself as he headed for the locker room.

Chapter 9

Chicago, Illinois, USA. Two hours later:

*T*he Grinson Building was the home of many businesses and organizations. However, the building also housed the headquarters of one of the county's largest criminal organizations—the Scorpio Syndicate. They had endured a divisive gang war after the death of Antonio Stavros at the hands of the Shadow Chaser, and a new leader had taken the reigns of the entire syndicate. He kept to the shadows, and few people had ever seen him before. All those who knew his true identity—are now dead. Everyone referred to the dark recluse as the One.

After the syndicate suffered defeat after defeat and sat on the verge of extinction, the One sold his soul to the Devil. With one chance at securing the continuity of his organization, the One made a deal with the most dangerous criminal organization of all time. They are the Group of 13. According to secret chronicles, they originated as a thieves guild during the Roman Empire of Julius Caesar. They grew during the new Christian era and in the Middle Ages. Many believed they supplied both sides during the Crusades. The rumours go as far as claiming they caused King George of England to lose his sanity during the American Revolution. Their ultimate objective was to start war and to profit from those wars, regardless of the victor. This organization supplied weapons the Nazis used during WWII and worked with terrorists in the Middle East. Their sole mission is to bring chaos to order, to engulf the light, and lead the world to utter darkness and anarchy. With the group's help, the Scorpio Syndicate won the war and owned a huge percentage of the North American market. This far surpassed anything Antonio Stavros could have ever done as head of the family. However, the syndicate now belonged to the Thirteen. They claimed sixty per cent of the take, which gave them the right to dictate policy. In return, the group provided protection and power. The One eventually demonstrated a legacy of success, resulting in a promotion. The group bestowed him the honour of becoming the chief inquisitor of the North American continent. Of course, that meant killing the previous chief inquisitor. This meeting was like no other assembly of the past. The One was about to make a public appearance.

The syndicate controlled the entire top floor where the meeting was to take place. Dressed as successful and legit businessmen, members of the syndicate vacated the elevator one at a time and waited in the main foyer. Two rugged gunmen began frisking each member until they were satisfied that their guests were clean.

"This way, gentlemen," The first one said, and they followed him towards the end of the hallway. A large, black door concealed the room. A man, dressed in an Armani suit, opened the door and escorted each lieutenant of the syndicate to the dark room. When they entered, they witnessed a solitary bright light that shone on the huge table. And then the man began to speak to the gathering.

"Good afternoon, gentlemen. I'm glad you could all make it here with us today. The One has an important announcement to make."

"Hey, Franky," they replied.

Franky Dice, one of the most dangerous men of the syndicate. Franky, the underboss, represented the One at the meetings. His colleagues, enemies, and the law referred to him as the Dice Man.

"There are some things we have to take care of first before the boss starts talking." Franky looked around the room. "One, no talking while the boss speaks, it's disrespectful. Two, what is said here doesn't even go to the rest of the boys, capice?" Franky said.

"Whatever you say, Dice Man," they replied.

"Then without further ado, please pay your respects to the One," he said. A chair in the corner rolled towards the table, showing everything but the crime lord's facial appearance.

"Thank you, Dice Man. My capos, we are entering the new millennium, and it's time to leave the old ways behind. It's time to extend our borders. We are stronger, and we will prosper," the One said, and nodded to the Dice Man.

"The boss is right, now's the time to move."

"Where are we locating, boss?" one of the capos asked.

"We are moving north of the border. Toronto, Canada. Their laws are more flexible on a lot of importing issues. My alliances have guaranteed we will prosper in Canada."

"But most of Canada belongs to the Nightingale Family. Are we invading their turf?" the capo asked.

"As of today, the Nightingale Family will no longer be a threat to us again," the One said. One of his soldiers stood and said in protest.

"Boss, we don't have the fire power to wipe out the Nightingales."

The One replied, "Quit wasting my time, Chucky." And then he looked at Franky. Within a few seconds, Franky pulled out his revolver.

"What, what are ya doing?" he shouted as Franky aimed the gun at him.

"Never question the boss." Franky pulled the trigger twice. The thug's skin rippled like a drop of water hitting a still pond as the bullets slammed into his chest.

"Antonio Stavros was a soft leader, that's why he is dead. Anyone who questions me, I will kill them. So, is there any more doubt of my abilities in this room?"

"No doubts, boss. Great Idea," they all said, fearing for their own hides.

"Excellent, now get this piece of shit out of my office. Get ready, boys; we're moving. Dice will remain here to oversee things in Chicago," the One said. The men feared their boss, and they complied with his orders.

"Oh, and boys, don't forget to watch the news. You will like what happens next," he added. With those parting words, the meeting came to an end. As the members made a prompt exit from the room, Franky remained with his hidden boss.

"The Group of 13 is going to destroy the Nightingales. When they're gone, nobody will be able to stop you." Franky smiled.

"I must say, it's good to be the king," the One replied. "What's next on the agenda?"

"The bookkeeper is here to see you, boss."

"Let him in."

Franky said, "Come on in, Cid." The door opened, and a little man entered the room. "Sit here and answer the boss's questions."

The bookkeeper looked a wee bit jittery, but replied, "Yes, sir."

"So, Cid, how are my investments?"

"We made a partner today, sir."

"Who would that be?"

"About two hours ago, Mr. Alexander Taylor of Taylor Enterprises has bought thirty-five per cent of Centurion Security Agency, which makes him your biggest minority partner in that company," he said while he looked at his papers.

"Ah, yes. One of my legit businesses; well, it's good to have a guy like Taylor involved. He's so clean he squeaks. Is there anything else, Cid?"

"Taylor always studies the market. He looks for companies that report losses, and then he investigates them. Once he's satisfied that he could turn them around and make a profit, he goes for the kill. Sir, when Taylor buys over thirty per cent of a company's stock, he has the tendency to buy out the other owners and in the long run—the entire company. He intends to take over your controlling interest," Cid said. He knew the One would react to the news.

"Then I guess we will buy from the others before he does."

"Well, sir, we may be too late. Your associate, Mr. Shapiro, told me that Taylor, just had a teleconference with the other shareholders to acquire the remaining fifteen per cent while on route to Detroit to meet them in person. If they accept his offer, he will become your full partner. Which means you will no longer be able to dictate policy without seeking his approval."

"How much do I tend to lose?"

"You tend to gain three billion in equity if he bids the market price, but your other ventures stand to lose over seven billion. With Taylor monitoring the company accounts, we will no longer be able to launder or redirect funds to the syndicate."

"In English, Cid. What do I tend to lose in total?"

"There is a high probability that you will lose over four billion dollars; and your biggest leverage against an IRS investigation."

"When do you expect him to strike?"

"As a rule, when he buys half of a company's stock, he leaves things in place for about seven months before he attempts a hostile takeover to acquire the remaining shares, which he may have actually initiated already, sir," Cid said before he placed the notes on the table.

"I will discuss this with the Group of 13 to see what they want me to do. For now, I guess we will tolerate Mr. Taylor for at least six months," the One said.

"Thank you for your time, Cid. Franky, please escort Cid to the door."

"Right, boss. Come on, bookkeep."

"Yes, sir," he said before he left the room. Shutting the door, Franky turned off all of the lights, except for the one that led to the door.

"Boss, what happens if the group wants to keep the company?"

"We will then approach Mr. Taylor and offer him a deal for his shares."

"What if he doesn't take the deal?"

"We'll make certain that our offer is too attractive to refuse. If necessary, Franky, Mr. Taylor, or his family, will die."

Chapter 10

Detroit Michigan, USA. February 15, 2007. 9:30 a.m.:

*O*ver the skies of Michigan, a placid Arthur Brown sat in his seat as the plane flew towards the airport. Brown wondered how his friend and his wife were doing. Brown hadn't seen them since the holiday season. Before leaving Canada, he received a written message from Virginia stating that they made arrangements to attend the winter carnival in Toronto. Brown found it odd because Alex knew he planned to stay with them while he attended a medical convention. But he did not want to mention anything to her in his text message reply in case Alex changed his mind. The last thing he wanted was to add more friction between them. Even though it wasn't the first time he stayed at the Taylor mansion without them present, the fact neither Taylor nor his wife called him personally, put him on edge. When Brown traveled to Detroit, the Taylors would offer him a guest room at the mansion, access to servants, and a driver. Whether they were in the city or away, they wanted their friend to feel welcome and at home. Taylor prided himself on the hospitality he could provide to his guests, especially Brown.

Alex is a creature of habit. He would have texted me forty-five times before I boarded the plane. Something isn't right. He thought. *For now, I can only assume he's arranged a driver and all is well. But I don't put much stock in assumptions.*

"May I have your attention please? This is your captain speaking; we will be landing at the Detroit Metro Airport in fifteen minutes. I ask that you fasten your seatbelts, please. I thank you for flying Air Canada Flight 144," the pilot said. Brown complied with the instructions.

Hopefully, I will get some answers. Brown thought.

Within a few minutes, the plane landed. Brown got off the huge craft and headed for the airport.

"I hope you have enjoyed your flight, sir," the airline attendant said.

Brown grabbed his luggage and smiled. "Yes, I did, ma'am. Have a nice day." Brown trekked around the airport and looked for Taylor's chauffeur. After searching in vain for about twenty minutes, Brown decided to do the smart thing—ask for assistance. Brown ambled towards the information centre. In front of him stood a beautiful, young woman. Her silk blond hair reminded him of his wife, Claire.

"Can I help you, sir?' she asked with a kind smile.

"Young lady, you remind me of my wife. She was a beautiful soul, much like yourself." Brown started to deliver the charm.

The lady could not help but feel attracted to the older gentleman. He may have been older than her, but he was without a doubt in her mind, a charmer, and an athletically, built man.

"Why thank you, sir. However, I doubt I'm the main reason for your coming here?" she smiled.

"I wish it were, but you are right." Brown returned the smile. "I'm looking for my driver. I'm afraid we may have crossed wires. Would you be so kind in paging him for me?"

"I would be delighted to, sir," she replied. "What is his name?"

"Maurice Beaulieu, thank you. And please call me Arthur, Arthur Brown. Sir was my father." He winked. She paged the chauffeur.

"If there is a Maurice Beaulieu here, please come to the information centre. Your passenger, Mr. Arthur Brown, is here. Thank you."

"Thank you, kindly."

"It was my pleasure, Arthur." Brown sat near the centre and waited for his driver to arrive. Seconds became minutes, and still the chauffeur failed to arrive.

It's has been twenty minutes, and no Maurice. Brown thought. *What the hell is going on?* After pacing for a few more minutes, Brown returned to the front desk.

"Arthur, you are still here?" she smiled.

"It appears so, ma'am. I was wondering if you can call me a cab. It looks like we did get our wires crossed," Brown replied.

"Consider it done. By the way, my name is Carolyn Walters. Ma'am was my mother." She winked while she made the call. Moments after the call, she handed him a piece of paper.

"Thank you, Carolyn. What's this?"

She gave him a teasing look and said, "It's my number, if you'll be in town for a while, I can show you around. Maybe we can go out. You're cute. Who knows, I may make you feel ten years younger."

"I'm afraid I may feel ten years older, Carolyn." Brown grinned when his cab arrived. "I got to go."

"Call me?" she asked.

"You bet," Brown said, and vacated the airport.

Brown entered the cab and thought. *So, this is how it feels to have a normal life.*

"Where to, chief?" the cab driver asked.

"Taylor Estate."

"Way up there. I don't get many calls to go by those parts. Traffic is busy. It's going to cost you double."

"Here's five hundred dollars, can we go now?"

"For five hundred I would tell my mother-in-law that I love her. Yes, sir," the cab driver said, and they drove away from the airport.

"I hope everything is all right," Brown said. "Hold on, folks—I'm coming." The cab headed towards the highway and Taylor Estate.

The yellow cab raced along the freeway closing in on its destination. Traffic problems meant the speedy cab took thirty minutes to get out of the interchange. The cab motored five miles further to a small rural area just outside of the Motor City. Brown tried to reach the estate, but with no success.

"This is peculiar," he said to himself. "Not even his servants are answering the phone. All of the lines are not answering, even his private ones."

"We're almost here, chief," the cab driver said. "Still can't reach your friend?"

"No, there is something wrong," Brown said. "Do me a favour?"

"Name it, chief," the cab driver said. Brown took out two cell phones from his jacket.

"Once you let me off, call the cops and find a place to hide. Take my other phone, and I will call you if I need help."

"Sure thing, but shouldn't you wait for the cops?"

"If we wait for the cops, it may be too late. Just call the cops and stay out of danger."

The driver drove towards the fence and asked, "Whatever—but what makes you think you can handle what's in there yourself?"

"I have experience with this kind of thing." Brown felt the urge of the samurai in the pit of his stomach. The attackers damaged the fence and disabled the electric circuitry. Brown knew something bad had happened.

"This is not good, chief."

"I'm getting off here. Call the police now—and hide. If you do not hear from me by the time the cops arrive, it means I'm dead. Got it." The driver tapped his fingers on the wheel and gave Brown a nervous smile. "You sure know how to make a guy feel good, chief."

Brown grinned. "It's the least I can do." And he stepped out of the cab and walked towards the main entrance. Brown kept a slow pace and advanced to the front doors, just passing the marble lions in-between each stairway that led to the door. Brown examined the lock on the front door; they picked it, and found three pair of footprints at the front.

The door is halfway opened. Looks like I'm facing at least three guns here. Brown gave a slight push on the door while he maintained an awareness of the entire area. *I have to be cautious; Alex, Genie, and Margaret's life—as well as the lives of the servants are in my hands.* Brown noticed the front foyer demolished and the family butler face down on the floor with a pool of blood next to him.

"Gilles, my God," Brown gasped as he approached the butler. Brown turned him around and noticed the bullet wound in the servant's right shoulder.

Trying to whisper, the butler look at Brown. *"It's just a flesh wound, sir. But I am still bleeding. I just came to, sir."*

"Rest, my friend. The police are on the way." Brown tried to reassure the old servant. "Are they still here?"

"Yes, Master Brown," he replied. *"One is with the staff in the study down here, and two of them are with Master Taylor."*

"Where are Virginia and Margaret?"

"They were not here when it happened, sir."

Brown replied, *"Stay here, my friend. I will handle this."* And then he tiptoed towards the study. He knew he had to be quiet in order to infiltrate and take out the threat. Brown held his cane rather than using it, to avoid the sound of the cane tapping on the marble floor.

Here's the game plan. If the gunman is holding his hostages away from the door, I can surprise him. If that doesn't work, then I will just have to trust my throwing arm. Brown turned the knob at a turtle's pace and opened a crack in the door far enough to survey the room. For now, luck smiled on him. He observed two servants, both tied up, and lying on the floor, except for Elaina, the nineteen-year-old maid was tied to a chair. The young girl's features kept the gunman distracted. The thug dropped his guard and ignored the door.

"Hey, you're something else, baby. Oh, your dress has been wrinkled, mind if I straightened it up for you?" he said to her with desire in his voice.

"Don't touch me," she begged.

"Too bad, I'm doing it anyway." He laughed. The thug placed his hand on her knee in a gentle manner and began to assault the young girl. The action brought Brown back to his wife and her assailants, and for the first time in over nineteen years; the Shadow Chaser entered the body of Arthur Brown.

"You heard the lady, creep," Brown asserted from behind him. "She said to leave her alone."

"What," the goon said surprised and confused. He spun around and noticed the silver handle of Brown's cane heading towards his face. With a powerful whack, the cane smashed his nose and knocked the gunman out cold. The blow left him on the floor—motionless.

"Are you okay, Elaina?" Brown asked while he untied her.

"Yes, Mr. Brown," she said. Tears flowed from her eyes.

"What happened here?"

"It was terrible. Three men stormed in and took us in here. They tied us all up, and the two of them took Mr. Taylor upstairs," she said, trying to stop herself from trembling.

59

"Help is on the way. Can you free the rest of them?" Brown asked.

"Yes, I can."

"Good. Untie them. Then get yourselves out of here," he ordered. "Take Gilles with you and do not make a sound. Understood?" In haste, he tied up and gagged the gunman.

"Yes, sir. But what are you going to do?"

Brown looked at the frightened maid and instructed, "Don't worry about me, just get all of them and you—out of here. Take this phone, and when you get out, press the memory 1 button. A cab is waiting for my instructions. Tell him to come and get you all. I will get Alex from the other two gunmen." Brown gave her the goon's handgun. "Here, take the gun. Just in case they get me, and they come out after you."

She pleaded with Brown to take back the gun. "Sir, you're going to need it more than me. If you're planning to get the other two."

"I hate guns; besides, I won't need it."

"But, sir, they are extremely dangerous."

"Really, Elaina." Brown smirked. "So am I." Brown sneaked out of the study. The young maid and the other two servants followed. Brown waited for the three to grab the wounded butler and leave the mansion before he proceeded towards the stairs. The staircase was long, and Brown knew he would need his cane. Brown wished he were nineteen years younger. Back then, he could have dashed to the top of the stairs with great ease, and with the reflexes of a ninja. But that's when he wore the mask of the Shadow Chaser, the dark spectre who leaped into the darkness and shared the night with the stars. But those days were gone. Now, he carried the cane of Arthur Brown, a fifty-seven-year-old cripple, in his mind. Nevertheless, he had to come up with a swift and flawless plan—or his friend could pay a dear price for his indecision.

I always hate this when they do this in movies, but I hope this works. Brown thought, but he had to play dumb. "Hey, Alex. Where are you? You did not have the limo for me; my bunions are killing me. Where the hell is everyone? Did you fire the help?" Brown acted out the role of a rich and ignorant colleague.

During that time, the two gunmen who were interrogating Taylor heard yelling from the stairs.

"Who the hell is that?" the first gunman asked while the other one punched a beaten and tired Alexander Taylor.

"How the hell am I supposed to know? Take a peek," the goon said, and he stopped the assault on his hostage; still tied to the chair. Taylor sat there almost lifeless; the blood oozed out of his lips.

"Some old guy with a cane, the fool can hardly get up. But he's on top of the stairs." The first gunman laughed at Brown.

"Who the hell is he, Taylor?" the other goon demanded. He raised his hand in the air, as if he would strike the billionaire.

Taylor argued with his pain and said, "It must be Dr. Brown, he's a scientist and a friend. He's here for a medical convention."

"I thought the boss took care of all of Taylor's commitments?" the first gunman asked. "How come Johnny didn't see him come in?"

"I would not be surprised if that dummy is still playing with the maid he tied up. As for the boss, he did, but somehow this old fart didn't get the message. Okay, Taylor, tell him where you are," the second gunman demanded. "But no tricks, or you and the cripple are dead, clear?" And he smacked Taylor's right cheek.

"Alright, alright," Taylor said to the gunman. "I'm here, Art, but I'm busy with a meeting right now. Meet me at the office in an hour." Taylor hoped his friend would not come in.

"Good one, Taylor," the second gunman said. "Is he leaving yet?"

"Nope, the dumbass is still comin'," the first gunman said.

Brown opened the door.

"Come on, Alex. I'm here," Brown said. "Why can't I come..." Brown spotted his friend tied to a chair with the second gunman adjacent to Taylor.

"Oh--oh mm--my G--g—od!" Brown stuttered, and waited for the first gunman to come up behind him. He prayed his performance would lead his adversaries into a false sense of security.

"Hands up there, cripple," the first one shouted.

"I will do whatever you want, sir. Don't hurt me, I'm just a scientist. Please, Alex, tell him I will do whatever he wants," Brown pleaded. Taylor knew Brown had a plan.

"Shut up, you old fool, and put your cane down," the first gunman shouted. That gunman stood to his right side. This gave him the perfect chance to react. Brown prayed he would have enough time to surprise the other goon as well. But if he failed, he knew the other gunman, next to Taylor, would have a clear shot at him; and this guy would not miss.

Brown replied, "As you wish." With all speed, he slammed his cane on the first gunman's right hand. The brutish thug's knuckle cracked like a firecracker; the blow forced the gun out of his hand. Before he had time to react, Brown used his cane as leverage for his left leg, and with his right leg, he delivered a forward kick to his opponent's head. The kick knocked out the first gunman, whose bulk thumped onto the floor. The second gunman could not believe what he had witnessed; the quickness of the attack astounded the thug. A cripple taking out one of the syndicate's best fighters; uncanny. But at the last second, he realized he had a clear shot at the lame senior.

The thug dithered for a moment; then he aimed his gun and said, "You son of a..." Brown took advantage of the thug's hesitation.

Brown muttered, "I hope this works." Instincts guided him as Brown turned with the quickness of a hare and tossed his cane towards the second gunman.

He had seconds to react, but he continued to practice his aim with his old Shadow Chaser fedora. But he hoped his accuracy with a cane was as good.

The cane flew through the air like a tomahawk. A skin-crawling *thump* sound followed as the handle of the cane impacted the gunman's forehead. The thug crashed onto the floor, his left foot quivering. The cane had split open his head, and blood gushed like water from a tap. The goon was still semi-conscious when Brown limped towards him. Looking for his gun, the thug tried to rise.

"Going somewhere?" Brown inquired, and punched him on the jaw. The thug collapsed for good.

"You still got it," Taylor said trapped in his chair.

"Alex, are you okay?" Brown untied his friend.

"I'm fine, but it happened so suddenly. How the hell did they get in?" Taylor asked while the circulation started to return to his arms.

"They disabled the security systems at the gate and around the building," Brown explained.

"How were you able to turn so fast?"

"I lifted my bad leg and used my good leg to twirl around. Then I used my bad leg for leverage to throw the cane at him. I'm glad the leg is getting stronger, or it would have been me with a hole in my forehead," Brown said.

A large *rumble* resonated from downstairs. The cavalry arrived at last.

"Police. Freeze," they yelled.

"We're in here, officer," Taylor yelled. The sound of footsteps invaded the stairs. The police stormed the room and assumed a defensive posture.

"Is everyone all right?" one of the officers asked.

"Were fine, officer. Thank you," Taylor said. The older officer approached him.

"We got the call from the cabbie, and when we arrived, your servants were with him," the policeman said while the other officers handcuffed the two gunmen, took their weapons, and escorted them out of the room. "Tell me what happened here, Mr. Taylor?"

"Well, those monsters attacked us and shot my butler," Taylor said. "How is he?"

"Don't worry, sir," he replied, "he's going to be all right. Mr. Brown, the maid said you saved them. Tell me what happened?"

"It's Dr. Brown, and your name please?"

"Lieutenant Davies, Detroit PD." The detective noticed Brown supporting a cane. "Now, can you tell me how you stopped these men?"

"Lieutenant, anybody, including a cripple can hit a man with a cane from behind. But, as for the other two, I got lucky."

"How lucky, sir?"

"Well, the first one tripped on my cane and fell on the edge of the chair; splitting his head and knocking himself out. His friend tried to help, so I took a chance and pushed him from behind, and he hit his head on the same chair."

"How the hell did he trip on your cane?"

"Well, I panicked and threw my cane on the floor. I am sorry to say I was afraid, and I begged him not to kill me. He was mad and tried to hit me. So, I guess he was not paying attention, and he tripped over my cane." Brown acted the part of a frightened man.

"So, then you panicked?" the lieutenant asked.

"Yes, I panicked. I'm a scientist. I'm not trained to deal with criminals. I'm not fighter. I leave that to the professionals. The ones I see capable to fight off these kinds of people are the men and women of the police force," Brown said, but in his mind—he laughed.

"I see, do you have anything else to add, Mr. Taylor?" he asked, but Taylor knew his friend did not want to know the true story of the battle.

"Of course that's what happened. Do you think the two of us staged this to get attention?" Taylor yelled. The lieutenant knew Taylor was influential, and the last thing he needed was to harass a billionaire who was also a victim.

"Not at all, sir. I will fill out my report. Thank you for your time. Oh, before I go, where are your wife and daughter?"

"I don't know. They left today for Paris for my wife's modeling agency. Art was coming here, and we were all going to meet in a week," Taylor said, but Brown intervened.

"Alex, I received a written message from Virginia saying that you, Margaret, and her were going to Toronto for the winter carnival. I found it somewhat odd that all of you would go without calling me. I was sure you knew that I was coming for the convention," Brown said. "But I just assumed you had changed plans and forgot to tell me."

"What are talking about?" Taylor wondered. "We were not going to Toronto."

"Well, that's what she said on the message," Brown said.

The lieutenant looked at Taylor and said, "We better find out their whereabouts, sir. This holdup may have been a diversion on the part of the criminals."

"What are you saying?" Taylor demanded.

"What I'm saying, sir, is that your family may be in terrible danger."

"I'm forced to agree with the officer, Alex. Who was taking her to the airport?" Brown asked.

"Maurice was supposed to take them there, then pick you up."

"You have better give him a call," Brown said. Taylor grabbed the phone and dialed his chauffeur. Taylor switched on the speakers, so the police could hear the conversation.

"Maurice, this is Mr. Taylor speaking."

"Yes, sir. How are you enjoying your trip to Toronto, sir?"

"Maurice, I'm still here in Detroit. You were supposed to pick up Dr. Brown at the airport after you escorted Mrs. Taylor and my daughter on the private jet."

"Yes, sir. However, your wife said Dr. Brown's convention was cancelled, and you were flying to Toronto instead. She said you told her to cancel her plans and meet you there," Maurice explained.

"I said no such thing," Taylor said, and started to panic.

"But, sir, she told me she talked to you. She said you wanted to spend some family time with her and Miss Margaret. She asked her assistant to take her place in Paris. Then she tried to catch a plane to Toronto," Maurice explained. "But she couldn't get one, so she asked me to drive her to Windsor, and she would grab a charter flight to Toronto. That is what I did, sir. I helped her on the plane with her luggage, and that was the last I have seen of them, sir. Monsieur, it is the God's honest truth." Maurice started to feel that something terrible had happened to his employers.

"I believe you, my friend. Where are you now?"

"I'm just entering the city. I should be back in twenty minutes."

The detective said, "Let me talk to him." Taylor switched off the speaker and handed him the phone. "Sir, give me your location, and I will have an escort meet you. We want to search the vehicle for clues."

"Of course, sir. I am on the Ambassador Bridge just entering Detroit. I'm the ivory coloured limo, and the licence plates are J4X E3P." The detective wrote the information the chauffeur provided to him.

"Thank you. We are on our way," the detective said, and he hung up the phone. "Anderson, get a squad car to escort this limo, here is the info. Tell them it's urgent. We are dealing with a possible international kidnapping."

"Yes, sir," the officer replied before he left the room.

"But how could this have happened?" Taylor asked in desperation.

"Voice manipulation and cell phone tampering can be done with the right equipment," Brown said in a sombre tone.

"They must have been planning this for a long time," the detective said. Brown ambled towards his friend and gave him a gentle pat on his right shoulder.

"Alex, I'm sorry this has happened. But you are hurt; you should go to the hospital. I will stay here in case the phone rings."

"Your friend is right. You have taken a serious beating by those gunmen."

"No, my place is here," Taylor shouted. For the first time in his life, he stood there, powerless to do anything but wait for a call.

"Well, at least let the paramedics treat you up here then, sir," the detective pleaded.

"Then treat me," Taylor yelled in rage. Brown sat by his friend.

"I know this is maddening, but you need to keep a clear head, Alex. The lieutenant is just doing his job."

Taylor rubbed his forehead and said, "You are right. I am sorry, sir. Just I don't know where my wife and daughter are—or if they are safe."

"No need to apologize, sir. Since there is a chance we are dealing with a kidnapping, we can waive the standard twenty-four-hour wait for missing persons and call the FBI." The detective grabbed his cell phone. "Yes, this is Lieutenant Isaiah Davies of Detroit PD. We are at Taylor Estate, and it appears that Mrs. Alexander Taylor and her daughter, Margaret, were abducted. We request the FBI be sent here immediately. The address is 1 Manor Drive, thank you." And he ended the call.

"What now?" Taylor asked.

"Now, we wait," Brown said when the phone rang.

"Turn the speaker on, I want to hear what they have to say," the detective said. After a quick nod, Taylor switched on the speaker again and answered. "Hello."

"Hey, Mickey. Is the rich stiff able to talk, or did you break his jaw?"

"No, it's me Taylor," he roared like a lion. "Your friends are not able to talk right now, but you are welcome to visit them in jail."

"What? How the hell did you get free?" the voice probed. "No matter, we will have to go with Plan B."

"What do you want, you son of a bitch?"

"Easy, old-timer. We got plenty of time. I just wanted to let you know we got your wife and your little girl. They're hot stuff. You're one lucky man." The caller laughed.

"What do you want?" Taylor demanded.

"We want you to be on the next plane to Toronto. We'll contact you by phone."

"Why there?"

"Because that's where they are. Gives you less time to get the cops organized. It's ten-thirty in the morning, so you got six hours to get there, or they're dead. I suggest you get on one of your fancy planes and fly up there," the voice said. "We were going to get the lads to bring you here in person, but that has changed since they are no longer with you."

"Alright then, damn you. Where do you want me to go in Toronto?"

"Your fancy Toronto office at Taylor Enterprises of course. We can make sure that the cops are not monitoring our calls from there. You got six hours, understood?"

"I understand."

"Good then. You better go, and if you're a good boy, I may let you talk to your wife—and that young daughter of yours. Time is ticking away. Talk to you soon."

"If you hurt them, so help me I'll…" Taylor threatened but the voice already ended the call.

"We better get to the airport, gentlemen," Brown suggested.

"Agreed," Taylor replied while the detective looked on.

"I will tell the FBI we are on our way to the airport. They will meet us there," the detective said. "In the meantime, I will call the RCMP and Toronto PD to advise them of our situation." And he stormed out of the room.

"We'd better follow, the faster we get to Toronto, the quicker I can find Genie and Margaret," Brown said, and helped his friend to the door.

"How are you going to do that?" Taylor asked.

"I'll explain on the way. Let's go," Brown said. And they left the mansion, leaving the police there to continue their investigation.

As they arrived at the airport, both Taylor and Brown were silent. Both men were trying to find the answer, but for now, whoever had Virginia and Margaret—were calling the shots.

"The FBI and the local authorities are already here," Brown said as the limo stopped near the private jet.

"You said you could find, Genie and Margaret earlier. How are you going to do that?" Taylor asked.

"You remember the set of jewelry I gave the three of you?"

"Yes, what about them?"

"Well, inside each of them is a tiny piece of circuitry that works as a homing beacon. When I get to my lab, I can find their location. Once I match the patterns of the signal from the GPS with the city map, I will be able to find them," Brown explained.

"You never told me you did that."

"Well, I always wanted to make sure you were all protected."

"You're a genius. That means the police will be able to get them back then."

Brown replied, "Odds sure looks that way, my friend." Brown and Taylor vacated of the limo, and the local detective introduced them to three FBI agents.

"Gentlemen, this is Agent Wise, Agent Marks, and Special Agent Flynn," the detective said as Brown faced his old nemesis.

"Gentlemen. Agent Flynn, good to see you again," Brown said.

Flynn looked at Brown and asked, "Have we met before, sir?"

"Last year at the charity event for underprivileged children, you were assigned to the Governor's detail." Brown smiled. But he remembered the man who tried in vain to put him, the Shadow Chaser, behind bars.

"Of course," Flynn replied, but the cane-carrying gentleman did not make an impression with the seasoned agent.

"We are going to join you on the flight to Toronto while the lieutenant will investigate things here," Agent Wise explained.

"I understand," Taylor said. The five men entered the plane. Minutes later, the jet took off for Toronto and for the unknown future that would soon unfold.

Chapter 11

Toronto, Ontario, Canada. 1:00 p.m.:

*T*wo and a half hours after the mysterious phone call, the players of this game of chess sat in Taylor's office on the top floor of Taylor Enterprises. During the time it took to travel by plane, the FBI in Detroit already made plans with the Canadian authorities to install surveillance devices at the office. Both police agencies formed an elite team to deal with the abduction. Toronto police had just completed the installation of their surveillance equipment when the FBI arrived. They were ready for the next phone call. And with a little luck, they will be able to trace their call and find those responsible for the abduction of Virginia and Margaret Taylor. While Taylor and the others went to his office to wait for the phone call and trace it, Arthur Brown prepared a plan of his own. Brown went to his lab and activated NIGHT. *I have to find them while I still have time.* Activating the homing beacon of both Virginia and Margaret's necklaces, Brown would be able to match their coordinates with the map of the city. In ten minutes, he would have their location.

This is going too smoothly. He thought and stood from his chair. Knowing he should be there with his friend, he grabbed his microphone.

"NIGHT, please notify me on my pager when the locator survey is complete."

"Yes, Dr. Brown," the computer replied. NIGHT's capability far exceeded the average computer. Dr. Brown had created the first ever self-aware neurotronic hybrid computer. The computer had the memory patterns of a human. NIGHT executed commands with flawless efficiency and accuracy; Brown programmed the computer to respond to both, Taylor's voice, and his own.

"NIGHT, do not demonstrate any verbal traits when the additional bio-signs arrive with me upon my return," Brown ordered. "They don't need to know of your existence."

"Acknowledged, doctor." Brown left the lab and headed back to Taylor's office.

Taylor waited and looked at the phone. His facial expression made him appear emotionless; but it was not so, his thoughts filled with sadness, regret, and pain.

"*Oh, things will be different,*" Taylor whispered. "*I promise I will make time for you both…just come back home.*" Agent Flynn and another plain clothed officer walked towards him.

"Mr. Taylor, we are ready for his call. We have our men all over the area. Our people are monitoring the phone, and we have state of the art devices for tracing their calls," Flynn explained. "Don't worry, sir. We will catch him."

"Thank you, Agent Flynn."

"Sir, my name is Inspector Joseph Somerville. I'm with the Toronto Metropolitan Police Services. I just wanted to let you know we're doing everything in our power to find your wife and daughter."

Taylor replied with a calm tone. "Thank you both, gentlemen." And he turned towards the huge window, looking for a miracle.

"Agent Flynn filled me in. I hate to make you relive this, but I must ask you a few questions," Somerville said.

With a slight turn of his head, Taylor looked at Somerville and said, "By all means, inspector."

"Thank you." Somerville nodded. "Do you know anyone who would want revenge against you?"

"No, not off hand," Taylor said. "I am a powerful businessman; I have made a lot of enemies in my life, but I can't believe anyone would do this." Taylor stepped towards his chair.

"Nobody at all? How about recently? Any threats or angry colleagues?"

"My last takeover took place two weeks ago. Seven months ago, I bought thirty-five per cent of Centurion Security Agency. The company was losing money, and the stockholders were desperate to sell. I studied the books and found no reason for this to happen. I called an emergency meeting with the board. Centurion chairman Mr. Tony Shapiro, myself, and three other owners were present at the meeting. I bought the three gentlemen out and became an equal partner with Mr. Shapiro. I ordered an investigation regarding the loss of revenue," Taylor explained. "However, I didn't know at the time about Mr. Shapiro's involvement with organized crime."

"Please continue, sir," Somerville said.

"Owning fifty per cent of the shares allowed me to make numerous changes to the company. About two weeks ago, the D.A. brought up Mr. Shapiro on fraud charges, and I took over Centurion in a hostile takeover. I took full control of the company. Four days ago, Mr. Shapiro's attorneys visited me and gave me an offer that I could not refuse; but I did refuse it, just the same."

"Shapiro is also being indicted for his suspicions of being the head of the Scorpio Syndicate," Flynn said. "You sure know how to pick your enemies."

"What did he offer you?" Somerville asked.

"He offered four billion U.S. dollars. I paid three billion for the company."

"And you turned it down?" Flynn gasped in astonishment.

"I know it is a lot of money, but I don't let criminals in my company, nor do I take their resources. I establish my own power and riches, but never at the expense of someone else," Taylor said as Brown walked inside.

"Any word yet, Alex?"

"Nothing. Art, this is Inspector Somerville. Inspector, this is Dr. Arthur Brown."

Somerville shook Brown's hand and said, "A pleasure, sir."

"Same here," Brown replied. He remembered Somerville. Back in the day, Toronto police assigned him to track down and arrest the Shadow Chaser. Brown felt like person who attended his high school reunion with all the old gang. If it weren't not for the abduction, he would've found this amusing. Seconds later, an officer moved towards the two senior officers.

"Agent Flynn, Inspector Somerville. We received a call from Detroit."

"Well, what is it?" Flynn pushed.

"The three gunmen were Johnny Gibbs, Mickey "Baby Eyes" Moreno, and Sammy Dawe. They are associates of the Scorpio Syndicate. But the best part is that Johnny Gibbs worked as a security analyst for Centurion Security Agency."

"It makes sense," Flynn said.

"Mr. Taylor, who set up your home security system?" Somerville probed.

"My company, Centurion. Oh my God," Taylor said with the shock of this recent discovery.

"Scorpio Syndicate, I thought they were losing the gang war," Brown said.

"Don't believe everything you see on the news, doctor. Ten years ago, they showed up with a new leader. He's known as the One," Flynn said.

"There is a possibility that Mr. Shapiro is the One. After hearing Mr. Taylor's story, I may agree with that theory," Somerville said.

"Shapiro? Not the 'Ice Pick' Shapiro. Alex, tell me you didn't go toe to toe with this guy," Brown said, but Taylor did not reply. The look on his face said it all. Brown knew the answer; and it disappointed him. Tony Shapiro, the former lieutenant of the late Antonio Stavros, survived the fire that claimed the life of his boss and the career of the Shadow Chaser.

"You sure know your mafias, Dr. Brown," Flynn said.

"I watch a lot of Court TV in my spare time, Agent Flynn."

"So, now we know that Gibbs disabled the security since he had the codes and the knowledge," Somerville said, looking for more clues.

"The first caller in Detroit asked to speak to Mickey, so we know they are all involved," Flynn said. "Mr. Taylor, did you recognize the voice on the phone?"

"No, I didn't. I never heard it before in my life."

"As I mentioned to the officers before, gentlemen, it's not hard to disguise a voice," Brown said.

"Sir, when did his attorneys say they would get back to you?" Flynn asked.

"They said Mr. Shapiro would be in touch with me in four days to see if I didn't have a change of heart."

"Now, he's making sure you do have a change of heart," Brown replied. At that moment, the phone rang.

"It can't be them, it's not six hours yet," Taylor panicked.

"It's just like the syndicate to change the rules," Flynn said. "They're trying to catch you unprepared, but they underestimated us. Pick up it, sir." Flynn nodded at the officer to begin the trace. Taylor cupped his hand around the receiver with a gentle, but firm, grip and raised it next to his left ear.

"Yes."

"Mr. Taylor, I see you're there waiting for us. Forgive the change of plans, but I figure you want to be with your wife and kid. So, I thought that now is a better time than any," the arrogant voice said.

"All right, I'm here damn you. What do you want?"

"First of all, your attempts to trace this call will fail. And, I know you involved the police. Just know we have eyes everywhere. When we say come alone; we mean what we say," the voice asserted. From the speaker phone, Taylor, the police, and Brown heard the sound of a gun reloading. A loud gunshot soon followed.

"What's going on?" Taylor yelled.

"I shot in the direction of your wife and girl. Don't worry, I missed, but I won't miss a second time. Are you ready to talk?"

"Yes, I will do anything you ask," Taylor pleaded.

"Then tell the feds to cut their tracing gadgets. Don't lie to us, Taylor. We'll know if you're lying," the voice said. Taylor looked at Flynn.

"Do it," Taylor ordered. Flynn nodded at his officer to cease the trace.

"You're a smart man, Taylor. Now, here's the offer. We want one billion dollars. But first, I want you to turn off the speakers, so this next demand will be for your ears only," the voice said. Taylor turned off the speakers.

"They are off."

"I can see that. Good man, Taylor. Now, we want you to dump the Centurion shares on the open market at half of what you bought them for. We don't want you owning this company. But before you sell your shares, you will send us an email. We'll provide you the email address. You just check your email account, and you will see that we sent you a message. Don't do anything fancy, Taylor. Just reply to it. Understood?" the voice ordered.

"Yes." Taylor checked his email and followed the caller's instructions. "I have done what you have asked. Now let me talk to my wife," Taylor demanded.

The voice replied, "Sure why not. Here's your wife." Taylor waited on edge until he heard his wife's voice.

"Alex, help us," she said doused in terror.

"I'm here, luv. I will do everything they want me to do. How is Margaret?" Taylor pleaded, but the thug took the phone away.

"Okay, Taylor. You heard enough. The account number is enclosed in the email message we sent you. Don't tell this to the cops. You got one hour to complete the transaction—or they're dead," the voice said before the line died. Taylor dropped the receiver. His whole life started to crumble in front of him.

"I don't know what to do." He lost all hope. His eyes gave an expression of fear, and he stared at the people in the room.

"Were you able to get a trace? " Somerville asked the officer.

"No, sir. There wasn't enough time."

"How did they know what we were doing?" Flynn said.

"Centurion did the security for this building as well," Taylor replied.

"My God, they could be monitoring everything and us as we speak," Flynn said. Silence filled the room for a moment. Then Brown felt a slight vibration coming from his coat pocket, followed by constant beeping. The sound caught everyone's attention. Brown knew NIGHT was on to something.

Brown looked at his pager and said, "Alex, Inspector Somerville, and Agent Flynn. Follow me, please."

"Where are we going?" Somerville asked.

"No questions, gentlemen. Just follow me, please," Brown requested. They followed him out the door.

Brown led the three men to his lab; the sealed door at the front entrance guarded its secrets. Centurion had no access to that corridor of the building; Brown trusted no one and administered his own security.

"This will only take a minute, gentlemen," Brown said, and he approached the retina scanner on the security panel.

"Dr. Arthur Thaddeus Brown. Access granted," the automation voice said.

"This way, gentlemen," Brown said. "Computer, secure the front door." And the door shut behind them.

Flynn stared at the machinery and the equipment before he asked, "What is this place?"

"This is my office. The door on your left leads to the Taylor Enterprises' laboratories. This is my private lab. The room is one hundred per cent secured. I built the system myself."

"This is impressive, but what does this have to do with the case?" Somerville probed.

Brown smiled. "I'm glad you asked." And brought them to his computer monitor. "Here is the location. Virginia and Margaret are right there." Looking at the monitor, they noticed two signals coming from the southeast end of the city.

"How did you find them?" Flynn asked.

"I think I can answer that, Agent Flynn. Art gave me and my family each a necklace. Inside, it contained a surveillance device in case such a thing as this would happened," Taylor said, and smiled at his friend.

"It took some time to pin-point the exact location, but now I have it. I will print it out for you, gentlemen," Brown said as he pressed the print button. Seconds later, the police received a copy of the map.

"Thank you, Dr. Brown. I will call for backup," Flynn said, but Brown grabbed his shoulder.

"Not yet, sir. I want make sure nobody could trace your call. I'm currently monitoring all the security systems in this building," Brown explained. "In one minute, I will be disabling their systems and reprogramming them through here." Brown typed in his codes.

"Could this be possible?" Somerville asked.

"Oh yes, Dr. Brown is the best in the field," Taylor said as the systems fell under their control.

Brown monitored the phones and said, "Done, I even left a ghost image in the computer's program, so they would believe they are in control."

"Now what?" Flynn said.

"I've just disabled all the phone bugs in the building except the one in Alex's office. This will give us the advantage now," Brown explained.

"Remarkable. Dr. Brown, could we synchronize our operational database with yours?" Somerville asked. "That way we can send the department the info you have on Centurion systems and the location of Mrs. Taylor and her daughter."

"By all means, you can get your equipment. You are free to move around the building and use any phone but Alex's phone," Brown said. "I have put a feedback loop in their system. They think we have returned to the Alex's office to await instructions. Page me when you're ready to come in, and I will open the door."

Somerville replied, "Excellent, we shall be back in fifteen minutes." And he and Flynn left the lab to make the proper arrangements. Taylor was about to leave the room as well until his friend grabbed his arm.

"Alex, I need to ask you something?"

"Sure, Art."

"I want you to go back to your office and set up the transfer. This way they think their plan is working."

"Done. Anything else?" Taylor asked.

Brown stood from his seat and said, "Follow me before the cops return." He led Taylor towards the bookcase. Brown pulled a book from the case, and a wall appeared.

"What's in here?"

"My real lab," Brown said. Taylor noticed a large viewing screen with state of the equipment and technology.

"What's this?"

"The second phase to NIGHT," Brown replied.

"Your super computer, it is bigger since the last time I saw it," Taylor said in amazement.

"NIGHT, say hello to Mr. Taylor."

"Good day, sir."

"The computer just talked to me," Taylor said in shock.

"Of course. I told you he liked his name. NIGHT, were you monitoring our discussions in the other lab?"

"Yes, Dr. Brown."

"Assuming the police could enter the building, what are their chances of rescuing the two bio-signs?"

"Without a comprehensive profile of the area to access, the highest rate of success would be in the fifty to fifty-five per cent range."

"NIGHT, scan the location of the bio-signs and locate via satellite, the exact appearance of the building?" Brown ordered as the computer displayed the structure.

"In 1966, the owners abandoned the building, sir. Tony Shapiro otherwise known as the 'Ice Pick' is the current owner. Would you like information on Shapiro?" the computer asked.

"Not for now, NIGHT. But search the municipal building library and locate the architectural blue prints of the building."

"Located and downloaded; now showing on display. The building has three floors. The detainees are held on the third floor, according to bio-scan readings."

"Good work, NIGHT," Brown said. "Now, with this new information, what are the odds of success for the police?"

"Odds have jumped to sixty to sixty-five per cent. However, it is my strong recommendation that they use a flawless diversion," the computer instructed.

Brown probed, "NIGHT, what are my chances of success if I was to attempt a rescue mission? Do a med scan on me." And a ray of light scanned him.

Taylor, confused by Brown's request, inquired, "What are you up to?"

"Scan complete. With the injury to your leg, success rate falls to forty-eight per cent," the computer replied.

"Wearing the Mark II battle outfit, and with the leg neural implant brace, what are my chances?"

"Warning! Both the brace and Mark II battle suit have not been adequately tested. Insufficient data."

"Search theoretical," Brown ordered.

"You have an eighty-five per cent success rate, but only if the brace and the Mark II meet and achieve your specified requirements. But I advise against such an attempt, Dr. Brown," the computer said.

"So noted, prepare the Mark II," Brown ordered. NIGHT complied with his creator, and the vault opened.

"Wait a minute," Taylor shouted. "You are not putting on that thing."

"Why not? I'm your best chance to save them."

"This isn't about saving them. This is about returning to your stupid cause. I saw the anger in your eyes at the mansion; you wanted that guy to shoot you. My wife and daughter will not be pawns in your private war," Taylor shouted.

"Before you start calling me cold hearted, who was the one who played ball with these scum bags. So, look in the mirror before you start pointing the finger," Brown fired back. Taylor's anger blinded him; he clinched his right fist, and acted on impulse.

"You son of a bitch," he shouted. Without hesitation, Taylor struck his friend. Brown couldn't believe it, but didn't fight back.

Brown licked the blood from his lip and inquired, "Does that make you feel better?" Taylor broke down in tears.

"Art, I'm sorry, but I'm on the verge of losing everything dear to me."

Brown held his friend's shoulder and said, "I know, my friend. That's why I want to help."

"I know, but can you guarantee that you can do this without risking their lives, honestly?"

"Twenty years ago, I could," Brown replied. "But no, not now." And he bowed his head.

"Then I am not risking my wife and daughter. Promise me you will not wear that costume and go after them. Promise me, or leave now and never show your face again," Taylor said in a cold-hearted tone.

Brown hesitated for a brief moment, but then answered, "I promise, Alex. Your friendship means more to me than anything. I just wanted to help."

"You have, my friend. We have their location, the plans to the building, and you saved my life and my servants. I thank you for that. Now, let the police deal with them. As it should be," Taylor said as Brown's pager went off.

"That's them. Let's go to the other room. Alex, don't mention this room to anyone, please," Brown requested.

"I promise," he replied. Upon returning to the main lab, the bookcase slid back to its original location and sealed the private room. Brown activated the door, and the officers entered the lab.

Brown said, "Officers, I have done further research for you. All you need to do is to upload some files to your database." And he granted the police access to his computer.

"Thank you, Dr. Brown," Somerville said.

"We are getting a team to join us here on our way out," Flynn said as Somerville walked towards him.

"We're ready."

"I will begin transferring the funds to their account. Then I want to go with you," Taylor said.

"It's too dangerous, you can't go, sir," Flynn said.

"That's my wife and daughter in there. And I am coming with you. Nobody is going to tell me what to do," Taylor demanded.

"Very well, sir. But you are to remain in the squad car until the area is secured, understood?" Somerville said.

Taylor replied, "Yes, I understand. Once I've completed the transfer, I will meet you in the main foyer." Taylor nodded at Brown for a brief moment, and then he left the lab.

"Gentlemen," Flynn said and followed the billionaire.

"I will stay and monitor things here with your officers, inspector," Brown said.

"Understood. Thank you again, sir," Somerville said.

"Bring them home, inspector. I know you can do it." Brown smiled. Somerville nodded and left the lab. Brown could not help but wonder what his friend had said.

"*I hope you're right, Alex. For your sake.*" Brown thought as he sat and monitored the area.

Meanwhile, a tall skyscraper in the core of the city held the man responsible for the entire abduction, the One. The shadowed figure sat with serenity and monitored the entire operation. His top man, Franky Dice strode into the room with further news. His boss, concealed in the dark part of the room, and his face hidden by a curtain.

"Boss, the transaction is being done."

"Excellent, Franky. Make sure they trace it all to Tony."

"Consider it done. Everything, from the company to the accounts, is in his name. The feds even think he is you." Franky laughed.

"Tony was a good soldier, but he used our money for himself, Franky. You know he was one of the last men who remained in the old family. That was a terrible night when we lost Mr. Stavros to the Shadow Chaser. It's hard to believe it's been close to twenty years since his death. But at least we know the freak is dead as well."

"Yes, sir," Franky replied. "Shall I show our hand to the cops and tip them?"

"By all means, but wait for Taylor to do his share. Then order Tony to shoot them at the first sign of trouble, understood?" the One instructed.

"Yes, boss."

"Thank you, Franky. That will be all." Franky turned around and left the room.

"Well, well, it looks like I have everything at my command. The best part is nobody, not even God himself, can stop the syndicate, the Group of 13, or me from taking over the crime world. Better yet, the entire world will be ours." He laughed as he poured himself a drink and cloaked his face in the shadows.

Chapter 12

Virginia and Margaret Taylor were trapped; tied up in a dark room, and the lone source of light came from a crack in the door. The area was quiet with the exception of the rapid beating of her own heart and the sobbing of her daughter. Virginia feared for her life, but most of all she feared for the life of her daughter. Evil left its mark in the room. The stench grew stronger. Trying to remain strong, she attempted to console her daughter.

"Margaret, are you going to the dance with that young man?" she asked. Her daughter looked at her mother with a puzzled expression.

"Mom, we are going to die. Why are you asking me that?"

"I know you are scared, dear. So am I, but we must have faith that we will get out of this. I don't want to die, but we can't let them get the best of us," she said, even though she did not believe they were going to survive, she had to remain strong.

"*Mom, I am so scared,*" she whispered. The tears fell from her eyes; dampened eye shadow streaked her cheeks.

"So am I, sweetheart. But we have to hold on for a bit longer. Your father will do everything in his power to get us back." It took Virginia all of her remaining courage to smile. "Just remember one thing, no matter what happens here today, I love you."

"I love you, too, Mom." A sound coming from the door ruined their tender moment together.

"Good afternoon, ladies. I trust that the both of you are being treated well." The thug laughed.

"What do you want?" Virginia asked.

"Just wanted to let you know that, at any moment now, we should be getting a response from your husband. Once he puts our money in the account, we will let you go." The thug stepped towards Margaret. "You got a lovely little girl here," he said. "I rarely get a chance to see a little lady who is so young and innocent." The thug smiled and stroked her leg.

"Get away from her, you monster!"

"What are you going to do? You're kind of tied up at the moment," he said when a second person entered the room.

"Leave her alone, Bruce. I'm in charge here."

"Sorry, Tony. I was just having fun."

"You had your fun, now get outta here," he ordered. The goon obeyed and left the room.

The man took out his gun and said, "Forgive my associate, ladies. It's so hard to find good help nowadays."

"What are you going to do with that?"

"This little thing, nothin' yet." He grinned. "I just wanted to let you know that you will either be alive or dead in fifteen minutes, dependin' on what your husband does next. See you both real soon." The stranger closed the door behind him, and the room returned to darkness. They remained silent while Virginia considered their options.

"Oh, Alex. Please hurry," she cried as she and her daughter awaited their fate, which was now fourteen minutes away.

Arthur Brown looked at his computer screen and waited for news on Virginia and Margaret's future. Two officers monitored the situation and the computers while Brown just sat there, defenceless and hopeless. One of the officers stepped towards Brown and shattered the silence.

"Dr. Brown."

"Yes, Constable Chin."

"The units will be there shortly. It will be all over soon."

"Yes, constable, it will be all over, but for whom?"

"Hopefully for the criminals, sir."

"You and me both, constable." Brown smiled.

"Sir, may I ask you a question?" she asked.

"You just did, but ask me another one," Brown said in a friendly gesture.

"Thank you, sir. Doctor, how did you come up with all of these ideas?"

"I would have to say ten per cent skill and ninety per cent luck."

"I see. But seriously, sir, how did you come up with all of these ideas?"

"Well, I do have my PhD in Engineering, Micro Engineering, Bio Technology, Nanotechnology, Computer Programming, and four other little degrees from those boring schools." Brown smiled at the female officer.

"Are you also a physician?"

"Yes, I specialized in microsurgery, but I left the health field to pursue my business in Engineering."

"What happened to it?"

"I was a poor business man." Brown grinned. "That's why I am here."

"One more thing, sir. Will the police department ever get some of this advanced equipment?"

"The military is our major buyer, but I'm sure this company would be more than happy to cut a deal with the provinces and the municipalities."

"Well, I will let you get back to work, sir. Once we hear something, we will let you know."

"Thank you, Constable Chin," Brown said. "Let's hope for the best." Brown turned around and looked at the bio-signs on his monitor. He hoped the police would get them out of there—and fast; for he knew time was running out on Virginia and Margaret.

Police cars were closing in on the location of the kidnappers, and with some luck, the two victims. Somerville followed the FBI vehicle belonging to Special Agent Flynn and his entourage, which included Alexander Taylor. The deafening sirens from the car reverberated between the high rises. Somerville feared the sirens would lead the kidnappers off to them.

If they hear us coming, they may kill the women. He thought. Somerville kept one hand on the wheel while the other one picked up the microphone of his police radio.

"Flynn, this is Somerville. Over."

"Flynn here."

"We have at least eight cars with their sirens on and screaming all over the place. Shouldn't we turn them off?"

"These sirens are telling people we need to get there in an emergency. The longer we take to get there, the worse it is for the women."

"I appreciate your position, sir. Just can we at least turn them off when we are about one block away from the building?" Taylor knew both men were right. They had to get there, but the element of surprise had to stay to their advantage.

"I'm forced to agree with the inspector on this one, Agent Flynn. Please turn your sirens off," Taylor pleaded with the FBI agent.

"Of course, sir. Okay, Somerville, we will play it your way. Just remember that it's the FBI's case, and not Toronto Metro. Understood?" he ordered.

"Crystal clear, Agent Flynn." Somerville lowered the microphone and turned off his siren. Seconds later, the rest of the squad silenced their sirens. They were just about a block away, and closing fast. Somerville knew this could become a dangerous situation for them all. This was one of those times he wished he could predict a positive outcome. But his experience taught him that situations such as this often ended in bloodshed. The sound coming from his police radio interrupted his train of thought.

"Somerville, it's Flynn. Over."

"Yes, Agent Flynn."

"We are stopping about fifty yards away from the area. We will get our SWAT team organized there. I have already notified the other squad cars."

"Understood." Somerville followed the car to the designated area. Somerville remembered a similar abduction that happened in the mid 70's. Toronto police at the time had some help; that help came from the Shadow Chaser. Despite his attempts to arrest the vigilante, he always knew the dark spectre fought on the side of justice.

I never thought I would hear myself say this. But I wish you were here right now, Shadow Chaser. He thought before he slipped out of his car. Within a few minutes, Flynn had the SWAT team ready for action.

"Okay, men. This is what we are going to do. Once I get confirmation the sharp shooters are in position, we are going to storm in and get the captives. We know, according to this homing beacon, they are on the third floor, so we have to rush up there and take out the kidnappers," Flynn said.

"Agent Flynn, I say we wait and increase our surveillance of the place. They have all the cards right now. Yes, we have the exact location, but they may shoot them before we get there, or they can get killed in the crossfire," Somerville explained.

"Sorry, inspector. We can't wait any longer. It's now or never. It's our case, not yours, inspector."

"I protest this course of action, and I will file a report on this."

"Do whatever you want, Somerville. But we are going in, either you come or stay. Your police chief assigned your unit to me. He knows his duty, do you know yours?"

Reluctant to proceed, Somerville agreed to follow Flynn's orders. "I'm in."

"Mr. Taylor, please stay in the car. We will notify you when the situation is secured. The Canadian officer here will stay with you until then."

Taylor looked at the rough FBI agent and said, "Of course, Agent Flynn. Please get my family out."

"We will do our best," Flynn said. The unit was just about ready to make their move when an FBI agent ran towards the unit.

"Special Agent Flynn."

"Yes, what is it?"

"We just received a call from an anonymous tip. The caller said there are three men guarding the women."

"How reliable is this tip?" Somerville asked.

"They gave the names of the abductors. Tony Shapiro, Bruce Whitaker, and Jamie Norrison," the agent answered. "The FBI and Canadian authorities did a check on them and found that they all have ties to Centurion. Of course we are all aware of Tony Shapiro's connections."

"Anything else?" Flynn asked.

"Yes, there is. We also know the three of them also have ties to the Scorpio Syndicate. We believe Shapiro is their leader."

"So, this tip is the real thing. Good work, Agent Moore," Flynn said.

"Thank you, sir." And the agent walked away from the unit.

"Well, that's it, people. We know there are only three guarding the women. Let's get them out of there. Everyone to their positions," Flynn said.

Somerville looked at one of his officers and said, "Constable, call dispatch and tell them we need an ambulance at this location just in case. And tell them do not, and I repeat, do not use their sirens. Understood?"

The officer replied, "Yes, inspector." With those final words, Somerville, Flynn, and the rest the officers, began a slow advance towards the building.

Jamie Norrison sat like a cat watching a mouse and guarded the first floor of the abandoned building. The door leading to their meal tickets was secure when Bruce took over from him. Norrison could tell that Bruce wanted a crack at the young girl. Norrison did not care, knowing either way—both women were going to die. Nevertheless, he knew Shapiro would be keeping an eye on Bruce. Tony Shapiro always followed the One's instructions. Except for when he was skimming profits; they were all skimming from the syndicate. Their scheme was so good not even the One's bookkeeper would know about it, or so they believed. Norrison began to remove his gun from his shoulder holster when he heard footsteps coming down the stairs.

"Relax, Jimmy. It's just me."

"Bruce, did you have your fun?"

"No, Tony stopped me. Too bad, I know she wants me." He laughed.

"You're such a lady killer, Bruce." Norrison laughed as well. "Hey, why aren't you guarding the second floor?"

"I got bored."

"Tony is going to have your head for this."

"Wanna trade for a while?"

"That means I gotta climb those stairs."

"Come on, Jimmy. Two beautiful women just one floor up, and Shapiro is guarding them like a nun in a convent—it's driving me nuts. If we are gonna kill them anyway, why not have some fun with them."

"You're sick, Bruce. Okay, okay, I'm on my way. Just pay attention down here. Don't daydream. Got it," Norrison demanded.

"Trust me, Jimmy." Bruce sat in Norrison's chair. "Thanks, bud."

"Whatever," he said, and sauntered up the stairs. Minutes later, Bruce started to get bored again.

Man, I wish there was something to do here. Bruce rose from his chair and walked towards the stained windows. He took a quick peak and noticed a young woman walking past the building. In awe of her beauty, Bruce Whitaker had to get a closer look, even if it meant going outside to follow her. Whitaker had escaped justice previously because the police lacked sufficient proof to lay charges against him for a series of premeditated assaults. He moved towards the door and opened it. He took a few steps outside, but before he could follow the girl, he noticed at least eight men running towards him.

"Damn it," he shouted. Bruce tried to get back into the building to warn his associates.

Somerville said, "I don't think so." And he speared him to the sidewalk. Whitaker's body landed like a hammer on the concrete. Three more officers ganged up on Whitaker and gagged him, so he wouldn't yell out.

"I have him, inspector," one of the officers said. Somerville strapped the cuffs on him.

"Thanks, Constable Akbar," Somerville replied.

"Nice move, Somerville," Flynn said.

"Thanks, Flynn."

"One down, two more to go. Okay, people, on the count of three we go in there quietly," Flynn ordered. The officers nodded, and then they crouched and crept towards the door. "One, two, three." With a slow turn of the doorknob, Flynn opened the door, and they skulked around the room. The officers scouted around and secured the first floor. Then they heard the sounds of footsteps coming from the second floor.

"*Okay, up the stairs,*" Flynn whispered. The officers followed with caution.

Norrison spent the last fifteen minutes cleaning his gun. The old chair he sat on creaked each time he moved. The sound annoyed him, but the silence annoyed him even more. Bruce, the noisemaker, was as quiet as a church mouse, and that made Norrison anxious.

"It's awful quiet down there, seeing that Bruce is guarding the area. That damn fool is always making noise, day dreaming, or even falling asleep," he pondered. "As soon as I'm finished, I better check up on him." But when he raised his head, four police officers were upon him.

"*Don't move, you are surrounded. Leave the gun on the table and be quiet,*" Flynn whispered as Somerville and the other two agents aimed their weapons at Norrison.

The officers started to approach him when he asked, "How did you find us?"

"An anonymous tip," Flynn replied. Norrison was now aware that the syndicate knew the truth. The One knew that three of his soldiers were skimming from his empire's accounts. Tipping off the police provided an elimination strategy for traitors. Once arrested, a jailhouse collaborator would complete the process. Norrison had no choice but to reach for his gun, death by the police was faster and less painful than death by the syndicate.

He screamed, "See you in hell." And he grabbed his gun. The officers fired at Norrison. The guns lit the room like a Christmas tree, and the shots echoed throughout the building.

"Nooo," Somerville hollered, but the damage was done.

From the top of the stairs, Shapiro screamed, "What the hell is goin' on?" And he spotted the police. Seconds later, Shapiro headed towards the women's room to finish the job. Somerville caught a glimpse of him and knew Shapiro intended to kill the hostages.

"Oh no! I can't let it end this way!" Somerville dashed for the stairs. He prayed to God he could reach the women in time.

Meanwhile, trapped in the dark room, Virginia and Margaret heard the gunshots. They knew they had to get out of their restraints—and fast. For the last ten minutes, Virginia and her daughter tried to free themselves from the ropes. Each pull and twist caused more skin to tear, and their wrists began to bleed, but they would not quit—for they knew their time was running out.

Margaret twisted her arm one more time. "I am almost free, Mom."

"Me too." Virginia tried to loosen the knot. "Got it." But at the same moment she freed herself from her restraints, Virginia heard the door open.

"Well, it looks like your husband got the police involved. That means you ladies are gonna die," Shapiro said, but noticed that Margaret appeared alone in the room, still tied to the chair.

"Where's your mother?" Virginia remained hidden behind the door and waited for the most opportune moment to surprise her abductor. Shapiro had his eyes on Margaret, and she knew her time to strike was now. Virginia shouted, "I'm right here." And attempted to strangle him with the same ropes that had bound her. With all of her remaining strength, she tried to cut the wind out of him. But alas, she was not strong enough to hold him. Her weakened condition saw to that.

"You stupid, stupid, woman!" Shapiro threw her off him and took the rope off his neck. "Now, watch your daughter die." Shapiro took out his gun and aimed it at Margaret. Almost free from the ropes, she yearned to escape, but the bonds kept her strapped to the chair. A sitting duck, and Shapiro had her in his sights.

Virginia screamed, "Nooo." And she flew in front of her daughter. Two shots fired from his gun. Both of them hit Virginia in the chest; but one of the bullets went through her body like paper and hit Margaret in the abdomen. Virginia Taylor's fragile torso fell onto the cement floor like dead weight.

"MOM," Margaret shrieked like a soul in hell. Even though the bullet hit her, she remained conscious.

Shapiro laughed. "Looks like you're next, sweetheart." And he paced towards the chair and aimed his gun. Death stared Margaret in her face; her final thoughts focused on her memories of her mother and her father.

"Drop the gun, Shapiro," Somerville roared, and he aimed his gun at the killer. Known as one of the fastest gunman in the syndicate, Shapiro thought he could outdraw the aging cop with great ease.

"Looks like it's my lucky day, pig." Shapiro turned towards Somerville. "Goodbye, pig." Both guns fired in unison. The bullets were on a collision course with each other like two knights in a joust. Somerville's bullet missed the opposing bullet by a fly's hair and pierced the air. After the smoke cleared, Shapiro saw Somerville bleeding from his right arm. But he felt a huge impact in his chest and smelled his flesh burning from the gunpowder.

"Oh….he's…. good…," he said; then he fell to his death. For he could not have known that Inspector Somerville had been one of the top five marksmen in the province. Seconds later, the rest of the officers arrived in the room. Flynn followed behind them when he spotted the bodies on the floor. He grabbed his two-way and called for help.

"Are those paramedics here yet?"

"Yes, sir."

"Then get them here, now. We have five people shot, two of them perps, both women, and Inspector Somerville is hurt as well," Flynn ordered.

"Get the women in the ambulance first; I will get one of the officers to drive me there. It's just a scratch. You better go see Mr. Taylor and take him to the hospital," Somerville said. Flynn nodded as the paramedics arrived in the room and treated the women.

"We have to get this one to the hospital and fast," the paramedic said after he analyzed Virginia Taylor's condition.

"We'll give you some room," Flynn said. The paramedics laid them both on the stretcher. Seconds felt like minutes to both Flynn and Somerville as the paramedics left with both of the victims. Flynn looked at Shapiro's dead body.

"I'll call the meat wagon for this scum," Flynn left the room.

Somerville looked around the room before leaving. Confused and angry—he screamed, "Why is it always the innocent who suffer?" Somerville tried to regain his composure. He shrugged his head and proceeded towards the door. *Somebody has to stop this syndicate once and for all, before they become unbeatable.* He thought, then left the room.

Just outside the building, Alexander Taylor sat in the police car and waited for an answer. A few minutes later, Special Agent Flynn walked towards the car. Taylor jumped out of the vehicle in haste and waited for a reply.

"How's my wife and daughter, Agent Flynn?" But then he witnessed the paramedics leaving the building with two stretchers.

"Things went bad, Mr. Taylor," he replied. "They are being sent to Mount Sinai Hospital."

"Oh my God," Taylor said.

Flynn said, "We will take you there, sir." Both men entered the squad car and followed the ambulance to the hospital.

Chapter 13

Alone in the waiting room, Alexander Taylor sat there stiff as a statue and in inexorable pain. He waited. Waited to hear an update from the surgeons who were trying to save the lives of his wife and daughter. Hatred filled his heart, but he reserved that loathing for himself. In his mind, he blamed himself for this mess. He danced with the Devil, and now his family paid the price. For the first time in his life, he knew what his best friend, Arthur Brown, felt like the night they killed Claire. Taylor wished he had allowed his friend go after those monsters who have torn his life apart, but he refused, for he forced his friend to stand down, and now his family have paid the price for his decision. The sanitary scent of the hospital burned his nostrils. He felt dirty, and the odour reminded him of it. But he knew that no disinfectant could take away the stench of poor judgment.

"I'm so sorry, Genie and Margaret. Please forgive me. Oh God, why didn't I see this coming?" he cried as Brown walked towards his friend with a cup of coffee.

"Here, Alex. Have a sip."

"No, I'm okay. What's taking so long?" Taylor asked with disgust.

"Take a sip, you need something right now. They are doing all they can for them. But they are not going to be any better off if you kill yourself here," Brown said. Taylor took two sips; then he placed the cup on the table in the waiting room.

Taylor lowered his head in guilt and said, "It's my fault they're in this mess."

"You can't talk like this. You never saw this happening. No one can, bad things happen—they just happen. It's those killers in the syndicate who did this—not you." Brown coiled his arm around Taylor shoulder.

"You were right, Art. I was swimming with them. I should have left you alone. You were the best one to deal with them."

"We don't know that, Alex. I could have been the worst thing that could have happened. I was thinking in the heat of passion. Things could have gotten worse. I know I was wrong, and you are not to blame. Besides, I don't know when to shut up," Brown said with regret in his voice. With a slight turn of his head, Brown noticed the surgeons walking towards them.

"Mr. Taylor?" one of the doctors asked.

"I am Alexander Taylor."

"Sir, I'm Dr. Walker and this is Dr. Goldmill. I performed the surgery on your daughter. The bullet went inside her abdomen and lodged near her spine. We were able to remove it, but she may be paralyzed from the waist down. If she is, we are hoping this will be temporary. But she will survive," he explained.

"Thank you, doctor. What about my wife?"

"Sir, I am the surgeon who performed your wife's operation. I am sorry to say she has lost a lot of blood. The bullet has done irreparable damage to her coronary arteries. Both left and right ventricles were damaged beyond repair," the doctor explained.

"What does this all mean?" Taylor asked.

"Alex, her heart has been damaged. They cannot repair the damage. She's going to need a new heart," Brown explained to his friend.

"Your friend is right, Mr. Taylor. We are looking for a possible match, but we have to try and keep her stable on life support. But in her condition, I fear the worst. I'm sorry, sir. I wish I could have done more."

"You have done all you can, gentlemen. For that you have my thanks," Taylor said.

"If there is anything you need, don't hesitate to call us," Dr. Goldmill said.

"May I see her?" Taylor pleaded.

"Of course, this way," Dr. Goldmill replied. The two doctors took them to her room in the ICU. As they walked in, both Taylor and Brown looked upon Virginia Taylor as she rested in her bed. Her eyes exposed her pain to her husband, her body supported by tubes with machines monitoring her vital signs. The beeping sounds grew fainter by the moment.

Taylor held onto her and said, "Genie, I'm here." His tears fell like rain, but he tried to act strong for her.

She tried to speak. "Luv...is....Mar...ga...ret...O...kay?"

"She's going to be fine, dear. Don't try to talk. Save your strength," Taylor begged. Virginia, in a feeble condition, turned her head towards Brown.

"Doc, take care of...them...for...me."

"You have my word, beautiful. But you will be all right," Brown said, but his knowledge as a physician told him the truth. Brown knew she was dying. With one glance at the monitors, he knew it was just a matter of minutes.

"I love...you...Alex," she said, and with her last ounce of strength, she smiled at her husband of over twenty-five years. "I am so proud...of...you. I wouldn't trade you for…anyth…" she mumbled, and the last pump of warm blood flowed through her arteries for the last time.

"I love you as well, my love," Taylor said as he felt her grip slipping away.

"No, it can't be," he cried like a child. "Somebody do something." The emergency crew arrived in the room and attempted to save her. The doctor rushed in, and for five minutes, he tried—but in vain. Virginia Taylor left the cold world of mortal existence to touch the face of God.

"She's gone, Art. My Genie is gone," Taylor sobbed like a baby. Brown hugged his friend and escorted him out of the room.

Brown replied with a gentle tone. "Come on, Alex. Let's go to see Margaret." And he wrapped his arm around Taylor's shoulder, and they walked away.

Toronto, Ontario. Canada: March 15, 2007:

Arthur Brown worked alone in his lab and prepared for tomorrow's meeting with the stockholders and the Canadian military. He finished working on the updates to the thermo suits as well as the introductions for his colleague's main presentation on the Darwin Vaccine. He opposed developing this new vaccine that would create the perfect human, but if it had been available at the time of Virginia's death—he would have used it to save her. It had already been a month since her death and funeral. However, he could not get her out of his mind, and seeing Margaret trapped in a wheelchair, haunted him at every moment. At least he would see his friend again. Taylor stayed away from the business and sold his place in Detroit. His current lodging was one of his country homes in Chicago. Watching his friend suffer, reopened a page in Brown's own history. For now, he had to focus on getting this project ready. He wanted to offer the military the Mark II combat suit. He confirmed it ready for testing. All the bugs were fixed, and ready to dance. Brown was going to call up the codes to open the vault when he heard a noise.

"Who's there?" he demanded. Taylor stepped into the lab.

"It's just me, Art," Taylor said. Brown walked towards his friend and hugged him.

"I missed you, my friend. How are you and Margaret doing?"

"I missed you, too, Art. We are holding out. But it is not easy."

"I know, Alex," Brown said in a dulcet voice. "I wasn't expecting you until tomorrow."

"Well, I have some news for you. I am moving to Toronto. Margaret wants to be close to her mother's grave. She even wants to go to public school. She needs a change. I cannot say no to her. Not right now," Taylor said.

"Excellent. I am glad to hear it," Brown said. "It's good to have a friend nearby." Brown returned to the vault and typed in his codes.

"What are you doing?" Taylor probed.

"Revealing the surprise of the meeting." The vault door opened, and in front of their eyes, the Mark II suit stood on display.

"Is it ready?"

"She sure is. I am going to surprise everyone. I even have the SSDO here tomorrow. I'm going to convince one of their agents to give it a dance."

"Do they know about this suit?"

"Not one bit. They are just here for the updated thermo suit and the Darwin Vaccine."

"Art, I need to ask you a favour?"

"Name it."

"Don't show them this suit."

"Why not? It's ready."

"How many more of these can you make?"

"By the end of this month we will have six made. Why?"

"Well, if you want to go on that proposition you requested so many years ago, we can't allow distribution to the public."

"What are you talking about, Alex?"

"You once asked me to bring back the Shadow Chaser. You have the knowledge and the training, and I have the money. You know what evil has done to the innocent. I laughed at you, ignored you, and I said you were obsessed with this vendetta. But it took Virginia's death and my daughter's condition to realize that we do need someone to fight for the innocent and against this scum."

"I don't know, Alex. You are in pain, you may not be thinking straight. What about the profits you'll forgo?"

"I based my whole existence on profit. Now, I've lost the meaning and direction in my life. Art, if you say no, I will understand, but please give me the chance to fight back," Taylor pleaded.

Brown looked at his friend, the suit, and at himself; then he replied, "Two conditions. One, I'm in command. What I say goes; I pick the Shadow Chaser. Two, once we are in it, we are in it. There is no turning back. Agreed?"

"Agreed." Taylor shook his friend's hand.

"I promise you, my friend. As of this day, Shadow Chaser, like the phoenix, will rise from the ashes and be reborn." Brown smiled. "As for the crime world, it will never be the same again." Both men left the lab to discuss the resurgence of the Shadow Chaser.

Chapter 14

Chicago, Illinois. USA: April 9, 2007:

*I*n a quiet suburban Chicago neighbourhood serenaded by the sounds of birds with shaded sidewalks for the occasional pedestrian, Arthur Brown strolled around the block. Brown took out a piece of paper from his pocket. He stopped for a moment and read. Then he turned towards a grey brick house. Indeed, a great feat of architecture, but Brown wanted to see the owner more than the house. For the last month, he began to rebuild his crime fighting empire, he had the suits designed, the technology at his command, and the financial backing of Alexander Taylor. However, he needed two more things to complete the operation. Agents to help his cause against evil, and indeed a champion. His first thought; find the child he saved during his last mission as the Shadow Chaser—Patrick Collins. Despite being twenty-five years old, Patrick had become a hero to his country. Patrick joined the military at eighteen. A few months later, they called him to serve in Bosnia. He later served in the invasion of Iraq where he saved the lives of five people from the brutality of three Iraqi soldiers. Patrick received an honourable discharge from the army and started his civilian career as a security advisor. He founded his own company; but he continued to serve his country as a reserve agent for the CIA. Brown kept tabs on the young man and learned that Patrick kept his word. He was proud of the young man he saved twenty years ago. Brown paced towards the front door, a little hesitant at first. For he never showed Collins his true identity, but he had to find people he could trust, so Brown had to take a chance. He went towards the door and rang the doorbell.

A little boy opened the door and said, "Hi!" The resemblance of the child astonished Brown. His features were identical, a spitting image of the five-year-old Patrick Collins.

"Patrick?" Brown pondered.

"Nope, you want my daddy," the boy replied. "I will get him. Bye, bye." The little boy closed the door. Brown smiled and thought about the innocence of the child, but his plan to choose Collins as his successor had changed. Minutes later, the door reopened.

"Hi, I'm sorry Jeremy shut the door like that. I'm Patrick Collins. What can I do for you?"

"I know who you are, Patrick. Do you know who I am?"

"No, I can't say I do, sir. Are you a friend of my father's?"

"No, I'm not. But I am a friend of the family."

"Sorry, I can't put a memory to your face, sir."

"That's okay. I was wondering if I could take you out for a coffee. There is much to talk about," Brown suggested.

"Sorry, sir. I am real busy at the moment. If there is some reason you came here, you can set up an appointment. I'm already behind in my business, and I have to get these damn accounts ready," Patrick said.

"Damn? You shouldn't say words like that." Brown smiled. "You make baby Jesus cry." Brown hoped those words would bring Patrick back to the time the youngster lectured Shadow Chaser on his choice of words.

"My mom and dad used to tell me that when I was young. How did you know that?" Patrick tried to guess the identity of this mysterious old man at his door.

"You told me that once, after I rescued you from the Scorpio Syndicate. Thank you for keeping your promise. You have done well, Patrick."

"It can't be," Patrick gasped. "You are…" Brown grabbed his shoulder with an air of warmth and gentleness.

"Yes, I am, Patrick. But I haven't been called that in twenty years," Brown said. "But for old times' sake, you can call me Mr. Red Eyes."

"My God. It's really you. Where have you been?" Patrick smiled and he shook Brown's hand.

"Retired; the leg injury finished me for good."

"You were hurt bad. I remember my coat was stained with your blood. I'm sorry you paid the price for saving me."

"I'm not. I took the risk, and I have no regret. I heard of your heroics, three medals for bravery, innocent people saved, and now a family. I think losing the strength of a leg is a good payoff," Brown said.

"My wife is gone for the afternoon. Would you like to come in for that coffee?"

"Yes, I'd love a cup of coffee. Thank you, Patrick," Brown replied. "There is much to talk about." And he entered the house.

For the last two hours, Arthur Brown retold the story of the Shadow Chaser to Patrick Collins. From his beginnings, to his problem with alcohol, his friend, and the recent tragedy that has brought forth the need for the return of the Shadow Chaser. Patrick Collins sat there and tried to absorb the awesome impact of Brown's story.

"So, you see why I have come here to see you," Brown said. "I need your help." And he took a sip of his coffee.

"You want me to become the Shadow Chaser?"

"I was going to, but I see you have a family. A wife and child do not deserve to have a husband and a father at such risk. My next Shadow Chaser has to be single and know what it means to lose something," Brown explained.

"Then what can I do for you?"

"I want you to be his eyes. You will gather six more people you can trust, and they will become the Shadow Chaser's agents. They will be his eyes and ears out in society," Brown explained. "You will lead them, and you alone will know who we are. We cannot afford leaks, and I alone will bear the risk. You, my friend, and I will know the identity of the Shadow Chaser. Understood."

"I understand, but how can you be sure you can trust me?"

"I followed your career with great interest. I even have a copy of a CIA hearing where you broke a conspiracy and took a chance of being the sole person to face the full weight of the hearing's outcome because you refused to name your sources."

"How did you get that?" Patrick said, then Brown smiled. "Forget it, you are the Shadow Chaser, you can do anything."

Brown said with softness. "If only that were true, Patrick." He pondered his past sufferings. "Now you know the truth. I need you—can I count on you? Will you be at my side? If you don't want to, I ask you never to talk about this conversation to anyone, and I will be on my way."

"How can I refuse the Shadow Chaser, I will do what I can to help." Patrick smiled.

Brown shook Patrick's hand and said, "Thank you, Patrick. I have to go, my plane will be leaving in an hour."

"Going back to Toronto?"

"Not yet, I have one more stop, Okinawa, Japan."

"Why Japan?"

"I have to see one more person for help. In the meantime, here is my number." Brown gave him his card. "As soon as you have a free moment in your schedule, call me, and I will make the arrangements for us to meet."

"Alright then. I will call you next week."

"Good, well until then."

"Do you need a lift to the airport?"

"No, thank you. My car is parked on the other side of the block. I look forward to hearing from you. Once again, thank you, Patrick," Brown said.

Patrick replied, "It's the least I could do for the Shadow Chaser." And he escorted him to the door.

"That's not my name anymore, Patrick." Brown opened the door.

"To me you will always be the Shadow Chaser," Patrick said. Brown grinned and walked away. Patrick, intrigued with Brown's story, shouted out.
"By the way, what's your friend's name?"
"You will find out soon enough." Brown grinned and continued on with his journey.

Okinawa Island, Japan: April 11, 2007:

For the last day, Arthur Brown spent most of his time meditating at his old teacher's dojo. The long trip had exhausted Brown, but he looked forward to meeting his old master. When he arrived, Tanaka's servants greeted him. His mentor was visiting the neighbouring city, but promised to return soon. Brown felt at home in the old dojo, for he spent much of his time training the art of ninjutsu, the art of stealth. Makoto Tanaka became more than his teacher. He became his mentor and friend. His training of the art and his philosophies were paramount to the success of Brown becoming the Shadow Chaser. As well, Tanaka taught him the samurai arts, the ways of the ninja, and the rare power of the martial arts he called the Shadow Art. The ancient art was a form of advanced combat and mental discipline. The history of the art originated when Cao Ping, a shaolin monk from China, became a victim of a shipwreck when a massive windstorm caused the lone boatman to veer off course. The monk remained adrift for seven days until a farmer found him off the shores of Japan. The farmer tended to the weakened monk and brought him back to health. In return, the monk helped the family at the farm. But he fell in love with the eldest daughter. He married her, and made Japan his home. Cao Ping took the last name of Tanaka in honour of his new family, and he taught them the art of his fathers. As the years passed, the art included the samurai and the ninja. The ancient scrolls indicated that on rare occasions the art could invoke fear and confusion in the dark shadows of a human soul. But for that to happen, the body had to be in full control of its emotions and eliminate its own hate. Brown remembered the first time his master told him the story of Tanaka's family who confronted the Dragon of Darkness. This story became Brown's favourite lesson. The Dragon of Darkness, an evil sect, attacked the innocent people of the village. Tanaka's ancestors, with the training of the shaolin, the ninja, and the samurai, confronted the darkness. They searched in the shadows for the dragon. When he found the sect, the battle for the village began. After a long battle, Tanaka's great-great-grandfather, Yoshi, knew the power of this cult and the evil it possessed. He decided he would use his abilities to protect the innocent. Yoshi, a powerful samurai, kept his identity as a ninja a secret. He used the art of fear and chased their shadow away from the village. The lesson motivated Brown to call his alter ego the Shadow Chaser, for he would continue Yoshi Tanaka's quest and chase fear into the shadows where evil resides. Brown never told his teacher he was gaining his skills to be a vigilante. He told Tanaka about his wife's death, but never told him he wanted revenge. A strong believer in controlling one's emotions and in the sanctity of law, Tanaka tried to impart these values to his students. In addition, he would never approve of any action that would result in the taking of a human life; something that Brown had done to save Patrick Collins from Stavros. Brown knew he had to save the child, but if he had to do it over again, he would've found another way. For his choice, he must live with the regret until his death. He needed Tanaka's help to teach his successor, but he had to come clean and tell him the truth about his life. Brown prayed Tanaka would help him.

"Master, it is good to see you again," Brown said, meditating.

"I could have been someone else," the voice said.

"I can recognize your essence anywhere." Brown smiled as he opened his eyes to look upon his teacher. Despite his bad leg, Brown sprung from the floor and bowed. The old sage returned the bow.

The old master hugged his student and asked, "How are you, my student?"

"I'm fine, Master Tanaka." Brown returned the hug. "It is so good to see you again."

"You as well, my young student."

"I'm not that young anymore, master." Brown smirked.

"Neither am I, my friend." Tanaka laughed. Makoto Tanaka, an ancient in every sense of the word. He was fifty when he first met a young Arthur Brown, and he taught the young doctor all he knew about the art and about honour. Now, at eighty, he walked a little slower, and his hair and beard were white as a snow-capped mountain peak. He had a softer voice, but his honour shined through like the sun, and he maintained the strength of a young lion in the jungle.

"Please sit down with me and have some tea," Tanaka said. Brown followed his master towards the table.

"Thank you, master," Brown said, and stood close to the table.

"Please sit, my young student."

"After you, master." Brown followed the traditions of the dojo.

"You are my equal in this house, my friend," Tanaka said. "No need to treat me as your teacher." Brown bowed and sat near the old master.

"I remember a wise man said that life was always a classroom, and that everyone around you is your teacher. To learn is to expand your wisdom and your respect for all life."

"Very true, Arthur-san. Who said those words?" Tanaka asked.

"You did, master." Brown smiled.

"I did? I see. Well, it appears you have a good memory."

"Well, you were saying that as you were flipping me all over the place. My head was hurting for a week." Brown laughed.

"At least you were focused." Tanaka beamed as he poured the tea. "So, Arthur-san, why are you here?"

"I need your help. I need you to train someone for me."

"Your new champion no doubt," Tanaka said.

Somewhat confused at his master's answer, Brown hesitated before he asked, "What do you mean, master?"

"Oh come now, Arthur-san. I know who you are." He smiled. "After you left here, the Shadow Chaser made his first appearance."

"You knew after all these years?"

"Yes, my student, I knew. I recognized your style. You were fast, brave, and heroic. You kept the traditions of my family with honour. I am proud of you," Tanaka said. "I followed your adventures in the paper and perceived the good you did for the people and for society."

"But I broke the law and killed a man. On my last mission, I rescued a child from a man motivated by evil and power. I was trying to escape when he had us both; he shot me, and I was losing blood. I had no choice but to kill him in order to save the child. Because of the life I lived, the damage to my leg is permanent. I dishonoured you by not telling you my true intentions—and I have broken your most sacred rule. I hope you could forgive me."

"Hai, you have broken the law, but by doing so, you have saved countless innocent lives; and you brought evil men to justice. Yes, you did take a life, and that life could no longer have a second chance at redemption, but the evil one chose the path to hell—and of his own free will. That injury there was your price for the life you lead. You are no killer, I am sure you had no choice. You have regret and pain for your actions, and for as long as you feel that regret of taking a life, you are still a man of honour." Tanaka held onto his student's shoulder. "This shows who you are, and I am proud to call you my student and my friend."

"Arigatou, master." Brown bowed to his teacher.

"Kochira koso, Arthur-san." Tanaka returned the bow. "Besides, I knew you wanted to learn the art of my fathers to fight back."

"How did you know?"

"You were a man who was hurt. And looking for an answer. I remember when I first met you; you were young and angry. However, inside that bruised shell stood a proud and honourable soul," Tanaka said. "I remember when my Yuriko was drowning, and you saved her. The tides were strong, and it almost took your life as well." Yuriko was Tanaka's little granddaughter.

"How is Yuriko?"

"She is well. Married with three kids. The youngest girl is training under her mother and myself." Tanaka smiled. "I remember when I asked you what you wanted for saving my little one."

"I observed you in your dojo, you were teaching your art to your students. I never saw a person move like that in my life. I knew if I learned your skill, I would be a force to be reckoned with," Brown said.

"Hai, and you ask me to teach you; teach you I did."

"But you could have refused me," Brown pointed out. "If you knew I wanted vengeance."

"I knew we were both men of honour, and I had to take the chance. And I made the right choice." Tanaka beamed.

"For that I'm thankful."

"Well, my friend, you said you want me to train someone for you?"

"Yes, master. I am bringing back the Shadow Chaser, and I need you to give him the same disciplines you have given me."

"You are able to train him with the art, my friend. There is little I can teach your champion."

"There is plenty you can teach, master. The problem is I still haven't found my champion, but when I do, I would like him to learn of the customs here and the benefits of your wisdom."

"You flatter an old man, Arthur-san." Tanaka grinned.

"There wouldn't be any other old man I would want by my side, master."

"It appears we have a lot of work to do, my young student." Tanaka rose from the table.

"Then you will do it, master?"

"Hai, I will train your chosen champion, but on one condition."

"Name it."

"You must spend the night as my guest. There is much I would like to show you, and I want you to dine with Yuriko's family and me this evening." Tanaka smiled.

"The honour is mine, master." Brown bowed once again to honor the ancient warrior.

"Then let us leave this place and return home," Tanaka said, and both teacher and student left the dojo.

Chapter 15

Toronto, Ontario, Canada: September 4, 2007:

Alexander Taylor contemplated business strategies as a new day began at Taylor Enterprises Canada. It was also the first day of high school for his daughter Margaret. For the last few months, he spent his time helping Margaret with her rehabilitation and treatment; but she remained trapped in that wheelchair. When he wasn't with her, he was either hard at work to improve his already successful company, or he assisted Brown with the rebirth of the Shadow Chaser. Since April, both he and Brown had been assembling the funds needed to finance the operation. While Brown designed the suits and improved upon the technology, Patrick Collins recruited four more agents. In the meantime, Brown's master organized the dojo in preparation for the training of the next Shadow Chaser. However, they were nowhere close to finding Brown's successor. Taylor became impatient and wanted immediate results in this endeavour. But he knew his friend would find the right person, and he had to leave it in his capable hands—still he hated to wait. Finishing his report, he received a call from his executive assistant.

"Sir, Dr. Brown is here to see you."

"Send him in please." The door opened.

"Hey, Alex. Are you ready for the briefing?"

"Just about." Taylor read the report. "It looks like the Darwin Vaccine is developing according to Dr. Simms's expectations."

Brown sat close to his friend and said, "Yep, all the tests prove positive in his favour, but I'm against this, Alex. I don't like the idea of playing God. I have to give you this, Alex." Brown handed Taylor a document.

"What's this?"

"It's my report on the vaccine. I cannot support this. I know I'm just one vote, but I have to express my opinion. I believe we are making a catastrophic mistake if we support this project."

"Art, you are my friend, and I trust you with my life, but we have the backing of some of the finest scientific minds on the planet. This breakthrough will mean billions for us. That's more money we can put into the Shadow Chaser program," Taylor explained.

"I understand your position on this; but I had to try."

"I understand, but you have to take the good with the bad, Doc. In business there are always risks," Taylor pointed out. But Brown noticed the vexed expression on his friend's face.

"What's wrong, Alex? Are you worried about today's test?"

"Not the test. I'm worried about Margaret's first day in high school."

"I understand. But don't worry, she'll be fine. How's her treatment coming along?"

"The good news is she has feeling back in her legs, and eventually, she should be walking again."

"That's great news, but what's wrong?"

"Well, she doesn't even try to walk. She said it hurts, so she doesn't try. The doctors examined her, and they could not find anything wrong with her legs. They say she's all right, but she's suffering from some kind of psychological breakdown. Well, that's what they say."

"So, she has it in her head she can't walk. Give it time, Alex. She will beat this."

"I know, but it's just so damn hard, Art. In her mind, her chair is the one thing that protects her. She still has nightmares of that day. Hell, I do as well." A tear fell from Taylor's right eye. "She wanted to move here because her mother is buried here. Virginia never left her side; but I did, so I can't blame her for not confiding in me."

"She loves you, Alex. Just stand by her and take care of her the best way you can. Things will work out." Brown smiled and tried to encourage his friend.

"I wanted her to go a private school, but she downright refused. She wants to go to a normal high school."

"Have faith, my friend. She'll be fine. By the way, look at the time. We better get to the presentation. We are making history today," Brown said before he stood from the chair.

"I'm ready," Taylor replied. And he followed his friend towards the door. "Before we go, I want to ask you how's your search for our chosen one?"

"It's getting there," Brown said. "I will give you some names after the meeting." Taylor and Brown left the office and headed towards the conference hall.

So began another school year for the students and faculty of Pierre Elliot Trudeau High School. Students started the morning with an hour-long assembly before entering their new homerooms. New students from junior high schools from around the city joined the few who hadn't yet graduated the previous year. The coach posted this season's football tryout notices inside the gym, hoping to find his next big star. The atmosphere, mixed with confusion and excitement, greeted the new students as they begin the school year while the Grade 12 students readied for their last year before graduation. Within a few minutes, the echoes of locks surrounding the steel rings of the lockers filled the halls; and Margaret Taylor witnessed the sounds of her new environment. Putting her school supplies in her new locker with the help of her portable handgrip, she wondered how the year, and her follow students, would treat her. She wanted a change in her life, but she feared they might look down on her because of her wheelchair. She wanted her peers to like her, but at the same time, if she acted friendly, she feared they would feel sorry for her. Indeed, the school year intimidated her, and she faced it alone. So far, she had all of her supplies put away in her locker, and she had one more binder to put in. But she had some room on the top shelf of the locker. She made a swift adjustment of her handgrip and attempted to put the binder onto the shelf. Raising her arm high, she was about to put it on there with ease—until it happened. The bolt of her grip had gotten loose, and the binder slipped from its grasp. The binder fell and landed on her other supplies, causing her things to slide onto the floor.

"Damn," she yelled. All the belongings, she had placed in a neat pile on the top of her locker, lay on the ground in a heap. She tried to wheel around the pile, but some of her papers had wedged in her chair.

Damn it, why is this happening. She felt everyone was watching her. A few seconds later, someone came to her help.

"Hi, I see you are in need of a hand," the voice said.

Her voice dripped with sarcasm. "What gave you that idea?"

"You're right, shut up and help. Got it," the voice replied with a touch of satire and wit in his tone. He bent to pick up the papers. She felt ashamed about her tone toward the young guy.

"I'm sorry. Thank you for your help," she said with a more docile tone.

"Apology accepted. Now, where do you want these things?" the guy asked.

"The binder was supposed to be on the top shelf when I dropped it."

"Cool." The guy placed the binder on the top shelf. "You know I got wood-working this semester, maybe I can make a shelf and install it in the locker, so you wouldn't have to use the top shelf."

"That's kind of you. Thank you," she said.

"No problem. All a part of the service." He glanced at her timetable. "I see your homeroom is 230."

"Yes, it is."

"Okay, well, give me your books, and I will take them there for you. My girlfriend is in the same homeroom, and I was planning to stop there anyway." He smiled.

"If you don't mind. Thank you. She's lucky to have you." She smiled.

"That's what I keep telling her. But she never listens," he joked.

"Is this your first year here?"

"Yep. For me, my girl Chloe, and our friends: Tommy, Cole, Julie, Tina, and Shauna," he said. The teens headed towards the classroom. Margaret realized she had yet to introduce herself to the young guy. She slowed her chair and extended her hand.

"Sorry for my manners, my name is Margaret, Margaret Taylor."

The guy shook her hand and said, "I'm no better, Margaret. My name is Kevin, Kevin Wolf. A pleasure to meet you." Some time thereafter, they entered the homeroom.

"Just put my stuff over there; I will find somewhere to sit."

"No way, Chloe is just over there. You can sit by her and Tommy," Kevin said.

But Margaret felt a bit shy. "You sure she won't mind?"

"Not at all, we are all new here. We should get to know each other," he said.

"Okay then," she replied. Kevin wheeled her towards Chloe Bellecoeur. Chloe was the epitome of the word beautiful. Her long red hair and sparkling green eyes lit the room and the souls that surrounded her. Beyond a doubt, she radiated all that was good in the human soul; modesty, dignity, and integrity.

"Hey, stranger. Wrong homeroom, Wolf." She smiled at her boyfriend.

"I know, I am just escorting a friend of mine here. Chloe, Tommy, this is Margaret," Kevin said.

"Hi there," Margaret said.

"Hi." Chloe smiled. "It's a pleasure to meet you."

"Likewise," Margaret replied.

"Same here. Welcome to PET high," Tommy said.

"Thanks."

"It's always cool to meet new people. Hey, are you free for lunch?" Chloe asked.

"Yes, I am," Margaret replied.

"Then let's all get together for lunch," Chloe said.

"Sounds like a plan," Tommy added.

"Alright then, I will," Margaret said.

"See, isn't this cool," Kevin said. "New school and a new friend, things are looking good for us." The young teen gazed at the love of his life.

Chloe pointed at the clock and said, "Uh, sweetheart, get the hell out before the homeroom teacher finds you here."

"I have plenty of time," Kevin said as the teacher marched in.

"Excuse me, young man. What is your name?" the stern looking educator queried.

"Hi, I'm Kevin Wolf." Kevin offered his hand. However, the old ice king ignored him and glanced at his attendance sheet.

"You are not on my list, Mr. Wolf."

"I was just leaving."

The tough-as-nails teacher replied, "That's a good idea, Mr. Wolf."

Kevin replied, "Bye." He smiled and blew a kiss to Chloe. Kevin was about to leave the room when the teacher enunciated.

"Oh, and Mr. Wolf."

"Yes, sir."

"I don't trust you. Your breed always gets into trouble. I will be keeping my eye on you, young man."

"Yes, sir." Kevin knew he overstayed his welcome and left the classroom. Margaret had a brief, but quiet laugh to herself. She looked around the classroom and felt happy. At last, she would fit in with her new school and her new friends.

The sounds of chatter filled the conference room as the members in attendance waited with patience for the briefing to begin. Brown and Taylor sat with the assembly and glanced at the clock, knowing the creator of the Darwin Vaccine, Dr. Simms, would soon arrive with the report. According to last year's preliminary report, Phase Two of the test should be in its early stages, which could result in the next step in the evolution of humankind. But Brown feared the implications. He felt he could be witnessing a twenty-first century Frankenstein. In a few minutes, they will have answers to all of their questions. If it worked, Taylor Enterprises will become the company of the millennium. The next step in the future of the human race will be at hand, but if the vaccine would fall into the wrong hands—it could lead to its destruction as well. Alas, Brown alone feared the outcome. The board members became accustomed to Simms's tardiness, but they believed his research overshadowed his lack of punctuality. The resonance of brief mumblings and pens tapping packed the room. They waited for several minutes when he walked in with a cart carrying his laptop computer and a stack of binders.

"Good morning, ladies and gentlemen. Fellow colleagues, members of the board, and Mr. Taylor," Simms said.

"Good morning, Doctor Simms," the crowed replied in unison. After they exchanged pleasantries, Simms prepared his presentation.

"Before I begin, I just want to thank you all here for attending," Simms said, "and I want to say that if it weren't for Taylor Enterprises' faith in my work, we would not be here today." Simms grabbed several copies of the report and passed them out to each member present in the room.

"I take it you have good news for us, doctor?" Taylor asked.

"Good news, Mr. Taylor? As of today, you can claim that your company is the gateway to the future of evolution." Simms smiled, and the applauds followed. The assertive scientist turned on his computer and began the presentation.

"As you can see here on the monitor, Phase Two of the project is now under way. After numerous tests and computer simulations of Phase One, we have developed a vaccine that is proven, without a shadow of a doubt, that it can turn the subject into the ultimate state of regeneration." The group watched the presentation on the widescreen. "To recap, last year we used the Darwin Vaccine on lab mice to see how the vaccine would enhance the DNA of these creatures. One of the mice was missing a limb. Once injected with the vaccine, within minutes, the mouse had a new limb. We have done another successful test with a chimpanzee that was near death," Simms explained. "Moments after the injection, the wounds had healed, and the damaged organs had regenerated. We have also tested the vaccine on numerous human DNA samples, and it looked promising."

Brown looked at the report and said, "According to this report, there was some other benefits as well, doctor."

"That is right, Dr. Brown. The chimpanzee showed an eighty per cent increase in agility, stamina, and strength."

"That's outstanding!" The response from the numerous people witnessing the recording of the test from the screen pleased Simms.

"Any side effects?" Brown asked.

"Well, not a side effect per se, but we do know the vaccine could be reversed within two weeks of it being administered," Simms replied. "We have an antigen that could break apart the genetic code of a subject who was administered the injection. The theory is it will either kill the subject or return it to its natural state."

"What happens if it is given to the subject after the fourteen-day period?" Brown probed.

"On the fifteenth day, the antigen will make the enhanced cells dormant, it could be reactivated by an injection of adrenaline," Simms said. "However, the cells would return to dormancy within six hours; but the strain of the adrenaline and the rebooting of the cells could be catastrophic. Therefore, I wouldn't recommend any more than two adrenaline shots per day."

"What happens after the fifteenth day?" Taylor asked.

"After fifteen days, the antigen would have no effect. The effects of the vaccine would be irreversible," Simms noted.

"You said you have tested human DNA samples, but has the vaccine been tested on humans yet?" one of the members asked.

"This is where Phase Three will begin. With the board's approval, we will begin our search for a viable human candidate and complete all prerequisite tests before examining the commercial viability. In my opinion, with the successful results from phases one and two, my staff certifies this vaccine is ready for human testing."

"How long will Phase Two take?" Taylor asked.

"Well, with the guidelines we are following, Phase Two will be completed by the end of this year. Then Phase Three, testing on a human being. We will be ready to administer the vaccine to a human subject by 2009-2010," Simms predicted.

Taylor said with a smile. "Excellent news, doctor." He looked at the board. "Any questions before we vote?"

"Just one. Dr. Simms, how does the vaccine work on a subject's mental capacity?" Brown asked.

"It improves the mental awareness and IQ in animals, but I won't know the true effects on humans until we complete the final test of Phase Two," Simms said. The rest of the board remained silent.

Taylor solicited, "Well then, can we take this to a vote?" And the members agreed to his request.

"All In favour of further funding to the Darwin Vaccine project?" Taylor asked. All but one raised their hands.

"All oppose?" Taylor asked as Brown raised his hand.

"I'm sorry, Winston. It is society I do not trust, not you. But it looks like the board approves of your work," Brown said. "Good luck."

"Thank you, doctor. You will see the benefits of this research someday."

"Well then, the motion is carried. You have your funding, Dr. Simms. Good luck, and we will reconvene in six months for a progress report," Taylor said.

"Thank you, ladies and gentlemen of the board," Simms said.

"Meeting adjourned." Taylor closed the meeting and the members left the room. Brown approached his colleague to congratulate him.

"Congratulations, Winston. I hope it works for you. I hope you don't think I'm jealous of your work, just don't trust the future I guess."

"That's okay, Art. Trust me, this will be the greatest finding in the history of the planet."

"I'm sure it will be." Brown smiled with false confidence.

"Well, if you will excuse me, I promised my wife I would pick up some tickets for the game tonight. It's Julie's first day in high school, and we want to celebrate her new beginning," Simms said.

"Julie already in high school. You are getting older, my friend," Brown said, shaking his hand.

"Aren't we all, Arthur." Simms nodded at his colleague and left the room. Taylor stayed and waited for his friend.

"You have that look again, Art."

"What look?"

"The 'we're all in trouble' look."

"Don't mind me, Alex. I just don't trust the human race."

"How about lunch at the private hall on me?"

Brown smiled. "Sure. Lead the way, Mr. CEO."

"After you, my good man." Taylor returned the smile, and they left the conference room.

As noon approached, Kevin Wolf headed down to meet his friends at the cafeteria. Even though he sought to adapt to his new surroundings, Kevin kept the pace. After a couple of wrong turns, Kevin found his way. He could have asked for directions, but he wanted to give the impression that he knew the school like the back of his hand. Besides in the midst of initiation week at PET, seniors watched for opportunities to play tricks on juniors. He may have been your average fourteen-year-old, but the teen possessed some extraordinary qualities. Raised by two exceptional parents, Kevin always believed that helping out others outweighed his need for personal gain in life. Kevin lived alone with his mother. His father died a few days after serving his country in Bosnia. The military had classified his death as accidental, but that still did not make things easier for his family. Kevin had a great brother who was ten years his senior. His brother worked as an architect and helped with the family as much as he could. That's when he wasn't busy with his own wife of two years and their little boy. For the most part, Kevin valued responsibility. He helped his mother after school with chores and various part-time jobs to help her pay the bills. His mother worked at a local sports bar and tried to maintain her own grades at night school. She wanted to be an accountant, but married life changed that for her. Ever since her husband's death, she had to find new ways to support the family. Kevin looked at his watch and noticed he was a few minutes late.

"Ahhh jeez! Chloe is going to shoot me." Kevin lifted his black hair away from his face. Kevin had been dating Chloe since the eighth grade, but they have been friends since the first grade when she moved here with her family. In kindergarten, Kevin used to have a huge crush on Julie Simms, but he never summed up the courage to approach her with his feelings. Instead, he became a close friend of hers and the rest of the gang she hung around with.

The hallway is clear. Maybe I can make a run for it. He took one more look around. The hall remained clear, so Kevin took a chance and began to increase the pace.

"Here goes nothing." He ran, passing locker after locker. So far so good, nobody noticed him. Getting closer to the exit at the corner, Kevin smiled.

One more turn; then I'm home free. He made a sharp turn around the corner.

Paff!

His body collided with another moving body. Within a few seconds, Kevin noticed what he had done.

"Do you realize it's forbidden to run in the hallways?" the teacher hollered. Kevin noticed Chloe's homeroom teacher; the same guy he had angered earlier.

"Not him. Not good," he moaned.

"Well, well, if it isn't Mr. Wolf. You do have a habit of finding trouble, don't you." The teacher stared daggers into Kevin's brown eyes.

"I'm sooo sorry, sir. I didn't see you there," Kevin pleaded.

He looked at the anxious student and replied, "Obviously not, since you were running like a madman."

"I was late for lunch," Kevin explained as he looked at his watch, "and I was trying to make up some time. I'm sorry, sir."

"You will be late for lunch, Mr. Wolf. You will be joining me in my class until the end of lunch hour," he ordered.

"But, sir, I have to go."

"You should have thought of that before you broke the rules of this school. Next time you will think before you act," the teacher said. "Now follow me."

"Yes, sir," Kevin obeyed. "Chloe is going to kill me." Kevin followed the teacher to the classroom and spent the entire lunch period there.

Time marched on for the rest of Kevin's friends. Chloe, Tommy, Cole, Julie, Tina, Shauna, and Margaret sat in the cafeteria and hung out. The gang spent the hour talking about the school, new adventures, their upcoming weekend—and the whereabouts of Kevin Wolf.

"You know lunch is just about over, and no wolf man," Cole said. Chloe tried to defend him.

"He probably lost track of time, as usual."

"Well, I got to split," Tommy said. "Tell Kev I will see him after."

"Sure thing, Tommy," Chloe said. The gang left for class for the exception of Chloe, Julie, and Margaret.

"I'm sure Kevin just forgot. You know how he can't keep things in his head," Julie said.

"Yeah, I know. So, are you going to the beach dance on Friday with Chad?" Chloe asked.

"Of course, silly. Hey, Margaret, why don't you come out with us?" Julie asked.

"I dunno. I don't have a date," she replied.

"Who needs a date? Just come on out," Chloe said.

"Yeah, why not?" Julie added.

"Oh…okay then, I will." She smiled. Margaret felt she had made a good impression on her new friends.

"Great," Julie said as she grabbed her books. "Well, I have to run, bye girls." And she left the cafeteria.

"Well, I guess we should get going," Chloe said, and grabbed her books. "I hope Kev at least shows up to class."

"How long have you and Kevin been together?" Margaret asked as she placed her books in her bag and attached it to the back of her wheelchair.

"For almost a year. He is so full of life, and he is just so caring." Chloe beamed. "How can I not help but fall in love with him." Margaret followed Chloe towards the exits.

"Yes, he does have a kind heart. He saw me there and offered to help."

"Kevin has this rare thing that he just wants to generally help people. Without profit or care to his own benefit," Chloe said. The two girls trekked the empty hall corridor, approaching the elevator. A voice from behind interrupted them. "Look what we got here. Two minor niners trying to get to class," the first voice said.

"Yeah, Luke. Look at them just ignoring us," another voice replied. The girls turned around and saw four seniors surrounding them.

"What do you want?" Chloe said.

"Let me introduce myself and my friends to you, baby," he replied. "I'm Luke Sampson, and this is Mich, Kyle, and Paul. We are the school."

Mich said, "That's right, kids. If you want to pass this section of school, you two are gonna have to pay a toll." The rest of the bullies acted tough and tried to overawe the girls.

"Get real, jerks," Chloe said.

"Pay now," Kyle said, "or we hurt your friend." He pushed Chloe out of the way. She crashed like a kite onto the marble floor; the four goons walked closer to Margaret.

"Get away from her," Chloe shouted.

Kyle looked at Margaret and said, "She is a cutie isn't she?"

"Cute and defenceless," Paul said. Margaret just froze. She could not speak; all of her thoughts circled back to the day of the kidnapping.

"I say you guys watch the red head," Luke said, "while I play a little game with her friend." His friends encircled around a defenceless Chloe.

"Stop it, don't go near her. Someone help us," Chloe pleaded, but the pleas for help fell on deaf ears, or so she thought. An irresistible force took Luke's legs out from under him. He crumpled onto the ground. The smack echoed down the hallway.

"I believe the pretty girl said for you fools to back off," Kevin said with a touch of satire in his voice, looking at the other three. "Hi, dear. Sorry I'm late."

"You're dead, punk," Mich vowed. The gang charged Kevin.

"Oh, dear; since the guys are running after me, so they can rip me in two, be a dear—and get some help," Kevin joked, but he feared the bullies. And he had every reason to fear them; he knew they wanted to hurt him.

Chloe replied, "Come one, Margaret." She grabbed the wheelchair handles and headed towards the elevator.

"Stop them," Luke yelled. "I got the pretty boy." The other three ran for the elevator, but they were unable reach the girls in time.

"Looks like it's just you and me, buddy," Kevin said. He hoped some of his father's self-defence training would work in his favour.

"I'm going to rip you apart, you little piece of crap!" Luke clenched his left hand and swung with all his might.

Kevin blocked the blow and countered with a right cross. The blow caught the larger teen off guard, and he fell onto the ground.

Kevin looked at the bully and replied, "The names Wolf, Kevin Wolf." Kevin felt like he had the advantage; but he forgot about the other three.

"Grab him," they shouted, and tackled him to the ground. Kevin tried to block their attack, but was not strong enough to stop them all. The teens continued the assault, and without mercy, they started kicking him in the abdomen. Luke jumped on top of him and unleashed a flurry of punches.

"Had enough, punk?" Luke boasted. In pain, Kevin remained on the floor. With his lip split opened, and his ribs bruised, his spirit wanted revenge. His words became his sole weapon.

"Oh, you guys are really something. Picking on a girl in a wheelchair and ganging up on me. You guys should be proud of yourselves. After you're done with me, there are a few babies in the maternity ward who need to be jumped on," Kevin said, but he knew this would result in further punching.

"You're finished, you son of a...." Luke said, but the teacher stopped him.

"That is it for you five. All of you, off to the principal's office," the teacher said. Kevin knew that voice

Oh jeez, not him. The teacher looked at him. It was none other than Chloe's homeroom teacher. The same teacher who warned him in the morning, the same one he ran into and missed his lunch period. Now, he knew him by his name—Mr. Elgin.

"Mr. Wolf. I see you live up to your reputation of being a trouble maker."

"Sir, I am the one getting beaten up. Didn't Chloe get you?"

"No, she did not. I was walking in the hallway when I saw you there making fools of yourself. Well, Mr. Wolf, this is strike three. Get up from the floor and follow me to the Mr. Brian's office," he ordered. Kevin staggered up from the floor.

"Of all the teachers who had to come to my rescue—it had to be him," he said. "Oh jeez, just stick a fork in me, I'm done." Kevin followed the teacher and the other four seniors to the principal's office.

After a delightful lunch at the private hall, Arthur Brown and Alexander Taylor relaxed over drinks. Taylor had a glass of red wine, and Brown a glass of iced tea.

"Thank you for the meal, my good man."

"My pleasure, Doc." Taylor took a sip of his wine. "So, how is our operation going?

"Quite well, I'm not sure who will be our guy yet, but I have my old base ready."

"So, it's up and running?" Taylor asked.

"She sure is. The keep is all equipped with the best equipment technology has to offer. Plus, it is where the rest of the agents will meet. I keep my private lab for our eyes, Patrick, and my new Shadow Chaser."

"Do you think Patrick has recovered from our meeting in May? Knowing that I'm the financial backer of the operation?" he probed. Taylor recalled his first encounter with Patrick a short time after Brown's initial visit with him.

Brown replied, "Your involvement had shocked him at first, but I'm certain he's looking forward to this new venture."

Before Taylor could say anything further, the Maitre 'D approached them with the phone and said in a modest voice. "Excuse me, gentlemen, but there is a call for you, Mr. Taylor."

"Thank you." Taylor took the phone. As the conversation progressed, Brown noticed Taylor's facial expression changed to a state of panic.

"What's wrong, Alex?" Brown asked after Taylor hung up.

"That was Margaret's principal. I have to go to her school. A group of bullies attacked her."

Brown sensed the trepidation in Taylor's voice and said, "I'm coming with you." Both men rushed out of the private hall and headed towards whatever faced them at the high school.

Chapter 16

Alexander Taylor and Arthur Brown waited eagerly for the principal to arrive. Still concern over Margaret's safety, Taylor paced all over the hallway.

"What's taking that fool so long?" Taylor demanded. Brown tried to calm his friend.

"Relax, he's talking to her and another girl. Once he's done, he will ask you to come in." But Taylor had different plans.

"I'm not going to let that pencil-neck geek intimidate her." Taylor marched past the secretary's desk and headed for the principal's door.

"Excuse me, sir. He's still in there with…" she said, but Taylor stormed in.

"Excuse my friend's behaviour." Brown smiled at her and followed him. As they entered, they noticed Margaret and a young girl talking to the principal.

"I want to know what has happened here," Taylor demanded. Brown had a more settled approach.

"Good afternoon, Mr. Brian. This is Margaret's father, Alexander Taylor, and I am his colleague and friend, Arthur Brown. Are you all right, Margaret?"

"I'm fine, Uncle Art," Margaret said. "Just a little shook up, that's all."

"What happened here?" Taylor probed as he sat with his daughter. The principal began to describe the incident.

"It appears that four students went after Margaret and Chloe here. I've talked to Chloe's friend Kevin. It looks like he started a fight with them as well," the principal explained. "I am truly sorry about this, Mr. Taylor. I assure you this will not happen again."

"What are you going to do about those punks?" Taylor asked.

"I've already heard their stories, but I'm going to talk Mr. Elgin; he stopped the fight," the principal said. "If you will excuse me for a moment." And he left his office. Taylor and Brown noticed the girls were dispirited and distressed.

"What's wrong, Margaret?" Brown probed.

"It's Chloe's boyfriend Kevin," she replied. "He saved us from those guys. Mr. Elgin arrived there before we could get help, and because he has a grudge against Kevin, the school will suspend him."

"Let me get this straight, this Kevin lad is in trouble for saving you both?" Taylor inquired.

"Yes, sir," Chloe answered. "Mr. Elgin has it out for Kevin. He busted him for being in our homeroom this morning, and Kevin told me, as we were going to the office, that Mr. Elgin had him for detention for running in the hallway."

"Where is Kevin?" Brown asked.

"He's in the other room next door to your right," Chloe said. "The other four are with Mr. Elgin in the room to your left."

"Alex, you think you can get the kid off the hook?" Brown smiled.

Taylor replied, "Count on it." He took out his cell phone and dialed a number.

"I am." Brown laughed. "I'm going to check up on the lad." Brown stood from the chair and sneaked in the other room. As Brown entered, he spotted the teenage boy with a fat lip and a bruised face. He held onto his ribs and sat there while he waited for his fate to be determined.

"Hi, Kevin. May I talk to you for a minute?" Brown asked.

"Sure. Are you with the school?" Kevin asked.

"Not exactly. I'm Dr. Arthur Brown."

"Oh cool, a doctor for my ribs," Kevin said. "Now, all I need is a priest for my last rights." The teen tried to laugh, but coughed instead.

"You have a singular wit about you. I like a guy who can deliver a good one-liner once in a while." Brown sat beside him. "But no, I'm a friend of Margaret's."

"How is she doing?"

"She and your friend are all right...thanks to you."

"Good, poor girl is trying to get accepted here, and you have those dumbasses ruining it for her."

"You didn't have to go and save her. You could have just got your friend out of there, or you could've gotten a teacher."

"What do you mean?"

"Simple, you didn't have to get involved. Now, you are getting suspended, and your parents are going to throw the book at you," Brown explained.

"I live with my mom. My dad died when I was six."

"Wolf! Lt. Duncan Wolf was your father?" Brown probed.

"You knew my father?"

"No, but I read about him and his actions in the Bosnian War. He was good man."

"Thank you, sir. So, you can see why I couldn't leave Margaret alone against those guys. She was an innocent person who needed help."

"You care that much about people do you?" Brown asked with interest.

"Yes, I do. I would have done the same for anyone. My father taught me that," Kevin said with pride, "but it looks like today the bad guys are going to win this one. Mr. Elgin has me looking like the instigator. It's just not fair. Have you ever had your back against the wall?"

"More times than I can count, my young friend." Brown smiled. "But don't worry, you won't be suspended."

"How can you be so sure?"

"Hey, you are not the only hero here today." Brown smirked and pushed himself from his chair. "I will be right back."

Kevin replied, "Alright." Brown left the room, past the secretary's desk, and heard Taylor's wrath coming from the principal's office. The oak door could not block the sound of his voice. Brown smiled and opened the door. When Brown entered the office, he watched his friend doing his magic on the principal.

"This young man has witnesses, including my daughter, stating that he had saved them from those young offenders. Now, you are going to suspend him?"

"I have no choice, I cannot condone fighting, sir," the principal replied as the phone rang. The principal grabbed the receiver without delay. "Hello, Mr. Chambers. It's always good to hear from the head of the school board. Yes, sir, Mr. Taylor is here right now. Of course, I will put it on the speaker." The principal turned on the speaker phone.

"Alex, they told me you would be there. Thank you for the donation you sent the board last week to finance the new sports facility," the voice said.

"You are welcome, Carl. But I feel that it will be the last one."

"Why would that be, Alex? Is there something wrong?" Chambers asked.

"Well, there is. My daughter and her friend were attacked by four students at the school, and a brave young man is being punished for stopping them and saving the girls from harm," Taylor explained. "So, if your schools are going to hurt a good kid for helping innocent girls, I'm pulling my daughter from your school, and my money from your board."

"Now, Alex, let's be reasonable. I'm sure Mr. Brian could give the young man one more chance," Chambers said, tripping over his tongue. "Isn't that right, Mr. Brian?" he added in a more authoritative voice to his employee.

"Yes, sir. I didn't call Mrs. Wolf yet, so I can close this matter," Brian agreed.

"And you don't have to call Mrs. Wolf, Mr. Brian. Let the lad go and punish the ones responsible. Do you understand me," Chambers ordered.

"Absolutely, sir."

"Good. Now, Alex, I hope that puts things back to order," he said.

"It most certainly does, Carl. Thank you for your time."

"No, thank you again for your generous donations, Alex," the voice said. "Goodbye." And the line went dead.

Taylor said, "Well, we shall leave you to your work, Mr. Brian" And stood from his seat. Brown, still standing, opened the door and lead the way.

"Certainly, sir. Margaret, Chloe, you may return to class now. On your way out, tell Kevin he is free to go as well," Brian said.

"Yes, sir," Chloe said. "Thank you." The girls left the office. Brown looked at his friend and smiled.

"How do you like that?" Taylor queried,

"I'm impressed, my friend," Brown said. "I see you called the school board while the principal was out, and you made good use of that wallet of yours." Minutes later, Chloe, Margaret, and Kevin greeted them in the hallway.

"Thanks, Dad," Margaret said. "This is Kevin Wolf."

"Mr. Wolf, my thanks." Taylor shook his hand.

"Thank you for getting me off the hook, sir," Kevin replied.

"Think nothing of it," Taylor said. "I will see you after school, dear." And he kissed his daughter's cheek.

"Bye, Dad. Bye, Uncle Art."

"Bye, Margaret," Brown said and looked at the other two teens. "It was a pleasure meeting you all." But as the teens started to walk away, Brown called out at Kevin.

"Excuse me, Kevin. I just want to say something before I go."

"Yes, sir."

"Thanks again for standing up to them. I won't forget what you have done for her." Brown walked towards him and shook his hand. "I hope to see you again."

"Same here, sir." Kevin walked towards the girls, and they headed towards class.

"Well, our work is done here," Taylor said, and they headed towards the main doors.

"So it seems, my friend." Brown opened the door. "I like him."

"Yeah, that Kevin kid looks to be a good lad," Taylor said.

Brown replied, "I have a feeling this won't be the last time we will hear from Kevin Wolf." And they left the school.

Chapter 17

Toronto, Ontario. Canada: Friday December 21, 2007:

*K*evin Wolf arrived home after a difficult school day. He had hoped to get some rest before school's Christmas party, but his mother saw things differently.

"Hello, dear. I'm glad you are here," she said, and gave him a kiss on the cheek. "Before you take off for your party, could you take the garbage to the bin?"

"Sure, Mom." Kevin grabbed the bag and placed it next to the front door.

"I have supper in the oven. I just received a call from your brother. He had to work late tonight, and Stephanie has the night shift at the hospital. So, I said that I would take over from the sitter," she explained. "After you eat, could you clean up the apartment for me before you leave?" She grabbed her coat from the closet.

"No problem, Mom." Kevin stepped towards the oven. "How are you getting there?"

"Ray is picking me up. I'm going to wait for him at the front." She blew her son a kiss and added, "Bye, sweetheart. Have fun at the party, but be back by eleven-thirty."

"I will, Mom. Bye," Kevin said before the door closed. *Man, there goes my sleep time.* Kevin took his supper out of the oven. He was not keen about cleaning the apartment, but his mother sacrificed so much for him and the family in general that he could not refuse such a simple request. She first met Kevin's father, Duncan, at college. Sophie and Duncan fell in love and got married. A bright accounting student, she ranked at the top of her class. But his career in the military meant a great deal of relocation. Sophie dropped out of college and followed her husband from post to post. Eventually they moved away from the base and bought a nice home. At the time, Sophie did not have a job, and the family depended on her husband's income. Sophie had to bear the

111

tragic news of her husband's death during a peacekeeping mission; killed in an accident on board the HMCS Halifax on his way home. After his death, the bills began to mount. She searched in vain for work. But in the end, the bank foreclosed on the house. She moved to Toronto with her children and took a job as a server at Shutout's Sports Bar & Grill. There she worked for years under Raymond Clayton's direction. In no time, the two became friends, and later they became a couple. The family liked Ray, a true gentleman to the core. Being the owner of the bar, Ray helped Sophie go back to college to complete her accounting degree. Sophie is expected to graduate in April. At times, she had to put her life as a student on hold because of her family and Ray. Kevin loved his mother and tried to help whenever he could—even if it meant cleaning the apartment for the third time this week. Lifting the top of the pot, Kevin looked at his meal.

Lasagna, how thoughtful, Mom. The scent of Italian spices billowed from the casserole dish. Kevin went to the cupboard to grab a plate and a glass. The young teen served his meal and drink, then placed the items on the coffee table. He was about to sit on the couch, when the doorbell rang.

"Hold on a minute," he shouted. Kevin sprung from the chair and mumbled all the way to the door. The doorbell rang again.

"I'm coming, hold on, hold on." Kevin said, his voice filled with aggravation. But he made a quick transition when he opened the door.

"Are you always in that kind of mood?" Chloe smiled.

"Hi, beautiful," Kevin said, and kissed her right cheek. "I didn't know it was you."

"Who were you expecting," she teased, "another girl?" And she stepped inside.

"Are you kidding? Angie isn't dropping by until tomorrow," Kevin returned the tease with his smile.

"Who's Angie?"

"Just joking. Besides, if we broke up, my mom would kill me."

"Damn straight, buddy," Chloe replied as she slapped his shoulder. "Just remember you're stuck with me."

"I think I can handle that," Kevin said. He tried to hug her, but the smell in the kitchen distracted her, leaving Kevin alone to hug the air. Chloe smelled the aroma of the melted cheese.

"Your mom made her lasagna, may I steal some?"

"Sure, dear. Help yourself." Kevin returned to his chair.

"Kevin Wolf, what do you think you are doing?"

"What?"

"You are sitting in the living room to eat. If your mom catches you, you are dead."

"She's not here right now. So, no one will know. Except for you."

"Sit at the dining table, or I'm going to tell your mom," she ordered.

"Fine then." Kevin stood with his plate and glass. "All I know is that Angie wouldn't tell on me," Kevin boasted.

"You jerk," she said, and threw her spoon at him.

"Relax, relax, pretty lady." Kevin laughed. Chloe couldn't help but smile.

"Why do I put up with you?" she inquired. She gazed into Kevin's brown, teasing eyes.

"Maybe because you like me."

"More than that, Wolfey," she said. "I love you." Chloe kissed his forehead.

"I love you, too, chere." The sound of Kevin's soft voice warmed her heart. After their meal, Kevin collected the dishes and brought them to the sink.

"Do you need a hand?" Chloe asked.

"If you don't mind." Kevin turned on the taps and started washing the dishes. Chloe applauded with polite sarcasm and flashed him a teasing look.

"Oh, you're real *cute*, chere." Chloe enjoyed Kevin's sarcasm.

"Don't you forget it." She smiled.

"I have to do the vacuuming here for my mom before I go," Kevin said. "The bus will be here in thirty minutes." He dried the dishes and placed them where they belong.

"Don't worry about the bus," she replied. "Lori is picking us up when we are ready."

"Oh, okay."

"But go and take a shower, and I will do the vacuuming. When you are ready, I will call her. But we will have to make a pit stop at my place. I have to make myself look beautiful in case some cute guy asks me for a dance," Chloe joked.

"Your parents love me. You do that, and I'll rat you out. So take that." Kevin gave her a smile before he went to the bathroom.

"Would you hurry up, big mouth." She giggled. Chloe sat in the living room and remembered the first time she danced with Kevin. During last year's teen dance, she and Kevin had been friends. She helped him that night to prepare for his date with Julie Simms. They were all close friends, she, Kevin, Julie, Tommy White, Cole Joseph, Tina Munroe, and Shauna Gibson. They all had dates for the dance. Cole dated Shauna, Tommy dated Sonia, Tina dated Dave, and she was with Matt. Kevin was doing the solo act, but at the last minute, Julie broke it off with Chad Carlson; a jerk even today in Chloe's eyes. Chad left Julie heartbroken. Kevin, in love with her since kindergarten, saw his chance to rescue her and be together. Chloe spent a week with him, trying to help him sum up the courage to ask her to the dance. That was the easy part. And when he asked her—she said yes. Then the fun part, Chloe helped him with what to say and what to buy her. Finally the night of the dance arrived. Things went well until Chad arrived and wanted to talk to Julie. She believed every word Chad said to her. Julie, happy that he wanted to be with her, looked at Kevin and asked him if she could spend the rest of the dance with Chad. Chloe felt the pain in his face. But maintaining a calm exterior, Kevin just smiled and told her to go for it. An hour later, Chloe's date brought some liquor to the dance and proceeded to get intoxicated. He ruined her evening. Kevin saw her running towards a bench near a pond to cry. Forgetting for a moment about his own hurt, Kevin followed her. They talked for about twenty minutes before they returned to the dance floor. And they danced. Something magical did happen for both of them; they realized how close they had become, and beginning that night, they started dating. Now, it has been a little over a year, and the two couldn't be happier. As her thoughts passed her by, Kevin finished his shower and had already gotten dressed for the party.

Kevin came out of his bedroom and asked, "Hey, how do I look?"

"You look great. Just great. You're always great in my books," she said with her gentle voice.

"It's because I have you. That's why I look so good," Kevin said. "You're good for a guy's morale." Kevin hugged her. He felt her warmth and the tender beat of her heart next to his chest. Contentment and love filled Kevin's soul. Chloe knew for as long she would be wrapped in his arms, Kevin would protect her. She tilted her head on his right shoulder and closed her eyes.

"I wish we could just stay like this forever." Chloe held onto him like a vice.

"Ditto, chere," Kevin said. "But we do have to go."

"Alright, I'll call Lori then." She walked towards the phone.

"I will get our coats," Kevin said. Chloe spent a few minutes on the phone, then hung up.

"All ready to go?" Kevin helped her with her coat.

"Yeah, Lori will be here in about fifteen minutes," she said. Then she opened the door and turned off the lights.

"Okay then, we will wait for her at the front," Kevin said.

Chloe strolled out of the apartment and asked, "You have everything, Kev?" Almost forgetting the garbage, he grabbed the bag at the door.

Kevin replied, "Yep. I have everything." And he locked the door and followed her towards the front exit.

Robert and Nancy Bellecoeur had just finished wrapping their Christmas presents when they spotted their oldest daughter's car pulling into the driveway. They thought they would have had all the gifts wrapped by the time she would have returned with her sister and Kevin. But the headlights shining at the front window proved otherwise.

"Quickly, hide them, Robert," she said. "I will keep them busy."

"I'm already at it, honey." He grabbed the bags.

"I will distract them." In order to buy her husband some time, Nancy dashed for the door and locked it. As the lock clicked shut, someone attempted to open the door.

"Hey, the door is locked," Lori said. Chloe pressed the doorbell button in rapid succession.

"I'm coming, girls," Nancy said. Once she knew Robert had finished hiding all the gifts, she opened the door.

"It's cold out here, Mom," Lori said. "Why did you lock the door?"

"Maybe me and your father were busy doing something?" She smiled.

"I doubt that. You guys are either watching TV or reading the paper." Chloe smiled.

"What's that supposed to mean?" Nancy replied.

"Don't listen to them, Mrs. Bellecoeur. You are without a doubt the prettiest girl here." Kevin winked.

"Oh, how I love this guy. Santa's going to give you something nice." Nancy smiled as her husband walked in.

"Hello girls. Hi, Kevin, how are you tonight?"

"Very good, and yourself, sir?"

"I am doing well, thanks. Are you all ready for Christmas?"

"Just about, sir. I have a few more gifts to wrap up, but I'm just about ready."

"I know one of those has my name on it." Chloe smiled.

"Only if you have been a good little girl this year," Kevin teased. Chloe gave Kevin a teasing look, and she climbed the stairs to get ready for the party.

Robert looked at Lori and said, "I see you are a chaperon for the party, dear."

"Yes, Mr. Brian asked me if I could help out this year," Lori explained. "So, I will be watching you, Kevin."

"I'll be good, but I would keep an eye on Chloe if I were you, Lori." Kevin smirked.

"Well, I'm sure that everyone will have fun tonight," Nancy said.

"I'm sure we will, Mrs. Bellecoeur," Kevin replied. A few minutes later, Chloe stepped down the stairs. She wore a stunning mauve dress and twirled like a ballerina.

"How do I look?" she asked. Kevin looked at the love of his life and replied in reverence.

"Like an angel, ma belle."

"Thank you, Kev," she said with an emotional tear in her left eye. Kevin grabbed Chloe's coat.

"Well, we have to meet Tommy and the gang at Margaret's place," he said.

"It's nice you all got together and rented a van to pick her up," Nancy said.

"We know her father could get the limo to drive her there, but we wanted to do something nice for her," Kevin replied. "Tommy's dad is driving the van."

"Well, she will love that," Nancy said as the teens were ready to leave.

"Have fun, guys," Robert said. "Honey, you look beautiful."

"Thank you, Daddy," she replied, and they headed towards the door.

"Have a great time," Nancy said. Chloe, Lori, and Kevin waived at them and entered Lori's car. Lori started the ignition, and they were off to Margaret's place.

Alexander Taylor stared at the Christmas tree and remembered happier times. He could still see his little girl running down the stairs of their Detroit mansion; jumping with joy when seeing the gifts under the tree. His thoughts haunted him also of the times when the first thing he would see when he woke was the face of his beautiful wife Virginia. The sadness and horrors of the present had replaced his fondest subjective memories of the past. This will be his first Christmas without his beautiful wife. Arthur Brown was no stranger to pain. This Christmas would be his thirtieth Christmas without his wife; as Brown once said to Taylor, "the hurt never goes away." The voice of his butler interrupted his reminiscences of his wife.

"Pardon me, sir. Dr. Brown has arrived."

"Send him in, Danforth." The butler escorted Brown into the study.

Brown smiled. "Thank you, Danforth." The butler took his coat and hat.

"My pleasure, sir. If there is anything else you need, I will be in the foyer, gentlemen." The butler left as quietly as he had arrived.

"How are you, my friend?" Brown asked as he sat next to the fireplace.

"Holding out the best I can. How was your trip with Patrick?"

"Well, we have our seven agents, the keep is built, and we are all but ready to put the ball in motion."

"Just no Shadow Chaser yet," Taylor said while he poured a drink of eggnog for his friend.

"It takes time to find the right person, Alex. I want the perfect person to wear that mask. I assure you, the wait will be worth it," Brown said, looking at his eggnog. "No rum in this, right?"

"No, alcohol free."

"Good." Brown took a huge gulp.

"Well, I know you will find the right person. Just I am so damn impatient. I want to get those bastards for what they did."

"I know, Alex. However, we have to find the right people we can trust. For now, let's just put the festive season as our priority for now."

Taylor replied, "I will, for Margaret's sake." Brown wanted to say more to ease his friend's anguish, but Margaret wheeled in and showed off her white dress.

"Hi, Dad. How do I look?"

"You look beautiful. Just like your mother." Taylor grabbed his daughter's right hand and kissed it.

"Thank you, Dad."

"I second that motion, dear," Brown said. "You look wonderful."

"Hi, Uncle Art. I didn't see you hiding in the shadows," she replied. "Thank you for the compliment, kind sir."

"My pleasure, my lady." Brown smiled. "Where are you going?"

"To my school's Christmas dance."

Brown replied, "Well, I hope you have fun then." Taylor wheeled her out of the study.

"I can call the limo for you?" Taylor asked.

"No, it's okay, Dad. My friends told me to stay here, and we will all go together."

"You seem to be happy, Margaret?" Brown asked.

"I am, Uncle Art. I couldn't ask for better friends," Margaret replied as the doorbell rang. Out of nowhere, the butler arrived to answer the door.

"Good evening, Miss Chloe and Mr. Wolf," the butler said.

The teens entered the mansion and Kevin replied, "Good evening, sir." Chloe nodded at the butler and they walked towards Margaret.

"My God. You look beautiful, Maggie," Chloe said with joy, hugging Margaret.

"You look smashing in that dress, Chloe," Margaret replied.

"No one is going to say anything about how I look?" Kevin smiled.

"You look stunning, young man. Don't you agree, Alex?" Brown joked.

"Oh yes, just stunning, Art." Alex laughed.

Kevin felt embarrassed and out of place. He tried to remain calm, but he stuttered a bit. "Wh--why, thank you, gentlemen."

"Are we ready to go?" Margaret asked.

"Yes, we are. Follow us," Chloe said.

"Where are you taking me?" Margaret probed.

"Just come with me to the door," Chloe said. "Kevin, open the door."

Kevin smiled. "Yes, me lord." And he opened the door. Margaret spotted a minivan filled with the gang and a place for her.

Margaret gasped. "You didn't?" And she put her hands on her mouth.

"We wanted to go there as a group, so we got together and rented a van," Kevin said.

"Thank you, guys," Margaret said. She reached out and hugged Chloe and Kevin.

"No problem. It's the least we can do." Kevin smiled.

"It's an early Christmas gift," Chloe said. "Let's get you inside."

"Let me help," Taylor said as they headed towards the van. Taylor and Brown helped her inside the van while Chloe joined her friend. Kevin took her wheelchair and placed it in the back of the van.

"Have fun, sweetheart."

"I will, Dad," she replied. "Bye, Uncle Art."

"Bye, my dear," Brown replied.

Kevin walked towards Brown and Taylor and said, "Well, that's it. Don't worry, Mr. Taylor. We'll take good care of her."

"Thank you for everything you and Chloe have done for Margaret." Taylor gave Kevin a warm handshake.

"It's our pleasure, sir."

"You are a good man, Kevin. Merry Christmas," Brown said.

"Thank you, sir," Kevin said. "Merry Christmas to you as well." Kevin entered the vehicle. Within seconds, the van drove away.

"I didn't think it was the best move for her going to a regular school. But look at her, Art, she is so happy," Taylor said with a tear rolling down his face.

"Merry Christmas, my friend," Brown replied; then he escorted his friend back inside the mansion to their meeting.

The crowd packed the school gymnasium. Students, teachers, and volunteers all played a part for the Christmas dance. The DJ played a combination of pop and a few Christmas tunes to celebrate the season. Kevin, Chloe, and the rest of the gang arrived at the dance. But as they entered, the teens noticed Julie Simms drinking a glass of punch. Kevin still had feelings for her. Ever since the first day of school, he watched her; mesmerized by her beauty. Even though Kevin wouldn't trade Chloe for anything, he couldn't help but feel something for the blonde, beautiful, and innocent Julie.

Chloe knew he felt something for her before, but she knew what kind of guy Kevin was. They had an eternal and unbreakable relationship.

"I wonder where that jerk is?" Chloe said, referring to Julie's boyfriend Chad.

"Who knows with him," Kevin replied. "Maybe we should go and say hi. I don't want to see her sad at this dance."

"I know what you mean. She's been talking about this dance all week," Chloe said.

"Hey guys, Jewel is over there. Let's go," Kevin said. In the first grade, Kevin had nicknamed her Jewel. With her looks and charm, the nickname stayed with her.

"Where's Chad?" Tommy asked Kevin.

"I don't know."

Tina bit her lip and said, "Don't tell me he stood her up."

"Well, we should just play dumb. In case he did," Cole said.

"Yeah, we don't want to hurt her even more than he already has," Shauna replied.

"Right, Cole," Margaret replied. "Let's go." The gang moved towards Julie.

"Hi Julie," Chloe said. "You look great."

"Hi, Chloe. I see the gang is here," she replied as they crowded her.

"Yeah, we just arrived," Cole said, trying to think of something to say.

"Party looks good so far," Shauna said.

"I think we are going to have a great time," Julie said.

Without thinking, Tommy asked, "Where is Chad?" Tina gave him an evil stare and elbowed his ribs.

"*Quiet you*," she whispered.

"Oh yeah, sorry." Tommy rubbed his ribs and remained silent.

"Oh, he's late. He's trying to save some money for Christmas. But he will be here. He promised," Julie said. Everyone felt bad, but they didn't know what to say. Margaret broke the ice.

"Of course he will. But in the meantime, you want to hang with us?"

"Margaret is right. There is plenty of room at our table, Jewel," Kevin said.

"Sure, I would like that," Julie replied. She joined her friends, and they headed towards an empty table. Not even ten minutes in the party, the girls decided to use the washroom.

"We are taking a powder break. You three stay out of trouble," Chloe said.

"Us—always. Right guys?" Cole said.

"For sure," Kevin replied.

"Absolutely," Tommy added.

Chloe said, "Yeah, right." The four girls giggled, and they left for the washroom. The guys waited until the girls were out of ear range to talk.

"Do you think Chad is going to show?" Tommy said.

"Who knows, with that idiot you never know. I don't know what Julie sees in him," Cole replied.

"Well, she loves him, and she's our friend," Kevin said. "So, we have to tolerate Chad for her sake and support her. I know it means putting on our poker faces, but that's what we should do."

"Well, speak of the Devil. Look who just showed up," Tommy said as Chad strode towards them. Julie's friends called Chad Carlson the ultimate narcissist. The guy had an ego a mile wide and the attitude of a banker on loan day. Chad was not familiar with the word 'no' because he always got whatever he wanted. And for some unknown reason, girls found him irresistible. He always played Julie around, but ever since he heard rumours that Kevin cared for her, he moved in just to boast and claim another prize.

"Hey, lads. Have you seen, Julie?" Chad asked while he combed his hair.

"She is in the ladies' room with the other girls," Kevin replied.

"She's trying to look good for me." Chad laughed. "That's cool. I will sit with you guys. Then maybe, after the girls see me and go wild, you guys may get lucky."

"What would we do without you, Chad," Tommy said.

"You know, dudes. I just don't know," Chad replied.

"Look at this guy, Kev," Cole whispered. *"Tommy just insulted him, and he takes it as a compliment."*

"I know, but what can you do?" Kevin grinned. The girls returned, and Julie spotted Chad.

"Hey, baby," Chad said with smug arrogance.

"Hi, dear," Julie said with a smile. "I'm glad you came." Julie kissed him and showed off her dress. "How do I look?"

Chad took a mere look at her dress and shrugged. "You look okay." And with a slight turn of his head, he glanced at the other girls in the gym. Chad greeted

119

a few of them with smiles and nods. Despite his actions, Julie remained attentive, as usual. When he finished scouting out the ladies, he turned his head towards her. "So, you wanna dance?"

"Sure, dear." Julie's face glowed with joy, and she followed him to the dance floor. The rest of the gang could not believe Chad's attitude.

"I can't get over this. Do you see how he's treating her?" Margaret queried.

"Yep, he's a real prince charming," Kevin replied.

"Well, I'm getting some punch. I can't bear the thought of him," Tina said before she left the table.

"Well, Margaret, do you want to dance? I might not be as smooth as Chad," Tommy said.

"Sure, Tommy. Maybe if we can get close to them, I can run over his foot," Margaret said.

Tommy replied, "Sounds like a plan." And he wheeled Margaret to the dance floor.

"Well, shall we join them?" Cole said, looking at Shauna.

"Sounds good to me, hun." Shauna grabbed Cole's hand, and they left the table. Seconds later, Chloe's favourite song echoed throughout the gym.

"Oh, Kev. It's our song. Can we dance?" she requested with the excitement of a child.

"Anything for you, chere." Kevin and Chloe strolled towards the music.

Chloe closed her eyes and said, "I just love this song." She felt comfortable in Kevin's arms.

"You are beautiful, Chloe," Kevin whispered to her ear. *"I don't know what I would do without you."*

"I love you, Kevin." Chloe started to sing like angel, and Kevin listened as intently as a child hearing a bedtime story. But halfway into the song, she came to sudden stop and asked, "Have you ever taken the time to listen to the words in this song?"

"A little bit," he said. "I listen more to rhythm than words." Kevin cradled her as they moved to the flow of the music.

"It tells us to live for today, for we don't know what will come tomorrow. Life is so precious, and that it could go in a matter of a heartbeat," Chloe said.

"I guess so." Kevin smiled.

"It's true. No matter what we do in life, our time does come, and we have to know that we have done all we can in life—as opposed to throwing it all away."

"Why all this tonight, chere?"

"I dunno, just felt like it. All of a sudden, I felt that things in my life won't be the same again this time next year."

"Of course they will. You are just getting emotional. Besides, I will never leave you. Who else would tolerate me?" Kevin smiled.

"I will tolerate you, Wolfey. I love you," Chloe whispered.

"And I love you," Kevin said. They were in love, and they danced throughout the evening.

As the evening progressed, so did the dance, an event considered a tremendous success. Lori Bellecoeur reminisced about her days in high school when she had true happiness in her life. But she soon learned the unpleasant realities of life. Two years ago, she had just graduated from university when she met a guy by the name of Graham Cassidy. Tall, dark, and handsome, a true specimen of manhood; he represented the appearance of a prince charming. However, Lori would soon learn the true substance of her prince.

Graham Cassidy, an up-and-coming star with the mafia family known throughout the world as the Scorpio Syndicate, a truth he kept hidden from Lori. Cassidy made it big with the local capo after he ran the gambling business for the family in Toronto. He had a good cover, and people would never have known about his connections to the syndicate. Lori started dating him about a year after they met, and at first, it was magic. Flowers everyday and gifts from exotic places. Then the curtain fell; the police caught Cassidy during a raid on one of the syndicate's clubs. He took the blame to protect the family. That move impressed the family, and with some legal trickery and a judge on the take, he received eight months for his crime. She ended the relationship with him, but he promised her he would return. It had been four months since his release, and he had yet to show up. Lori hoped it would stay that way. Looking at her watch, she knew the dance would soon be over.

"This is the last dance, folks," the DJ said. Lori took one more look around to see how things were going, but then she heard a voice from her past.

"Hey, darling. How about we share this one," the voice requested. She turned around on the spot, and to her surprise and apprehension, Cassidy stood there all dressed up and grinned.

"What do you want?" Lori asked.

"Hey relax, doll. I just want a dance. How are you?" he asked with a flower in his hand.

"I'm fine," she said. "Now please go." Her blood began to freeze in horror.

"Go? I'm here to give you a flower and tell you I still love you, baby," Cassidy said. "Now, let's be together. I got so much money I want to share with you."

"I don't want you in my life, Graham. Please go," Lori replied, but Cassidy refused her plea and took her by the hand.

"You're coming with me, doll."

"Leave me alone," she screamed. The whole room saw what happened. Kevin and company were no exception. Chloe was well aware of what he represented in her sister's life. She was twelve going on thirteen at the time when she first met him, but she knew her sister was in serious danger.

"It's Graham. He's back," she said.

"Go get help, I'll keep him busy," Kevin said.

"What do you want us to do, Kev?" Tommy asked.

"Just back me up in case I get in trouble." Tommy and Cole nodded in agreement.

"Be careful, Kev. He's dangerous." Chloe left to get help. Kevin ran with all his speed to get to Lori.

"I said for the last time, baby," Cassidy said, "you're coming with me." Kevin stepped in front of him and looked at Lori.

"Is there a problem, Lori?"

"I'm okay, Kevin."

"You heard the lady, snot face," Cassidy said.

"Well, Chloe is getting help, and I know the cops will be here at any moment now," Kevin said when the school's security guard walked in.

"Is this man bothering you, ma'am?"

"I was just leaving. This isn't over, Lori," Cassidy said. "I'm coming back for you." He backed away from her at a snail's pace; his eyes targeted Lori as he grinned like a fiend.

"Leave me alone, Graham," Lori said. "And never come back."

"Oh, I will be back. I promise," he vowed. "And don't think I forgot about you, snot face. I will get you for this." Cassidy stormed out of the gym.

"Alright, folks. The show is over," the security guard said, and the dance resumed. After the smoke cleared, Chloe ran towards her sister.

"Are you all right, Lori?"

"I'm fine, Chloe. Let's go home."

"Go ahead, Chloe. I will make sure that we follow you," Kevin said when Cole and Tommy advanced towards him.

"He's back, just great," Cole said.

"Yeah, and as charming as ever," Tommy added.

"We are going to follow them home. Once they are safe, we will leave," Kevin said. "Tommy, call your dad and tell him we are ready to go."

"Alright then. While I do that, Cole can get the girls," Tommy said.

Cole nodded. "You got it." He returned to the table and explained the situation to the girls. Within an instant, the gang followed Kevin to the parking lot and waited for Tommy's father to pick them up. Twenty minutes felt like hours, but in the end, the van arrived. Chloe stayed in the car with her sister, and Kevin and the gang were right behind them in the van. Kevin was certain Cassidy meant business—and knew his group's young lives would never be the same.

122

Chapter 18

Toronto, Ontario. Canada: May 23, 2008:

*R*ay Clayton prepared his bar for another weekend. His beloved establishment, Shutouts Sports Bar & Grill, was his life. The restaurant, bar, and dance club served great food and offered a family atmosphere to its patrons. Local country bands performed on Saturdays for the live music-loving crowd. He started the business eight years ago, but he began losing money. A great person of the people, but a lousy businessman with the books, Ray came close to losing his business on a number of occasions. However, luck would change his fortune for the better when he hired Sophie Wolf. He liked her since the first time he saw her. The kindness of her demeanour enhanced her physical attractiveness; she became his angel of mercy. The two became friends from the moment they met. Before they knew it, their friendship evolved into a relationship. She had a gift for numbers; Sophie had done miracles with the books and budgeted the business into the black. He made her the manager. Sophie took the position, but she continued to serve the patrons, because she loved the interaction. Today, he prepared a meal for her family at his best table. Kevin wanted to surprise Chloe with dinner because she won a summer job at a legal clinic. After all what Chloe's family went through these past five months with Graham Cassidy, Kevin wanted to make things good for Chloe. He asked Ray for help, and Ray pitched in with his usual enthusiasm. He had the table set for Kevin, Chloe, Sophie, and himself. At the last second, he remembered to add three more chairs, one for Kevin's brother, Mark, his wife, Stephanie, and their little boy, Logan. With Chloe's parents out of town, and Lori at work, Kevin's family filled the guest list. Sophie walked in as he finished the seating arraignments.

"Hey, handsome," she said, walking towards the door with the cake.

"Hey there." Ray kissed her right cheek. "That's a nice cake."

"Thank you, luv. I thought putting a scale of justice on the cake was a nice touch." Sophie placed the cake on the table. "Mark, Steff, and Logan are outside with the decorations."

"I'll give them a hand," Ray said, and headed for the door. Sophie went into the kitchen to see how the meal was coming along.

"Hi, Phil. How are you?" she asked the cook.

"Not bad, Sophie, and yourself?"

"I'm doing well, thanks. How are our lasagnas looking?"

"I just put them in the oven. But I'm sure they will look great."

"Thanks, Phil." Sophie returned to the table.

"Hi, Nana," little Logan said as the rest of them were putting the decorations up.

"Hello, my little man." Sophie picked him up. "How's my favourite guy doing?"

"Good. When is Uncle coming?"

"He will be here in another hour," she replied. "He's keeping Chloe busy at the library. Then he's going to bring her here."

"I like her. She always plays hide-and-seek with me," he said. "Is Uncle going to marry her?"

"Well, they both have to graduate from high school first and go to college." She smiled.

"Well, after that can he marry her?"

Sophie looked into his sweet, baby blue eyes and asked, "You would like that, Logan?"

"Yes, I would, Nana. Then I can call her auntie."

"Well, I'm sure if you call her that now, she wouldn't mind."

"Okay then, I will," the boy said as she put him down. "Can I go and play now?"

"Go ahead, dear."

"Thank you, Nana. Bye, bye." Logan ran around the dance floor and played with the balloons. Mark and Ray had just finished hanging streamers.

Mark remained on the ladder and asked, "Well, Mom. What do you think of the decorations?"

"They look great, dear."

"Kevin put a lot of effort into this. I'm so happy for him and her. They make a cute couple," Stephanie said.

"They sure do," Sophie said.

"You always had a soft spot for my brother," Mark joked.

"Well, yeah. If I hadn't baby-sat him, I would have never met you, silly," Stephanie replied.

Mark replied, "You're right." And he winked at his wife.

"Well, we're all set. We just have to wait for Kevin's phone call," Ray said.

"Well then," Sophie said, "let's grab a drink here while we're waiting." Sophie and her family stepped towards the bar and waited for Kevin's call—which was now fifty minutes away.

Kevin looked at the clock on the library wall and noticed that he had to make his phone call; he had to get Chloe to join him at Ray's for her surprise supper. He took his mom's cell phone and made his call. After a few words with his mother, he noticed Chloe walking with a stack of books.
"You found all of the books you wanted?" Kevin asked.
"Just about, dear," she replied.
"Here, let me take them for you," Kevin offered.
"You are a sweetheart aren't you?" She smiled and handed him the books.
"Well, I try," he said. Kevin glanced at the book on top.
"Capital Punishment in Canada," he read. "I thought you were just doing a little light reading?"
"Well, I'm trying to get as much reference as I can on the subject. I hope to impress my bosses," she replied.
"I see. Well, we should have that back here again," Kevin added.
"What do you mean?"
"I mean we should have the death penalty here again. If you kill someone, you should pay for it."
"But, Kev, it won't bring the person back. Two murders don't bring retribution, it brings more sadness, darkness, and pain," Chloe said.
"You mean even though some scum bag killed someone you cared for or loved, you would not support the death penalty?" Kevin queried.
"I would be mad, and I would want justice; but vengeance is not the last memory I would want to hold of a person who has been lost to me," Chloe said. "I want to remember the life of the person, and I want my loved one's life to be honoured by the way that person had touched my heart, and not by the death of a criminal," she said.
"I understand what you are saying, chere, but shouldn't the law have the right to take away that life?"
"No one has the right to take away life, hun. Only God can do that. I for one do not want to be accountable for the death of anyone—even if I were killed by someone, that death would not bring me back. If someone was to be put to death because of my murder, I don't think my soul could rest," Chloe said.
"If you say so, dear." Kevin smiled.
"It's true, only God can take a life. Not me, you, or society."
"Well, this discussion won't end in an afternoon." Kevin smiled. "Are you ready to go?"
"Yes, I am. Sooner I get home, the faster I can get to read these books."
"Before we go to your place, we have to make a pit stop at Ray's. I have to pick up my mom's papers," Kevin said.

"That's fine," she replied.

"By that time, we can catch the bus. But before we go, I want to give you something," Kevin said.

"You have something for me?" she teased.

"Yep, this is to say congrats on your new job." Kevin gave her a little box he took out of his coat pocket.

"What is it?"

"Open it, chere." Chloe acted like a child on Christmas morning and opened it.

"Oh my God, Kev," she said in awe, taking out a gold chain with a charm attached to it. "It's beautiful." The charm—the scales of justice in gold.

"I thought it would be a perfect gift for you at the legal clinic." Her expression of joy pleased Kevin.

"I love it so much. Thank you, sweetheart." Chloe glowed and hugged him tight. Kevin dropped her books, causing a loud slam onto the wooden floor. The sound caught the librarian's attention. She looked at them with a sombre expression and placed her index finger on her lips.

"Shhh!" They both giggled like children in the playground and kissed.

"For you, I would give you the stars, chere," Kevin said, releasing his gentle grip around her waist. "Here, let me help you with it." Kevin attached it around her neck.

"I'm never going to take it off."

"It's you." Kevin smiled, then looked at his watch. "Jeez, look at the time, we better go to Ray's and pick up those papers." Kevin grabbed the books from the floor.

Chloe held his left hand and replied, "Lead the way, handsome."

"Let's go then, chere." And they strolled together hand in hand together as one and in love.

Sophie waited near the window to act as the lookout for Kevin and Chloe. Fifteen minutes passed since she received a call from Kevin saying they were on their way.

"He's five minutes late," Stephanie said.

"You know Kevin, he's always late." Mark shrugged.

"They're coming," Sophie said, "get ready and light up the cake." Sophie and her family gathered together and waited for Kevin and Chloe to walk inside. As the door opened, they shouted.

"Surprise."

"What's this?" Chloe said in shock.

"Congratulations of your new job," they cheered.

Chloe looked at Kevin and asked, "Oh my God, did you plan all this?"

"It's all for you." Kevin smiled.

Sophie hugged Chloe and said, "Congratulations, dear."

"Thank you, Mrs. Wolf," she said with a tear in her eye.

"All the best, Chloe." Ray greeted her with a handshake and a warm smile.

"Thank you, Mr. Clayton."

"Now I will know where to go for my parking tickets." Mark smiled.

"Well, I'm not a lawyer yet, just a clerk." Chloe grinned.

"Oh, that will happen soon enough," Stephanie said.

"Hi, Aunt Chloe," Logan said, raising his arms to her. The action filled her heart with joy.

"That's the sweetest thing anybody has ever said to me, Logan." She smiled and hugged him. "Thank you, sweetheart."

"I love you, Aunt Chloe."

"I love you, my little man," she replied as the waitress brought in the main course.

"I know how much you like my lasagna, so I had it made for you just the way you like it," Sophie said.

"Thank you, all. I don't know what to say," she said overwhelmed with emotion.

"Just take my brother away from home someday. That will be payment enough," Mark joked.

"To have a family like you have as well," Chloe said, "it's a deal." And they all sat for the meal. The cheese bubbled and the aroma of sauce caught their attention. Kevin was about to grab the pan when his mother and Chloe slapped his hand.

"Kevin," they both scolded him. "The blessing first."

"Yes, bosses," Kevin replied as the group laughed.

"Chloe, would you do the honour?" Sophie asked.

"Thank you, Mrs. Wolf," she replied and started the prayer.

"Dear Lord. Bless this table, the food prepared, and our family surrounding this table tonight. And may we be always happy and together in your grace forever. Amen."

"Amen," the group answered.

"That was beautiful, Chloe," Sophie said.

"It was my pleasure, Mrs. Wolf." Kevin raised his glass and stood.

"To Chloe, my best friend," Kevin said. "May you succeed in everything you do." Kevin's family lifted their glasses and toasted her.

"And for keeping Kevin out of our hair," Mark said, getting a laugh from the table. From that moment, the meal, and the good times, began and continued through the hour.

Two hours after the meal, Kevin and Chloe traveled on the bus from Ray's. They had the back seat to themselves. Kevin sat with his elbow on the window sill with Chloe's head, next to his shoulder. She held him like he had saved her from an emptiness; in many ways, they had both saved each other.

As the bus drove closer to her stop, she asked, "Are you going to church tomorrow?"

"I dunno, I had a long day today, I may just sleep in," Kevin said. He knew it would get her talking.

"Kevin Wolf, what would your mom say?" She glared at him with an unyielding look.

"The old gal would probably throw her slipper at me," Kevin teased.

"Old gal," she hollered. "I would like to look that good at forty-five. Plus, she's not old." Chloe punched his arm.

"I'm just joking, chere." Kevin smiled.

"Well then, you will meet me here tomorrow then for mass," she said.

"Do I have to?" Kevin asked.

"We're Catholics, so we have to act like Catholics," she said. "When I'm a mom someday, I want to bring my family to church," she said.

"Is it that important to you?" Kevin probed.

"It is, hun. We got to have something to believe in. It's a matter of faith," she explained.

"Ahh, I see." Kevin shrugged the topic.

"Sometimes you piss me off, Kev. You sound like you don't believe?"

"I do, chere," Kevin said. "It's just that you are so cute when you are mad and talking philosophy. I couldn't help it."

"You're cruisin' for a bruisin', pal," she said.

"How about a kiss?" Kevin solicited.

"I think I can handle that." Chloe gave him gentle peck on the lips. Their stop was arriving at a rapid pace. "I better pull the string." Chloe grabbed the cord and tugged. Kevin grabbed her books and his backpack.

"I have your books," Kevin replied as the bus slowed to a crawl. The bus came to a complete stop, and the young couple disembarked. The bus started to depart from its stop. The engine sounded like an asthmatic lawn mower, leaving the teens clouded in diesel exhaust. Kevin handed her the books.

She glanced at them and asked, "Is that all of them?"

"Yep, Capital Punishment in Canada, Justice of Society, Canadian Law for the Twenty-First Century, Pocket Criminal Code, and The Shadow Chaser: Blind Justice," Kevin read. "What's this Shadow Chaser book about?"

"He was a vigilante in the mid 70's," she said. "He fought criminals who were untouchable by the law. They say he was dressed in black and wore a mask. The cops tried to arrest him, but according to the book, he was never caught."

"He's a fictional character in a novel, cool. Kinda like a super-hero," Kevin said. "I didn't know you were into that kind of stuff."

"He's not fiction; he existed for real. The book said the last time he was seen was back in 1987," she said.

"He was for real," Kevin said with puzzlement as they walked towards her home. "I never heard of the clown."

"Why do you call him a clown?"

"Come on, chere. A guy dressed in black and hid his identity, I mean it's cool for a movie, but for real," Kevin said. "Who would be stupid enough to do something like that?"

"I see what you mean, Kev." Chloe took out her key.

Kevin noticed the car was not in the driveway and said, "It looks like your folks are not home yet."

"They should be back in a bit," Chloe said, and she unlocked the door.

"Well, I will stay until they arrive." Kevin followed Chloe inside and dropped his backpack by the door. Chloe looked at Kevin and beamed.

"I'll be fine, Kev. Aren't you supposed to be going to Tommy's to study for your Algebra test?"

"I was, but I'm not going to leave you here alone. Not with Cassidy out there bugging your sister," Kevin said. "Your parents will be here soon enough."

"Kev, go ahead. I have some studying to do with these books. I'll be fine. Nobody has heard a peep from Cassidy in over four months." Chloe coiled her gentle arms around Kevin. "Besides, how can I study with you around?"

"Are you sure?" Kevin inquired. "I don't know..."

"I said go, I'll be okay. Now, get out of here." Chloe smiled.

"Alright then," Kevin said. "I'll be on the bus tomorrow morning at ten." Kevin gave her a quick kiss on the cheek.

"See you then, Wolfey," she said before he headed towards the door. Kevin was just about to put his foot on the step when a gentle voice stopped him in his tracks. "I love you." Kevin turned around and caught a glimpse of Chloe smiling at him and giving a gentle wave goodbye.

Kevin walked towards her and asked, "Why did you say those words with such beauty? How can I leave now when I get a send off like that?"

"I do love you. You're the best thing that has ever happened to me," Chloe said as Kevin hugged her.

"I love you, too, chere." Kevin gave her a soft peck on the upper lip. "If I could be reincarnated, I would be a tear. So, I can be born in your heart. Seen in your eyes, touched by your cheeks, to die on your lips."

"That is beautiful." Chloe wiped a tear from her eye. "You should be a writer."

"I can stay," Kevin said.

"No, I have to study. I will be all right," Chloe said. "I will see you in the morning."

"Alright then, good night, chere." Kevin smiled and walked away. Chloe locked the door; then she turned on the lights in the house. Still excited about her new summer job, she wanted to catch up on some reading, preparing to impress her new bosses. She brought the books inside the living room, so she could relax at the same time. Placing the books on the table, Chloe sat on the couch and took the first book from the top. Chloe read for about five minutes. Then a long, bone-chilling *crack* came from the hallway and disrupted her reading.

What was that? She dropped the book onto the table. "Mom, Dad. Is that you?" But there was no reply. Cautious as a mouse, Chloe rose from the couch. "Lori, are you here?" Again, still no reply. "Kevin is that you?" The silence continued to haunt her. "If it's you, this is not funny." Chloe, scared, but determined to find the source of the noise. She ambled towards the sound, but found nothing. *Must be my imagination.* Chloe rechecked the locks on the door and the window. *Everything is still locked.* After a thorough exam of the house, Chloe returned to the living room. But when she ambled towards the couch—she heard the rocking chair rocking back and forward. She moved closer to the couch and noticed someone was sitting there. Chloe was about to turn around and head for the front door, but a hand grabbed her wrist.

"Now where do you think you're going?" the voice asked. Chloe turned around and witnessed the face of Graham Cassidy.

"Graham, what are you doing here?" she cried in apprehension.

"Well, sis. I'm looking for Lori." Cassidy threw her on the couch. "She won't come back to me. So, I'm taking one of the girls from this family with me."

"Get out of here, or I'm calling the police!"

"Go ahead, sis." He laughed. "I've cut all of the phone wires. I was sort of hoping it would be Lori here instead, but oh well, life is not always fair." Cassidy sauntered towards the couch.

"What are you going to do to me?" she cried.

"You're a big girl, sis." Cassidy grabbed her. "Figure it out." Chloe waited for the right moment to fight back. As Cassidy pulled her closer to him, she kicked him in the groin. Cassidy screamed in pain. "I'm going to kill you, you little tramp." Chloe was able to get off from the couch, but she tripped onto the table and fell face-first onto the rug.

Cassidy jumped on her and said, "Now I got you." With every ounce of strength in her body, Chloe freed her arms and scratched his left cheek.

"My face," he roared like a wounded bear. "You little slut." But before Chloe could free herself from him, he struck her in the mouth.

"Get off me, you monster," she shrieked, bleeding from the mouth.

Cassidy screamed, "Say goodbye, sis." And he took out his switchblade and raised it in the air.

Kevin had been walking for the last three minutes before realizing he had forgotten his backpack. He turned around and ran back to Chloe's place. *Pretty hard to study without the book, dumbass.* Kevin thought to himself before he arrived at the front door. He tried the doorknob, but found the door locked. Kevin rang the doorbell and wrapped at the door, but heard no response.

"Chloe, it's me," he shouted. "I forgot my backpack." Then he heard the unthinkable. A scream that seemed to resonate from the depths of hell came from Chloe's lungs.

"Chloe," Kevin hollered back. Fearing the worst, he took out a key Chloe had given him when he used to water the plants for her family when they were out of town. Kevin unlocked the door and dashed inside.

"Chloe, where are you?" Kevin hollered. When he got closer to the living room, he caught sight of a man, hidden in the shadows, by the back door.

The voice said, "See you around, snot face." The door opened, and the person walked out. Kevin caught a glimpse of the person. His worst nightmare had come to life; Graham Cassidy had returned. Kevin ran inside the room and found Chloe on the floor. She had two stab wounds in her upper body and bled profusely.

"Oh my God," Kevin panicked as he went towards her. "Chloe, can you hear me?"

"Kevin…it…was…Cas…si…de…y." Chloe felt the life draining out of her.

"Don't talk, Chloe. I'm going to get help." Kevin looked for the phone. Clutching the receiver, Kevin attempted to call for help, but the line was dead. He still had his mother's cell phone. Kevin took it out of his coat pocket and dialed 911.

"911 dispatch, please state the emergency?"

"I need an ambulance now, the address is 1975 Davisville Avenue. Hurry! My name is Kevin Wolf. My girlfriend was attacked and stabbed in her home. The attacker was Graham Cassidy. The family has a restraining order on him," Kevin said. He tried to keep calm, but anxiety overwhelmed him.

"We are sending an ambulance now, sir," the voice replied.

"Please hurry!" Kevin dropped the phone.

"Kev…in…it…hurts," she wept. "I…. feel…cold."

"It's going to be all right, chere. I'm here, and the ambulance is coming," Kevin said, staying by her. He tried to stop the bleeding, but he couldn't. The sirens screamed louder and closer. A powerless Kevin watched her coughing and praying. It felt like an eternity while Kevin waited for the paramedics to arrive. In the background, Kevin heard the tires squeal on the asphalt and the ambulance doors slammed in unison. The paramedics ran inside with a stretcher and their equipment.

"What has happened?" one of them asked.

"Her sister's ex boyfriend stabbed her," Kevin said.

"You will have to get out of the way, lad. We have to stabilize her," the second one said. Kevin moved while the paramedics tried to stabilize her. His body trembled, and the images in his mind scrambled his thoughts. He stared at the two paramedics as they patched her up the best they could. One of them tried to ask her questions while the other one called the dispatch on his radio. Before Kevin knew it, they had her on the stretcher, and they carried her out.

Kevin looked at the paramedics and said, "I'm coming with you."

"Alright then," the first one said. On the count of three, they lifted the stretcher and placed her inside the ambulance. The crowd formed around the area and looked on with concern.

"Let's go," the second one said, slamming the back doors of the ambulance. In a flash, the ambulance accelerated to the closest hospital.

Chapter 19

*M*argaret Taylor spent the day looking over summer outfits with her care worker. Janet Briggs had been working for the Taylors since Margaret's confinement to her wheelchair. But she also became like a mother figure to her. Margaret cared for Janet a great deal and trusted her judgment.

Margaret looked at the book and asked, "Do you believe the blue would look better than the red?"

"I believe the red one would bring out your eyes better, Miss Margaret," she replied. Taylor stepped inside the study and noticed the ladies looking over the latest fashions.

"Hello ladies." Taylor smiled. "How are the both of you this evening?"

"Hi, Dad. Okay, just checking the Paris fashions."

"Good evening, Mr. Taylor. I am doing fine, sir."

"Good, good. I'm going to the opera this evening with Art. Here is the number you can reach me in case of an emergency, Janet," Taylor said, passing her the note.

"Very well, sir."

"Dad, how did you get Uncle Art to go to the opera?"

"I lost a bet," Brown said, walking into the room, followed by the tapping of his cane. He turned towards the mirror and whispered a few colourful metaphors at his tie.

"Having problems with your tie, Art?" Taylor smirked.

"I hate ties, but when you have to wear one, you have to wear one." Brown made a vigorous effort, but the tie continued to annoy him. Taylor smiled and took over for his friend. By the time Brown stopped mumbling, Taylor had completed a Windsor knot.

"Well, you look rather distinguished, Uncle." Margaret smiled.

"Thank you, dear," Brown replied before he took one final look at his features and grabbed his cane.

"Besides, the board will be there, and we have to make a good impression," Taylor said when the phone rang. Janet headed towards the phone and answered it. She turned towards Margaret.

"It's for you, Miss Margaret." Margaret grabbed the phone. She held the phone for about thirty seconds; then her face turned ashen white, and her hands started to shake. She dropped the phone and began to cry. Taylor went to his daughter's side.

"What's wrong, dear?"

"Oh, Dad, it's terrible." Her eyes watered. "It was Tommy on the phone. He told me Chloe was stabbed by her sister's ex-boyfriend, and she is in surgery." Taylor held onto her daughter.

"When did this happen?" Taylor asked.

"About a couple of hours ago, everyone is there right now. Poor Kevin."

"That's terrible," Janet said.

"What hospital is she in?" Brown asked.

"Toronto General," Margaret said. "I want to go."

"I will take you," Brown said.

"We are all going," Taylor said. "Janet, please call the board members and inform them about the situation," Taylor said.

"Of course, sir."

Brown said, "Let's go then." And they headed for the door. Once outside, Taylor said to his driver. "Maurice, please take us to the Toronto General Hospital."

"Understood, sir." The driver opened the door for them and placed Margaret's wheelchair in the trunk. With all speed, the driver entered the limo, started the engine, and drove away from the mansion.

Kevin sat like a blindfolded man in front of a firing squad. His bloodstained fingers folded on the back of his neck, and his head hung low in distress. Still blaming himself for leaving her, he waited desperately for an answer. Chloe was in surgery for over two hours while her parents and sister were in the OR waiting room. He ignored the clutter of voices in the room. But he could not shake the constant crackling of the hospital intercom. Each announcement reminded him of his present nightmare. Fortunately, Kevin did not face this crisis alone. His mother and brother were at his side; his friends were there as well. Tommy held onto Tina, and Cole cradled Shauna. Julie had just arrived to find them all there.

"Hi, Mrs. Wolf," she said.

"Hi, Julie."

"Any word on Chloe?" she queried. She tried to hold back from crying.

"Nothing yet."

"Hi, Kevin." Julie sat by him.

"Oh, Jewel," Kevin said. "He really hurt her." The tears rushed out.

"It's okay, Kevin. I know." She hugged him. "We're all here, Kev. You're not alone."

"Thank you, Jewel," he said, sobbing. Margaret and her entourage had just arrived as well.

"Hi, Kevin," Margaret said. Kevin tried to smile.

"Hi Margaret. I'm glad you're here. Chloe would be…happy," he said, but then he started to cry again. Sophie moved, so that Margaret could wheel beside him.

"Mrs. Wolf?" Taylor asked.

"Yes, I am."

"My name is Alexander Taylor. I'm Margaret's father. This is my friend, Dr. Arthur Brown."

"Hello, I have heard so much about the both of you." She greeted each of them with a brief handshake. "This is my other son Mark." Mark nodded at them, but he focused his attention on his brother.

"You have good son, ma'am. If there is anything he needs, just let me know," Taylor said.

"That goes the same for me," Brown said.

Sophie replied, "Thank you both." But her attention shifted when Chloe's family walked towards the room.

"How is she?" Sophie asked.

"Not good. The doctor said that most of her organs were severely damaged by the attack," her father said.

"She's in her room now, and she's in pain. They drugged her up, but she's crying for Kevin," her mother said. Kevin sprung from his chair.

"Can I see her?"

"This way, dear," she replied. Kevin followed them to her room.

"I'm so sorry for leaving her. It's all my fault," Kevin said.

Her father held onto his right shoulder and said, "It's not your fault, Kevin. We should have been there as well."

"Mom, I should be the one in there, not her. He was coming for me," Lori said.

Her mother stopped in the middle of the hallway and grabbed Lori's shoulders. "Don't ever talk like that, Lori. You didn't ask for this."

"Your mother is right. Don't worry, that bastard will pay for this," her father said. "The police have a tip on his whereabouts." And they resumed their trek to her room. Upon opening the door, Kevin watched the love of his life, fighting to survive. The smell of medicine lingered in the room. Tubes were attached all over her; she continued to breathe with the help of an oxygen mask. The thrust of Cassidy's blade caused severe damage to her left lung. With his heart in his throat, Kevin went to her bedside and held onto her hand.

"*Ke...vin,*" she whispered.

"I'm here, chere." Kevin held his tears and tried to remain strong for her benefit.

"I...am...sorry...that...I...won't...be...with...you," she cried as a tear fell from her right eye.

"Yes, you will be, chere. You are going to fine. I prayed that you will be fine; we are always going to be together." Kevin looked at her eyes shifting everywhere.

"I...am...scared...Kev," she said.

Kevin tightened his grip on her hand and vowed, "You're not leaving me."

"I...love you...all." She coughed. Her parents and her sister were crying in the background.

"No, don't leave us, chere," Kevin begged. Chloe looked at the ceiling.

"Look...Kevin.... it's...beautiful." She smiled.

"No, God. Don't take her away. Please," Kevin cried.

"Don't...cry...Kev," she said with one final tear falling from her face. "If I could be reincarnated...I would be a tear," she said. "So, I can be born in your heart. Seen...in...your...eyes, touched...by...your...cheeks, to...die...on...your...lips." And she closed her eyes.

Beeeeeee!

The flat line registered on the monitor.

"No, you can't go," Kevin cried. Her parents helped him to his feet, and they left the room. When they approached the waiting room, everyone watched the expression on their faces. They knew they had lost a caring person with the soul of an angel. They all united together and cried a waterfall of tears. They held each other with tenderness and warmth, for they knew they would never see the smile or hear the voice of their loved one and friend, Chloe Bellecoeur, again.

Chapter 20

*I*t was a beautiful day; the birds sang in the distance, the blue sky offered the promise of hope, and the white clouds floated like cotton in the sky. The sun's radiance captured the scene. The green grass covered the ground, and the flowers around stood guard over the wide field. Chloe Bellecoeur loved a sunny day. On a beautiful day like this, one would usually find Chloe sitting next to a large tree curled up with a book. Now, they will find her resting beneath a tree again—this time for eternity. Family and friends surrounded the site, for on this day, they will lay her body to rest. Mourners surrounded the area as far as the eye could see. They were around the fences and outside of the cemetery. Chloe had made a tremendous impact on her community in her young life. She had given to everyone who needed help, and today they were all there for her because they loved her and needed her; and they still do today.

"She may be gone from this world, but we will never forget her memory; a promise we vow to keep," the priest said as he read the sermon. Her parents and sister were in the front row. Kevin, his family, and her friends joined her family at the service. Kevin just stared at the coffin, knowing that this would be the last time he would ever see her. Sorrow flooded his heart, but he did his best to maintain a brave front to honour her memory. The scent of the flowers resting near the coffin perfumed the air. The substance of the priest's sermon fell on deaf ears, because Kevin's mind journeyed back in time to the first day he had seen her.

February 12, 1999:

Even in Grade 1, Kevin had a crush on Julie, and he was running to give her a Valentine card. He tripped on a rock and fell into the mud. The puddle next to the mud stained his card. He cried for several minutes; then out of nowhere, an angel came to rescue him.

"Why are you crying, buddy?" her sweet voice said to him.

Kevin showed her the card and said, "My card is ruined."

"That's okay, I got a spare card." She smiled. "Do you want it?"

"Yes, please," Kevin said with glee. "Oh, thank you, you're a nice person."

"I know. My name is Chloe, I just moved here a week ago," she said. "Do you want to be my friend?"

"Okay, Chloe," he said. "My name is Kevin."

"Hi, Kevin," she replied. "The school bell is ringing, we got to go." And they walked inside the school.

His thoughts shifted back to the present when the priest took out a vial of dust. The old cleric opened it and sprinkled dust on the coffin.

"My child, you were made from dust, and you shall return to dust." Kevin's eyes began to smart. Before he could rub them, two tears fell from each of his eyes. The priest finished the service with a blessing to the coffin. Kevin saw the actions of the priest, but again he revisited another moment in time.

August 25, 2006:

The final teen dance of the summer, and with Chloe's help, Kevin had a date with his dream girl, Julie Simms. The evening was going great. Kevin and Julie were about to dance, for this was going to be his big chance to let out his feelings for her. Chloe was dancing with her date, Matt, when she noticed Chad walk into the hall.

What is he doing there? She pondered to herself as he strode towards Kevin and Julie. Chad said some words, and in an instant, Julie excused herself from the dance. Minutes later, Julie walked towards Kevin.

"Kevin, Chad is sorry, and he wants me back." She smiled.

Kevin hid his emotions and said, "I'm happy for you, Jewel."

"Do you mind if I finish my evening with him?"

"Why would I mind? Go on." Kevin smiled. "Enjoy yourself."

"Oh, thank you, Kev." Julie hugged him. "You're the best." And without delay, she joined Chad, and they started to dance.

"I'm not that good," Kevin muttered to himself. "He still has you." Kevin felt a little hand grabbing his shoulder.

"What happened, sweets?" Chloe asked.

"Oh, the happy couple is back together. I guess it's for the best." Kevin smiled, but inside he wept.

"I'm sorry, Kevin," she said, her soft voice filled with affection. "I know how much you've put your heart into this evening."

"It's okay, Chloe. Really, I'm fine. Thanks for everything." Kevin gave her a quick peck on the cheek.

"If you ask me, she wouldn't know a good guy if it hit her on the side of the head," Chloe said.

"Thanks. You better get back to your date, he looks impatient." Kevin smiled. "Oh, he's impatient alright; he's waiting for his friend, Sam," she said with a bitter tone in her voice.

"Are you all right?" Kevin asked.

"Yeah, I am," Chloe said. "I'll talk to you later." And she returned to her date. As the evening progressed, Kevin and the rest in attendance watched Matt and Sam get drunk. The alcohol made them act crazy. Before they could finished their fourth flask, Matt started to vomit. The foul stench of liquor and vomit saturated the air. Security guards grabbed the two troublemakers and escorted them out the door. But the damage was done; Matt ruined Chloe's evening. Kevin watched her storm out of the hall in tears. He followed with brisk steps. Kevin turned to his left and spotted her sitting on the bench next to a pond. He moved towards her and said, "Hi, Chloe. Beautiful view out here."

"Yeah, it is," she replied, trying to hide the tears with her tissue.

"Hey, beautiful. Don't hide your pretty face." Kevin smiled and sat beside her. "I know this hurt you bad, but don't let this ruin your evening." Kevin took the tissue and wiped her tears.

"Why does this happen to me? I thought he was the guy, Kev. I loved him. Matt's father was an alcoholic. Now, he has started to experiment with alcohol as well. But he promised he would quit drinking. He just went out there and made a fool of himself and of me."

"He's not worth your love, Chloe. You will find another guy." Kevin smiled.

"Sure! Who is going to go out with me? I'm not as pretty as Julie, Tina, or Shauna."

"No? Well, I beg to differ, chere," Kevin said. "I had to fight off twenty guys just to sit here with you. These guys were high school seniors."

"Oh you did, so where are they?" she asked, and gave him a little smile.

"Well, they knew I was going to kick their butts, so they left," Kevin teased.

"You're bad, Kevin Wolf." Chloe smiled.

"Well, I do have my moments, now come on. You have a dance to finish."

"Well, kinda hard to find a date now," she replied.

"Well, since I was dumped, wanna be my date?"

"Well, you do look good in that outfit." She smiled.

"Then it's settled, but if you don't want to, I will under..." Kevin said, but Chloe interrupted him with a kiss that Kevin would never forget. Her lips had Kevin in a magical spell of happiness and amazement. He looked at her and said in astonishment. "Wow."

"I'm sorry," she said.

"Oh, don't be, I take it you want to be my date?" He smiled.

"Yes, silly. I was the one who prepped you, remember," she teased.

He replied, "Yep, well then, lead the way." Kevin held her hand and helped her rise from the bench.

"Thank you, Kevin. You're the best," she said, holding onto his arm. Kevin felt her affectionate touch and smiled.

"I've been told that once before." And the new couple returned to the hall, and the song "Dust in the Wind" began to play.

"Oh, I love this song," she said.

"Then why are we standing here, chere," Kevin said. "Shall we dance?" Kevin and Chloe walked towards the music and to their future, which began with that one dance.

The song of that beautiful night shifted to "Amazing Grace" at the cemetery. And once again, Kevin found himself trapped in the present, in this reality he loathed—in pain and alone. With the priest's final blessing, the services ended. The gathering, weary from the loss of this remarkable soul, began to disperse from the burial scene. Kevin realized the time had come to say goodbye and leave her there all alone—buried in the ground. But he couldn't walk away and leave her to face eternity alone. Sophie walked towards her son and hugged him like she did the first time he fell off his bike. Back then, all it took was a Band-Aid and a kiss to heal his wound. But this time she feared that her love could not heal the pain within his heart.

"Come on, son," he soft voice said. "It's time to go."

"No, Mom. I am not leaving her here alone," he replied. "I am not leaving at all. She needs me." Sophie tried trying to console her son.

"She's in a better place now, and she's not suffering anymore, Kevin. But you have to let her go."

"Mom, I know what you are trying to do, and I love you for it, but I have to stay. I just can't leave her here alone, not right now," Kevin begged. Mark walked towards the two of them, and Kevin felt his brother's gentle grip upon his shoulder.

"Go ahead, Mom. I will stay with him. Steff is waiting for you in the car. The rest of the people are getting together at the hall for the meal," Mark said. She gave a gentle nod towards her older son, stroked Kevin's forehead, and gave him a tender peck on the cheek.

"I'll see you later, pup," she said.

"Okay, Mom." Sophie headed towards the car. With each step forward, she glanced back at her son until she arrived in front of her vehicle. Opening the door, she took one last glimpse at her son and the grave. A tear welled up in her eye, and she said, "Goodbye, Chloe. You will always be in my heart forever." And with those parting words, she leaned into her car and drove way.

A few steps away from Kevin, Chloe's closest friends all huddled together remembering their friend.

Cole held onto Shauna and looked at the grave. "She would have been a great lawyer," he said, his voice faint. "We used to talk about the law, and where it was going." Cole had come from a long line of police officers. His plans were to join the force after graduation; something Shauna was not crazy about, but Chloe always supported his dream.

"Why her?" Shauna asked.

"Chloe, I will join the force; and I will make you proud of me," Cole said. Shauna tilted her head towards Cole and said, "Hun, now is not the time to think about being a cop. I don't want to be standing here looking at your casket being lowered to the ground." The tears welled in the corners of her eyes. Cole remained silent for the moment, but he knew someday he and Shauna would have to deal with his decision, but now was not the time. Tina stood alone and stared at the coffin. She had asked her boyfriend, Dave Carrington to come to the funeral, but he refused. She was having problems in her relationship, and more than just the occasional verbal arguments. Chloe alone understood the torment he put her through. Chloe became Tina's closest confidant, but now she was gone. Two weeks before the tragedy, Chloe warned Tina about Dave's temper, and that she should end the relationship before something terrible could happen. But little did Chloe know, her own life was about to come to a tragic end fourteen days later.

"What am I going to do without you, Clo?" she cried. Tommy observed the pain on Tina's face. He wanted to do more for her, but he kept his emotions distant from her. He ambled towards her and slipped his hand into hers. His voice subdued by grief, he asked, "Is there anything I can do for you?"

"I will be all right. I was thinking of something Chloe told me a couple of weeks ago." Tina kept quiet, and Tommy did not pursue the matter. When the gang slipped away, Tommy followed; but he noticed Kevin there alone with his brother.

Tommy looked at the gang and said, "You guys go ahead to the hall. I'm gonna stay with Kev."

"Maybe we should stay with you," Julie said.

"No, Julie. Chloe's family needs her friends right now. I will stay with Kev. But give them my best," Tommy said.

"Alright, Tommy, but first we just want a few words with Kevin," Julie said. Tommy nodded in agreement, and they all stepped closer to Kevin and his brother.

"Kevin, we are so sorry for your loss," Cole said, and gave his friend a brief hug.

"Thanks, buddy. It's your loss, too. I know she loved you all so much," Kevin said.

"If there anything you need, sweetheart, let us know," Tina said, then kissed his left cheek.

"Thanks, Tina."

"Same here, Kev. Just give me a call," Shauna said, and followed Tina's action. "You are the best group of friends a guy could ask for," Kevin said. Julie and Chad walked towards him.

"Oh, Kevin, I miss her so much," Julie cried. "I don't know what to say?" And she hugged him.

"It's okay, Jewel. Being here is good enough. She cared for you." Kevin tried to smile, but his face, exhausted from crying.

"She was one of a kind, Kevin. I'm sorry for your loss," Chad said. For the first time since he knew him, Chad sounded like a human being. Kevin appreciated his action and nodded.

"Thanks, Chad," Kevin said. "That she was, there will never be another one like her." And they walked away. He noticed that Tommy remained with him. "Aren't you going to the hall?" Kevin asked.

"No, I'm needed here."

"I will be fine, no use for you to stay, too."

"Chloe was my friend, and you are my best friend, Kev. You would do the same for me." Tommy smiled.

"Did I ever say you were the best, Tom?"

"Nope, but now is a good time." Tom grinned.

Kevin looked at his brother and said, "Thanks, Mark. You didn't have to stay."

Mark held onto Kevin's shoulder and said, "I'm your brother, man. Didn't I teach you how to play sports and to dress in style? Besides, after Dad died, you were more than a brother to me, Kev. You were like my son."

"I remember what you did for me, Mark. I'm glad I have you here with me now," Kevin said as a tear fell from his eye. Margaret wheeled herself next to Kevin and grabbed his hand.

"Kevin, my thoughts and prayers are with you," she said. Her makeup ran down her face from the tears.

"Thanks for coming, Margaret. I know this must be hard for you with your mother and all," Kevin said, recalling the story she had told him about the day they shot her and killed her mother.

"Of course I would be here. You and Chloe were the friends I never thought I would ever have," she said. "If you ever need someone to talk to, you know my number."

"Thanks, Margaret. Take care," Kevin said.

"Do you need a ride to the hall?" she asked.

"No, I'm staying. I don't want to leave her alone."

"Alright, dear. I will call you later." Margaret smiled at him one last time and wheeled away. Taylor and Brown kept their distance and waited for Margaret to approach them. Chloe's death affected Brown; in her own way, she reminded him of his wife Claire. Both were young, beautiful, energetic, and taken away before their time at the hands of a killer. Taylor looked at his friend and saw the pain in his eyes.

"It always seems that we end up here," Taylor said. His eyes glanced around the cemetery. "Are we cursed with these ongoing losses of our loved ones?"

"I don't know, my friend," Brown replied. "How are you holding out?"

"Okay, I guess. It hurts me to see such a young girl die like that. She was also a special friend to Margaret. She has now lost two people who were dear to her in just over a year."

"I know," Brown said, then paused. Looking at Kevin, he traveled back in time. "Look at him, Alex. So young, and already he knows the pain and the burden that we have to face every day."

"He just turned fifteen in April. He's lost without her. So young and so alone," Taylor said. "Well, I'm going to have a scholarship created in her honour. And as for the school gym I donated funds to, well, I'm going to have it named in her memory."

"That's noble of you, Alex."

"Well, the poor dear deserves that much. She was like Margaret's sister," Taylor replied. Margaret wheeled towards her father and Brown.

"I'm ready to go to the hall, Dad."

"All right, dear. Does Kevin need a ride?"

"No, he's staying there. He's not ready to say goodbye yet."

"Poor soul. Well, we should be going then," Taylor said, but Brown remained still.

"You two go ahead, I will stay with him."

"Are you sure?" Taylor probed.

"Yeah, I'm sure," Brown said. "The family needs the both of you right now. I'm going to stay here with our young friend." And he walked towards them. Mark recognized the older man and extended his hand.

"Dr. Brown, I presume?"

Brown shook his hand and replied, "That's right, you must be Mark, Kevin's brother. I am sorry for your family's loss."

"I am, and thank you for coming."

"Is that Tommy standing by his side?" Brown asked.

"Yes, he's Kevin's best friend."

"I know them well. They are all Margaret's friends. I see them a lot at the mansion."

"Mr. Taylor was indeed generous with all the arraignments he made for the funeral. We and her family are all in his debt."

"Think nothing of it, that poor soul was an angel from Heaven. The sad thing is that sometimes angels are called back because they were too good for this world." Brown's voice turned to sadness for a moment. Then he cleared his throat and contained his emotions once again.

"It seems you are no stranger to death, doctor?"

"You have a keen intuition, Mark. I lost my wife thirty-one years ago. She was murdered like Chloe."

"Oh…I am sorry; I should have kept my mouth shut."

"Don't be, I can't get her out of my mind. Today more than ever."

"Well, thank you for coming, doctor."

"In all honesty, Mark, I wanted to stay as well. I wish to give my support to Kevin and honour Chloe."

"You don't have to do that, sir."

"I know, but I want to if it's all right."

"I don't see a problem with it."

"Thank you, Mark. Shall we join them?" Mark followed Brown to his brother's side. The four of them stood side by side and watched the coffin being lowered to the ground that will become her final resting place.

Six hours had passed since the burial, and the four continued to stand by the gravesite. The caretaker left four chairs after he cleaned up from the service. On occasion, the others took time to rest while Kevin stood steadfast—never taking his eyes off the ground below. It got cloudier during the day, and the rain was about to come. Mark and Tommy knew the time had come to leave.

"It's going to rain soon, Kev. We should get going. Everybody will be worried sick," Mark said.

"He's right, bud. It's time for you to go back home," Tommy added. Brown sat there and remained silent during their conversation.

"I can't just leave her here alone, guys. If you want to leave, that's fine. Thanks for staying as long as you could," Kevin said before he kneeled to grab a handful of the fresh tilled dirt that covered the casket.

"We just can't leave you here, Kevin," Mark said as the rain began to come down.

"Mark is right, Kev. It's pouring out here, and you can't bring Chloe back. She wouldn't want you to put yourself through this," Tommy pleaded, and the rain grew heavier.

"Don't you understand?" Kevin roared. "I am not going." Brown stood from his chair and approached Mark and Tommy.

"You have done the best you could, both of you," Brown said. "But our young friend is in pain, it will not go away."

"But we just can't leave him here," Mark said.

"I will stay with him. Both of you go home to your families," Brown said.

"What will I tell my mother?" Mark asked.

"Tell her I am looking after him. I will bring him home before dark. I have been through this before. I will get him to come back home," Brown said.

"Thank you, doctor. For everything." Mark shook his hand and nodded.

"Think nothing of it. Now, bring Tommy home and tell your mother Kevin will be home tonight." Mark and Tommy glanced at Kevin, then left the cemetery. Kevin did not hear his brother or his friend leave. Kevin, not aware that someone stayed with him, kept a silent vigil for Chloe. He knelt and watched the ground grow muddy and wet. He tried to talk to Chloe's buried body, but a painful scream came from his chest. Brown stood there and watched him. The old vigilante relieved his pain and his loss. The teen needed someone, and he decided to intervene.

"Do you have many loved ones in this cemetery?"

"What?" Kevin turned to confront the face behind the voice.

"Don't be alarmed, Kevin. It's just me."

"Why are you still here?"

"For almost the same reason as you. So do you?"

"Do I what?"

"Do you have many loved ones at this cemetery?"

"My dad—and now Chloe."

"My wife is here as well. She's about twenty metres in that direction," Brown said. His finger pointed to the east of the cemetery. "She and Chloe had a lot in common."

"Why do you say that?"

"They were both beautiful, kind, caring, loved life, and were murdered."

"Was her killer ever caught?"

"You can say that." Brown grinned. "But the main thing is you can't go on staying here."

"But I can't leave her here alone."

"Only her body is here, Kevin."

"Oh, don't give me that crap—she is in a better place! I let my mom and her family say that because they are religious, but I don't have to take it from you."

"So, we have an angry young man here."

"That's right, I am angry!" Kevin rose from his knees. "I prayed and prayed that she would live, but she's not alive, she's dead. Can you answer me that?"

"No, I can't; but to blame God for society's trash won't bring her back either."

"Listen, I tried to believe that she's in better place, but night she died, I begged God to save her. Despite my plea, I still lost her. So, I seriously doubt that God or heaven truly exists."

"I guess she is really lost then."

"What do you mean?"

"Well, as long as you believe in God—or a heaven, she will always be alive. But since you, in your infinite wisdom, say that neither of them exists, then in your heart you have truly lost her."

"So, you believe there is a God?"

"Yes, I do."

"Then why did he let her die like that at the hands of a killer?"

"Well, Kevin. There is the other power within the equation."

"What other power?"

"Evil, son. The Devil; he does exists."

"So, you think the Devil did this?"

"Not physically, no. But his deeds are accomplished by the scum of our world."

"Where's your proof in God or the Devil?"

"There is a God because I'm still alive, and the Devil exists because I have faced him on more occasions than you can ever imagine, kid," Brown said. His cold voice could have frozen the sun itself.

"That was enlightening," Kevin said, his voice reeked with sarcasm.

"I'm glad you're still using your witticism. Your response is a great coping mechanism," Brown said.

"So, answer me this then. Why didn't God stop this guy?"

"Listen, kid. I'm not a philosopher, but I will tell you this. Sometimes evil gets the upper hand early in the war, but good always finds a way to equalize the playing field. Sometimes evil does win the battle, but I can assure you it never conquers," Brown said. The cold rain grew stronger, turning more into a downpour, and fell like tears from Heaven. Brown raised his cane, pointed it at Kevin, and said, "Besides, he has done something; he's sent you to stop them."

"What are you talking about? I don't understand?"

"You will soon enough, but for now, it's time for you to go home. Your mother is worried sick about you, and the last thing you want is to bury another loved one," Brown said.

Kevin nodded and said in a reluctant tone. "Alright, you win. I'll go."

"Very well then," Brown said. "I will drive you home." And they headed towards his car. Kevin looked at the plot one final time before he opened the car door behind him.

"I love you, chere." Kevin swallowed his heart.

Brown smiled. "She loves you, Kevin. In this world and the next." They stepped into the car and drove away, leaving the rain and the wind to the departed dead.

Chapter 21

*I*nspector Somerville of Toronto Metropolitan Police's Homicide Unit spent most of the morning chasing leads on the whereabouts of Graham Cassidy. Since the murder of Chloe Bellecoeur, Somerville had personally been tracking leads and compiling all the evidence in the case. Still after three weeks of searching, they faced continuous new roadblocks each time they found a clue. The sole evidence he had—the killer's DNA from his skin. Thanks to Chloe's brave efforts, the forensic team found skin samples under her fingernails. The coroner indicated that she scratched him, and a few layers of his skin remained inside her nails. The police arrested Cassidy before for charges of Racketeering, and he had a history with the Bellecoeur family. If only he could catch and compare the DNA with Cassidy—he would have him. On the night of the murder, he collected statements from the victim before her death and her boyfriend. Plus, he had signed statements from students and teachers who saw him at the school gymnasium on the night of their annual Christmas dance last December. According to his files, Cassidy stalked the victim's older sister and threatened to get even with her. Somerville wanted to nail him for this crime, and he would do anything within the law to find him. Also, if he could break him, he may be able to get Cassidy to admit his ties to the Scorpio Syndicate. And that would lead to a major strategic advantage for law enforcement in their battle against organized crime. While he reread the files, one of his officers interrupted his research.

"Inspector Somerville."

"Yes, constable. What can I do for you?"

"It's what I can do for you, sir. We've just received this from the FBI. They caught our guy in Detroit."

"Excellent," he cheered and jumped out of his seat. "When did they catch him?"

"About two hours ago, sir. He had just left the Canadian border and arrived in Detroit via the Ambassador Bridge. When he arrived in Detroit, he met a colleague of his, but the feds were watching his friend at the time. When they found out who he was, they tailed him to the casino and arrested him there."

"When are we getting him back?"

"They will be sending him back tomorrow. They are questioning him about the guy he visited."

"Thanks for the news, constable. I will go and tell the superintendent," he said before the constable walked away. Somerville grabbed the phone and made a few calls. First, he called the Crown, then the forensics team. After he finished his phone calls, he stormed towards the superintendent's office. The superintendent was on his way out the door when Somerville met up with him. The superintendent noticed Somerville's nonchalant behavior.

"Inspector, you look like the cat that swallowed the canary," he said.

"Better than that, superintendent. We got the son of a bitch," Somerville said with a huge grin on his face.

"You will have to be more specific, inspector. We are after a lot of sons of bitches in this department." The superintendent smirked.

"Graham Cassidy, sir." Somerville filled in the blank.

"The killer of the fifteen-year-old girl?"

"That's the one."

"Where did we find him?"

"Well, the FBI caught him in Detroit. They arrested him in the middle of one of their stakeouts."

"Excellent news, inspector. When will we have him?"

"The feds are bringing him to Toronto tomorrow, sir. May I go and welcome him at the airport, sir?"

"I will do better than that, Joe. You will take the next plane to Detroit and meet up with the FBI there. I will arrange it for you. You think you can handle that order?" The superintendent grinned at his inspector.

"Yes, sir. I'm on my way," Somerville said with zest and panache. "But first I have to do one more thing."

"What would that be?"

"Let some grieving parents know they will have justice."

"Understood," the superintendent said. "I will see you with the prisoner, inspector." Somerville ran back to his office and made the call he was praying he could make since the night of the murder.

Ray Clayton took out a gourmet meal out of the oven when Kevin walked inside the apartment. Ever since Chloe died, his family and friends tried to comfort Kevin out of his misery. They visited, took him out, and called just to keep him occupied. So far, none of them had any success. Sophie had to work on her college project, so Ray offered to stay with Kevin until she returned. He spent most of the afternoon cooking some fettuccini with some veal, topped with and a creamy alfredo cheese sauce. Ray hoped he could get Kevin to eat a little. For the last three weeks, bowls of cold cereal became Kevin's main meal. Most the time he put his unfinished bowl in the sink. Kevin walked in and dropped his school bag next to the door.

"Hey, Kevin. How was school?" Kevin crashed on the couch and closed his eyes.

"Hi, Ray," he replied. "It came and it went."

"Well, I have supper ready, and the Jays are on the tube. So, I thought we can watch the game." Kevin wanted to say no, but he knew Ray tried his best to help out.

Kevin replied, "Alright then." Ray took off the oven mitts and prepared a dish for him. He sprinkled some parsley on top and brought the plate to the coffee table.

"Looks good, thanks."

"My pleasure." Ray grabbed the remote and turned on the TV for the ball game.

"So, where's Mom?"

"She had to hit the books, so I decided to make us all supper," he said, taking a bite from his dish. "Dig in before it gets cold, Kev." Kevin took his fork and tasted the fettuccini.

"It's good, Ray." The rich aroma of the sauce could not bring Kevin back to normal. Kevin remembered when his sense of smell brought happiness to him, but with Chloe dead, he lost the connection to her fragrance. And he never wanted to inhale the scent of happiness again.

"Just good?" He smirked.

"It's great, Ray. This is one of your best."

"Why thank you."

"I'm sorry I'm not the best company right now."

"Don't be, Kevin. I can't imagine what you are going through. Take all the time you need," Ray said, then the phone rang. "I will get it."

"No, it's okay, Ray." Kevin stood from the couch. "I will get it." Kevin headed towards the phone.

"Hello. Oh, hi, Mrs. Bellecoeur. What can I do for you, ma'am?" he asked. Then Ray noticed the change in Kevin's face.

"You mean they caught him?" Kevin probed, his attitude started to brighten. "That's great news. Thank you so much for calling. Take care." Kevin slammed the phone, anxious to tell the news.

"What's wrong, Kevin?"

"They arrested Cassidy, Ray. They caught him! And they are bringing that monster back to stand trial, so he can rot in jail for the rest of his damned life," Kevin proclaimed. The tears of vindication came down his cheeks. Ray walked towards Kevin.

"Then it's over. Thank God," Ray said.

"Finally, Chloe will get some justice," Kevin said.

Ray hugged him and said, "That will be a day I will look forward to seeing as well." Kevin returned to his seat, and for the first time since the murder, he believed that Chloe would finally get the retribution her memory and her soul deserved.

Detroit, Michigan. USA:

Inspector Joseph Somerville had just got off the plane when the FBI greeted him inside the airport. One of the agents he remembered well, Special Agent Flynn led the entourage and greeted the inspector with confidence.

"Welcome to Detroit, Inspector Somerville."

"Thank you, Special Agent Flynn," Somerville acknowledged. "I heard how your agents caught my fugitive. On behalf of my department, we thank you."

"Well, we had no proof about his role in the Viny Family that's why we couldn't keep him. So, if we can help nail him for that murder case of yours, so be it," Flynn said. "So, do you have a case against him?"

"I think we do, we have statements from her boyfriend and from the victim— just before she died. Cassidy dated the victim's sister and had sworn revenge upon her. We have an abundance of witnesses there. We may not have the murder weapon, but we do have DNA samples taken from the victim's nails, proving that she scratched him. If they match up, we've got him," Somerville said. "According to the report, she had significant amounts of his skin in her fingernails. Are the scars visible?"

"Yeah, he has four deep scratch marks on his face," Flynn replied, and they walked out of the airport and towards the parking lot. "I hope you put him away, but if we find something about him and his mob connections, we want a crack at him as well."

"You got it," Somerville said. The entourage walked towards two vehicles. Flynn escorted Somerville to his car while the entourage entered the second car adjacent to Flynn's black Cavalier. Both engines started in harmony and drove away.

Graham Cassidy sat with his feet on the table and relaxed while the guard in the interrogation room watched him with abhorrence in his eyes. The guard heard of the murder he committed; he wanted to see him out of his precinct and his city. Cassidy, on the other hand, remained conceited and supercilious as he stared into the eyes of the guard.

"Tell me, copper, do you think I should be wearing the blue suit or the black one back home?" He laughed.

"You will be wearing orange before you know it, buddy. So, it doesn't matter what you want," the guard said.

"Oh, you're a funny guy. I guess the doughnut shops must pack 'em in when you're telling jokes." He snickered at the guard. The guard wanted to grab him and ram his skull through the table, but he held his composure.

"What, nothing else to say? Oh, too bad," Cassidy said. "I was having so much fun." A knock on the door interrupted his amusement. The guard opened it, and he saw Agent Flynn and another police officer.

"We need a minute alone with the prisoner," Flynn said. The guard nodded and left the room.

"What's this? One pig goes out; two more pigs come in."

"Cassidy, this is Inspector Somerville. He will be taking you back to Canada for your murder trial."

"Oh good, you're going to take me back home. Well, it will save me the money for the ticket." He laughed. Somerville slammed his fist on the table.

"You won't be laughing long, you son of a bitch!" Somerville vowed.

"Oh, a pig with spirit. I like that. What kind of games will we be playing on the plane?" He smirked.

"More like what kind of games will you be playing in prison," Somerville said when they heard a knock at the door.

"Busy place." Cassidy laughed. Flynn opened the door and noticed a small man in an Armani suit.

"Yes."

"I am Salvador Fuchetti, Mr. Cassidy's lawyer. He called for me."

"Come in, Mr. Fuchetti. This is Inspector Somerville. He will be taking your client back to Toronto," Flynn said.

"Ah yes, inspector, I did not see you at the extradition hearing," he said. The greasy lawyer offered a limp hand, but Somerville ignored the gesture and refused to soil himself with the stench of the rat who stood before him.

"No, you didn't," Somerville said. Fuchetti's arm returned to his side.

"Pity, well my client called. And wishes to consult with me before his trip to Canada."

"So, you will be representing him there as well?" Somerville asked.

"No, inspector, we are a huge firm. One of my colleagues will have the opportunity to acquit Mr. Cassidy of the charge." He smiled.

Smerville replied, "Don't count on it, mister." And he stormed out of the room.

"You can talk with him for at least an hour," Flynn said. "Then he's out of here with Inspector Somerville." The FBI agent headed towards the door.

"Thank you, Agent Flynn." The lawyer waited for Flynn to leave before he said a word to his client.

Once the door closed, Cassidy asked, "So, what do they got on me, Sal?"

"Well, Graham. They have collected DNA from under her fingernails," he explained. "And we both know it's your DNA."

"Can't you stop them?"

151

"We can't stop the prosecution's investigation. You got sloppy, Cassidy. And once you're back in Toronto, they will match the samples with your DNA. Then you're finished, my friend."

"You got to help me, Sal. Tell Dice that I need their help. I am a faithful soldier to the syndicate. I even delivered the plans to the Viny Family for them. That's how I got arrested," he stated.

"We know what you have done for us, and it's not forgotten. We already have a man inside the forensics team waiting to do the test, and he will destroy the DNA samples they have. So, when we demand the samples for the defence, they will not be able to provide what they cannot have. Then our guy will admit they tampered with the DNA samples during the test. Thus, leaving a ruling for reasonable doubt or a mistrial due to lack of evidence. Oh, by the way, we know that Judge Reinhardt will be presiding. One our guys." The lawyer laughed. "And if that doesn't work, well, we will have a way to convince the jury of your innocence."

"Thank you, Sal. Give the One my compliments and my gratitude," Cassidy said.

"The One always rewards his most loyal people, Graham," he said. "He looks forward to seeing you at his side when this is behind you." The lawyer rose from his seat and knocked on the door. "Enjoy your trip back home, Cassidy." The door opened, and the lawyer left the room. The guard returned inside.

"I'm taking you back to your cell," he said. Cassidy stood and grinned.

"Lead the way, officer." Cassidy laughed while the officer handcuffed and returned him to his cell.

Toronto, Ontario. Canada:

Two weeks after the extradition of Graham Cassidy, the court date had at last arrived. Everyone anticipated this moment; Arthur Brown included. He followed the case in the media and from what Margaret heard from Kevin. Brown hoped Cassidy would receive the punishment he deserved. Brown vacated the elevator and headed towards Taylor's executive assistant.

"Hello, my dear. How are you today?"

"Good morning, Dr. Brown. I am fine, and you?"

"I'm well, thank you. I'm just here to see Alex for a minute."

"You know you don't need any invitation, sir. Go on in."

"I wouldn't take no for an answer anyway." Brown grinned. "Thank you." Brown opened the door and found Taylor drinking a cup of coffee; looking over spreadsheets.

"Morning, stranger. Is that coffee warm?"

"Yes, it is. Help yourself, old man."

"Why thank you." Brown grabbed a cup and poured coffee into it.

"How are things in the department?"

"Good and good. We are ahead of our production schedule," Brown said. "But that's not why I am here." And took a sip his coffee.

"I'm sure you will tell me why." Taylor smirked.

"I'm taking some time off during the trial. I want to follow this. It could help us in our own battle against the syndicate."

"That's fine with me, so who will replace you?"

"Dr. Hammer. He's a good man."

"Alright then. Keep me updated on the trial." Brown finished his coffee in a gulp and placed the cup onto the table.

"You bet," Brown said. "Talk to you later." And he left the office.

I hope they put him away for a long time. Those butchers can't always get away with murder. Taylor thought as he finished his coffee and looked out of his office window.

Chapter 22

Kevin and his mother kept their composure and waited with Chloe's parents and her sister as the preliminary hearing began. The packed courtroom became the most popular place in the city. People waited with anticipation to catch their first glimpse of Graham Cassidy. And at that moment, he entered with his defence attorney. Brown kept a low profile and sat in the back row of the courtroom. He watched both Kevin's expression and Cassidy's arrogance when the judge entered the room.

"All rise, the Honourable Justice Quentin Reinhardt preceding," the bailiff proclaimed, and those in attendance stood.

"Please be seated," he replied, then looked at the Crown attorney. "Your opening statement, member of the Crown."

"Thank you, Your Honour. On the night of May 23 of this year, fifteen-year-old Chloe Bellecoeur, a girl with promise, beauty, youth, and innocence, became a victim of a soulless monster. Taken away from her family by none other than *that* man right over there—the defendant Graham Cassidy," the Crown said. "This man had a relationship with the victim's sister, until the police arrested him in 2007 for Racketeering. To this day, he is still under investigation as a member of the Scorpio Syndicate. On the night of the murder, the victim bravely tried to defend herself, and with her last ounce of courage, scratched Mr. Cassidy. We have DNA evidence that places the defendant at the scene of the crime; the proof tells us how the incident unfolded. Mr. Cassidy stabbed the victim repeatedly until her boyfriend returned to her home. Mr. Wolf witnessed the defendant leaving the scene. She then told him and the police officer at the hospital, just before surgeons tried desperately to save her, that Cassidy attacked her. So, I will prove to this court, beyond a shadow of a doubt, that there is substantial evidence for a conviction. Thank you." The Crown attorney returned to his seat.

"Thank you, Mr. Reed. Does the defence wish to begin its opening statement?" The defence lawyer stood and looked at the judge with an air of self-righteousness.

"Well, Your Honour. Before I begin, I wish to bring to the court's attention that I wasn't given full disclosure of the evidence presented by the Crown."

"Your Honour, I have given him the list of the witnesses I have for May 23, 2007, the night of the murder, and witnesses for the night of December 21, 2007. That is the night the defendant allegedly threatened the victim's sister, Lori Bellecoeur. We do not have the murder weapon, but we gave the DNA test results to the Defence, and we have the sole remaining samples of the DNA the forensics team extracted from the victim's nail," the Crown protested.

"We are not arguing your witnesses. However, we never received the test results from the Crown. Naturally, I did a follow up, and they sent the results about a week ago, like the Crown said. However, we learned that the DNA found from the nails of that poor sweet girl was mishandled accidentally by one of the members of the forensics team," he stated. "So, the only proof that could demonstrate my client's guilt or innocence was contaminated. In addition, the results of this test never reached my office."

"Your Honour, I didn't hear any of this from the people at forensics?" the Crown protested.

"They were not aware of the mix up," the defence lawyer said. "If I may continue, Your Honour?"

"Proceed, but make a point to all of this please."

"Thank you, sir. We have Dr. Lucas, an assistant to Dr. Mitchell here to explain what had happened to the original samples. I know the Crown has the floor, but with his testimony, we can clear up this matter right now and save the taxpayers' money."

"I want to hear what this man has to say. Proceed," the judge said.

"Objection, Your Honour."

"Mr. Reed, I am allowing this, now sit down," the judge ordered. The doctor took the stand, and the bailiff swore him in.

"Dr. Lucas, please get to the point of all this. What happened to the test results?"

"The original DNA samples that came from the victim's nails were destroyed accidentally moments before comparing them with Mr. Cassidy's DNA."

"You are telling me *that* the original DNA was destroyed before the test? By who? And how were you able to perform the test; then give those results to the Crown?" the lawyer queried.

"Well, sir, I'm ashamed to say that I contaminated the DNA accidentally. I noticed that the Crown and the police had a good case against Mr. Cassidy, so in fear of the repercussions, I used Cassidy's own DNA. Then I did the test. I made it look like that I discovered his skin from the victim's nails," Lucas told the court with his head bowed.

"So, you are telling me that you, doctor, took my client's DNA and used it against him; to save us from knowing about your incompetence?"

"Yes, for that I am sorry. I hope everyone can forgive me."

"Well, you have soiled the people's belief in the efficiency of police science and forensic research, doctor. You know that your career is over. But thank God, thank God almighty, we discovered the truth here today. Your Honour, the Crown has no murder weapon and no DNA to prove my client's guilt. All he has are the testimonies of people at an incident that happened months ago and the last words of a dying girl who, no doubt was delusional from the loss of blood. The witness, her poor boyfriend spotted a shadow of the true monster who killed this poor flower," the defence lawyer said.

"Do you have any other proof, Mr. Reed?" the judge asked.

"Your Honour, it was a miracle we were able to get the DNA we had from the victim's nails. Those were the only samples we had," the Crown said.

"Then I am sorry, without the DNA, all you have is uncorroborated evidence. I have no choice but to dismiss this case," the judge said.

"No, sir. He is guilty, you can't do this on the basis of this testimony from *this* doctor," he pleaded.

"Dr. Lucas, until now, was one of the most respected members in his field. The Crown has trusted the testimony of this man for over fifteen years. I see no reason to doubt him now. Case dismissed," the judge said, lowering his mallet. Chloe's parents yelled in pain and in disbelief. People in the room booed the decision.

"Bailiff, clear the courtroom," the judge ordered. The bailiff complied with his order.

"He killed my little girl," her mother cried as her husband held her tight.

"You can't let him get away," Chloe's father yelled. The court guards escorted them out. Kevin sat in shock. He could not believe it. This man, this murderer, had escaped justice; a free man in the eyes of the courts while Chloe will remain alone, buried in that cemetery for eternity. Sophie gave him a gentle tug on his arm and said, "Come on, dear. It's time to go."

"It can't end this way, Mom. It just can't." Sophie coiled her arm around his shoulder and tried to console her son.

"God will see that he gets what's coming to him, dear." She held onto his hand and escorted him out of the courtroom. Brown sat motionless as the bailiff walked towards him.

"You have to leave, sir."

"I was on my way, sir. It was too crowded for me to use my cane," Brown said, using it as an excuse.

"I understand, sir. Do you need a hand?"

"No, thank you." Brown stood and followed the people towards the exit. Journalists hovered like vultures outside the courthouse and yelled questions in all directions to both the Crown and the defence.

"What happened to the Crown's case?"

"All I have to say is that today we all became victims of blind justice. I have no further comment." Furious over the judge's ruling, the Crown attorney ended his statement and returned inside. An officer escorted Chloe's family to a black minivan, preventing reporters from flooding them with questions. But the defence team and Cassidy remained outside on purpose, so they could gloat to reporters. The members of the media formed around Cassidy like a pack of seagulls chasing breadcrumbs.

"What is your reaction to the hearing?" one of them asked over the shouting.

"All I have to say is that Justice Reinhardt, an experienced trial judge, perceived the evidence before him and made the right choice. Thank God that justice was served," he said.

"Mr. Cassidy, do you have anything to add?"

"Yes, I do. Free at last, free at last. Thank God Almighty I am free at last." He smiled, and they headed towards a black limo. Kevin, in a fit of pure rage, marched in the direction of the limo.

His mother said him. "Kevin, what are you doing?"

Kevin replied, "He's not going to get away with this." And he stood in front of Cassidy and the limo.

"Kevin don't," she yelled as he confronted Cassidy and his lawyer.

"Can we help you, sir?" the lawyer asked.

"I know you did it, you son of a bitch, and I will get you for what you did."

"Mr. Wolf, I know you are in pain, so I will ignore what you've said to my client, but next time you will face our judicial system if you repeat those words again," the lawyer said. Out of nowhere, Brown stepped in front of Kevin.

"We were just leaving. Come on, Kevin." Brown grabbed Kevin's right arm.

"See you later, snot face," Cassidy mocked Kevin. Brown sent the young teen towards his mother. Once Kevin left the area, Brown turned towards Cassidy and his lawyer.

"Gentlemen, will you excuse me," Brown said in a diplomatic tone.

"Yeah, you're in my way, old man," Cassidy said.

"Enjoy the time you have left." Brown smiled with a sense of superiority and walked away from the limo. He followed Kevin and his mother to her car. Cassidy and his lawyer slipped into the limo and closed the door.

"Thank you, Charles," Cassidy said.

"Don't thank me, Graham. Thank the One and his friends in the Canadian judicial system, including our good friend Dr. Lucas." A few seconds of silence smothered the back of the limo before both men snickered as the limo drove away.

September 2, 2008:

Another school year was upon Kevin Wolf and his friends, but this time Chloe would not be there with her daily morning smile to lift their spirits. Kevin spent most of his summer working as a temp at the Toronto Guardian, one of the city's up-and-coming newspapers. He hoped that working for the paper would help him gather intelligence on the whereabouts of Graham Cassidy. After the preliminary hearing, Cassidy left the city without a trace. For the whole summer, Kevin heard nothing, but with just one week left before school started—his bet paid off. Sources told one of the journalists that Cassidy would soon return to Toronto and open a new nightclub called the Lover's Rose. With the money Kevin made from his job, he had enough cash to buy a gun from one of the local sellers off the street. He already had all the info he needed from one of the school's troublemakers, Todd Sterling. Sterling, a known contact for pushers and other entrepreneurs of the city's crime world, brushed with trouble daily. Tonight's grand opening of the club would provide the opportunity Kevin needed to bring justice to Chloe. Kevin opened his locker and took out his homework for the evening when Margaret wheeled beside him.

"Hi, stranger. What's new?"

"Hi, Margaret. How was the last period?"

"Long and boring, but I'm glad it's three-thirty. Are you going to Julie's house tonight?"

"Why?"

"Don't you remember, Kev? She invited us for the BBQ and pool party. She planned this for weeks."

"Oh, yeah, sorry," Kevin said. "No, I can't—something came up, but I hope you have fun."

Out of nowhere, Sterling appeared and said, "Hey, Wolf. I got some info for you."

"Be right there. Talk to you later, Margaret."

"Kevin, this guy is bad news. What are you doing with him?"

"Thanks for the speech, Mom. Talk to you later." Kevin left her there and walked towards Sterling. Margaret had never seen Kevin act this way before. She watched Kevin and Sterling walk towards the corner. Margaret followed her friend, but kept a cautious distance. She wheeled herself away to the other side of the hallway. Kevin looked around before they talked and saw that the hallway was clear. Unaware that Margaret was hiding close by, he began to speak.

"So, what's the news?" Kevin asked.

"I've talked to Fast Eddy, and he's got your merchandise for you."

"What's his price?"

"He wants eight hundred dollars. Plus, he's giving you the bullets as a free gift." He laughed.

"I have the money, and I need the piece tonight."

"No problem, we will meet him tonight at the Stargaze Plaza at eight."

"All right. I will meet you there, first table at the right corner of the food court, by Sub Hunt Sandwiches," Kevin said.

"Sounds good. Later, Wolf," he said, and walked away. Margaret could not believe Kevin wanted to buy a gun, but she could imagine his intended victim. Kevin wanted to kill Cassidy, and tonight his wish would come true. She waited until he left; then she wheeled as fast as her arms could push. She proceeded towards the main exit. And to her father's limo that waited for her.

"Good afternoon, Miss Margaret. Are we going to the library before home?" the chauffeur asked.

Margaret wheeled herself adjacent to the back door and said, "No, Maxwell. Take me to my father's building. I have to see him right away." She clutched the armrests of her chair and hoisted herself into the back seat.

"Very well, Miss Margaret." The chauffeur grabbed her wheelchair, placing it in the trunk, and he entered the limo.

"I've have to stop Kevin before it's too late," she said, and the limo drove away from the school.

Chapter 23

*D*ecision day had arrived for Arthur Brown as he headed towards Taylor's office. He had a meeting with him and their recruiter, Patrick Collins. For the last eighteen months, Brown searched for the next Shadow Chaser. Despite a long a vigorous search and weighing all of his options—Brown had chosen his heir to the Shadow Chaser name. He already made the arrangements with his former master; he and his successor would be in Japan by the end of the month.

"Good morning, Dr. Brown, they are expecting you inside," the executive assistant said.

"Thank you, Wanda," he said. He opened the door.

"Hello, Art. Now, the party can begin," Taylor said.

"Gentlemen," Brown said, and he sat on the chair. "So, Patrick, what have we got?"

"Well, folks, it's like this. I have your seven agents. From Mexico, Eduardo Ramirez, former soldier and master of the Mexican martial arts, the dealers killed his family because of a drug related act of retribution. He is an honourable man and good friend. Gabriel Cardieux from France. He is a master of deception and disguise. Lance Maxwell from Her Majesty's Secret Service," Patrick read on from his list. "Tasha Borisnov, she is a former government agent with the KGB and a master in the art of Sambo. Caitlin McGregor, from Australia. I have never seen anybody with a better shot than her. And last, but not least, Mashudu Mulaudzi from Africa. He is a long-time hunter and a top survivalist in the wild. With myself included, we are your seven agents."

"Excellent news, Patrick. The equipment is ready, the secret keep is set up, the resources are invested, and all we need now is to hear who our new Shadow Chaser is, Art," Taylor said. He turned his head towards his friend.

"I have a name," Brown said. "Are you ready?" Both men nodded, then Brown reveled his successor. "His name is Kevin Wolf."

"Kevin Wolf, I never heard of the guy," Patrick replied.

"WOLF. You can't be serious, he's just a boy," Taylor said with a touch of protest in his voice.

"He's fifteen years old, true. But he can be nurtured to be an irresistible force. Like the ancient Shadow Art warriors of the past, most of them began their training as children. We can train him, and teach him discipline the right way, our way. In return, we will get years out of him. He is a person lost to both himself and to the world. He lost his one true love like us, and the justice system failed to protect him. Crushed, by the same syndicate that hurt you, Alex; you can't take away his right to vengeance as well."

"Well, it's worth a shot, but we will have much work to do," Patrick added.

"All right then, Wolf it is. Heaven help us if you're wrong, old friend," Taylor said and then heard a buzz from his phone.

"Yes, Wanda. Oh, alright then, send her in." And before Taylor could look up, Margaret wheeled inside.

"Dad, I need your help." Margaret ignored Brown and Patrick in the room.

"Well, I'm busy at the moment, dear."

"Damn it, Dad, it is important. Kevin is in trouble. He knows Cassidy is back in town, and he's buying a gun to kill him!"

"When did you hear this?" Brown asked.

"I heard him talking to a guy after school. He's meeting the guy and the dealer tonight at the Stargaze Plaza at eight. He will be by the Sub Hunt Sandwiches."

"All right, dear. We will do what we can." She looked at her father and Brown.

"I know you are the only two who can stop him," she said.

"Patrick, would you wait for me in the lab, please," Brown requested. Patrick nodded and left Taylor's office. "Why do you say that, Margaret?"

"I know what the both of you are up to, I heard you both talk on many occasions. I know who you were, Uncle Art. So, I know you and my father can stop Kevin from ruining his life or getting himself killed."

"All right, Margaret, say no more. I will go with Patrick. Once I hear anything, I will let you know, Alex. Can't have our boy get taken away from us," Brown said before he stood from his chair.

"No, we can't. Good luck," Taylor said as Brown gave him a devilish grin and walked away.

"What does he mean by that?" Margaret asked.

"I will tell later, dear," Taylor said. "Come on, I will buy you dinner." And he stood from his chair and wheeled his daughter out his office.

Arthur Brown and Patrick Collins spent the last hour waiting to see if Kevin Wolf would arrive to meet the illegal gun dealer. Patrick had tremendous respect for Brown; after all, the former Shadow Chaser saved him as a child, but he second guessed Brown's decision to burden a teenager with this extraordinary undertaking.

Patrick looked at his watch and said, "Almost eight, and so far nothing, boss."

"He will be here, I know it." Brown looked around the mall.

"How do you know for sure?"

"Because I would have done the same thing," Brown replied.

"Why do you have so much interest in this lad? I know Cassidy murdered his girlfriend, but why?"

"Because life and the justice system cheated him. Most of all, he has a unique quality you don't see anymore."

"What would that be?"

"He cares about people. Without thoughts for himself, he wants to help people, with no strings attached. A trait you don't find in this day and age," Brown said. "How many people you know who are like Kevin?"

"Just one, boss." Patrick pointed his index finger at Brown. "You." Brown tipped his flat cap at Patrick. Then he spotted Kevin approaching their area.

"Okay, Patrick, it's show time," Brown said. Patrick walked towards Kevin, and he stumbled in front of the teen. Exhaling an ooof groan, Patrick bumped into Kevin and grabbed his left shoulder.

"I'm so sorry, lad. I must have tripped on something." Patrick dropped a bug inside Kevin's jacket. The teen had no idea what had just happened.

"No problem, sir. No harm done," Kevin replied, and went on his way. Brown observed the drop, turned on his miniature hearing device, and placed it in his left ear. Within minutes, he spotted Kevin talking to two other guys; one matched Kevin's age, and the other one was a local dealer by the name of Fast Eddy.

Still in the game, Eddy. Brown thought. He waited to hear something that will help him know Kevin's next move. So far, he knew the price of the gun and witnessed the exchange of the bags. He watched Kevin look inside the bag and nodded. And they exchanged their final words to each other.

"A pleasure doing business with you, kid." He laughed. "Now, if you'll excuse me, I have to get ready for the opening night of that new nightclub, the Lover's Rose. Who knows? I might get lucky." Fast Eddy and Sterling left the area, leaving Kevin with the package.

"Yeah, it's going to be one hell of a night there for Cassidy, number one with a bullet," Kevin whispered, but Brown picked up every word. Looking at his watch, Brown turned a circular dial counter-clockwise and muttered, "NIGHT, authorization: Brown, alpha-three-omega-two." The codes activated the computer from his lab, and Brown waited for a response. Within seconds, he received an answer from his hearing device.

"Yes, doctor," NIGHT replied.

"Information on the following nightclub in Toronto. The Lover's Rose."

"Accessing…stand by…. The Lover's Rose; building approved by council in 1998. Originally called Aquarius Nightclub and Bar, but Graham Cassidy bought out the building in 2006. Grand opening tonight at ten p.m.," NIGHT noted. "Would you like additional information on Graham Cassidy?"

"No, thank you, NIGHT. Just the address of the club."

"The corner of Yonge and Main."

"Thank you, NIGHT. End program," Brown said. Patrick glanced at him.

"We have to go to the Lover's Rose nightclub."

"That's where they are having their grand opening," Patrick said.

"Yep, and Cassidy will be there, so we have to stop Kevin before he makes a huge mistake. Let's go." Brown and Patrick rose from their table and left for the nearest exit in the hopes of catching Kevin before he pulls the trigger.

The block-long lineup made security a nightmare. The smells of cigarettes, cologne, leather, and marijuana brimmed the perimeter of the snaking lineup. Everyone wanted to party in the newest nightclub in Toronto. The bouncers controlled the mob from passing or trying to get inside before the owner could arrive. He made it crystal clear that he alone would start the opening ceremonies. Two limousines pulled up to the curb in front of the red carpet, and Kevin looked on from across the road. He saw four guys and six women get out of the first one. They looked like something that came out of the Godfather movie. The second chariot had five women and two guys; one of them was the man he wanted. Graham Cassidy had two women by his side, each of his hands were full as he coiled his arms around their waists like a snake.

"Hello, everybody," Cassidy screamed. "Who wants to party?"

"We do," the crowd cheered in one huge, thunderous roar.

Kevin replied, "So do I!" He pulled out his gun and began to amble across the road. But when he made his first step towards the road, he felt something grab his hand and yank him away.

"Heeyy!" Kevin lost his balance and fell onto the ground. As he got up, he noticed the gun on the ground and the identity of his assailant. Dr. Arthur Brown stood in front of him with a devilish smile. He realized the old man used the handle of his cane to pull him back.

"What the hell are you doing here?"

"I was about to ask you the same question," he replied. "What the hell are you doing with that gun?"

"I'm going to kill him for what he did. Now, do me a favour, you old goat; get the hell out of my way and stay the hell away from me." Kevin attempted to grab the gun. But in an instant, Brown used his cane and flipped the gun into his hand.

"I can't let you do this, Kevin."

"Why are you protecting him?"

"I am not protecting him, boy. I am protecting you. See all those guns over there. They will kill you after you take the first shot."

"I don't care. At least justice will be done."

"Listen to yourself, you're not making sense. What about your family?"

"They will survive."

"I thought you were smarter than that, boy. But if you want your gun back, you're going to have to go through me."

"That can be arranged," Kevin said in anger. Without a thought of the man's age, Kevin charged Brown with all his might. Without effort, Brown evaded Kevin's charged and tripped him with his cane. Kevin fell like a log onto the ground. Brown towered over the teen.

"Now, are you done yet?" Brown asked

"I have just begun, old man!" He jumped right back and started swinging. Brown moved each time, and at last he decided to finish this mess. With one block, Brown took the offence and struck Kevin in the mouth. Within a heartbeat, Kevin fell back onto the floor.

"I'm sorry about that, kid. But if an old man with a cane could beat you, what makes you think you've got a chance against Cassidy and his goon squad?" Brown said as the teen staggered back up to his feet. "See what this has done to you, Kevin. You are acting like the scum you hate the most." Kevin realized the terrible wrong he had done; he attacked an old man for no reason at all.

"What have I done," Kevin began to bawl. "I'm sorry, sir."

"I know, kid. I'm not mad at you, but you have so much potential."

"But he's going to get away."

"No, he won't. I can help if you let me."

"How can you help? I know you said that you lost your wife to a killer like Cassidy, but you didn't see your loved one die in front of you," Kevin replied.

"Oh really! Proves how much you know, lad. I was right next to my wife on the night they killed her. I was a surgeon, and I just started my own technology company. I was in love, and had plans for a great future," Brown said. "Then those monsters came." Kevin watched the tears coming down from Brown's eyes. "There were three of them, but I was no fighter. I wouldn't even harm a mosquito, but the first one attacked her. I tried to fight, but I was weak; I never threw a punch. The two of them held me; they beat me up like an old dog while they assaulted and stabbed my wife. They continued to beat me up. Then they left me there to die. But someone found us and called the police. I survived, but my wife didn't."

"I'm sorry, sir. May I ask what happened next?" Kevin asked.

"Well, the three had just escaped from a mental institution, and they were already there from previous assault charges. But they were connected to a local mob family. So, they stood trial. But bribery, threats, and extortion influenced the outcome. And again, they were found innocent due to reason of insanity. From there, I decided I would make them and others like them pay for hurting the innocent in the future. I spent four years in Japan and when I returned, I used the technology I created and waged war on crime. Now, come with me, Kevin, and you will have your chance to face them with honour and with power." Brown looked at Kevin.

"What must I do?"

"First, you must leave your anger behind you and follow me," Brown said. A Midnight black Ford Mustang pulled up in front of them. Patrick, from behind the wheel, gave the young teen a gentle nod. Kevin remembered him from their brief encounter at the mall.

"Get in, Kevin." Brown entered into the car.

Kevin looked at Cassidy entering the building and said, "I will be back, Cassidy. I promise you." Kevin entered the car and wondered what Arthur Brown had to offer him for his quest to stop Cassidy from escaping justice.

Chapter 24

Kevin followed the two men inside a dark hallway. The cracked and uneven ground made it difficult to walk, and the smell of mildew ruled the room. Before he stepped inside the abandoned building, Kevin wondered what could an old structure on the verge of collapse have to offer him.

"You still haven't told me what this used to be?" Kevin probed.

"This used to be my company. I lost it, and the new owner abandoned it for many years, but I just repurchased it," Brown said. "This will be your home now." The three men entered the main room. With the exception of some huge steel shelves at the end of the wall, the three of them stood alone in the empty area.

"Looks nice, Doc. Great, when do I get to move in?" Kevin mocked. "Lots of space. But it kind of lacks a woman's touch."

"This is just a mirage, kid, an illusion," Brown replied. They walked closer to the steel shelves. Their footsteps echoed across the room.

Kevin pointed at the shelves and asked, "You wanted to show me this?"

"No, this." Brown placed a firm grip on the tip of his cane, and a button appeared on top of it. He pressed it, and a whooshing hum began to fill the room with sound. The shelves moved to the side of the wall, and in front of them—an elevator presented an entrance. Patrick looked at the young teen with a childish grin on his face.

"Impressed yet?" Patrick asked.

"Way! Where does this lead?"

"Before we go further, I must ask upon the honour of Chloe's memory that this room will stay with you and you alone. Your word," Brown warned.

"I swear, but what is it?"

"It's an elevator that leads to your destiny and the protection of the innocent. It's the gateway to your keep, your arsenal, and your shelter. But you may call it the Shadow Crypt." Brown pressed various buttons on the keyboard, and the elevator doors opened.

"Are you coming?" Brown asked. Hesitant at first, Kevin paced inside the elevator with Brown and Patrick. The elevator descended for about a minute before it stopped. The doors opened wide. Kevin could not believe the image his eyes were witnessing. The room resembled a military base command centre. To his left, a giant monitor attached to sophisticated computers and machinery. To his right, chemicals and various weapons, a virtual armoury. Incased in solid steel, the walls shone like a knight's armour. Four additional steel doors appeared straight ahead. Brown walked towards the first automatic door to the far right, and it slid open.

"This way, Kevin," he said, and the young man followed. Once inside, Kevin saw twelve motorbikes of futuristic design and seven black minivans. And ahead of him, a long tunnel that appeared to have no end.

"I will show you the other room, kid." Brown returned to the main centre and opened the door adjacent to the one he had just entered. Without a doubt, Brown designed this room as the ultimate training facility. It hosted a gym, a swimming pool, a dojo, and a combat simulator room. Also, the room had a vast number of books and a computer archive.

"What are those books and disks?"

"These are all on international law; also, the dossiers of every major criminal in the world. The black books are my chronicles. They are used to help fight the scum of society." Brown escorted Kevin back to the main room again. Kevin pointed at the far one on the left.

"Where does this door go?" Kevin asked.

"That door leads you to the Provider," Patrick said.

"And who is this provider?"

"That would be me, Kevin," Taylor said.

"Mr. Taylor," Kevin said in shock. "You're a part of this with him."

"Yes, I am. Patrick, I will take it from here now, thank you."

"Until then, Mr. Taylor. Doc, Kevin." Patrick nodded before he took the exact door that Kevin wondered about.

"The door leads to my company, Kevin. That is the second command centre of this operation," Taylor said.

"What are you two talking about? What is this all about?"

"It's about fighting back, Kevin," Brown said. "This may help clarify things." And the middle door opened. "This room is the vault." Brown and Kevin walked inside, and to the youngster's amazement, a hallway full of costumes of identical design surrounded him. The costumes brought back a memory in Kevin's mind.

"This costume looks somewhat like that Shadow Chaser guy Chloe was reading up on," Kevin said, then paused, realizing where he was. "Oh my God. This is the Shadow Chaser. You were the Shadow Chaser!"

"I was, but that was over twenty years ago. Unfortunately, the war is not over. This was mine for a long time; then I lost it. But thanks to Alex, I got it back and made a few modifications in the keep; now, it is ready. We are just missing one thing," Brown said.

"What's that?" Kevin asked.

"You!"

"I don't understand."

"In my last mission, I rescued Patrick when he was a child from Antonio Stavros; the head of the Scorpio Syndicate. I had to stop him, and I did, but at a price. The cost of his life and the use of my leg, even though I have sufficiently recovered—I could never do this again. That's why I have the cane."

Taylor entered the room and said, "I became involved with the operation after the same syndicate murdered my wife and paralyzed my daughter. A few months later, we have teamed up to resurrect the Shadow Chaser."

"But I wanted someone who has experienced hurt and loss; and because of your legacy, you know that someone has to protect the innocent at all costs. Now before you say yes, listen to me carefully, Kevin," Brown said. "Once you are in, there is no turning back. You will have to leave the country for at least a year to learn an ancient art in Japan. We will educate you in matters you would have never tried to comprehend in your life. We will take care of you financially by providing you with a position at Taylor Enterprises. You will work the night shift; this is when you will fight this war for us."

"But my mom will never let me leave for Japan," Kevin pointed out.

"Leave that to me, Kevin," Taylor said.

"Kevin, if you say yes, I promise you we'll make them pay for what they've done. You will bring honour to her memory. This will be long campaign, and you will be a combatant in this war. I am a strict general and I demand only the best from you. You are wearing my honour, and I insist that it remains a glorious one," Brown said. "With my mind, Alex's resources, and your courage, the underworld will never be the same again. Do you accept?" Kevin took his necklace off and showed it to Brown.

"On one condition. You make as many of these as you can. This will be my calling card, and I want one just like that as the seal on my chest," Kevin said. "It's a duplicate of the chain I gave Chloe. I want her presence to travel with me in this war."

Brown replied, "Agreed." And with his palm down, Brown extended his hand towards his friends. Taylor smiled and placed his palm over Brown's hand. Kevin nodded and placed his palm over Taylor's hand, completing a three-way team handshake. "Welcome to the war, kid. Now, we take back our city," Brown said with a gothic tone in his voice as the new trinity cemented their covenant against evil and the Scorpio Syndicate.

Chapter 25

September 29, 2008:

*T*oday brought forth a new beginning for Kevin Wolf and his family. He looked over his checklist with a diligent eye before Brown picked him up for his greatest adventure and challenge ever. He packed his luggage, having already said his goodbyes to his friends the previous night at Ray's. They had a farewell party for him; a night he would never forget. However, now he had to face his destiny and master the skills he required in order to assume his role as the Shadow Chaser. With a tear in her eye, his mom watched him zip up his last sports bag. Kevin turned his head and saw her there.

"Hi, beautiful. You know the sun captures your eyes in the morning." He smiled, and his mother hugged him.

"Oh, you're a charmer, pup. Just like your father. You look like him right now, packing to go overseas. Thank God you are not going to some war like he did," she said.

"Me, in a war?" Kevin laughed. "That's a good one, Mom." A sudden knock on the door interrupted their small talk.

"Come in," Sophie said.

"Hi, Mrs. Wolf," Tommy said. The gang followed him inside.

"Hey guys, here to say one last goodbye?"

"Yes we are, Mrs. Wolf. I know we agreed not to do it, but we couldn't resist," Tommy said.

"Hey guys, now you miss me." Kevin grinned.

"Well, I can't stay for long, Kev. Just wanted to wish you the best and come back home soon." Cole gave him a brief hug. "Oh, and if you can find me a geisha girl there, I would appreciate it." Shauna slapped Cole's arm.

"I don't think so, buddy," Shauna said. "Don't listen to him, Kevin."

"I won't, dear."

"Now, you take care and come back to us, hun," Shauna said before she kissed him on the cheek.

"Thanks, dear. It's all a part of my new job as Dr. Brown assistant, but once he's done with his project over there, I will be back." Kevin winked.

"Stay out of trouble, Kev." Tina hugged him.

"No promises, Tina." Julie approached Kevin with a tear in her eye.

"Bye, Kevin. Take care of yourself," she said, holding his hand.

"I will, Jewel. What's with the tears?" Kevin asked. His concern for her showed.

"Just that I lost one of my closet friends, and now today—I'm losing another one."

"You haven't lost me, Jewel; just going away for a while. I will be back before long, but with all of this going on and Chloe's death, this may be the right move for me right now," Kevin said.

"I know, just take care and come back to us." She smiled.

"I will." The gang left for the exception of Tommy.

"Well, this is goodbye," Tommy said.

"For now, but not for long, bud," Kevin said.

"You're the best, man. I don't know what I'm going to do without you," Tommy said.

"I'm asking the same thing right now as well. You were always in my corner, bud." Tommy tried not to be sentimental, but he found it hard to hide his emotions.

"You know I'm not into this mushy stuff, so I'm off," Tommy said.

"You, emotional? That will be the day." Kevin smirked. "Take care of the gang for me."

"You bet. Later, Kev." Tommy took one last look at Kevin and walked away. Kevin felt the tears welling up in his eyes, but wiped them away with a swift swipe of his right hand. Just as he finished, the door opened again. This time Ray, Mark, Stephanie, and Logan came in to say goodbye.

"Hey, Kevin." Ray hugged him. "I just want to wish you the best."

"Thanks, Ray. Take care of Mom for me."

"That's a promise, Kevin. All the best."

"Now, don't get accustomed to that country, little brother. We want you back here as soon as the project is done." Mark hugged his bother hard.

"You bet, Mark. Keep an eye on the family."

"I will. Watch yourself out there and call us, will ya?"

"I will, bro."

"Take care, dear. Stay out of trouble and don't stay up late." Stephanie kissed his forehead.

"I will, sis. Now, you keep that lughead brother of mine out of trouble."

"I will."

"Uncle, why do you have to go?" Logan said, the tears fell from his face. Kevin picked up his little nephew and smiled.

"Well, buddy. Uncle has this neat job, and he has a chance to learn from the best people and places. But once Uncle's boss is done with the project he has to do, I will be back. I will be home for Christmas, that's a promise."

"But I don't want you to go, Uncle," he cried.

"I don't want to go either, bud, but I have to. But in Japan is where they created Pocket Monsters. I will get you some cool stuff there. Is that okay?"

"Oh, okay, but you have to come back home," he said.

"I promise, half-pint. I love you."

"I love you, too, Uncle." Kevin lowered him to the ground. A few moments later, they heard a second knock on the door. Sophie opened it and greeted her next guest.

"Good Morning, Mrs. Wolf. How are you this fine morning?" Taylor asked.

"Mr. Taylor, I am fine," she said, surprised to see the billionaire inside her little apartment. "I'm so embarrassed, the place is a mess."

"Not at all, you have a nice place." He smiled. "I see your family is saying their goodbyes to Kevin. Just let him know I'll be waiting for him at the front."

"Certainly, Mr. Taylor. Thank you for giving my son this opportunity in your company," she said, unaware of Taylor's true intentions.

"No, thank you for letting us bring him aboard. The Toronto Guardian spoke highly of him. Besides, he is a good friend to Margaret, and I owe him this chance for a good future," he replied. Kevin grabbed his luggage; Mark and Ray helped as well.

"I will call you when I reach Okinawa, Mom." Kevin looked at his mother. "I love you, Mom."

"I love you, too, pup. Take care." She had no control over the tears that ran down her face. Kevin winked and headed for the elevator. After it descended, Kevin exited the building and waited in front of Taylor's limo.

"Allow me to take those, gentlemen." The chauffeur smiled and grabbed the remaining luggage from Mark and Ray. After one more goodbye from his brother and Ray, Kevin stepped into the back of the limo. Taylor looked at Kevin and smiled.

"Are you ready?"

"I will miss them."

"They will be well-cared for, Kevin," Taylor said. "I promise you." The limo drove away and headed straight for the airport.

Arthur Brown and Margaret Taylor waited by the company plane for the black limo to arrive. Margaret for a long time knew what her father and Brown were trying to do, but she felt uncomfortable about the fact that they asked her friend to join them in this quest.

"Uncle, you will take care of him, will you?"

"I will, Margaret. I know you think we are wrong to put your friend through all of this, but he's our last hope."

"Just protect him, that's all I ask," she said. The limo arrived.

"Well, it's time," Brown said. Kevin slipped out of the limo. The chauffeur opened the trunk, and Kevin picked up two suitcases and a sports bag. The chauffeur grabbed the remaining three bags. Taylor joined his daughter.

"Take care, Kevin," Taylor said.

"Thank you, sir. Bye, Margaret."

"You don't have to do this, Kevin. It's not too late to change your mind," she said.

"I have to, Margaret. For all of our sake, I have to," Kevin said just before he entered the plane. Brown and Taylor parted with a handshake.

"Take care, old friend," Brown said.

"Be safe, Doc."

"Bye, Margaret."

"Take care of yourself and Kevin, Uncle." Margaret wheeled in the direction of the limo.

"I will." Brown entered the plane and sat next to the teen. He stared at Kevin while the teen surveyed the tarmac from his window.

"Are we ready?"

"We are," Kevin replied. The plane started to move. Within a few minutes, it took off to the sky above and headed for the land of the rising sun otherwise known as Japan.

Okinawa, Japan. September 30, 2008:

After a long journey over the Pacific Ocean, Arthur Brown and Kevin Wolf arrived at Tanaka's shrine. This was Kevin's first trip outside of Canada. He experienced Japan in photographs and on television, but never in person. Amazed by the architecture, the monuments, and the culture, Kevin stood there and felt humbled by a country he would soon call home for the next couple of years. He hoped Japan had the answers he needed to become this warrior for justice; but doubted the potential remaining in his sorrowful heart.

"This is the home of my teacher, Master Tanaka. Honour it, and it will honour you." Brown took off his shoes outside at the front of the entrance. "Follow my lead." Without hesitation, Kevin took his shoes off as well and followed Brown inside. Kevin noticed numerous documents covering the walls of the shrine. The paper resembled parchment; filled with Japanese symbols and drawings foreign to him. In front of the room, there stood a giant drawing of an elderly man. The drawing hung on the wall like a holy relic. The picture appeared to have been painted centuries ago. Kevin pointed at the painting. "Is he your teacher?"

"No, he was his great-great-great-grandfather. Yoshi Tanaka was one of the last remaining samurai warriors of his clan. They lived in the village after the last feudal wars. They painted this portrait around 1790," Brown replied.

"Did he create that fighting style?"

"You could say he brought it to the next level. The Shadow Art was entrusted to their family for centuries before the Tanaka family reached their eventual level of nobility among the samurai. He was a warrior and a pillar to the village. Then the darkness came. A sect called the Dragon of Darkness was attacking his village. In order to defeat them, he had to use the ancient discipline of his ancestors. He combined his samurai code, the art ninjutsu, and the rare discipline in the teachings of shaolin to fight the sect. His ancestors called it the Shadow Art. He embraced and developed the ability of chasing their shadows away from the village," Brown said. "So, technically he was the first Shadow Chaser."

"That's where you got the name," Kevin replied as an old man ambled inside.

"Konnichiwa, my student. Forgive my lateness." Tanaka smiled.

"Konnichiwa, master. No forgiveness is necessary." Brown bowed to the elder. "This is the boy I told you about, master."

"You must be Kevin Wolf. It is an honour to meet you." Tanaka bowed, but his eyes remained locked on the teen. Kevin was not sure what to do, but at the last second, he followed the old man's lead.

"Thank you, sir," Kevin replied, after a quick bow.

"I see you will be with us for a while."

"As long as it takes."

"You have fire in your spirit, reminds me of another young kohai who stumbled into my door not so long ago." He grinned.

"We are ready to start the training when you are, master," Brown said. "He's enrolled in a private school just about a block away."

"Excellent, but for now the evening will be ours to enjoy and to learn from each other," Tanaka said.

"What can I teach you?" Kevin asked.

"Many things, chosen one. As your teacher, you will learn from me. And as my student, I will learn from you." Tanaka grinned.

"I don't understand," Kevin said with a confused expression.

"Hai, chosen one," he replied. "You will, but for now, I will show you to your rooms." He ambled towards a long cord and yanked at it. Kevin had blinked once when a young Japanese female seemed to have appeared out of nowhere and walked inside.

"You called for me, Great-Grandfather?"

"Hai, Mariko. These are our honoured guests. They will be living with us for a while. You remember, Master Brown?"

"Yes, master. It is good to see you again."

"Arigatou, Mariko. Oai-deki-te ureshii-desu," Brown replied. "How is your mother?"

"She is fine, thank you, master." Kevin did not know what they were saying, but it sounded like good news. So, he remained silent until someone introduced him.

"This is his young friend, Kevin Wolf. He will be my new student," Tanaka said.

"Hi."

"Hello, Kevin-san," she replied. "I will take you to your rooms." Kevin grabbed his bags with a confused look on his face.

"Does something trouble you, chosen one?" Tanaka asked.

"I just have this feeling that the world is a tuxedo, and I'm just a pair of brown sneakers right now."

"You will feel welcome here, my friend. Now, tend to your room, and the three of us will talk later," Tanaka said. Kevin followed Mariko out of the dojo.

"So, what do you think, master?" Brown asked.

"He has a lot of work to do, he looks lost and unsure of his potential," Tanaka said, "but we shall see, my student." Brown followed his master to the garden and contemplated the future.

Chapter 26

Okinawa Island. Japan. April 9, 2009:

Kevin Wolf spent most of his sixteenth birthday sitting by the river, reflecting on his life. For the last six months, he spent about eighty per cent of his waking time training, fifteen per cent in school, and the remaining five socializing. He found the training onerous, and half the time he was not succeeding. He ran obstacle courses, studied pain tolerance techniques, learned proper balance, and practiced gymnastics while wearing traditional samurai battle armour. The tasks and exercises steadily grew more difficult and began to take its toll on him. Brown appeared critical of his every move; he never once encouraged his young student while attacking his physical and emotional levels of tolerance. He knew his spirit would soon begin to shatter like glass, and he felt trapped in a self-imposed abyss. As for Tanaka, he remained silent, shook his head, and frowned every time Kevin completed a required task. Kevin wanted to quit; his one moment of happiness out of all this was meeting Mariko and her boyfriend Yori. They were good friends, and they reminded him of his friends back in Canada. Mariko and Yori spotted Kevin sitting by the tree alone and walked towards him.

"Hello, Kevin-san." She smiled.

"Mariko, Yori. What's new?"

"We are going to the village tonight. Would you like to join us?"

"I would like to, but I can't. Master Tanaka and Doc want me to redo my Bo training."

"You are lucky to learn from Master Tanaka, Kevin-san," Yori said.

"You wanna trade?" Kevin joked.

"I wish, but he will never give me that honour."

"Why is that?"

"You see, Kevin-san, my great-grandfather believes the Shadow Art belongs to the Tanaka bloodline. The tradition passes from father to son or daughter.

Yori is learning other disciplines with Great-Grandfather, but not this one," she explained.

"But why is he teaching me?"

"Because he considers Master Brown like his son. My grandfather died at a young age, and he had no other son. Master Brown saved my mother, and Great-Grandfather could refuse him no favour," she replied.

"So, you see, Kevin-san. I truly envy you." Yori smiled.

"And I envy you, Yori," Kevin replied.

"Why?"

"Because what you and Mariko have is something special. Something I once had with Chloe. I would give my soul just to look at her again, but she's gone." Kevin bowed his head. "Now, everything else means next to nothing."

"Mariko told me about your love Chloe, Kevin-san. I am sorry for your loss. I am sure she was a beautiful person."

"That she was, Yori. That she was," Kevin said. Mariko watched a tear rolling down from his right eye.

"We can stay with you if you wish, Kevin-san?" Mariko asked. Kevin tried to appear unaffected and smiled.

"No, go on you two. Have fun. I will see you tomorrow."

"Alright then," she said. "But before we go, we want you to have this for your birthday." She gave him a small box wrapped in paper.

"Thank you. You guys didn't have to do that." Kevin said. The teen ripped the paper and opened the box. He found a silver wolf ring in the centre. The head, handcrafted with painstaking accuracy, and the eyes had two red gems.

"We hope you like it."

"Like it! I love it, thank you." Kevin smiled.

"Well, we should be going then. Take care, Kevin-san," Yori said.

"Sayounara, Kevin-san," she added.

"Sayounara and arigatou," Kevin replied. Yori and Mariko left, holding each other by the hand. Kevin looked towards the river and wondered how lucky they were. Kevin would never again hold Chloe by the hand. Yori and Mariko had each other and their love. Alone, Kevin faced his cold, harsh reality. However, unaware to Kevin, Tanaka heard the conversation and saw the pain Kevin was putting himself through. He sauntered behind him.

"A beautiful sight, is it not?" Kevin sprung from the ground.

"Master, I didn't hear you coming."

"Ta, ta, ta, chosen one. I am here to enjoy the view with you. That is all," he replied. "How are you feeling today?"

"The truth, master, I feel broken inside. I think I made a mistake by coming here."

"Oh, how so?" Kevin poured his heart out with one breath.

"I've been doing this for the past six months, and all I feel is your disappointment in my efforts. Doc is always shouting at me, and I see you just withdrawing after every attempt I make. I don't blame you, I guess I just don't have what it takes. I'm not sleeping well either."

"You miss her, my friend?"

"More than ever, master. She's in my dreams and in my thoughts. But that's all gone now," Kevin replied. "She's dead, and I'm here—so I have to live with it." Kevin looked at the river as a strong wind blew through the trees.

"She will always be with you, chosen one. They say the spirit of a loved one can speak to you through the wind. They will talk to you in your time of need, that's what they say," Tanaka proclaimed.

"Spirits don't exist, master. Once we are gone, we are gone."

"You have a lot to learn, chosen one. They do exist, just because you cannot see something does not mean it does not exist. To think like that, is to think like a baka."

"A baka?"

"An idiot, chosen one." He laughed. Kevin grinned.

"I know I have failed you and Doc, for that I'm sorry. I'm not what the both of you expected."

"I am not disappointed in you, chosen one. You are not me or Arthur-san. You are Kevin Wolf. That is all you need to know. In order to seek the prophecies of the future, you need to acknowledge them in the past."

"You have me there, master. I'm not following you."

"In order to proceed to the next step, you must except who you are and the life you have led to this point. But then again, what do I know, I'm just an old man in pyjamas as you westerners would say." Tanaka laughed.

"I would never say anything bad about you, master." Kevin grinned. The rain started to come down, and the wind grew stronger.

"I suggest we return to the dojo and finish your training there this evening, chosen one," Tanaka said.

"Agreed, and one more thing, master. Why do you keep calling me chosen one?"

"Because you are the one who will continue what Arthur-san had started, my young friend," Tanaka said, and they headed for the dojo for more training and shelter from the rain.

The storm grew stronger as the evening progressed. But Kevin continued his training, and after each attempt—Brown kept on pointing out the teen's mistakes. Kevin, tired of the criticism, tried one last time to please his trainer. To disarm his opponent, Kevin attempted a forward swing with his staff, but ended up being blocked. With one counterattack, he disarmed Kevin, and the teen kissed the mat on the way down.

"You are extending your leg too far, leaving yourself unbalanced," Brown roared. "How many times will it take to get it through your head?" Kevin could not hold his anger anymore; he roared back at him.

"Damn it, Doc. I'm trying! What do you want from me?"

"Better than this, kid. You do stuff like this, and they will eat you alive," he shouted. "I think this was a mistake. I'm beginning to believe I have made the wrong choice."

"I think I made the wrong choice as well, Doc. I should never have come here," Kevin said, discouraged and broken.

"For once we are in agreement," Brown replied. Tanaka could no longer bear to witness this attack on Kevin and interrupted the dispute.

"Enough," Tanaka hollered. The old master looked at Kevin and said with a softer tone in his voice. "Kevin-san, you may leave for this evening. We will continue your training in the morning before school. As for you, we have to talk, Arthur-san." Kevin bowed at both of them and left the room.

"Master, I know you think I'm hard on him but..." Brown said, but Tanaka raised his voice.

"I am the master here. You will remain silent and hear what I have to say. Do you understand me?"

"Forgive me, master," Brown said, for he knew he angered his master.

"I know you are trying to prepare the child for your war, but you are doing more harm to him than those criminals could ever do. You are killing his spirit," Tanaka said in a softer tone. "When you do that, the person is truly dead. You may hide your feelings better, but that doesn't mean you can attack him, I will not allow it in my home."

"Forgive me, master. The last thing I want to do is offend you and hurt the lad. It's just I feel he's failing. Maybe I should just call this whole thing off," Brown replied.

"If that's your wish, so be it. But if he failed, the dishonour is not his alone. It falls to us for failing to mentor him. Remember that, my student."

"I'm going to go talk to him," Brown said. "I will tell him it's time to go back home." Brown was about to leave the dojo when they heard a huge blast.

"What was that?" Brown pondered, and then one of Tanaka's servants entered the room.

"Master, Tanaka-san. Yori-san's car has been hit by a falling tree, and he swerved into the river."

"My Mariko," Tanaka cried.

"Young Kevin-san was outside going to his room when he saw the accident. He has jumped into the river," the servant said.

"Let's go," Brown replied. The three men moved as fast as they could to the river. The accident happened about one hundred feet from the Tanaka home, and they could see the air bubbles from the river.

"Mariko, Yori," Tanaka screamed.

"Kevin," Brown screamed as well.

"I will call for help," the servant said, and ran back to the house.

Kevin had at last reached the car, still sinking to the bottom of the river. He tried to open the door, but the damage to the front end jammed the door. He tried the other doors, also jammed. He looked inside the car through the side window and saw Mariko, aware of his presence, but Yori, bleeding from the forehead, appeared unconscious. The cab filled with water, and Kevin knew he had to free them before they drowned. He knew it was next to impossible to break the car window, but he remembered his training. Tanaka taught him that every object and person had pressure points, and if you can locate those points, you can break it—or them. Kevin felt the need to breath, but concentrated on the matter at hand. He closed his eyes and touched the glass, focusing on his sense of touch. Thanks to his training, he discovered a minor weak point. With no concern for his own safety, Kevin smacked the window with an open hand punch. The glass split in two pieces giving Kevin the opportunity to kick out the rest of the glass. Kevin grabbed Mariko and motioned to her to swim to the surface. He knew if he followed her, the car would descend to the bottom so fast, and he would never be able to catch up to it, losing Yori. By the grace of God or luck, she was not injured. She nodded at Kevin; and then she began swimming to the top. Trying to reach the surface, she fought with all of her strength to stay on top of the current.

Brown and Tanaka yelled and yelled again until they saw air bubbles rising from below. Brown dived into the water and helped Mariko to the surface. She gasped for air like a newborn baby.
"I have you, Mariko," Brown said, and helped her out of the water. He passed her to Tanaka. The old man grabbed her. He kept a tight grip on her arm and carried her to the shore. When Tanaka placed her on the grass, Mariko started to cry. Tanaka hugged his great-granddaughter firmly.
"I thought I lost you, Mariko," he cried on her shoulder.
"No, Great-Grandfather. I am here. But Kevin-san is still down there with Yori!" She sobbed, fearing for the worse.

Kevin felt his chest tightening and his lungs collapsing. He needed air, and soon. He had to think fast, or he would be swimming with the fishes along with his friend. Kevin looked at the tires and remembered what Brown taught him about thinking on his feet.
Remember, kid, sometimes you have to leap beyond logic and do the impossible, because sometimes the impossible is all you've got. Kevin swam towards the front of the car. He took the air seal off one of the tires, cupped his hand above the valve, with his thumb beneath his lip, and his fingers along the upper lip, and released some air inside his mouth. But the airflow mixed with water, and Kevin could not inhale enough air from the tire. His lungs tried to heave as he began to lose his oxygen supply. But Yori's life remained Kevin's main concern. He may have lost Chloe, but he would die before allowing Mariko to share his

curse. Kevin used the Shadow Art to focus his mind and body. The meditation allowed him to control the capacity of his lungs. Each time he took a breath, his lungs adapted to the air pressure. To his amazement, *it worked.* The air tasted awful, but he had little choice. After inhaling more of the stale air, he breaststroked back towards the front of the car. Yori's face was turning blue, and Kevin knew he had little time to bring him to the surface. Yori's seatbelt remained attached. Kevin pulled with all of his might, but he could not release the belt. Kevin grabbed a sharp piece of glass from the edge of the windshield and used it to sever the belt, but not without accidently cutting his own hand. He grabbed the back of Yori's kimono and peddled with his bloodied hand to the fresh air above. Exhausted, he had to continue. He needed air desperately as he almost blacked out.

Brown returned to the water and spotted a wavy silhouette, he plunged like a dolphin towards Kevin, struggling to hold onto Yori. Brown dove underneath and pushed them both to the surface. Brown dragged Yori to the shore. Kevin coughed and gagged. Brown returned for him and he noticed the blood from his hand.
"Are you okay?"
"I'm fine, tend to him," Kevin replied. Brown moved as fast as his bad leg could take him and administered CPR to Yori. Time seemed to stand still while they waited for Yori to respond. Then he began to cough. Water came out of his mouth, and the colour returned to his face. His breathing and his heartbeat returned to normal. An ambulance arrived at the scene, and a paramedic ran towards them to tend to Yori and Mariko. Brown and Tanaka helped Kevin up from the ground.
"How did you get them out of there?" Brown asked.
"I broke the windshield thanks to a technique I learned from Master Tanaka. Then Mariko was not tied to her belt, and she was conscious, so I directed her to go ahead and swim to the surface." Kevin tried to get his breath back. "After that, I needed to get some air to breath, so I took the top off of the air seal from the tire and took in some air. Once I had enough, I tried to get Yori out of the car, but he was stuck, so I took a sharp piece of broken glass, cut his seatbelt, and the rest is history."
"You have saved the pride and joy of my life, my reason for living, Kevin-san. Arigatou, you are indeed the chosen one." Tanaka bowed to the young teen.
"You honour me, master." Kevin returned the bow. A second ambulance arrived at the scene. Tanaka followed Yori and Mariko into the first one as it drove off to the hospital.
"You better get that cut checked out, kid," Brown said. He helped Kevin towards the ambulance. "Kevin, could you forgive a stubborn old man?"
"I think I can. Too bad it took saving two lives to do so, but yes I can." He smiled.

"Alright then. Let's get your hand fixed up, and tomorrow we'll go back to the training. Great work, kid," Brown said. Kevin nodded and stepped into the second ambulance and drove away.

Okinawa Island. Japan. April 13, 2010:

A year had gone by since the accident, but it seemed like days. Kevin had transformed into the ultimate combat weapon. He had just completed his Grade 11 exams, and already knew how to speak English and French, but now he had Japanese and Latin added to his linguistic curriculum vitae. He studied history, chemistry, and law; passing them all with honours. But most important of all, he learned the Shadow Art. He became skilled in the ways of Tanaka's ancestors. His reflexes and combat techniques were phenomenal. His instincts, his willpower, his wits, and his grasp of the new knowledge taught to him were impeccable. His training helped him improve his hearing, his touch, and taste by a factor of three. The herbs he drank improved his vision from a twenty-twenty vision to a twenty-fifteen vision. He could now spot the red laces of a hundred-mile-per-hour fastball coming at him. He stood ready for the role destiny had bestowed upon him as the Shadow Chaser. Today, he headed home to begin his quest. That quest; to find Graham Cassidy—the killer of his beloved Chloe. Kevin spent most of the morning in the dojo meditating when a familiar scent captured his attention.

"Hi, Doc. Come on in." Kevin smiled with his eyes closed.

"How do you know it was me?"

"The smell of the wood from your cane. Plus, the English Leather cologne was a giveaway." Kevin opened his eyes.

"Excellent, kid. Are you ready to go back home?"

"You bet I am, but I will miss this place and this country. A lot of culture and history here."

"You've got that right, an adopted culture and history that will come to define you. Before we leave, Master Tanaka wants to see you," Brown said. "He's waiting in his shrine for you." Kevin rose from his meditation and headed for the door, and Brown followed. Kevin arrived at the shrine and removed his sandals before entering. Mariko, Yori, and Tanaka stood in front of the Yoshi Tanaka painting. He motioned his hand towards Kevin, signaling for him to approach. Kevin stepped towards him until he stood next to the three.

"You wanted to see me, master?"

"Yes, Kevin-san. I wanted to give you this celebration before you left for home."

"What celebration would that be, master?" Tanaka took out a katana from a chest.

"Kevin Wolf you have become one with my home, my land, and my family. The Tanaka name was one I was honoured to have borrowed in my life here. Now, I give you that name as well. I have taught you all that I know; my strength, my speed, the art of my fathers, my wisdom, and my spirit is now with you," Tanaka proclaimed. He took out a katana and displayed the blade in the air. "You will be the last student I will ever teach the Shadow Art to. For that I am honoured. You have the courage of the samurai, the skills of the ninja, and the soul of the shaolin. You are now, and forever will be, a Tanaka. This blade will remind you that this house, and its traditions, are with you."

"Thank you, master. I don't know what to say?"

"Keep my teachings in your heart and never allow yourself to adapt to the ways of the evil ones—or you will fall to their spell. Now, go and meet your destiny, samurai." Tanaka handed the katana to Kevin.

Kevin looked at the white wolf's head handle of his sword and vowed, "I shall—for you and your name, master."

"Good luck, chosen one." Tanaka bowed to Kevin and walked away.

"Take care, Kevin-san. Dance at our wedding." Mariko kissed his cheek.

"Count on it, Mariko. Take care." Yori shook his hand.

"Take care, my friend. Thank you for everything you have done for us."

"Anytime, Yori. Now, I want you both to come to Canada for a visit real soon. You two will always be welcome."

"We shall," she replied, and they left the shrine. Brown hugged his old teacher before he joined Kevin on his trip home.

"Thank you, master. For everything," Brown said.

"It is I who should thank you, my student, for bringing back the passion to my family. Good luck, Arthur-san," he said, and he ambled away. Brown moved towards Kevin and looked at the blade.

"Congratulations, kid. Not many people have one of those."

"I bet you've already received one from him."

"Of course I have." Brown grinned. "Now, let's go home."

"For sure," Kevin replied. The two men walked outside of the shrine; their next stop—the airport and the way back home.

Toronto, Ontario. Canada. April 14, 2010:

After a long flight home and a night's sleep at Taylor's mansion, Kevin arrived at his apartment building. Kevin kept his arrival a secret and wanted to create a surprise. He stood in front of his door, his right hand on the doorknob with a gentle grip, and he pushed the key into the keyhole. With a slight twist, he opened the door. He tiptoed inside the hallway and found his mother watching her morning talk shows. Looking at her, Kevin realized how much he missed her, and how much a year and a half had taken away, precious time he could have spent with her and his family; but that opportunity has now passed. Cassidy took so much away from him, but now he could make things right. He kept his word and returned home. Kevin smiled as he heard her talk to herself. Sophie took a quick peek at her watch.

"I better get going," she said.

"What's the hurry, beautiful?" Kevin inquired. Her face froze in wonderment; then she turned her head in the direction of the voice.

"Kevin! You're home!" Sophie jumped from her chair and hugged her son. Kevin held onto her and laughed.

"Hi, Mom. I take it you missed me." She poked at his chest and smiled.

"My God, look at you! You're all grown up, and hey, is that muscle tone?"

"Just a little, Japanese cuisine is high on soy-based products. But it's still the same old lovable me."

"Well, I will have to tell everyone you are back," she said, and headed towards the phone. "I will call Ray and take the day off. I guess you will be leaving again before long."

"No, I'm back for good. I'm home, Mom," Kevin said. "But could you hold off for at least another day to tell everyone. I had a long trip, and I'm beat."

"Sure, pup. I will tell them tomorrow morning that you just arrived," she said.

"Thanks, Mom. Listen, I'm going to get some sleep for a while. I have to work tonight at the lab for Mr. Brown."

"You just came home, and he has you there already?"

"The money is good, Mom. Don't worry; I'm all finished school for the year. I have a pretty good report card as well." Kevin placed his bags into his room. "So, go ahead to work. I'll be here when you get back."

"Alright then, Kevin," she said. "But I want to know everything, okay." Sophie kissed him on the cheek.

"Alright, Mom. Talk to you later," Kevin said. She grabbed her purse and left the apartment. Kevin went back into his room, took out his katana, and placed it on top of his shelf. *One more place to go, then the game begins.* Kevin unpacked his clothes and reflected on his time in Japan.

Chapter 27

*L*ori Bellecoeur ambled along the path of the cemetery and listened to the birds singing in the distance. The snow had just melted, leaving the ground damp and muddy. Her first visit to her sister's stone since November, Lori yearned to see her again. Even though she could never hold her in this life, she wanted to be as close to her sister as possible. Last summer, Lori spent her afternoons keeping Chloe's grave maintained. She blamed herself for getting involved with Graham Cassidy. Upon arriving at her grave, she noticed the green grass growing again and the few flowers blooming next to the stone. She filled her lungs with the scent of the season. Lori could see the birth of spring in the lifeless cemetery.

Lori shared her sombre thoughts with her sister. "Oh, Chloe. They are blooming for you, my little sister. I can't believe you're there, it should be me, damn it. It should have been me." And the tears trickled down her face. Out of nowhere, a voice came from behind her.

"She wouldn't want you to feel this way, Lori." In shock, she turned around and saw Kevin holding a red rose. Lori hugged him with all her might.

"Kevin, it's so good to see you again."

"It's good to see you, too, Lori. How are your parents?"

"They're doing the best they can. Dad is working on a new project at work to keep his mind off things, and Mom is working on a committee that protects the rights of crime victims. I, on the other hand, am doing much the same; just working and coming here."

Kevin held onto her shoulder and said, "You have to move on with your life. Chloe wouldn't want you to blame yourself for this."

"But it's my fault she's dead," she said. "I brought Graham into our lives, and I ruined my family." The tears continued to roll down her cheeks. Kevin, with a gentle touch, wiped them from her face and smiled.

"You had no idea what this guy was capable of, and you can't go on blaming yourself." She glanced at her sister's grave.

"I met a guy last week; kinda reminded me of you a bit. He asked me to go out, but I was just afraid to."

"You have to get back on the horse, Lori. You cannot live in fear forever. Besides, if he's like me, he can't be all bad." Kevin had succeeded in putting a smile on Lori's face.

"Thank you, Kevin. We missed you a lot. When you left, I felt that I had taken your life as well."

"Nope, I just needed some time to grow and to adjust to my new life. Now I'm back," he said. "If you or your family need anything, call me." Kevin placed the rose on Chloe's grave.

"I will give you a moment alone." Lori smiled and walked a few feet away from the grave.

His soft hand touched the top of the headstone and he whispered, "*Now it begins here. You will have justice; I promise you.*" Kevin kissed the top of Chloe's monument and walked towards Lori.

Kevin held her hand and said, "It's getting late, and I have to go to work now."

"Thank you, Kevin. For everything," she said. Kevin started to walk away, but at the last second, she cried out.

"Kevin!"

"Yes." Kevin turned around to face her.

"Why do people like Cassidy get away with stuff like this?"

"I wouldn't be so sure if I were you, Lori," Kevin said. "Do you still read the newspaper?"

"Yes."

"Then keep reading, I guarantee you may find the news to be...let's just say...interesting." Kevin grinned. Lori turned her head in the direction of Chloe's grave, then glanced back at Kevin.

"What do you mean by that?" she asked, but Kevin disappeared like an apparition. "Kevin, where did you go?" She received no reply; the cemetery was empty except for herself and the rows of tombstones in the field.

Arthur Brown had placed the final touches on his suit when Kevin Wolf entered the room.

"Well, Doc, I'm here. Nine on the nose."

"Good, have a seat. I want to see if you remember how to operate your gear," he said. Kevin looked at his Shadow Chaser suit.

"Mark II battle suit. A first layer is made from computer circuitry and the second layer is made from molecules you call Night Fabric. Meaning that this fabric will fit the wearer, and it can be used as a more advanced form of body armour, which you have already designed. The suit is linked to my DNA, so no one could wear the suit, but me unless it's reprogrammed," Kevin said.

"Not bad, now describe the goodies."

"The suit is equipped with neural muscular implants that enhance my strength and the thrust of my punches by a factor of three. In addition, it is possible to upgrade the suit to a higher level if necessary. The suit is designed with a thermo device, so I can wear it in heat and cold. It's flame resistant and protects the skin against gas and radiation exposure as well.

"Don't forget the ten-hour compressed oxygen supply for an underwater or vacuumed environment," Brown added. "As well as your battle jacket that can transform into a cape for gliding and hiding. Thanks to its nanotechnology-based design."

"I was getting to that. The suit is equipped with impact dampeners to protect me from sudden stops when I use a rope to break my fall; it also protects me from attacks," Kevin added. "Plus, this baby has an electromagnetic force that redirects steel and lead bullets at long range."

"You forgot to mention you can reverse the magnetic flow to attract items or to cling to steel. Also, remember the golden rule. Do not use the field when bystanders are around, or they could be the ones hit by the bullets in a crossfire," Brown said. "As for the rest of the weapons, gadgets, and devices—well, you already have a grasp on them. Any questions?"

"When do we get to play smack the bad guys around?"

"Step into my parlour, young man," Brown said, and they entered the vault and the war.

Packed to capacity for another night, patrons of the Deuces Wild nightclub welcomed the darkness of the evening night. University and college students celebrated the end of exams. However, a few of them still had a few more to write, Sandy Benjamin included. She fit the profile of a shy girl-next-door type with a compassionate heart. Not one for the bar scene; but some of her friends had finished all of their exams, and they were leaving town for the summer. So, after some convincing from her best friend Jill, she decided to go out until midnight. With one exam left to write tomorrow afternoon, Sandy wanted to leave early and finish off some last minute studying. An accomplished student with no danger of failing, she wanted to be prepared nonetheless. Jill approached her with a topped-up shot glass in hand.

"Hey, Sandy. Have some."

"No, I have my exam tomorrow. I want to be ready and sober."

"Oh, come on, live a little."

"It's just about midnight, I should be going," she said when an attractive male with the looks of a movie star approached them.

"Good evening, ladies."

"Hi, Craig," Jill replied. Sandy gave a shy wave and remained speechless. The gentleman, Craig Keller, a good guy with great looks. Sandy had a crush on him since the first semester, but she could never muster the courage to tell him the truth.

"Sandy, I hear you're staying in Toronto for the summer?" he asked.

"Yes, I am, Craig. My parents are moving up here in a week," she replied, surprised that he would take the time to speak to her.

"That's great. Most of my friends are gone home for the summer, but I'm staying here. I don't know many people, and since you will be here, maybe we could grab a coffee sometime at Fresco, if you like?" he asked. Sandy could not believe he wanted to go out with her; her enthusiasm showed.

"Sure, I would love to. Would tomorrow night be good?"

"That's super. Here's my number, give me a call. Well, I have to go, goodnight, ladies." And Craig left the bar. Sandy hugged Jill in excitement.

"I can't believe it! Craig is having coffee with me!"

"I know, you lucky girl you," Jill said. Sandy looked at the time.

"Well, I have to run. Take care, and I will see you in a couple of weeks." The girls hugged one last time before they parted ways. Excited about her date of a lifetime, Sandy walked outside of the nightclub. In her exhilaration, she took a wrong turn and entered the darker part of the city. When she realized her error, Sandy stopped and turned around with a sudden air of anxiety and fear. While attempting to backtrack, she heard two sets of footprints behind her. She started to walk faster, but the sounds of the footsteps accelerated as well. A minute ago, she felt like she landed in heaven, now she felt trapped in hell. She decided to run for it and prayed she could get back to the nightclub. Half a block away from the nightclub, she started to walk faster, but the footsteps continued to echo behind her. Fear raced through her veins and the echo made her anxious and wince. Out of nowhere, a pair of hands grabbed her— and threw her into the dark alleyway. Her body crashed onto the garbage cans in the alley. The scents of garbage and rotten fish permeated the atmosphere. One of the men hiked her up and shook her like a rag doll. She found herself surrounded by three men.

"What do you want?" she cried.

"Shut your mouth," one of them screamed, and punched her. The other two checked her purse and took a few dollars from her wallet. "Do you want another one?" he hollered, waiving his fist in the air.

"N...nn..o," she cried.

"Now, we're going to do our thing, and you're going to enjoy it, baby," he said, his voice consumed by lust. "When I'm done, one of my buddies is next." The thug took out his knife and ripped her buttons off her blouse one at a time.

"Pl...ea...se, stop."

"You hear that, Rob. She asked you to stop." The second one laughed.

"She sure is nice and young, we hit the jackpot, Johnny." The third one salivated over the young girl.

187

"You see, baby. We been doing this here for a long time, and no one will ever find us here," the first one said, trying to rip her blouse off. But a strange fog came out from nowhere.

"Don't be so sure, boys," the voice said in the distance.

"What the hell was that?" the second one asked. The voice echoed throughout the alley.

"That's your soul telling you tonight is judgment night for you three clowns!" The three men started to sweat. Before they could react, they saw movement in the darker part of the alley.

"Johnny, go find that jerk and kill him."

"Why me, Rob? It was your idea to jump the skirt," he panicked.

"I said go find out, Johnny!" Rob repeated his order.

"Alright, alright. I'm going." Johnny took out his gun and walked towards the end of the alley.

"Do you see anything?"

"Nothing, maybe it was some punkass kid. Whoever he was, he's gone now." But the other two noticed a pair of red eyes behind Johnny.

"Johnny, look out behind you," the second thug warned. Johnny turned around and spotted the red eyes looking at him.

"SWEET JESUS," he yelled.

"No, but you may be seeing him before long!" The spectre picked him up by the throat and lifted him three feet above the ground. The dark stranger held him there for several seconds. Johnny gasped for air. The stranger threw Johnny, six feet into the air, right past the other two thugs, and into the sidewalk next to them. His back collided with the steel pole, knocking him unconscious.

"Kill him, Brad," Rob yelled. The other thug grabbed his gun and fired at the stranger. The bullets travelled like a magnet on metal towards the target, and the stranger fell onto the ground. The smell of gunpowder saturated the air.

"Good work, Brad," Rob said and turned towards the girl. "Now, where were we?" Fortune was not smiling on them, for they did not see the stranger leap back up to his feet.

"Forgetting someone?" the stranger asked.

Brad turned around and shouted, "He's still alive. Oh dear God, Rob, he is still alive." Brad knew that this person, or thing, should have died, but there he stood—and from the sound of his cold voice, they made him or it angry.

"My turn!" The stranger delivered a sidekick to Brad's groin. Brad moaned in agony and fell to his knees. The dark stranger delivered a roundhouse kick to Brad's left cheek as a final touch. Now, Rob, all alone with the dark stranger, grabbed the girl at knifepoint.

"Let the woman go, and I may not kill you," the stranger commanded. Rob pushed the girl towards the garbage bags and challenged the stranger with his knife.

"I'm going to cut you good, you son of a...." Rob lifted the knife to the stranger's chest.

As the knife came down, the stranger commanded, *"Magnet."* All of a sudden, the knife came to a complete stop midway between them. An unknown force held the blade. Despite his best efforts, Rob couldn't push it into his adversary's chest.

"What the hell is this? Some force is holding me back." He screamed like a wild animal and stared at the stranger in frozen terror. "Who are you?"

"Having problems with your toy?" The stranger asked. *"Here, let me take a stab at it."* And he karate chopped the blade of the knife with his right hand. The blade broke off, and all that remained of the knife—was the handle. Once the blade broke, so did the hold he had on the knife. Gravity led Rob towards the ground, and his face made a clear collision with the cement. Rob staggered his way up, and he tried to wipe the blood from his face. Extreme fear had set in; flight became his only option.

"Where do you think you're going, junior?" the stranger asked as he clinched his fist. Out of nowhere, a cord that resembled a steel cable flew towards Rob. The hook snapped onto his jacket, and the stranger pulled him with one swift yank.

"Oh God," he shouted, and fell onto the ground. The force from the hook dragged him towards the stranger. Turning around, he noticed the black hands of the stranger wrapping around his throat and lifting him up into the air. The dark spectre held him there like he did to Johnny, and Rob believed the stranger would kill him soon.

"Oh please, man! Don't kill me, please don't!"

"On one condition, buddy," the stranger said. *"You're going to be my messenger."*

"Sure, whatever you want. I will do it!"

"Tell your friends that for over twenty years I have slept while you all ran around in my realm; but because of you, I have awakened to reclaim my world. If you do not tell them this, I will find you—and I will finish you."

"Sure, man. I will tell them whatever you want," he cried. The stranger dropped him.

"Good, now say goodnight." The stranger punched him in the jaw. The blow knocked out Rob for the ten count, and the threat was over. The stranger took out three manacles for each of the thugs and strapped them together around the steel pole. Once he finished with them, he turned his attention towards the girl. She sat on the ground all curled up as he slowly approached her. She looked up and spotted two red eyes in black with a jacket and a hat. Her emotions took over and whimpered like an abused puppy.

"Please don't hurt me."

"I'm not going to hurt you, miss. I'm not the bad guy, believe it or not, I'm one of the good guys," he said. *"You shouldn't be in this part of town this late at night, miss."*

"I was trying to run away from them." She tried to pull herself up. The stranger offered his hand, but she refused it.

"Are you hurt?"

"Just a bit, but I will be all right."

"Good. Then go to the coffee shop across the road and call the police," he said. Sandy started walking towards the coffee shop. However, her curiosity took over.

"Who are you?"

"Just a friend." Before the second had passed, smoke filled the alley, and within an instant, the stranger vanished. When the smoke cleared, she stood alone in the alley. The thugs—still tied up, and next to them were three necklaces. Taking a closer look, she noticed the scales of justice charms in solid gold. She sprinted across the road and into the coffee shop to call the police. Unknown to her, the stranger remained close by. He stood on the rooftop of the building to the right of the alley and watched her entering the coffee shop. Once he knew she was safe, he tapped himself just behind the ear with his index finger.

"Did you see it, Doc?" Brown sat next to his super computer NIGHT and watched the entire event from the Shadow Crypt.

"Saw the whole thing from your eyes to my monitor, even the mini-spy device caught it. Not bad, kid. But some advice if you wish?" Brown queried

"Sure."

"Next time, if you want to use a verbal command, you could just simply use your tongue to silence your voice equalizer. The feature acts like a soundproof barrier, so the enemy doesn't have to know what you are planning to do, or if you wanted to talk to me privately as well. They won't see you do it since it's all done inside of your mask," Brown explained. "Then use your tongue again to click back to channel. Alright?" Kevin clicked the silencer with his tongue. In this mode, Brown heard Kevin's actual voice, and not the artificial voice by the equalizer.

"Understood, Doc," Kevin replied "Anything else?"

"Yeah, two things. One, don't increase your strength to second level, first level is sufficient enough for thugs. You don't want to kill anybody, understood."

"Got ya, and two?"

"Two, there is a bank robbery happening at the First National Bank. Emissary confirmed that there is a heist in progress. I have already given the coordinates to your NIGHT I bike; the bank is about five minutes away from your location." Brown named his mini-spy device Emissary. The probes circled the city at supersonic speed searching for criminal activity. The spheres were no larger than a softball, but they were as resilient as a diamond.

190

"Understood." The teen clicked his voice speaker on to channel. *"Time to get the rest of my stuff."* And he dove from the roof. In mid air, he gave the voice command for his jacket to transform into his gliding cloak without broadcasting it into the open. He glided sixty feet to the ground with great ease. Upon landing, he grabbed the mini-amps he used to echo his voice to the thugs. He glanced at the road, and the bike pulled up on auto driver.

"I'm on my way to the bank. Time to make a personal deposit." And he rode away from the alley. As he cleared the scene, he heard sirens in the distance, heading towards the coffee shop.

While waiting for Kevin's arrival, Brown probed his computer for any strategic advantage.

"NIGHT, I need a lock on the bank and the bio-signs inside." The computer downloaded the information it received from one of the Emissary devices. The devices had a unique ability; besides, the digital camera and recorder, it could position itself to monitor precise areas. It possessed the ability to bend light and merge colour with an object close to it. It worked almost on the same principals as the defence mechanism of a chameleon. Taylor entered the room to see if the operation's first night was going according to plan.

Taylor sat next to Brown and asked, "How's our boy?"

"So far, so good. He's stopped a gang of thieving rapists earlier," Brown replied. "Now he's attempting to stop a bank robbery." Brown's computer displayed the information he needed.

"There are six bio-signs, doctor. However, one of them appears unconscious," NIGHT said.

"I'm willing to assume that one is the security guard," he said before the turned on his com-link. "What's your ETA, kid?"

The young vigilante replied, *"I'm right in front of the bank now."* And he switched to silencer mode.

"Good, now there are five of them, one guard is down," Brown instructed.

"I'm switching to x-rays now." The light of his visor switched to a dark yellow. "I see them, you're right, Doc. Five of them are emptying the safe, and one is one the floor—and he's not moving," Kevin said.

"They got inside through the top window. I suggest you do the same."

"I'm on it." He fired his launcher to the top of the roof, and in a flash, he ascended like a rocket.

With his silencer mode turned off, he said, *"It's play time."* He looked down on the action inside the bank. Two of the five were guarding the area while the other three were busy cleaning out the vault.

"I can get them from up here, Doc." He took out two guns from his side holsters.

"Do you have a clear shot at them?"

"Ohhh yeah."

191

"Take them out." The darts produced an almost silent hum as they were released from the barrel of the gun. The projectiles hit both of their targets in simultaneous fashion; the dart carried a sleeping compound that could induce unconsciousness for three hours.

"Ouch!" the both of them said. The two felt an urge to scratch, and they grabbed the back of their necks. In a matter of seconds, their eyes began to glaze over, and a sudden dizziness came over them. They fell asleep and thumped onto the floor. The other three inside the vault were using drills at the time, so they did not hear their colleagues fall. This gave the young vigilante a chance to dive from the top roof window and land without alerting the remaining conscious robbers. Instead of turning his cape back into his jacket, he left it loose, so he could see how well he could fight with it on him. He spotted the guns of the other three on the ground. He took out a capsule from his belt and applied a mist to them. The guns dissolved before his red eyes. Meanwhile, the three robbers were relishing the fruits of their labour.

"Look at all of this money, man," the first one said with greed in his eyes.

"I know. I told you we wouldn't have any problem getting in here," the second one replied.

"Of course we can do it, we are the best of the best," the third one said while he took out the precious jewels from one of the safety deposit boxes.

"Look at this, guys. We hit the jackpot!" The other two were in awe of their find.

"Yes! I wonder what we're going to get for this baby?" the second replied. Then a fog filled up the vault.

"Twenty to thirty years I think. Maybe a little less for good behaviour!" the chilled voice said from behind them.

"Who the hell said that?"

The vigilante appeared from the mist and said, *"I did!"*

"Who the hell are you?"

"Your worst nightmare, punks!"

"Get our guns!" one of them said, but noticed the melted steel on the floor.

"How the hell did that happen?" one of them asked. "No matter, grab our gear, boys." And the bank robbers came after him.

"I see Moe has a crowbar, Larry has a sledgehammer, and Curly has a huge torch." He took out a thick rod about the eight inches in length. *"Well, I have a weapon, too; can I play?"*

"What the hell are you gonna do with your little stick, freak?" the first one demanded, and the other two laughed out loud.

"Oh, this little thing here," he replied. *"Well, maybe…this."* The stranger squeezed the rod. It extended in both directions and extended into a staff. They charged him with their weapons, but the dark hero blocked all of their moves. The third one turned on his flamethrower and released the flames at the dark stranger.

"Watch him burn, guys," he said as the flames smothered the dark one. However, the flame extinguished when it made contact with his suit. *"You fools, you can't kill what you can't understand!"* the stranger said. The three robbers could not believe the flames went past him and inflicted no damage to the dark stranger whatsoever.

The first one gasped. "Did you see that?" And he fainted from the intense fear that consumed his body and the root of his soul. The other two tried to continue the battle, they were afraid as well, but they knew they had to fight for their lives. They tried to outmanoeuvre him with their weapons, but the dark figure with the red eyes moved like lightning and blocked each attack with his staff. With one quick jump over their heads, he disarmed the both of them with one forward thrust. The first one, fearing for his own safety, pushed his partner right into the dark spectre.

"What are you doing?" The second one shouted and fell into the stranger's arms.

The first one replied, "I got to do what I got to do." And started running for the exit.

"Why, I never had a guy fall for me before, Heh, Heh. But don't worry, your friend will be back with you soon enough." The stranger knocked him out with one punch. And then he looked at the final one trying to escape through the front door.

"Where are you going? I thought we had something." He took off his fedora. *"Target, lock, hostile!"* And he threw it towards the robber. The speed of the fedora accelerated as the guidance system inside it followed the robber and struck him in the back. Similar to Brown's old boomerang, his fedora had more accuracy and could engage multiple targets. The robber screamed in pain and fell onto the ground. With a little gesture from the vigilante's hand, the hat returned to him. He walked towards the robber and tied him with manacles. He rolled the crook over on his back with his foot.

The robber in pain, looked at his red eyes and yelled, "Who the hell are you?"

"I'm the innocent you can't hurt anymore. Tell your friends I have returned." The stranger headed towards the bank alarm and turned it on. The alarm cried out, and the dark stranger dropped necklaces on each of the four men on the ground. He returned to the last robber he had just trapped and laughed.

"Number of robbers knocked out: five; money stolen from the vault: zero; getting their butts whipped by the good guy: priceless." The dark stranger dropped a necklace on the robber's chest. The robber noticed the gold scales of justice matched his crest on his chest. *"Good night."* The dark stranger tipped his fedora to the robber, and a smoky mist filled part of the room. All of a sudden, he disappeared, and the front door opened. A laugh haunted the robber as the door closed behind him.

"What was that thing?" he cried, and his heart rate increased. He tried to look around, but all he could see were the shoes of police officers arriving at the scene.

Already three blocks away from the bank and the police, the young teen received another transmission from Brown.
"How are you doing, kid?"
"Pretty good, Doc. Is it time to come back to the crypt?"
"Sorry, kid. We got one more call that just came through."
"What have we got?"
"Some nut about three miles from your position is holding three kids hostage in his ex-girlfriend's apartment. He has a bomb, and he's going to use it. He's on the top floor, the cops are trying to get to him. However, he's barricaded the front door, and he has the lights off—so the sharp shooters can't get a clear shot."
"I hope I can get there on time."
"Look at your control panel. There is a red button just underneath your view screen."
"I see it, Doc."
"Good, press it and hold on, kid." Kevin obeyed his order. The button ignited the turbo boosters of the bike.
"Wow!" The engine made a powerful zoom, and the bike accelerated beyond the teen's imagination. At this rate of velocity, he would arrive within minutes.

Max Aspen became the master of his world as he held his ex-girlfriend's children at gunpoint, with a bomb attached to his chest. The police were in the hallway next to the open door, but the road towards him—barricaded. All they had were glimpses of him and the bomb, nobody knew if he had already initiated the timer. He engaged in a firefight with the police for the previous thirty minutes. Inspector Somerville of homicide was headed for home when he received the call, and until the negotiator arrived, he assumed command of the situation. He and three officers were trying to get a better look at him while the mother stood at the far end of the hallway with an officer. Aspen wanted her to speak to him on the phone, so Somerville arranged for her to talk to him while they thought of a plan to save the kids and disarm the bomb before he activates it or much worse—it explodes.
"She has the phone now, Aspen," Somerville stated to the madman. "She's calling you!" The phone rang, and he tightened his grip on the receiver and picked it up.
"Hi, Mary. I got your kids. I told you that you were never going to leave me. You took away a huge piece of my life, so now I'm going to take a piece away from yours," he said with a strange smile on his face.
"Don't do it, Max. I beg you, please don't hurt them!" she begged.

"You got to be taught a lesson, Mary. I am sorry. Say goodbye to the children," he said. In one vile act of revenge, he moved the receiver next to the kids. They were all under six years old, and were terrified.

"Mommy! Mommy! Mommy!" they all cried in a horrified harmony.

It tore Mary apart, and she yelled at him on the phone. "For God's sake, Max, don't do this."

"But I have to, Mary," he said with a calm voice. "Goodbye." And he hung up the phone.

"Listen to her, Aspen. You don't have to do this," Somerville shouted back. The officers waited for the word to storm in.

"Shut up, pig! If you come in here, we are all seeing the Devil tonight!" he roared back. Somerville took his two-way radio and contacted the sharpshooters at the building across the street.

"Singh, do your men have a shot?"

"Negative, inspector. It's too dark. Wait! I see something moving on the roof of the next building. It's hard to describe."

"What do you mean?" Somerville asked.

"My God, it just jumped across; how could that be possible?"

"Is it one of our guys?"

"No, I doubt it, inspector," the shooter said, zooming his lens and searching for what he thought he saw. "We are searching the area now."

"Anything?"

"Nothing, sir. With all the activity, I must have imagined it. We are returning back to our previous target." However, the shooter did indeed see something or someone on that roof. The young vigilante used his cape to glide to the next building. He hid from the shooters thanks to the sensors in his suit that warned him of any movement that came from the rooftop across the road. Using his x-rays, he scanned the area. In the blink of an eye, he discovered a man with a handgun and three children who were sitting in the corner. The gunman stood near the window in the dark. The young hero crouched in haste and crawled to the edge of the building; he dropped a mist capsule to the ground. The mist covered the whole rooftop and the view of the shooters.

One of the shooters asked, "Hey, where in the hell did the smoke come from?" The young hero clamped a hook on the edge of the building and swung down towards the window. The mist covered him from both Aspen and the sharpshooters. Approaching the main window, he kicked it with all of his might.

The window shattered like a failed dream as he crashed into the room.

"What the hell was that?" Somerville said, trying to get a glimpse inside.

The dark room kept its secret. The attacker surprised Aspen, and the madman hesitated for a brief second. The dark vigilante spotted the gun thanks to his infrared vision.

He shouted, *"Factor of three."* And the suit augmented his strength to triple the force. He disarmed Aspen with a swift roundhouse kick to his gun hand. He finished the attack with a rapid forearm blow to his neck. The strength of the blow flipped Aspen to a perfect three hundred and sixty degrees in the air before landing on his stomach. Aspen's body collapsed onto the floor. The dark one spun Aspen around like a top and ripped the bomb and the straps off of his chest. He noticed the bomb had already been activated; and that he only had forty seconds to disarm it.

"The kids are safe, but the bomb is ticking. Everyone get out now and take the kids with you!" the stranger said. By the time the police breached the barricade to grab the kids, the stranger had already vacated the apartment.

"Susan, you're with me," Somerville said. "The rest of you, take her and the kids and get out of here." The remaining officers followed his orders and vacated the premises.

"Where are we going, inspector?" the constable asked.

"Up on the rooftop, I bet whoever this guy is, he must be trying to disarm the bomb," Somerville replied. Two officers ran towards the stairs that led to the rooftop of the building.

The young vigilante tried to dismantle the bomb with his teacher's guidance.

"Okay, kid. Good move, but next time, watch your strength. You nearly took his head off," Brown said.

"Alright, Doc. But right now, I have bigger problems. I have twenty-five seconds left. I tried scanning the wires, and I cut all the right ones, but it triggered a backup timer."

"Alright, kid. Just relax and remember your training. Take out a vial of liquid nitrogen and freeze it," Brown said. The young vigilante took the vial from his belt and poured it all over the bomb. Within seconds, the liquid froze the timer and the battery, deactivating the bomb.

"Thanks, Doc. We did it with just three seconds to spare." The rooftop door slammed open with a crash. He turned his head towards the clatter and said, *"Got to go, I have company."*

"Alright, stranger. Freeze." the young officer shouted.

"Calm down, officer. Here is your bomb." He threw it towards her. The bomb smashed into pieces upon hitting the ground.

"Hands up and don't move," she ordered as Somerville spotted the dark spectre.

"It can't be," he said in awe.

"You know who this clown is, inspector?"

"Oh, he knows, constable," the stranger said. *"I am the night, and we shall meet again."* The stranger jumped to the edge of the building.

"You're not going anywhere!" the young officer said.

"Care to join me?" The spectre laughed as he lifted his hands in the air and fell backwards into the streets below.

"I can't believe he just did that!" The officer freaked out and rushed towards the edge of the building. "This can't be!"

"Let me guess, he just disappeared, right?" Somerville smirked.

"Yeah, how did you know?"

"I saw him do that over twenty years ago, constable." Somerville returned towards the stairs.

"You know who he is?"

"Yep. And I know this will not be the last time we will see him."

"Then who is he?" the officer queried. Somerville took a few more steps forward to the stairs, turned around, and faced the officer and smiled.

"You know I was thinking of retirement, but now that he's back; I'm going to stick around for awhile longer."

"But you still didn't tell me who he is?" The officer grew impatient.

"His name is the Shadow Chaser." Somerville smirked, "and as of this moment, the nights in this city are going to be pretty different, constable." Somerville returned to the stairs and abandoned the rooftop.

Chapter 28

Sophie woke up to an unfamiliar sound coming from her apartment. The kettle whistled as she entered the kitchen.

"Morning, Mom," Kevin said, walking towards the table. "Have a seat, breakfast will be ready in a sec." She could not believe her eyes; Kevin had set the table and placed the kitchen utensils in the proper order. Kevin loved his mother with great devotion, but he never took the time to prepare breakfast for her in his life, nor did he ever use proper table etiquette.

"Wow, Son." Sophie beamed. "Where did these new qualities come from?"

"Well, it was part of my training in Japan. They honour their parents there, so I thought we could use some of that custom here." Kevin smiled and handed her a plate.

"Bacon and eggs. I'm impressed, pup," she said. Kevin placed the toast next to her.

"Don't forget the tea, the croissants, and the jam, Mom." Kevin joined her at the table.

"Look at the kitchen," she said, "it's the first time it's been cleaned up without me asking you to take care of it." Sophie grabbed her fork and sampled some of Kevin's cooking.

"Well, don't expect this every day, but since I am home, I just wanted to show you a little bit of what I have learned."

"Now that's something I haven't seen in a long time, a smile from my son's face." She held onto his left hand. "I missed your smile."

"I still feel her loss, Mom. But I found a way to deal with it; this new job makes me feel I'm doing something important."

"Well, I know the money is good. Six hundred dollars a week is good for a guy who hasn't finished high school yet, but I don't like you working late at night."

"I finished school for the year, Mom. I will be returning in September."

"Alright then, but those hours are going to change in August. Do I make myself clear, pup?"

"Yes, ma'am," Kevin said. "Do you want me to turn on the TV for you?"

"Sure, dear," Sophie replied before she took a sip of her tea. "Might as well find out what's happening in the world." Kevin grabbed the remote and turned it on to the local station.

"News is on right now, Mom." Kevin returned to his seat.

"Leave it there, pup," she replied as the anchorman spoke.

"Good Morning, Toronto. In our city, our outstanding police officers face danger on a nightly basis, but last night they had a little help from an unknown stranger. Cecil Owens reports on how these events may mean that an old vigilante may have returned to play judge and jury on our streets." The scene switched to the reporter on the scene.

"Last night was a typical night for the Toronto Metropolitan Police Services with the exception of three cases, an attempted rape, a bank robbery, and a madman holding hostages while tied to a loaded bomb. What's so different you may ask? These criminal actions were stopped by a dark stranger in black with a black hat and red eyes who appeared and disappeared into a cloud of smoke and mystery," the reporter said while visual scenes of the alley, the bank, and the building where the madman was holding the hostages appeared. "Some have added that he had a cape, some said no. But for those of us who remember the same descriptions of a certain vigilante in the 70's, one would might ask if he has returned? Could it be the Shadow Chaser, after all these years? Well, according to Sandy Benjamin, a student at the University of Toronto, she owes her life to a stranger in black with red eyes. We caught up with her at the hospital with her friend, Craig Keller, this morning to discuss the events of last night." The scene turned to the young girl and her friend at the front exit of the hospital.

"I took a wrong turn after I left the pub. Two men followed me while a third one hid in the alley and grabbed me as I walked by. They were going to rape me and maybe even kill me; then some smoke materialized, and this dark thing with red eyes appeared," she said. "After he took them out one by one, he tried to help me up, but he scared me and I got up myself. I know now he was trying to help, and I wish to say thank you." Her friend intervened before she could add more to the story.

"Alright that's all! She needs her rest, and she's been through enough," he said, taking her away from the reporters. The clip returned to the reporter on the scene.

"Police also are investigating a bank robbery where the robbers claimed that a monster in black with red eyes appeared and stopped them; then he disappeared. According to early reports, one of the robbers tried to burn the dark stranger with a flamethrower, but the fire did not even affect him. Police say they are still investigating as well as taking statements from two officers who witnessed a dark stranger on the rooftop disarming a bomb after he knocked out a man holding his ex-girlfriend's children at gunpoint. The abductor had a bomb attached to him with a timing device that had been activated. Police are not giving any comments until they have finished their investigation. As for the madman, the woman, and children involved, the police are mum on that information as well. Has Shadow Chaser returned? Only time will tell. Cecil Owens, RJBTV Toronto." Sophie switched the channel twice, and each time there were talks about this unknown stranger. She clicked on for about twenty channels before she found her game show on the air. Kevin placed the dishes in the sink.

"Wow, what do you think about that, Mom?"

"I remember hearing about this guy when I was younger, back in 85, I believe. Mark was four at the time."

"This is the first time I ever heard of this guy," Kevin said. He put on his best poker face as he grabbed a glass of orange juice.

"Well, we have enough trouble in this city without some psycho in a black suit coming back again. I would love to meet the parents of that freak," she said. Kevin choked on his orange juice. "Are you okay, pup?"

"I'm fine," Kevin said, "just went down the wrong pipe, Mom." He placed his glass in the sink and started to do the dishes. "Once I am done with the dishes, I have to go to PET and pick my courses for September and to say hi to the gang."

"Don't worry, dear. I will do the dishes, you go ahead; remember to be at Ray's for noon. The rest of the family would like to see you again. I called them last night and said you will be in Toronto this morning at six just as you asked. Ray is setting up a welcome home dinner."

"I will. Thanks, Mom." Kevin passed the washcloth to his mother. "I will see you in a little while." Kevin gave his mother a peck on the right cheek, grabbed his jacket, and left the apartment.

"Welcome home, Kevin." Sophie beamed and started washing the dishes. Happiness filled her soul, for her son was home.

Caught in a whirlwind of news, the Toronto Guardian scrambled to find the truth as journalists sought out more information on the events of the previous night. Downstairs in the press room, the place reeked of ink. The printing press ran for most of the night. And for the first time in the paper's short history, the morning edition sold out. The Guardian's most experienced reporter, Mike Smith, was no stranger to the Shadow Chaser case. A cub reporter at the Toronto Gazette in the mid 70's, his editor assigned him to the Shadow Chaser beat. Each time they confirmed a Chaser sighting—a phrase he coined, he would investigate the scene and read any reports no matter how bizarre. He drove Staff Sergeant Somerville nuts with barrages of questions regarding the Shadow Chaser investigations. However, in 1987, the sightings had faded as suddenly as they began. By 1988, the paper transferred him to the crime beat. He stayed with the paper until last year when he joined the Guardian. As time passed by, the public and the media just disregarded the dark stranger, and the legacy of the Shadow Chaser vanished into the abyss; but he had always wondered if the vigilante would ever return. Thus, last night's events were like a calling to him, and he swore this beat would belong to him again, no matter what the cost. Smith stepped inside his editor's office and hoped he would get the assignment.

"Mike, did we get anything from Metro yet?" the editor asked.

"Nothing yet, Peter. They are as tight-lipped about last night's Chaser sightings as they were twenty years ago. But I know how to get them talking; I know this guy's pattern."

"I know what you want, Mike. You want this story, but Mike you are my most experienced reporter. I need you at Queen's Park, not in the slums of Toronto chasing an enigma," the editor said.

"Just listen to me for a minute, Pete," Smith pleaded. "What if it is the Shadow Chaser, and we get the scoop ahead of the big boys like the Star, the Post, or the Globe? That would certainly give us an edge. Besides, you can't trust something like this to one of the younger guys like Dave or Randy. Don't get me wrong, they're good, and that's why they should be bugging the Premier. I want the Shadow Chaser, I think you owe me that much."

"I don't know, Mike. It may be nothing, and we can't afford to stay on this for long."

"Give me two weeks. If nothing comes out of it, I will volunteer to pull out. Come on, Peter. If I am right, you may become Canada's most famous editor. You gotta love the sound of that?"

"Alright, you old con artist. You have your two weeks—not a day more. Got it?"

Smith jumped out of chair and said, "You won't regret this, Peter. I promise you."

"I'm already regretting this, now get out of here before I change my mind," the editor said. Smith smiled and ran out of his office. Two other journalists watched Smith ran past them as he headed for the elevator.

"Where's the fire, Mike?"

"Sorry, can't talk, off to chase a shadow. Give my best to the Premier," he said. Then he entered the elevator to begin his hunt for the Shadow Chaser.

Tommy, Cole, Julie, Tina, Margaret, and Shauna were hanging out in the school hallway before they headed towards their next class of the morning. The group had done a lot of maturing over the last two years. The unbearable murder of their friend, Chloe, reminded them of the evil that existed in the world. And to add insult to injury, her killer had been acquitted. Graham Cassidy gained his freedom and walked back onto the streets with the blessing of the court. The final blow occurred when they witnessed Kevin leaving the fold behind to follow a new life in Japan. Margaret remained silent about the reasons for Kevin's departure, for she knew that, above all else, she had to protect his secret.

"It's just not the same anymore, guys," Tommy said, and gang nodded in agreement.

"I know what you mean, Tommy," Cole said.

"I still can't believe Chloe is dead and Kevin is gone," Tina said.

"I thought this group would always be together," Shauna said.

"It's just not fair. The one who should be suffering is free somewhere," Julie said.

"I know it's hard, but we have to remain strong for the rest of us. Besides, Kevin wouldn't want us to be sad," Margaret said when a familiar voice joined in the conversation.

"She's right, I wouldn't." They looked back in amazement and hollered like children.

"KEVIN!" The gang hugged him each in turn.

"It's good to see you again, hun," Tina said.

"It's good to see you, too, folks," Kevin replied.

Julie hugged him and said, "I missed you, Kevin." Kevin looked into her blue eyes and noticed how much more beautiful she had become.

"I see the girl I once knew in the young women who stands before me now." Kevin smiled.

"Yep that's Kevin, the smarmy poet." Shauna grinned. "He's back."

"You've gotten bigger, Kevin. What the hell did they put you on?"

"Soy products." Kevin laughed.

"Good to see you, bud," Cole said, and gave him a playful slap on the chest. Little did he know, last night, one of thugs shot and wounded Kevin in the same location where Cole had slapped him.

"Oww!" Kevin moaned.

"Are you okay, Kev? I didn't mean to hit you that hard," Cole said.

"It's okay, bud. It's just a strained muscle I injured before I left Japan." The bullet did not penetrate his armour, but a bruise remained from the impact.

"So, how long are you in Canada for?" Tommy asked.

"I'm here for good, except for the occasional business trip."

"That's great news," Tina said, happy to hear the good news.

"So, when do you start class again?" Shauna said.

"I'm all done for this year. The advantages of going to the private schools in Japan."

"You lucky son of a...." Tommy said, but Tina covered his mouth with her hand.

"Watch the potty mouth, buddy," she said.

"But I'm taking Grade 12 here in September. That's why I'm here to pick my courses. Then I'm off to Ray's for a family get-together," Kevin said, looking at Margaret. "Hey, sweetheart. You're kind of quiet. Where is my hug?" Kevin crouched, and Margaret hugged him.

"*You were a bad boy last night,*" she whispered. Kevin gave her a teasing look and smiled.

"*I wasn't the bad boy, they were,*" he whispered. And he got back up and looked at the group. "Well, I have to hit the road, so many things to do, so little time."

"Well, let's get together tonight then," Cole said.

"Sorry guys, I have to work late," Kevin replied.

"Well, there is a school dance on Friday; it starts at eight. Since I am on the student council, and you are coming back in the fall, I can get you a guest pass. I'm sure you can come for a few hours," Julie said in her usual charming way. Kevin did not want to commit, but he could never say no to that girl. The class bell rang, and Kevin had to decide.

"Sure why not, I will catch up with you all tomorrow night." Kevin waved to his friends. They returned the wave and took off for class. Kevin walked away with a quick step, storming for the exit and his dinner date with his family.

Inspector Somerville spent the entire night and most of the morning looking over the events that transpired just twelve hours ago. He could not believe he had seen the dark stranger again. The stranger recognized throughout the law enforcement and the crime world as the Shadow Chaser. The costume appeared different, and he had a crest on his chest that looked like the scales of justice, but the red eyes and voice were the same. He never thought he would see him again. After having vanished for twenty-two years, Somerville thought Shadow Chaser had met his death in some unknown battle; yet, after what he witnessed last night, it seemed the force, and he himself, had made a premature assumption. In another hour and a half, he had to join the police chief and other officers at a press conference about last night's sightings. He was looking over the reports from the attempted rape and the bank robbery when an old face from his past walked up to his desk.

"Good morning, inspector. It's been a while," the voice said. Somerville gave a slight tilt of his head and smirked.

"Mike Smith, I thought you had retired."

"Nope, just working at the Guardian as a political columnist," he replied. "Well, I was—until we had a Chaser sighting after twenty-two years."

"Now hold on, Smith. We cannot confirm this. All we have are a few witnesses who claimed to have met something that they could not explain. But before we take their word for it, let's look at our witnesses. The first one: Sandy Benjamin, the victim of a possible rape attempt. The poor thing was so traumatized she could have imagined anything. Then we have her three attackers. They were known and convicted drug users. As for the bank robbers, they were using toxic chemicals to break into the vault, the fumes may have gotten to them," Somerville explained.

"Okay, let's just say you are right for those two cases. It's the third one I'm interested in. The madman with the bomb, the one you were involved with." Smith grinned. "While on the rooftop, two of you witnessed a man in black with red eyes and a cool voice dismantling a bomb. Then doing a Peter Pan leap off the building and disappearing. I'm willing to say you and the young cop are reliable witnesses." Somerville rose from his seat.

"To tell you the truth, Smith," Somerville said, "I don't know what I saw."

"Yes, but your young officer said in her report that you thought he was the Shadow Chaser."

"How did you get access to a police report?" he asked, but noticed Smith smile at him. "Never mind, you know I could charge you for that."

"But you won't because you're a nice guy."

"If I'm a nice guy, then leave me alone, Smith. I have work to do."

"Just give me something, come on."

"We have a press conference in seventy minutes." Somerville grabbed his coat from the top of his chair. "You and your fellow bloodhounds could ask us anything you want there."

"Okay, inspector. But off the record, just between you and me. You know I will not print this," Smith said. "You know you can trust me."

"If it means you will get off my back, alright—but it better not be printed," he said. "What is it?"

"Is it him, is it really Shadow Chaser?"

"I don't know, Mike. But it sure looks that way," Somerville said, and he left the area—leaving Smith alone with his thoughts.

Chapter 29

*K*evin's family had finished the final touches for his welcome home dinner at Shutouts. Upon hearing the news of Kevin's return, Ray and Mark spent the morning decorating the bar. Mark took the day off work, and Ray left the daily operations of the bar to his staff. Stephanie left to pick up Logan at school around noon, and Sophie would soon arrive with a cake. The family had not seen Kevin since Christmas, and they missed him like crazy. But his mother missed him the most. While he lived in Japan, she stayed alone in her little apartment, but it felt like an empty mansion with all the children gone. She prayed for his safe, speedy return. She knew one day he would find his road home, and in her mind, God had answered her plea.

"Well, the streamers and the banners are up. What do you think?"

"Looks good, Ray," Mark said. "It will be good to see him again."

"It sure will," he replied. "I bet you miss him, Mark."

"Yeah, he always followed me when he was a little kid; sometimes I felt like ditching him, but most of the time he was okay for a little kid. Things changed when Dad was killed overseas, I became more of a father figure to Kev. He was a good kid then, and he still is today."

"You and your mother have done well with him, Mark."

"We had a lot of good times together. I just started college when Mom hired Stephanie to baby-sit for her. When I was visiting home for Thanksgiving, I met her for the first time. We fell in love and got married. So, I guess I owe that to my brother as well," Mark said, reminiscing about the past.

"You two reminded me of Kevin and poor Chloe," Ray said, his face sombre.

Mark replied, "Yeah, I know. What makes me even angrier with this damn mess is that son of a bitch didn't even pay for the crime. There is just no damn justice anymore." Sophie walked inside with Stephanie and Logan.

"Hello, ladies and our young gentleman. Are we ready to celebrate?" Ray asked.

"Yes, we are," Sophie replied, and placed the cake at the centre of the table. Stephanie enjoyed the aromas of soup, shrimp, and fresh bread. The happiness of the moment filled her soul with warmth and hope.

"That smells great, Ray," she said.

"Why thank you, my dear. It's all ready. All we have to do is wait for our guest of honour to arrive."

Logan looked at the adults and asked, "Can I help?" Ray looked at him and smiled.

"We're all done, buddy. But maybe you can watch for your uncle at the door."

"Okay!" He ran towards the door and waited for several minutes—then he screamed, "Uncle."

Kevin opened the door and said, "Hey, half-pint. You missed me?"

"Yes, I did!" he said, jumping. Kevin picked him up and carried him into the room. .

"I missed you, too, Logan." The rest of the family ganged up on Kevin.

"Hey, little brother. You look good, but you are still ugly." Mark hugged him.

"You don't look so good yourself." Kevin laughed.

"What about me, bro?" Stephanie said, holding her arms out for him.

Kevin hugged her and smiled. "Of course. Besides, you deserve a hug everyday for putting up with this guy."

"Good to see you again, Kevin," Ray replied, and he extended his hand.

"It's good to see you, too, Ray." Kevin returned the handshake.

"Well, let's all sit down, the meal is ready," Sophie said. Kevin took his backpack off before sitting.

"Before we start, I have some gifts for you all." Kevin handed them each souvenirs from Japan. They all enjoyed the marble dragon statue they each received from Kevin. Logan, empty handed, looked up at his uncle.

"Where is my gift, Uncle?" he asked with a sad face.

"Well, half-pint. I thought I would give you this instead." Kevin took out a assortment of Pocket Monster collectables.

"WOW," he cheered. "Thank you, Uncle." Logan said, and hugged Kevin.

Kevin replied, "I'm glad you like them, buddy." Sophie and Ray placed the meal on the table, and the family gathered around the feast.

"Alright let's sit down and say grace," Sophie said, and they all followed suit. Kevin still did not support his mother's religious beliefs, but he went along. "Dear Lord, we thank you for the food we are about to receive, and we thank you for having Kevin back with us. We pray that this family will see happier times in the future. Amen." After the reply—the celebration commenced. Kevin watched his family at the table, and he temporary felt his spirit rejoicing, for he missed his family with all of his heart while he lived half a world away. But reality had set in, and once again, his heart began to break. The last time they were all together as a family was on the day Chloe died, and she was with him there. From that moment on, he knew things would never be the same again. After the meal and the cake, they took pictures and relaxed in the dining lounge for the afternoon.

"Do you want me to put on the ball game, Kevin?."

"Sure, Ray." Ray turned on the TV. But a press conference preempted the scheduled game.

"What's this?"

"I heard about this, Ray. It's that vigilante guy who was seen all over the place last night," Mark said. Ray turned up the volume. Their attention focused on the conference already in progress.

"Inspector Somerville, can you tell me what exactly happened last night?" one of the reporters asked.

"Well, it is true that a young university student, Sandy Benjamin, was brutally stalked and assaulted, but before her three attackers were able to inflict any additional damage, an individual did stop them, using brutal force of his or her own. The suspects were subdued and confined with some kind of manacles before this mysterious individual placed gold scales of justice charms in front of them," Somerville read the report.

"Why did he do that? We also heard that there were shots fired in the ally?" Another reporter blurted out.

"Yes, there were shots fired, we have found some casings in the ally, now there are two of them that are not accounted for. According to one of the perpetrators and the victim, the suspect fired two shots at the individual, and he fell; but the person got back up and appeared unharmed. However, I cannot imagine that would be the case. The alley was dark at the time, and we will eventually recover the unaccounted for bullets. As for the charm, it must be some kind of calling card," Somerville added.

"What about the other two events?"

"Yes, there was another sighting of this individual at the First National Bank shortly after the attempted rape of Sandy Benjamin. Five world-renowned bank robbers, you may know them by their trade name, the Blackhawk Five, were in the process of robbing the bank when this individual appeared and stopped them. The same manacles and five charms were found at the scene, one for each of the suspects."

"One of the robbers claimed to have used a flamethrower on the individual. But he says the flames didn't do anything to him. Could you verify that?"

"No, I cannot. Next question."

"Inspector, Mike Smith for the Guardian. What I want to know is what can you tell me about the situation you were involved in last night?" Somerville gave a reluctant answer to his query.

"Last night, I was on my way home when I received a call to go to a hostage situation. When I arrived, the suspect, Max Aspen, was holding his ex-girlfriend's children at gunpoint. He had a homemade bomb strapped to his chest. Aspen told the mother he was going to kill them and himself because she had left him. He then turned off the lights and barricaded the front entrance, so we couldn't get to him. One sniper on the roof of the building across the street believed he saw a dark figure, but couldn't get a proper visual. However, just after Aspen activated the timing mechanism in the bomb, a mist appeared from the roof of the building, and the window smashed into pieces. We couldn't see what went on, but within seconds, the suspect was down and the bomb removed from his person."

"Did you see the individual?" Smith redirected.

"Not at first. We heard an eerie voice that said the suspect was down, but the bomb was still armed. He told us to take the kids out of there. When we broke down the barricade, he was gone. I figured he was trying to disarm the bomb. So, one of the officers and I went up to the roof. When we arrived, we witnessed this person in black with a cape and a hat. We tried to hold him there, but he jumped off the roof and disappeared," Somerville said.

"So, are you telling me it's the Shadow Chaser? He's back, isn't he?"

"Now, Mr. Smith, I'm not saying anything of the kind. But we have reopened the file on him in case it's either a copycat or something else."

"Inspector, I have a letter that was sent to the Guardian, and it was also sent to other media outlets around the city," Smith said. "This is what it says." And he read the letter. "*For those whose travels embrace integrity, guided by an enlightened awareness, respectfully roaming the narrow path of self-determination, the shadow you cast is my refuge and my stage. For those that create fear out of uncertainty, exploiting gloom while promising deliverance, ensnaring your prey as they stumble through the fogs of self-doubt, you may consider me your adversary. For those of diminished faith and compromised temperament, my hand is out reached, to elevate you above your apprehension and out of the shadows. Yet, in the shadows, I must remain a ghost of justice filled with a need for retribution, burdened by an anger never fully constrained. I am confined by the wall that divides joy from sorrow and conquest from loss, never to be released. Stand Back: the shadows are mine! I am the Shadow Chaser.*" Somerville looked at the rest of his fellow officers and the police chief. And with all promptness, the chief took over the podium.

"Well, thank you, ladies and gentlemen, we will look into this. For now we have nothing further to add." The reporters acted like hungry dogs turned loose in a butcher shop and demanded answers. But the officers dashed out of the room, and the press conference came to an abrupt end. Ray turned off the TV and sat next to Sophie. They, for the exception of Kevin, were in utter amazement.

"Can you believe that?" Ray said. "Is it really that guy from the 70's?"

"He must be a dinosaur now the old freak," Mark said.

"I didn't hear much about this Shadow Chaser thing. Who was he?" Stephanie asked.

"He was this vigilante dressed up in black and trying to make himself appear like a ghost to criminals," Sophie said.

"What did he do to the bad guys?" Logan asked, listening to their conversation.

"He used to confront them and tie them up for the police to take them away." Kevin smiled. "Kinda like the comic books."

"Wow, he's a super-hero. Cooool," Logan replied with excitement, but Mark wasn't happy.

"He's a freak! There is nothing cool about this guy, Logan. Uncle Kevin should know better than to glamourize someone like him to a little boy."

"I didn't mean anything bad, Mark," Kevin said.

"Then don't promote the guy, Kev. He's trouble, and I will not have my son thinking that this freak is some kind of role model. I won't allow it," Mark scolded his younger brother. Kevin wanted to say something in retaliation, but he could not say much for the sake of the family. He had to keep his secret that the freak, his brother thought of as nothing but scum, was none other than his *own* younger brother.

"Okay, boys. We are not here to fight over this clown," Sophie said.

"Your mother is right. How about we have a few more drinks, and a sundae for the half-pint," Ray said. Kevin stood and looked at the time.

"I'd like to, but I have to get to work in another hour." Kevin looked at his family. "Thanks for the welcome home party. I'll see you all later." Mark felt bad about the outburst.

"How about I pick you up after work, Kev," he said.

"No, thanks. I'm working late." Kevin opened the door.

"Why are your hours so late?"

"It's not my fault." He grinned. "It's the company I keep, bro." Kevin walked away from the bar and headed for the crypt for some early training before another night of reckoning as the Shadow Chaser.

The Mark II battle suit hung there on the wall while Arthur Brown confirmed its power supply before Kevin would don it and once again assume the name that Brown had adopted for all of these years, the Shadow Chaser. An energy battery cell powered each suit with a ten-hour charge, along with thirty minutes of emergency power. The suit came with three more energy cells; each of them supplied with an extra three hours of reserve power. So far, Kevin expended three hours of power; thus, the original cell would last for at least another night.

Kevin entered the vault room and asked, "Hey, Doc. What are you up to?"

"Just doing a diagnostic on the suit, kid," he said, scanning it for damages. "You have seven hours of power left in the suit."

"Why don't you just recharge it then?"

"If you would have remembered the briefing, kid, you know that for every hour the suit is used, it takes two hours to recharge it. So, I want to use the remaining power left."

"How are all of the other suits working?"

"The five are ready to use when needed. Your weapons are at full inventory, so you won't have to worry about running out of something in the field."

"So, are they all linked to my DNA now?"

"Ah, so you do pay attention at times." Brown smirked. "Yes, they are all in sync with your DNA, and nobody can use them; unless I reprogram them, but I don't have forty-eight hours to do that."

"Sorry about pushing my strength the other night, Doc. Just I panicked."

"Don't worry about it, kid. Just next time watch it because the strength increase can drain power levels faster, and prolonged increases can make it painful for your muscles."

"So, tonight, could I use the other goodies?"

"You mean the chameleon effects, the holo-spheres, and recorders? Sure, knock yourself out," Brown said.

"Cool, so when do I go after Cassidy?" Kevin probed with interest.

"Well, kid, I got NIGHT to do a search for him, and it appears he's left the country for the moment, but don't worry I have our agents looking for him. Once we hear something, we will plan to get him."

"You mean we lost him? With all of this high-tech equipment, and our agents monitoring the entire planet, we still lost him?" Kevin asked, his voice damped with anger and cynicism.

"It happens, kid. Don't worry—we will get him. But for now, the night is coming, and we have other scum to fight." Brown grabbed Kevin's left shoulder and said with a gentle tone. "Kevin, we will get him. It just takes time."

"I know, Doc. I'm sorry for the attitude, just had a rough day with the family," Kevin said.

"How did the welcome back party go?"

"It was great, until we turned on the TV and watched the police's press conference on the Shadow Chaser. My family thinks I'm a greater threat than the criminals, and my brother lectured me for telling his son that Shadow Chaser was an okay guy," Kevin replied.

"Well, get use to it, kid. A lot of people don't like us. But we are not in this war to be loved or admired, just to fight the stench of injustice."

"I know, Doc. Just don't like the feeling that my family thinks I'm scum."

"Not you, Kevin, Shadow Chaser," Brown pointed out.

"But I am Shadow Chaser."

"You may dress like him, but you haven't earned that name yet in my eyes. You have a lot to learn, remember that," Brown said.

"Thanks for the vote of confidence, boss. It's nice to know you have faith in me," Kevin said with some bitterness in his voice. "So, when are you going to call me Shadow Chaser?"

"When you are ready, and when you have earned it. But that's enough for now. I have something for you." Brown gave Kevin a box.

"What's this?"

"Open it, kid." Kevin opened the box and took out a fancy sports watch.

"Nice, Doc. What do you want me to do with it?"

"The watch has four major functions. It serves as a location beacon for me to find you. If you turn the rings clockwise, you will have a mini-laser in case of emergencies. Turn the rings counter-clockwise, and you have a com-link to me and NIGHT at all times," Brown explained.

"Cool." Kevin fastened the watch on his wrist. "What's the fourth function?"

"This!" Brown pressed a button on the computer terminal.

Kevin received a shock and hollered, "Yeoow. What did you do that for?"

"It's my way of getting your attention. It's just little shock, but it tells you that Shadow Chaser is needed." Brown smiled. "Think of it as your personal pager."

"You're one sick guy, Doc," Kevin said.

"I know I am." He grinned. "Now, come with me, I have something to show you."

"What would that be?" Kevin asked.

"You'll see." Brown took Kevin further into the room and eventually revealed to the young teen a piece of Brown's history. "There she is, kid. My suit, the first Shadow Chaser suit; the Mark I." The suit resembled the first one, with the exception of the golden crest on the chest and the cape did not turn into a jacket.

"Wow, she looks good. Does it work?"

"Yes, she does. The suit has a battery cell that powered the suit for 4 hours. Quite limited in features compared to yours, but she would be the top of the line in today's market. I created her in 1975. This suit was thirty years ahead of its time, like yours is today," Brown explained.

"I'm impressed, Doc. But it's missing the mouth piece, the equalizer."

"I took it off and put it on the first Mark II suit. The one you are using right now. I thought by putting it on the new suit, it would make me feel that I am still out there."

"Makes sense to me, Doc." Kevin stared at the right pant leg of the suit. "Where did the hole come from?" Kevin queried.

"That's where Antonio Stavros shot me and granted me early retirement. I never fixed that part of the suit. I wanted to remind myself that all things come to an end," Brown said. Kevin tried to change the subject when he noticed two miniature buttons on the left glove that resembled his own.

"What does that do, Doc? They look like the same ones I have."

"You're a keen observer. I was attempting to put the electromagnetic force technology in my suit just before my last mission. I had not yet finished the modification, and I held off at the time. Maybe if I would have had it that day, I wouldn't have this leg today."

"Does it work?"

"It does, a few weeks after the incident I finished the link up. I couldn't have it as part of the suit, but the link up could transfer the upgrade from my computer at the time. But I was never able to put it to the test. My leg didn't want to play, so I never used it. But today, it can be upgraded by your suit or by NIGHT. With your access codes, you can transfer your field to this suit, and then the wearer of the suit would be able to use it as well," Brown demonstrated. "The one down side is the field only has a five second burst, so it would fry my circuitry within seconds after the transfer."

"Why don't you upgrade your suit, Doc?"

"Because I want to keep this suit just the way it is as part of my history. The Mark II is your history," Brown said. "Well, we used enough time on this subject. It's already eight; and it will soon be getting dark."

"Alright, I will get to the simulation chamber, Doc," Kevin said. "Oh, before I go, I'm going to a dance for awhile on Friday night."

"Kid's stuff."

"Well, I am still a teen, Doc."

"You can go, but be here for midnight. You will have stay out until 4:00 a.m.," Brown said. "Now, get going."

Kevin replied, "Right." And he left for the simulation chamber and prepared himself for another night in the concrete jungle.

Friday April 16, 2010:

Julie Simms and her friends were already at the school gym for the student dance, waiting for Kevin to arrive. For the last two days, the topic of conversation remained on the dark character who traversed the city during the night and stalked criminals. The guys in the gym were sharing stories they heard on the TV, radio, and the newspaper. However, the girls found it to be a waste of their time when there were more interesting subjects to talk about, such as guys.

"So, do you think he's going to strike again tonight?" Tommy asked.

"I don't know, but did you hear what he did last night?" Cole replied.

"No."

"He stopped a rapist who was stalking girls in the city," Cole replied. "According to police reports, he just appeared out of nowhere and knocked the crap out of the pervert."

"That's nothing, he stopped three gunmen as they were getting away from the police. This Mike Smith guy wrote that they were seen being chased by him on this cool bike of his. They were shooting at him; then he disappeared. As they turned their heads to the front, they spotted him in the middle of the road challenging them. They accelerated, and at the last second, he flicked his hand and the windshield shattered. Something grabbed the wheel and forced them right into a street pole," Tommy said, acting out the story. "Then he ripped off the doors with his bare hands, fought them all, and put the cuffs on them."

"He also leaves behind gold scales of justice charms, must be his calling card," Cole said. "My dad said the department keeps on getting calls about this guy, and if he's working with the police."

"So, what does your dad think about the guy?"

"What do you think? He's a vigilante, even though he's done some great things, my dad says he can't be allowed to run violently on the street like that. Somebody is gonna get hurt."

"But what do you think, Cole?"

"Hey I want to be a cop. It's my calling," Cole said, but noticed the look on Shauna's face. "I'm sorry, dear. But you've always known I wanted to be cop. But anyways, I can't support this guy either." Shauna tried to change the subject.

"Are you guys done yet?"

"Yeah, what's so special about this guy anyway?" Julie inquired. "Besides, we've got to concentrate on being there for Tina tonight."

"That's right. She broke up with that boyfriend of hers. Dave—Dave what's-his-last-name? Well, I never liked him anyway," Cole said.

"Julie is right, we have to be there for her," Tommy said. Tommy had a crush on Tina as much as Kevin had one on Julie. "We'll talk more about Shadow Chaser later, Cole." Kevin had just arrived when the conversation ended.

"Hey folks," Kevin said with glee as they approached him.

"Hey, Kev. Glad you could make it," Cole said.

Kevin replied, "I told you I would be here." He turned his head and looked at Julie. "Where is Chad, Jewel?"

"Oh, he was busy." She tried to hide the hurt in her voice. "His new job has him working late hours, and his boss demands a lot from him." Kevin acted like he believed her story.

"That's cool. So, he may show up after work. Where's Tina?"

"She should be here at any time. She had just broken up with her boyfriend before you returned from Japan," Tommy said.

"She's taking it hard, so maybe we could cheer her up. So, guys don't mention his name alright?" Shauna said.

"No problem," they replied. A few minutes later, Tina joined the fold.

"Hey sorry I'm late. I hope you guys weren't waiting long," Tina said. Kevin spoke for the group.

"No, not at all, we've just arrived."

"Wait, where is Margaret?" Julie asked.

"Oh, she will be here in a bit. Danny is picking her up. I told her we would save them a table," Kevin replied.

"Her and Danny are getting friendlier," Julie said.

"She's happy," Kevin replied. "So, shall we go in, folks?" And the gang followed him inside the gym. Tommy, looking at Tina alone in her thoughts, decided to make the first move.

"Tina, I know you are going through a tough time right now, so if you need a friend, I am here." He smiled.

"Thank you, Tommy. I'm lucky to have friends who care," she replied.

"Well then, would you like to dance?" Tommy asked.

Tina replied, "Yes, I would." The teens strolled onto the dance floor.

"Well, are you coming, sweetheart?" Shauna said to Cole.

"I'm right behind you, dear." Cole and Shauna joined Tina and Tommy. Kevin witnessed the sadness in Julie's eyes, but before he could ask her to dance, she said, "I have to go to the bathroom, I will be right back." Julie wanted to get away from the table before she began to cry.

"Sure, Jewel," Kevin said. Julie stood from the table and left. Kevin slapped his own forehead for his slow reaction to the situation.

Come on, Wolf. Now's your chance. Last night, you were fighting the world, now you can't even get up the courage to ask her for a dance. Margaret and Danny joined him at the table.

"Hi, Kevin."

"Hey, Margaret. You look great tonight."

"Why thank you. Kevin, this is Danny Mason. Danny, this is Kevin Wolf," she said. Danny greeted Kevin with a brief handshake. Danny Mason, PET's newest student, caught Margaret's eye from the moment they met on the first day at school. With his good looks and kind heart, Margaret could not help, but feel something for him.

"It's good to meet you, Kevin. Margaret has told me a lot about you," he said. Kevin still lived in Japan during the time Margaret met Danny.

Kevin replied, "Same here, Danny. She can't stop talking about you." Margaret blushed and gave Kevin a humourless look.

"Do you want me to get you a drink, Margaret?" Danny asked.

"Sure, please."

"Kevin, can I get you one?"

"No thanks, Danny. I'm fine for now."

"I will be back in a bit." Danny left the table and headed for the punch bowl. Margaret took the opportunity to encourage Kevin to talk to Julie.

"I see Tommy is spending time with Tina during her hard time," she said. "She got hurt by Dave again."

"That's what I heard. So, you and Danny are getting along quite well I see."

"You're in that mask too long, Kevin. You see things that are not there. We are just friends."

"Oh, of course," Kevin teased.

"What about you? Julie is coming out of the bathroom, and Chad is not here again. This is the third time in the last five weeks that he's a no-show. She doesn't even dance with anybody. She just sits there and watches everyone else have fun."

"Well, that's going to change," Kevin said.

"Good, now I'm going to wheel myself over to Danny to give you some privacy. Excuse me." She smiled, and she wheeled away. Julie arrived at the table. She spent the last few minutes fixing up her eye makeup because of the tears she shed in private.

"Hey, Jewel. I know Chad is not here, but since you're alone, I would be more than happy to have the next dance with you. We're friends, so you are not dating behind his back, it's just a friendly dance. You're here, so you might as well have fun," Kevin said.

"You don't have to do this, Kevin."

"But I want to. Next dance, okay."

"Alright then. Thanks, Kevin." She grinned.

"All a part of the service, Jewel," Kevin returned the smile, and the song ended. They were about to dance, when the song "Dust in the Wind" played. Julie knew that song belonged to Kevin and Chloe. Kevin stood there frozen like a statue. Julie took immediate action and grabbed his arm.

"Come on, Kevin. We will get the next one."

"Thanks, Jewel." Kevin felt if he danced with another girl to their song, it would betray Chloe's memory. However, unknown to both Kevin and Julie, Chad entered the school gym. In other dances, he stopped by from time to time just to see if Julie ever danced with anyone else while he claimed to be at work. But each time he arrived, Chad would see Julie sitting there like a log— while the others had fun. He enjoyed the control he had over her, but this time he spotted Kevin there, and he knew Kevin cared for her. So, he had to act before they could get even closer.

"Hey, baby," he shouted, and jogged towards the table.

"Hi, Chad." Julie glowed as she sprung up from the table and hugged him. Every time Julie looked at Chad, it brought the best out of her. And Kevin could sense her happiness increase tenfold when he entered the room. Kevin could not stand him for the way he treated her, but remained silent because he knew how much she loved him.

"Hey, Wolf. I heard you're back in town for good," he said.

"That's the rumour," Kevin replied.

"Listen, baby. I have few minutes to spare; then I have go," he said, "so let's dance."

Julie looked at Kevin for a brief moment before she turned her head towards Chad and said, "Oh, I can't dance to this, honey. This was Kevin and Chloe's song. I can't leave him here alone."

"But, baby, I only have time for one dance. I'm sure Kevin won't mind. Right, Wolf. You want her to have some fun before I go." Chad smirked.

"Go ahead, Jewel. You heard him, he's not staying for long," Kevin said. "So, go and enjoy yourself." But his heart shattered like glass.

"You don't mind?"

"No, go ahead."

"Thanks, Kevin," she said. "You're the greatest." And the couple left for the dance floor. Kevin felt like giant spear went through his back. He watched Chad danced with Julie and wished he had an excuse to leave. But he did not—that is until he felt a slight shock from his wrist meaning one thing; somewhere the innocent needed help from the Shadow Chaser. His instincts took over like a light switch as he turned the rings counter-clockwise and pressed his right shirt collar.

"Yeah, Doc."

"Sorry to ruin your party, kid. We have a situation in New York. I already asked Alex to call your mom and say you are spending the night at the mansion. Now, I know you asked for the evening off, but this is…" Brown said, but Kevin interrupted him in a brisk tone.

"I'm on my way." Kevin ceased the com-link and stood from the chair. Margaret wheeled close to him to see if he needed a friend to talk.

"I saw what that creep did. Are you okay?"

"I have to run. Tell the guys I got paged to go to work after all."

"What's wrong?"

"Bad guys again. Take care and have fun."

"Be careful, Kevin." Kevin knew by the soft sound of her voice that she worried about him and feared for his safety.

"Always." He winked. Then he left the gym and headed for the danger that awaited him in the abyss of darkness.

Sixteen hours had passed since Kevin left the teen dance to face an unknown evil in New York. Once again, Shadow Chaser removed another foul creature from the streets. Alexander Taylor watched the news coverage from south of the border about what had transpired last night.

Taylor appeared pleased with Brown's creation as well as the effort Kevin had put into the operation. However, Taylor knew the war would escalate and get tougher as they chased more dangerous offenders. He had just switched the channel when Brown entered the study.

"Hello, Alex. Sorry I'm late," Brown said, and poured himself a cup of coffee.

"Hi, Art. You just missed our boy on CNN."

"CNN? Wow I'm impressed."

"Well, at least you can catch this one," Taylor said, and they listened to a second news report.

"The citizens of New York City will be sleeping soundly now after the arrests of the notorious Head Hunter and his biker gang the Demon's Circle. This gang was wreaking havoc all across the United States for the past eight months. The leader of the gang, Damien Hunter, other known as the Head Hunter, wanted for forty-five counts of homicide as he and his gang continued their murderous rampage across the city," the reporter explained, and the image flashed on the TV. "Last night, the murderers were chasing three university students when a black spectre known as the Shadow Chaser appeared out of nowhere. After stopping the biker gang, the stranger fought a dangerous fight against the Head Hunter. This Shadow Chaser overpowered the large butcher and detained him and his gang until the police arrested them all. The FBI is now looking into the case. They have assigned Special Agent Jackson Flynn to the case. Agent Flynn was the former head of the vigilante task force; he is a leading authority on the Shadow Chaser. He said that if it is the Shadow Chaser, they will arrest the vigilante once and for all. Susan Haines, WRJB New York." Taylor turned off the TV and looked at Brown.

"How's the lad?" Taylor asked.

Brown applied pressure to his cane and got off his chair. He turned towards Taylor and said, "He's cut up a bit, but he will be fine. But that's not what's worrying me."

"What's wrong?"

"Flynn is back on the case, and that means he won't rest until we are stopped," he replied. "Alex, my friend, the war has just gotten that much harder on the Shadow Chaser and us." Brown walked out of the study to prepare for Flynn, for he knew things were about to become more complicated in the days to follow.

Chapter 30

May 14, 2010:

Arthur Brown and Alexander Taylor spent the afternoon in his office looking over the progress reports for the high-tech wing of Taylor Enterprises Canada. Already a month had passed since Kevin Wolf, the Shadow Chaser, had been clearing the streets of Toronto of crime. However, despite the name he had made for himself, his victories were against common criminals. With the exception of the Head Hunter and his biker gang, Shadow Chaser had yet to face his ultimate test, and Brown knew the time for a more challenging conflict might come sooner than later. Taylor dropped the report on the table and grinned.

"Well, Doc. It looks like we are way ahead of schedule. Profits have gone up another one per cent."

"Great news, Alex." Brown continued to read the document. "And it looks like Dr. Simms's Darwin Vaccine is ahead of schedule as well," he added with a touch of discomfort in his voice.

"Still worried about this vaccine thing, aren't you?"

"You've read my report. I don't think we should play God that's all."

"So, what are we doing now? By resurrecting Shadow Chaser aren't we playing God?"

"How so?"

"He is the judge. He chases the people whom we deemed guilty."

"But we don't take a life or try to alter life. Even though we fight against the system, we still use it when we gather enough evidence against the criminals we fight."

"I could never get the best of you, could I?"

Brown smiled. "What can I say? I hate to lose, Alex." The intercom buzzed.

"Mr. Taylor, Patrick Collins is here to see you," the voice said.

"Send him in please," Taylor replied before the door opened.

Patrick entered the room and said, "Good afternoon, gentlemen." Both men gave him a brief nod; then Taylor stood and glanced upon him.

"Mr. Collins, you have something for us?"

"Yes, Mr. Taylor. Arthur, do you remember the rumours we were hearing about a terrorist sect trying to purchase weapons of mass destruction?"

"Yes, everybody from NATO to INTERPOL is looking for the suspects."

"Well, our agent Gabriel has been watching the harbours in Europe, and he may have something for us," Patrick said.

"When is Gabriel contacting us?" Taylor asked.

"He's going to reach us in thirty minutes."

"Then we better go to the crypt," Brown said. Taylor pressed numerous buttons on his desk. Before time could react, the bookcase slid across, and the elevator that led to the crypt appeared.

Taylor asked, "Shall we go, gentlemen?" But just before he joined his friends, he contacted his executive assistant on the intercom. "Wanda, I'm going to be here for a while longer, but you can call it a day. I will see you tomorrow."

"Very well, sir. Have a good night, sir."

"You as well, Wanda," Taylor said while the other two waited for him in the elevator. Taylor followed with confidence in his footing, and the door closed. The elevator descended a hundred feet below the underground parking lot. When the door opened, the three entered a tunnel made of titanium. Brown and Taylor had built the tunnel as a short cut to get to the crypt. Sealed off from the rest of the building; so nobody would be aware of its existence. In front of them was a hybrid cart that would drive them to the crypt. A fifteen-kilometre distance separated the crypt from Taylor's Enterprises. On average, the trip took about twelve minutes. The whole process was a magnificent feat of ingenuity and engineering. Before they knew it, the three were facing the door that lead to the crypt. Brown typed in the access codes and then the door whooshed open. They entered the main room and waited for Gabriel's message. Brown approached the console.

"NIGHT, we will be receiving a visual communications from Agent Gabriel Cardieux, codename: Hawk. Prepare screen for protection one protocols and set up Provider Alpha program."

"Acknowledged, doctor. Protection one protocols are in effect, and beginning Provider Alpha program," NIGHT answered.

"I know protection one protocols are for authenticity of messages, voice matching, and blocking tracking systems, but what is Provider Alpha?" Patrick asked.

"Like I said, no one knows the identity of Alex or Kevin. The Provider and the Shadow Chaser are a mystery," Brown explained. "So, when I'm using visual communications with them in the room, NIGHT alters their appearances and their voices."

"I understand," Patrick replied. Within seconds, NIGHT intercepted the signal. "Incoming hail from Hawk."

"Patch us through." The screen activated, and the French agent appeared on the screen.

"Good morning, gentlemen. Or should I say good evening, non," he said with a Parisian tone in his voice.

"Good to hear from you, old friend," Patrick said.

"Good to see you, mon ami." He smiled. "I see dat we have zee docteur and zee Provideur with nous as well."

"We're one big happy family, Hawk. What do you have for us?"

"My government has been monitoring ships coming to our harbeurs considerably since zee onze de Septembre, and just recently we have had a small, but manoeuvrable diplomatic ship from Saudi Arabia called the Shiva's Bead, entering one of our harbeurs to deliver supplies to dere embassy as well as pick up cargo," he explained. "Dey cleared most of zee cargo, but a few of dem were diplomatic crates, and dey were not allowed to be opened. Dey stayed here for about tree days before leaving for Canada. Zee goods are supposed to be shipped to zee Saudi Embassy in Ottawa, but they will be delivered at zee consulate in Toronto. From there, they will be place on a avion to Ottawa."

"But you wanted a closer look at those diplomatic crates." Brown grinned.

"Exactly, docteur. So, I went in zee coveur of darkness and found dat zee crates had different kinds of weapons, but dey also had uranium in big amounts," he said.

"They had weapons-grade uranium?" Brown probed. Taylor and Collins were shocked with disbelief.

"I am afraid so, mon ami. I did a further examination in the ship, and I saw manuals on how to construire a mini-nuclear bomb in a suitcase."

"Is the ship run by the Saudis and the terrorists?"

"Da ship is Saudi, but I found dat zee ambassador is an agent of zee Group of 13, and he's got associates on zee ship. So, after making zee sale with zee terrorist in zee North American cells, he will deal with zee legal goods for his government." Taylor turned towards Brown.

"Group of 13? I heard about them once before didn't I?" he inquired.

"Yeah, I first ran into them in 76. They are extremely dangerous. Is the ambassador on the ship?"

"Oui, and he will remain with zee shipment during zee journey to Canada and until zee deal is completed. Once he has his compensation, zee ship will sail back to his country. He's currently on leave from his duties."

"But why bring them here to Canada, why not the States?" Taylor asked.

"Because our port security is considered more vulnerable than that south of the border. In addition, there is a perception that we have some considerable loopholes in our customs legislation," Brown pointed out.

"Dat is why dey are coming to Canada. Dey have already left about tree days ago," he added.

"So, that means they would arrive here tonight around midnight. The group supplied the goods, and the syndicate will make the transaction with the terrorists," Patrick said.

"Oui. Tell zee Shadow Chaseur to be extremely careful because of zee danger both to him and to zee city," Hawk added.

"He will. Thank you for the report, Hawk," Brown said.

"It's always a pleasure to help. Bonne chance, mes amis." And the screen went blank.

"What's the game plan, Art?" Taylor asked.

"Patrick, get me a layout of the harbour. I want to know which port the Saudi ship will be docking in," Brown ordered.

"Understood," he replied, and then he left the room. Brown looked at his friend.

"Alex, get on NIGHT and see what you can dig up on this Saudi ambassador," he said.

"Right on it. What are you going to do?"

"Get the suit ready and wait. Once we have what we need, then it will be time to call our boy to do some house cleaning," Brown said. While Taylor worked on the computer, Brown entered the vault to prepare the combat suit for its greatest test.

Another busy night at Fresco Café Grill as Kevin and Tommy walked inside for a warm cup of coffee, and a chance to catch up on lost time. In the past, the two friends were there on a constant basis, but after Chloe's death and Kevin's departure to Japan, Tommy just felt the place wasn't the same without his friend. Even though it's been over a month since Kevin's return from Japan, they only went out twice, and both times to the grill. Tommy knew Kevin had changed, but he kept silent. He feared Kevin would go further into isolation. Kevin sat at their usual table toward the left-hand corner of the pub while Tommy grabbed two menus from the main counter.

"Here ya go, sir." Tommy smiled and handed Kevin the menu.

"Most kind, my good man," Kevin returned the smile, and Tommy sat across from his friend.

"It's great we're finally getting to do this again, Kev. It's been long time."

"I know, bud. I'm sorry I have been neglecting you all lately. I'm just trying to adapt to my new job. You know I wasn't trying to avoid you guys."

"I know, bud. I just wish Margaret's dad would give you some time off. Especially that stoneface doctor friend of his. He gives me the creeps," Tommy said; his skin tingled just thinking about Brown.

"He's not a bad guy, Tommy. He just takes some getting used to." Kevin smiled. A familiar friend walked next to them, wearing a waitress uniform.

"Here is something I like to see. Two great guys hanging out here again," Julie said, opening her pad.

"Hey, Jewel." Kevin's face radiated with joy. "How's the shop's prettiest waitress doing tonight?"

"Not too bad, hun." She smiled. "What can I get you both tonight?"

"Just a coffee for me," Kevin said.

"Same here, but add one of those ham and Swiss sandwiches for me," Tommy added.

"One coffee for homecoming guy and a regular for his faithful sidekick," Julie teased. "Coming right up, gents." She left the table and headed for kitchen. Tommy noticed the look in Kevin's eyes; for he knew his friend had feelings for Julie.

"So, Kev, why don't you make your move?"

"What do you mean, Tommy?"

"I mean she fought with jerk-face again. You're back now, bud. You can make a move. I'm certain you could get her."

"If it were only true, bud. But right now, she don't need me trying to satisfy my feelings, and I have a lot on my plate right now," Kevin said, trying to ignore the subject.

"You're working for Taylor, not living a monk's life, man. Get with it." Kevin tried to change the subject.

"How about you and Tina?"

"Well, she's still kinda hurt about what happened to her and Dave. I will try to ask her out, but I want to give her time," Tommy said.

"Well, don't take long, bud," Kevin warned. "Or you will become like me, alone."

"I know you love and miss Chloe, but you can't stay like this, man. She wouldn't want you to," Tommy said. Kevin remained silent and turned his head towards the big screen TV.

"The game is on," Kevin said, changing the subject again. Tommy followed Kevin's lead. Before they could talk about the game, Julie brought the order to them.

"Here you go, guys." She smiled.

"Thank you, Jewel," Kevin said.

"Thanks, Julie," Tommy replied.

"No problem, gents. Hey, Kevin, are you going to Margaret's pool party on Saturday?"

"Tomorrow? I don't know, Jewel. I may be busy."

"Come on, man. Live a little." Tommy took a huge bite from his sandwich.

Julie gave him a look with her teasing eyes and said, "Tommy is right, Kevin. I would like to see all of us go. Please."

"You know I can't say no to those eyes, dear. Alright, alright—I will go," Kevin said when the manager called for Julie.

"Julie, phone call for you."

"Okay, talk to you later, guys," she said, and left the area. Kevin smelled the fresh coffee from his mug, but aroma could not overcome the scent of Julie's perfume that remained in the air.

"See I told you, she wants you there. You know what that means?" Tommy said.

"It just means she wants the gang together that's all," Kevin stated.

"Sure, bud. If you say so," Tommy mocked. "So, what time are you working tonight?" And he took another bite from his sandwich.

"My night is cleared tonight," Kevin said until he felt the minor electric shock coming from the watch. "Or maybe not. I better phone in and see." Kevin got up from the table and went outside to use his cell phone. Within seconds, he received a reply.

"Sorry for the shock, kid. But we have a real situation on our hands. We need you here ASAP!"

"What's up?"

"Serious, real serious. What's your location?"

"I'm at Fresco."

"Alright, walk about a block or so east, and we'll pick you up there," Brown said. "See you in a few, kid." The line went dead.

I wonder what I am getting myself into. Kevin thought as he entered the coffee pub. Tommy had just finished his meal when Kevin approached the table.

"I have to run, Tommy. An emergency at the office has just come up. I'm sorry, buddy."

"That's okay, Kev. It was fun while it lasted." Tommy grinned. At that moment, both teens noticed Julie wiping a few tears from her eyes.

"What's wrong with Jewel?" Kevin asked.

"I dunno. She started to cry after she received that phone call," Tommy said.

"I better see what's wrong before I go. I'll see you tomorrow at Margaret's."

"You bet, see you later," Tommy said, and Kevin walked towards Julie.

"Hey, stranger. Why the tears?" Kevin asked, his voice docile.

"It's Chad, we had another fight. I will be okay."

"Listen, I have to run now, but I'll give you a shout tomorrow morning, okay." He smiled.

"I would like that. Thanks, Kevin, you're the best." She smiled.

"That's my girl," Kevin said. "See you later." And he ambled out of the coffee pub.

If this keeps up, Chad may be history. Then maybe I can try my luck once again. He remained pensive and walked away. Kevin Wolf knew, for the moment, his worries would have to remain in check; allowing Shadow Chaser to take control of the reigns towards the unknown road that Brown had in store for him.

Chapter 31

*T*wenty minutes after the call, Kevin took the elevator down to the Shadow Crypt. Kevin had been in this elevator a hundred times before, but this was the first time he had ever heard Brown so secretive about a night mission; that alone created a degree of anxiety and even a bit of fear in him. When the door opened to the command centre, Kevin knew he would soon understand 'why'.

"Hey, Doc. What's up?"

"Have a seat, kid. We are in major trouble," Brown said.

Kevin complied with his teacher's instruction and said, "Your voice says it all, Doc. You have my full attention. What are we up against?"

"I just received word from one of our G7 agents that a Saudi vessel is sailing into Toronto, and it is carrying weapons and a significant shipment of enriched uranium."

"G7? Oh, right, the seven agents who provide eyes and ears for the Shadow Chaser. Patrick is in command." Kevin smiled.

"Boy you catch on fast, kid," Brown said, mimicking some of Kevin's sarcasm. "But seriously, we are in trouble. We've established that Saudi Arabia's Interim Ambassador to Canada has connections to the Group of 13."

"Who are they?"

"They are an ancient guild of extremely violent thieves, murderers, and extortionists from the Dark Ages, according to legend. They are the driving force behind the underworld on our planet. Not all gangs and mobs are associated with them, but a chosen few are permitted to join the Thirteen," Brown explained. "The descending numbers represent levels of power within the organization. Number one is known as the Overlord, and the others members two through thirteen fill out the hierarchy. The majority of the general population has no knowledge of this secret society or believes the group's existence is simply a myth. But believe me, they are for real."

"So, they're in control of the ship, and they're sending the goods here. Using the diplomatic powers this guy of theirs has, customs will not open those crates labeled as diplomatic property," Kevin added.

"You catch on quick, kid. That's right, so they will not be intercepted by the coast guard. But they are bringing them here to Canada because the perception is that security is not as beefed up here as it is in the States. The ambassador will be staying on the ship and will be returning to the Middle East with the crew."

"So, is the group here as well?"

"No, the Scorpio Syndicate will arrange the shipment and financial transfers for them here. They are affiliates of the Thirteen."

"Oh, nifty, that's Cassidy's gang. How long have they been between the sheets together?"

"After my last mission against the syndicate and the death of Stavros, the syndicate was in the middle of a gang war, and they were in a serious decline. One of the top lieutenants from Scorpio came from out of nowhere and assumed control of the syndicate. Realizing he couldn't win the war alone, he arranged a meeting with the Group of 13."

"How did he know about them if it's a secret guild?"

"Well, Stavros knew about their existence because his mentor made the mistake of picking a fight with the group. Stavros took the opportunity to contact the Thirteen, offering to kill his boss, and in return for immunity for the syndicate. They agreed, so Stavros killed his boss and assumed the leadership role in Scorpio. And the group left him alone."

"What a piece of work Stavros was."

"He sure was, now this 'One' person is no better, in fact he's worse. His boys will be arranging the sale, and the buyers are cell members of a very dangerous terrorist sect, Kevin."

"If they get their hands on that uranium, they will try to make a nuke," Kevin said, his face turned chalk white.

"They also have the blueprints to make suitcase-sized nukes. If they are able to deploy them, a lot of people will die. Many, many innocent people will die," Brown said, then paused.

"They are not going to die, Doc, because we are going to stop them." Kevin rose from the chair. "Just tell me the name of the ship, where they are docking, and what time."

"The ship is called the Shiva's Bead, and it's docking in pier 14 in the harbour. The ship is due to dock at midnight, but I want to wait until the whole crew arrives, so we can nail them all to the wall," Brown said.

"I understand." Kevin nodded, and he walked towards the vault. "Doc, do you think Cassidy will be there?" Brown looked at his young student.

"I don't know, kid. But right now, the shipment is more important than your quest for vengeance. Put Cassidy to the back of your mind and concentrate on the task at hand. We can't allow another terrorist attack to occur."

"I know, Doc. This time it won't happen," Kevin said.

"Oh, and, kid—don't always rely on your suit to get you out of trouble, that's why you were trained in the Shadow Art."

"I know what you mean. The magnetic effect didn't work during my battle with the Head Hunter in New York. The blade of his axe did nick my shoulder," he said, feeling his recent war wound.

"That's because the blade was made from granite as opposed to steel. And the diamagnet does not work on granite. Don't assume anything in combat."

"I'm beginning to learn quickly, Doc," he replied. "Now, if you will excuse me, I have some terrorists to catch." Kevin entered the vault and suited up for his most challenging and most dangerous mission.

Shadow Chaser spent the last two hours scouting the harbour and the pier, hoping his surveillance would pay off. His suit provided a great deal of protection from the frigid night air. The smell and the waves of the water brought with them a sense of serenity, but only for a fleeting moment. Thoughts of the mission ahead brought him back to reality. *How could something so peaceful bring fourth so much terror?* He expected the ship would soon arrive. The first hour and a half went by without incident. But over the last thirty minutes, several groups of men arrived, getting out of three separate vehicles. They entered the warehouse as the ship moved closer to the pier. Without delay, Shadow Chaser contacted Brown in stealth mode.

"Doc, we have company."

"I see them, kid, from the monitor. Can you fasten a bug onto one or two of them?" Brown asked. The dark hero aimed his right hand towards one of the men and clinched his fist like a boxer.

"Got him in my sights," he said. With a quick flick of the wrist, he fired a device, and it lodged itself in the back of the target's jacket. Colour-recognition sensors allowed the device to blend with the colour of the thug's coat. "He didn't even feel a thing."

"Okay, kid. Now, we listen and wait for the rest of them to arrive," Brown said. The duo watched the ship docking and the unloading of the crates. The dealers ordered their goons to move the shipments of both illegal and legal goods into the warehouse. They were opening the doors when the young vigilante had an idea.

"Doc, I have five nano-cams left, I can fire them on the four crates while they are being carried inside, so we can get a better view than just my x-rays and the audio from the bug," he pitched.

"Good thinking, kid. Just make sure they don't notice you."

"I'll be careful." He fired one nano-cam at each passing crate. Each time, the device blended with the colour of the crates, mimicking the traits of a chameleon. He fired the final one just inside the building at precisely the moment when the door closed. The device grazed the door and made an almost inaudible sound.

"*tick!*"

"What was that?" one of the thugs asked.

"It's just the door behind us, Carl, a creak in the hinge, or two pieces of wood in the door rubbing together. Lennox is outside guarding the front. He would have yelled if something was wrong," he replied.

"Yeah, you're right," he said. "We better finish this before Johnnie Eyes gets here." And the door closed. The dark guardian got lucky on that last shot.

"Too close. Way too close." He took a deep breath and exhaled. "Doc, are you getting anything?"

"Yes, I am. The last one hit a wall inside, and I have a good view of them all," Brown said. "I'm patching the signal to your visor." From the corner of his left eye, the young vigilante surveyed the room. After listening to some conversation for a few minutes, he contacted his mentor for further insight.

"They keep on talking about Johnnie Eyes. Do we have a file on him?"

"Funny you should ask that, I just got NIGHT to display his profile," Brown said. "Jonathan Myers, aka Johnnie Eyes. He's one of the top lieutenants in the syndicate. Only Franky Dice is higher up than this guy. He's a dangerous and formidable foe. Watch out, he's psychotic."

"Dealing with maniacs and killers is a part of my job description, Doc," he replied when another vehicle drove in front of the warehouse. Two men jumped out of the car and opened the back door. A tall man with a fancy suit and a fedora stepped out. The three men walked towards the guard.

"Lennox, has everything been arranged for our clients?"

"Yes, sir, Mr. Myers. Everything is in there, and the guys are waiting for you inside," the guard said.

"Good boy, Lennox. You keep your eyes open and let our clients in."

"But, sir, what are we going to do with the legal goods? The Saudis are expecting them."

"The ambassador will notify the consulate to pick up the goods in a few hours. By then, the deal will be done, and we will be long gone," Johnnie said. "Oh, and, Lennox, please remember to use the password." He looked at his watch before he entered the building. His entourage followed him inside.

Lennox replied, "Yes, sir." Shadow Chaser looked on and waited for the clients, which of course were the terrorists, to arrive, so he could put an end to this distressing situation.

"It's almost one in the morning. What's taking them?"

"Take it easy, kid. They'll be here. When they arrive, do not attack them right way. Let them go inside the building. Once they make the sale, we go in.

With our surveillance equipment, we will have some bonus evidence against theses bastards; then we will nail them."

"Alright, Doc. Just getting a bit edgy." In that same moment, a different car drove in. "Hello, it looks like we have the final piece of the puzzle, Doc." Four men, Middle Eastern in origin, walked towards the door.

"The sons of freedom are here to walk on the path of victory," one of them said. Lennox knew they had the correct password. He wrapped at the door three times, and a buzzing sound followed.

"What is it?" the voice on the speaker asked. Lennox gave them the password, and within seconds, the door opened. The four clients walked inside, and Lennox returned to his position. Both Brown and Shadow Chaser listened to the conversation that transpired inside the room.

"Mr. Jaffer. So good to see all of your associates with you here tonight," the voice said.

"Thank you, Mr. Myers. Now, I trust you have our merchandise," the client asked.

"Of course, Mr. Jaffer. It's right here. We have the firearms you need and the chemicals; I didn't forget the supply of anthrax and vials of smallpox. And last, but not least, the main dish, the piece de resistance, the enriched uranium." Johnnie smiled and opened the crates. "You have enough uranium there to make two bombs or twenty mini-bombs for suitcase nukes; which we have the plans for right here."

"Victory is at hand! We will crush the infidels and win our war against the West, bringing their governments to their knees," Jaffer exalted, and his friends smiled along.

"Of course you will, but first our payment," Johnnie said.

"Here is our account number," he said. "My brother Abdul will transfer the three hundred million dollars to your account." Abdul took out the laptop, logged in, and began the transfer.

"Excellent," he replied with zeal. "Carl, give them our number." The henchman stepped in front of the computer and typed in a code.

"Transfer will be completed in fifteen minutes," he said.

"Well then, Mr. Jaffer, that will give us time to enjoy each other's company," Johnnie said, and they all laughed. Meanwhile, Brown contacted the young vigilante.

"Okay, kid. We have what we need, now is the time to act."

"I'm on it," he said and turned off his stealth device. *"Now, it's my turn!"* Shadow Chaser fired his grappling launcher. The cable hissed across the sky, and the hook lodged itself into a rugged roof beam supporting the building adjacent to the warehouse. After securing one end of the cable, he snapped on a special trolley, adjusted the handle, and gave the cable a tug. Grabbing the zip line, he glided towards the structure. Once on the rooftop, he surveyed the area one more time. Lennox, unaware of the coming assault, kept his stare on the gigantic ship. Shadow Chaser still had the advantage for now. *If I can put him to sleep, I can bring him back up here and extract the password from him.* He thought. Using his blending ability, he made a slow descent from the roof tight against the wall, just behind Lennox. The thug didn't notice a thing as Shadow Chaser took him by surprise. He gagged and subdued Lennox before he had a chance to respond. A pellet of knock out gas ensured that Lennox fell fast asleep, enabling Shadow Chaser to haul him to the same rooftop for a further interrogation. Time became his main adversary, with the arms dealers and the terrorists ten minutes away from completing the transaction. Shadow Chaser activated a holo-sphere and utilized smelling salts to revive him. The little sphere emitted a laser-like beam that transferred thought suggestions directly into his neurons, interacting with his brain waves. The images created had Lennox believing he was dangling from the top of the CN Tower.

"What am I doing here?" he screamed. Then he looked into the red eyes of the Shadow Chaser.

"I want information from you, and you are going to give it to me, or I will drop you now." Shadow Chaser held onto him with one hand in the air.

"What do you want to know? I will tell you! Just don't kill me!"

"Alright then. Tell me your name?"

"My name?"

"Yes, you idiot, tell me your name!"

"It's Lennox Alders," he cried in terror.

"Stop your whining. Now say it again calmly like this; it's me Lennox, let me in." Shadow Chaser dangled him in the air and screamed, *"Say it."*

"Okay, okay, it's me Lennox, let me in," Lennox replied. Little known to the mortified thug, Shadow Chaser's voice equalizer recorded his voice patterns, so the dark guardian could replicate his words and sounds.

"Good little boy. Now, what's the password? Not the terrorists' password, yours!"

"I can't tell you that! They will kill me!"

"You brain dead fool. I will kill you right here if you don't tell me," Shadow Chaser said, and started to lose his grip on Lennox. *"My grip is slipping."* And moved his fingers away one by one.

"Alright," he screamed for his life. "I will tell you. The hawk soars to the sun!"

"Thanks, have a nice trip!" Shadow Chaser released his grip, and the thug dropped to the floor. But Lennox believed he was falling to his death.

"Noooo," he yelled. Lennox's back landed hard onto the ground, but he found himself on top of the roof next to the warehouse.

"You bastard, you tricked me!"

"So I have." Shadow Chaser knocked him out with a rapid jab. After he tied him up, Shadow Chaser jumped off the roof, his jacket morphed into his cape, and he glided to the surface. Landing like a feather next to the door, he

noticed he had three minutes left before the transfer would be complete. He decided to launch the attack. He rang the intercom and waited for a reply.

"What it is it?" the voice asked. The dark guardian's voice equalizer, set and ready for action.

"The hawk sores to the sun. It's me Lennox, let me in," Shadow Chaser said in Lennox's voice.

"Alright." The door unlocked. Without a thought, Shadow Chaser kicked it open.

"What was that?" one of terrorist wondered, and they spotted a black warrior with red eyes knocking out two of Johnnie Eyes's men.

"You're not Lennox," one of them shouted.

"No, I am not; but I did stay at a Holiday Inn last night." Shadow Chaser laughed. Before the shooter could react, Shadow Chaser jumped over the goon and back-kicked him in the shoulders—sending him into the crates and burying another thug beneath them. Johnnie Eyes and the rest of them ran towards the noise to find three of his men knocked out—and the other one buried.

"I remember you," he shouted. "You're Shadow Chaser."

"It's nice to be loved. Now, I hate to ruin your fire sale. But you see, I have this thing about innocent people getting killed while monsters like you make money. So, consider this your Going-Out-of-Business sale," Shadow Chaser said, his voice chilled the room. But despite his threat, the four terrorists took out their weapons and fired.

"Kill the infidel," one of them screamed.

"You heard the man, boys," Johnnie said with gusto. "Kill the freak." And they fired at the red-eyed warrior. Shadow Chaser activated his magnetic/diamagnetic device, and the bullets began to fly everywhere while he ran towards them.

"The bullets are flying towards us, boss. Tony is hit," one of them cried out.

"Cease fire," Johnnie yelled. "Grab him."

"You want to spar with me boy, sounds like fun." Shadow Chaser jumped over them and took out his rod. Landing on his feet, the rod extended and he began to fight all seven of them. But the terrorists continued to fire their guns.

"You dummies. He can deflect them," Johnnie yelled, but they ignored his warning.

Shadow Chaser replied, *"I have to take them out and fast!"* With all speed, he dropped several mist capsules. The huge mist engulfed the room.

"I can't see a thing," one of the thugs cried out as Shadow Chaser skulked right behind them.

"That's funny, I can see you two clowns quite well," Shadow Chaser said before he knocked them out with a double forearm smash. He sprinted towards the terrorists.

"I cannot see a damn thing, Abdul," he shouted, and then two red eyes appeared out of nowhere.

"I'm not Abdul, but I think you know that, ugly." Shadow Chaser disarmed him. Using his staff like a baseball swing, he sent him flying towards the wall. Abdul heard the noise, but could not see a thing.

"Hussein, where are you?" Abdul continued searching for his brother. But before he could call out his brother's name for a second time, a body flew right at him.

"Arghh!" The brothers collided with each other and fell hard onto the floor.

"Hey, Abdul. Your brother was looking for you. It looks like you found each other." Shadow Chaser laughed and looked at the two of them lying there unconscious. Brown contacted Shadow Chaser from his com-link.

"Don't get too cocky, kid. This is going too easy. Never underestimate your enemies," Brown warned.

"What show are you watching, Doc? I'm walking away with the prize here," Shadow Chaser boasted.

"Focus on the mission damn it! You have seven more to deal with, including the terrorists."

"I'm on it, Doc. The computer is in front of me. If I can get close to it, could you freeze their accounts, so the police could identify and access them?"

"Consider it done."

"No one is near the computer, and I have two minutes left of mist," Shadow Chaser said, approaching the computer. *"There is still thirty seconds left before the transfer is complete."* Extending his right hand, a small cyber cable extended forward out of his glove, and it connected to the computer.

"What do you mean two minutes? You have five capsules left!"

"I used them all to create a bigger fog."

"One capsule alone would have done that, now what are you going to use if you get into trouble?" Brown pointed out to the rookie vigilante.

"Nothing is gonna happen, Doc. I'm in control of the situation," Shadow Chaser proclaimed.

"I hope you're right, hero," Brown said. "Okay, kid. I have the computer, and I'm hacking in. Transfer is now frozen. We have the money for the cops. Now get back to work."

Shadow Chaser replied, *"Yes, sir."* But unaware to Shadow Chaser, the huge mist travelled at an accelerated pace towards the smashed door, leaving a vacuum of air outside to clear the room. Behind him, one of the thugs approached an opened crate.

"He's killin' us! There must be somethin' in here to kill him with." He scanned the inside of the crate and found a silver case. He snapped back the clasps and opened the case. The item caught his attention, and his eyes were hungrier than a lion after its prey.

"It looks like a bazooka! This must be your lucky day, Stewie. Now, the freak is gonna get it," he smiled to himself, crediting his discovery, and grabbed the weapon from the crate.

Shadow Chaser, still unaware of the impending danger, noticed the mist had dissipated.

"I still have a minute left. What's going on?"

Brown replied, "Your mist went out the door so to speak. Okay, so you lost your main concealment, and thanks to your little stunt, you're in the open," Brown said with aggravation. "But you still have several targets to take down. Get on with it and get out of there."

"I just love to hear you talk, Doc," Shadow Chaser said when he noticed one of the terrorists holding a knife.

"Tonight you die, Infidel!" he cried as he prepared to throw his hunter's blade at the young vigilante.

"You still haven't learned yet about my power!" Shadow Chaser laughed.

"Throw your fedora at him!" Brown intervened.

"No worries, Doc. I got this one!" Shadow Chaser said. Still behind from the ghost of justice, and thanks to the knife thrower, Stewie finally had the vigilante distracted.

He aimed for his back and said, "Say goodnight, big black!" And then he fired. But nothing seemed to have happened. Shadow Chaser was still standing. Shadow Chaser, unaware of what had happened, looked at the knife as the blade left the thrower's hand. At that precise moment, he noticed a quick flash emulating from his suit—and then all went black.

"What the?" he said, his voice equalizer had been disabled, and his red eyes faded. At the last second, he remembered the knife. *"Oh hell!"* But it was too late. If it were not for the distraction, he would have evaded the flying blade. Alas, the knife penetrated his suit and his right shoulder blade.

Meanwhile in the Shadow Crypt, Brown watched as the nano-cameras from within the building and Kevin's visor flashed into darkness, and his audio devices turned to static. His last view was the knife leaving the terrorist's hand. "Kid, respond! Respond," Brown yelled. "Damn it, Kevin! Respond!" But he received no reply. He lost his perception of the action, and worst of all, he lost Kevin.

"We have lost all contact with Kevin, doctor. I am unable to detect his bio-signs or any other activity within the building," NIGHT stated.

"Locate the source of the disturbance," Brown demanded.

"Unknown, doctor. The disturbance emulated from a power source that is not recorded on any known device on file," NIGHT replied. Taylor arrived to get an update on the mission, but noticed Brown in a panic state.

"What's wrong?" Taylor asked.

"NIGHT, locate Kevin's tracer! Launch Emissary to scan the area," Brown ordered.

"Acknowledged," NIGHT replied. Brown switched his com device to Patrick's frequency.

"Patrick, we have a situation. For some unknown reason, we have lost contact with the nano-cams, and we lost Kevin's signal."

"I'm on it," Patrick said before Brown glanced at Taylor.

"We have lost all contact with Kevin," he said with a stern tone.

"Oh my God!" Taylor said in shock. "Was Kevin in the building?"

"Yes, and the last image coming from his visor showed that he was under attack."

"So you're telling me you can't find him?" Taylor probed with a touch of anger in voice.

"I just told you that!" Brown fired back. Taylor waited for a brief moment to sum up the courage to ask his next question.

"Is he hurt?" Taylor probed, but Brown did not reply. "Damn it, Doc—answer me!" Brown maintained a dead stare and remained silent. Taylor, realizing the direness of their situation, asked the question he had always feared to ask.

"Is he dead?"

Brown swiveled back towards the screen and said with air of desperation. "I don't know."

Chapter 32

*M*inutes seemed like a merciless eternity for Brown and Taylor. Both men, unaware of Kevin's fate, tried desperately to find out what caused the disturbance that had severed communications between the vigilante and the Shadow Crypt. So far, NIGHT, the most advanced computer on the planet, had no explanation. Brown replayed the last recorded moments prior to the blackout. He had come to accept his successor and student was in grave peril. Brown tried in vain to reestablish communications with Kevin, but the silence screamed nothing but disaster.

"NIGHT, what is the ETA of Emissary?"

"Emissary probe will arrive at the scene in approximately two minutes," the computer replied. Brown switched his com-link to Patrick's frequency.

"Are you almost there, Shade?"

"I am about a minute away from the current location. I'm approaching the rear of the docks," he replied.

"Okay, get in position and let me know the moment you see or hear anything," Brown said with a concerned, but calm tone.

"Acknowledged." Taylor stared at the screen.

"What's going on out there?"

"I don't know, but we will find out."

"How could this have a happened? Is it a glitch from the suit?"

"It can't be. The suit was fully operational and performing with an eighty per cent power rating. The nano-cams are out as well. Something or someone has caused the blackout."

"Damn it! I hate being left, *literally*, in the dark," Taylor sneered. "I knew this was going to happen." Taylor had never made a secret of his opposition to Kevin's recruitment and warned Brown of the dangers his choice imposed upon the entire operation. But Brown was not in the mood to have Taylor point a self-righteous finger at him.

"Well, maybe next time you can inform me in advance since you appear to have a crystal ball perpetually at your disposal," he fired back.

"Damn it, Doc, we have placed a teen in the middle of a war. And we don't know if he is dead or alive," Taylor said. "What am I going to tell his mother? Oh, Mrs. Wolf, I'm sorry for the loss of your son. Oh, by the way, we turned him into Shadow Chaser, and sent him out to confront murderers and terrorists! We felt, as a mature teenager, he could handle the danger."

"He's not dead," Brown shouted; then he lowered his voice and glanced at the black screen. "He's not dead."

"How do you know?" Taylor said with force. "So, now it's you with the crystal ball."

"He can't be dead. He's a survivor, and he's been trained in the Shadow Art. A teacher feels these things. We'll get to him. We'll find him." Brown tried to focus his energy while glancing at the screen. "We have to find him."

"Well, I'm asking the police to move in," Taylor said, and grabbed his smart phone. Brown yanked it away from him.

"Are you crazy! They will take him in!"

"Better than having him dead!"

"This is not the stock market, man! We can't just cut and run at the first sign of trouble. We are at war. We need to give Patrick time to infiltrate the area." Reluctant to comply, Taylor turned away from his friend for a moment, took a deep breath, and nodded.

"Very well. We'll do it your way. I sure hope you know what you are doing."

"So do I." Brown let out a dispirited sigh.

Without warning, NIGHT said, "Receiving data from Emissary probe, doctor."

"On visual," Brown ordered. The screen activated and both men scrutinized the visual signal emitting from the probe.

"Emissary reports no power outages in the area." NIGHT said. "However, there is an electrical storm in the vicinity."

"Could the storm have caused the blackout?" Brown queried.

"Negative, doctor. The warehouse appears to be lit. Confirming the detection of bio-signs."

"Is one of them Kevin?" Brown said.

"Unknown, doctor. Probe is still two hundred metres from the programmed position and unable to differentiate between the bio-signs."

"When will be able to positively identify his bio-signs?"

"Once Emissary approaches forty metres, we will be able to capture an accurate data set and be able to distinguish between individual bio-signs," NIGHT explained when they received a hail.

"Crypt Keeper, it's Shade. Come in." Patrick said, using his code name.

"Crypt Keeper here! What's going on out there?"

"I'm closing in on the warehouse. It appears they are still in there. I am about fifty metres away, behind some crates and barrels. The front door is smashed open, must have been from Shadow Chaser's arrival."

"Do you see him?"

"It's hard to tell. The room appears to be lit up with lanterns. I do see a few of the suspects in a circle. They look like..." Patrick said, looking through his military binoculars, then hesitated.

"What do you see?" Brown asked.

"They've got SC. It looks like they have him restrained with metal chains. Do I have the green light to engage?" Patrick lifted his night vision goggles.

"No, Shade. There are too many of them. Not without backup," Brown said. Taylor looked at the screen and said, "Are there any other G7 agents in the area?"

"Negative, Provider. Shade is the only resource accessible," NIGHT replied before switching back to the probe. "Emissary is now sixty-five metres away and closing."

"Once Emissary is in range, we will be able to fill you in on what's going on inside, Shade," Brown said.

"Got ya, boss. In the meantime, I have plenty of concealment with these crates surrounding me. I'm going in for a closer look," Patrick said.

"Be very discrete, Shade," Brown said as NIGHT began the countdown. Taylor and Brown watched the visual probe closing in on the warehouse.

"Fifty metres," NIGHT continued. "Forty-five, forty-four, forty-three, forty-two." Before NIGHT could finish the countdown, they heard a thunderous clash.

"What the hell was that?" Taylor said.

"The screen just went blank," Brown said. "NIGHT report!"

"It appears a bolt of lightning may have struck the probe, positioned exactly forty-one metres away from the warehouse, doctor." Taylor noticed the link with Patrick had been severed as well.

"Shade! Shade! There's no answer. What happened to Shade?" Taylor said with a panicked tone.

"It appears his bio-signs were last recorded at approximately forty-one metres," NIGHT said.

"Could the explosion be responsible?" Taylor asked.

"Unknown. Both Shade and Emissary were close in proximity. However the storm could have played a role in the communications black out," NIGHT said.

"Son of a bitch!" Brown said with anger, and slammed his fist on the console.

"Profanity will not be productive in the current situation, doctor," NIGHT stated.

"Stick to the facts, NIGHT!" Brown exclaimed.

"Yes, doctor. The fact is, without the probe, we are unable to distinguish the individual bio-signs and obtain an accurate account of what is transpiring within the building," NIGHT explained.

"What about their computer we've hacked, NIGHT? Do we still have contact?" Brown inquired.

"Checking, checking….negative. I have additional information. I can confirm a lightning strike has caused a blackout in the area. Unable to achieve a successful connection. It's possible it may have been destroyed during the previous battle."

"Then it's back to square one. Damn it!" Brown exhaled.

Taylor glanced at Brown and asked, "What do we do now?" Brown kept his eyes on the black screen.

"We wait. And pray that Kevin remembers his training."

"What about Patrick?"

"The explosion of an Emissary probe would not likely cause a serious injury. But it could short circuit his com-link. It's a defence mechanism in case someone found one and tried to access stored information on the device. That way, no one could try to trace its origin or reprogram it."

"But he's left in the dark without us."

"Yes, he's in the dark, as are we."

"Okay let's just say Patrick is okay as you claim, but what about Kevin," Taylor pointed out. "What if he's unconscious?"

If that's the case, Patrick has only minutes to save him." Both voices hushed to a dead silence. They waited.

Patrick barely moved away from the fragments of what was left of Emissary. *Too close for comfort.* Patrick thought as he glanced at the debris on the ground and clicked on his com-link.

"Doc, Emissary was hit by a bolt of lightning. Wait, someone's on the move," Patrick said. "Five or six of them are carrying him towards the river." Patrick held his tongue for a brief moment. "They just threw him in." Patrick received no reply. "Crypt Keeper! Provider!" No response resonated from his request. "Damn it. It must have been the explosion. Well, I guess I am on my own." Patrick kept his eyes on the scene and waited for his time to strike.

Johnnie Eyes and four of his men had just tossed over their unwelcome intruder when four members of the terrorist sect approached them. The rain came down in buckets, soaking their clothes, but no water could wash away the stale stench of evil that corroded their souls.

"Who the hell was that guy?" Jaffer demanded.

"He's nobody. Just some freak in a black suit, but he won't be botherin' us anymore," Johnnie said.

"Your guys should have shot him," Jaffer said.

237

"Hello! Bullets were firin' all over the place and comin' back at us, remember! We don't need to attract any more attention down here. Your knife throwin' brother got lucky. Fortunately, for us, we were able to take him down with a few crowbars when he tried to remove the knife. After a few swings, he was out like a light. We tied him up in chains, and now he's swimmin' with the fishes. By the way, weren't you knocked out at the time? I didn't see ya offerin' up any insightful ideas when we could have used 'em," Johnnie said.

"So what if he was still breathin', I gua-ran-tee dat he ain't breathin' anymore."

"Well then, should we continue with our business?" Jaffer inquired, the rain fell harder than ever. "We are getting soaked just standing here."

"I thought ya'd never ask." Johnnie smiled. The same thug who had taken a shot at the Shadow Chaser, still carried the weapon he had grabbed from an insulated crate, headed towards his boss. His arrival could be distinguished by his clumsy, splashing feet.

"Stewie, nothin' damaged in the crates?" Johnnie asked.

"Nah, everythin' checks out, Johnnie. But this damn thing don't work. I tried to use it on the freak, and all it did was light up. It's still lightin' up," Stewie replied, examining the gun.

"Hey! Watch where ya pointin' that thing, ya dummy!" Johnnie scolded the lackey.

"If that's not working, we are not paying for it," Jaffer proclaimed as lightning danced across the sky.

Fuhgeddaboudit, Jaffer. We'll tell the boss, and he'll see you get a discount." Johnnie smiled.

"Very well, it is our wish that we continue the negotiations. Let's get out of this accursed rain." Jaffer and the rest of the thugs returned to the building. Johnnie stopped Stewie before he continued a step forward.

"You stay here and make sure the freak doesn't try to get back up to the surface."

"But Johnnie, my gun is in the warehouse, and all I have is this funny gun that does nuthin' but light up like a Christmas tree." The wind grew stronger, and the cool air made him shiver.

"Then throw it at him if he swims up," Johnnie said. "Quit yer worryin' will ya? We tenderized him like a steak at Billy's Butcher Shop. And the chains are gonna sink him to the bottom. So no worries. If you see bubbles coming up, then yell at us. But that's not gonna happen."

"But, Johnnie, it's freakin' rainin', and I don't have nothin' to cover up with. I don't want to catch pneumonia."

"Do you want to tell the One you didn't stay and guard the stiff because you were afraid to catch cold? You know what would happen to you."

"Okay, Johnnie, you made your point." he said. Johnnie gave him an annoyed look and returned to the warehouse. Not too far away from Stewie, hid Patrick who took one last peek around the perimeter before springing into action. The sound of the massive downpour slapping the concrete concealed the sound of his footsteps. Stewie spent most of his time playing with the various buttons on the weapon, unaware of the assault he would soon face. Quieter than a whisper, Patrick skulked behind Stewie and surprised him with a carotid sleeper hold. Stewie, trying to fight back, dropped the flashing weapon onto the concrete ground. The repeated claps of thunder acted as a silencer. Within a heartbeat, he fainted from the lack of oxygen. Patrick dropped him with a reluctant gentleness to prevent the buyers and sellers from hearing a sound. Out of instinct, he kicked the weapon into the river. The device started blinking as it released puffs of smoke before sinking to the bottom. To his astonishment, Patrick heard a signal from his com-link.

"Shade! Can you hear me?"

"Loud and clear. It's good to hear from you."

"What happened?"

"I was moving in when Emissary just whizzed by me. Before I could take another step, a bolt incinerated the probe, and I lost contact."

"Are you hurt?"

"Nah, but my ears are still buzzing. But that's not important. I have some news for you."

"I'm listening."

"*SC is in the brink, and he's still wrapped in chains. I may have to take a swim,*" he whispered. The dark water hid its secrets well. Patrick could barely see beyond his wavy reflection.

"We are not picking up any..." Brown said, then shouted, "Wait a minute. I can't explain this, but his costume is back online! And I am getting a faint bio-sign!" At that same moment, Patrick noticed a red glare ascending from the depths.

"I think I see him. But he's down deep."

"I have the suit back online, but he's still restrained," Brown said when they heard a faint cough.

"Kid, can you hear me?" Silence mitigated their hopes. The tension shattered when they heard a weak voice followed by a cough.

"Doc, the...oxygen...is...coming...back...to...the...mask. But I can't break these chains."

"Hold on, kid. I'm coming for you," Patrick said.

"It's too deep for you, Shade. Stand by." Brown switched his attention to the young vigilante. "Your suit is still repairing itself. Kid, where are your feet?" Brown asked.

"Towards the bottom. The water is so dark, Doc, I can't see the surface."

Brown, assessing the damage to the suit, noticed the teen's oxygen supply was running low.

"Okay, kid, I know you're disoriented, but we have a lot of damage to the suit. You have some oxygen now, but only for a few more minutes. Don't worry,

I'm gonna get you out of this. But you have to do everything I say," Brown said.

"No argument out of me," he replied with an air of uncertainty. "Doc, if I don't make it, tell my mom I love her."

Brown gave out a heartless reply. "Shut up, kid. Now, it's just like what you did in Japan. Position your body until your head is directed towards the bottom. Use your training to breath properly. Relax and meditate." The teen followed Brown's word to the letter, and was now looking further into the darkness. Brown activated the firing devices in Shadow Chaser's gloves; his target, a wooden pillar on the dock. "Brace yourself." The steel-like cables fired through the water like a spear gun. The streams propelled through the water until it connected with the pillar. Like a fish on a hook, his body lurched towards the surface. Shadow Chaser, uncertain of the vague images from his visor, felt a tug as Patrick grabbed the cable and pulled him onto of the wooden planks of the docks.

"Are you alright?"

Shadow Chaser spoke, but it sounded like gibberish. He removed his mouthpiece and coughed.

"Ah, air. Arrhhgh...argghhh," he groaned and spit out a combination of saliva and blood. "Thanks for the lift." His suit smelled of moss and some sewage. But the only odour he could perceive was the scent of unfinished business.

"My pleasure. What happened?"

"I don't know. One minute I was knocking them out like Barry Bonds, the next minute someone took away my steroids," Kevin said, attempting to stand. "What happened to the suit, Doc?"

"We don't know yet, kid. NIGHT is investigating." Taylor joined in the on the link.

"You gave us quite a scare, young man."

"Scared me, too, sir." Kevin felt a sudden burn emanating from his right shoulder. "What's going on?"

"Relax, kid. It's just the nanites cauterizing the knife wound. I'll fix you up properly upon your return."

"Well, those little buggers. They do love to burn a guy worse than a bad relationship."

"At least his sense of humour is back," Patrick said.

"All right then, you're safe. We'll call the police, and they can arrest them," Taylor said.

"No!" Kevin replied. "I still got a job to do."

"You can't be serious," Taylor said with astonishment.

"Damn serious, sir. I have this thing about people trying to kill me," Kevin replied as the rain pounded down stronger and the thunder exploded louder than war itself. "How bad is the suit, Doc?"

"It's at seventy per cent, and you can still double up your strength," Brown said. "But you have no weapons, kid?"

"I think I can supply him with a few," Patrick said. "I have some mist capsules and a holo-sphere we can use."

"All right then. Kid, you go through the front, and, Patrick, you engage from the back entrance. Let these bastards know they can't eliminate the ghost of justice," Brown said. Kevin connected his mouthpiece and activated the equalizer. Thunder cracked the battle cry of vengeance, and Shadow Chaser stared at the warehouse.

"Round two," Shadow Chaser said, and with that proclamation, the ghost of justice and Patrick headed towards the warehouse to spread the trap.

The deal between the terrorists and the syndicate had just been finalized and all that remained was for the merchandise to be received and transported by the terrorists. The light from the kerosene lanterns started to fade as a gale force wind blew through the front exit. Jaffer looked at Johnnie Eyes and smiled.

"Thank you for an interesting evening, Mr. Myers. We must do this again some time."

"Indeed, Mr. Jaffer. A pleasure doing business with you and your men." Johnnie returned the smile. Thunder rumbled, and the lighting flashed in all directions.

"Give my regards to the One. Now, if you will excuse us, we have a war to win," Jaffer said. Before Johnnie could answer, he heard something rolling across the ground.

"What's was that?" he said. Out of nowhere, a giant fog enveloped the room once more.

"Oh no, not again!" one of the thugs said with a touch of newfound anxiety in his voice.

"Oh yes, again!" Shadow Chaser said, the lightening flash shadowed him and amplified his red eyes. Turning around to face the dark stranger, the roof began to shake in front of their eyes. The building creaked and groaned.

"But you're dead. We killed you," one of the thugs yelled, trembling in terror while the rest of them stood mesmerized in horror. Water dripped from his fedora as the wind chilled their dark hearts with the Devil's fear.

"I have been dead before, but evil always resurrects me. Now it's your turn to face your fate," Shadow Chaser roared with vengeance.

"This cannot be!" Jaffer said in fear.

"Oh but it is, scum," Shadow Chaser said. The fog filled the entire room, and the ceiling crumbled. The men tried to protect themselves from falling debris. They were not aware the danger only existed in their very minds. The rolling sound came from a hollow-sphere that Shadow Chaser released before making his appearance. Just as he had created an illusion for Lennox earlier,

the rest of the crew now believed the roof was about to crash down on them. Patrick crashed through the back exit and fired a series of knockout darts at his confused foes.

"I can't see a thing," one of the men cried out as one by one they fell onto to the floor. Shadow Chaser began his frontal assault and took out the first two terrorists with a combination of punches and forward kicks. His shoulder burned from the pain, but his anger fueled his rage, and he continued with the attack. Within moments, both the terrorists and the syndicate members laid still on the dark, cold floor. The mist began to clear, and Patrick withdrew to the shadows, leaving Johnnie Eyes alone with the Shadow Chaser. Johnnie noticed the roof, still intact, and his associates on the floor defeated and cuffed. "You son of a bitch," Johnnie screamed. "You tricked us all. I swear to God, I'm gonna finish the job this time." And he took out a butterfly knife. Johnnie charged the vigilante, but Shadow Chaser removed his hat and threw it at the mobster's knife.

"Blades," Shadow Chaser commanded. The rim of the hat turned into rotating blades and sliced the blade from its handle. Johnnie could not believe what he had witnessed and stopped, just looking at the handle—in shock. Shadow Chaser flicked his wrist, and the fedora returned to him.

"What are you?" The thug asked, stunned with disbelief.

"I am a tortured soul that has lost much thanks to your kind," Shadow Chaser said. *"For I am your Reckoning."* He jumped in the air and delivered a kick to Johnnie's chest area. Johnnie flew two feet into the air before landing onto the floor. Shadow Chaser approached him and used his manacles on him. Before he vacated the scene of the crime, he sprinkled a number of scales of justice charms throughout the room.

"Not this time, boys," Shadow Chaser said. He tipped his hat for his own amusement and walked out of the warehouse. Patrick, already outside, waited for the ghost of justice.

"You did great, kid," Patrick said. Shadow Chaser saw another thug tied next to the door. Patrick smiled. "While you were dropping your charms, I moved old Stewie closer to the door." Shadow Chaser nodded and tapped his com-link.

"We're done here, Doc."

"I'm sorry Cassidy wasn't with this group, but we will get him," Brown said.

"That's okay, Doc. Call the cops and tell them about a pickup. Also, the ship is on its way back home. We can't let the ambassador get away."

"Already on it, kid," Brown said. "Shade, get his cycle back into the battle van. I've just disintegrated the nano-cams from the wall. Now let's get out of here before the police arrive." Shadow Chaser pressed his remote button on his belt, and his cycle arrived. By that time, Patrick had pulled the van up next to

Shadow Chaser. The young vigilante loaded the bike and what was left of Emissary into the van before speeding off into the stormy moonlight.

Chapter 33

*F*ifteen minutes after Brown placed the call to the police—they arrived at the scene. The storm vanished as swiftly as it had arrived, and the rain faded to a light drizzle. Parked in front of the building, four cruisers, two special units vans, and a team of bio-terrorism technicians surrounded the area. After receiving an anonymous tip, Constable Chan was the first on the scene. He updated Inspector Somerville and Special Agent Flynn on the limited information he had gathered. With one guy still tied next to the warehouse door, the officers entered the building with extreme caution. Inside, they found eleven members of the Scorpio Syndicate and the four terrorists tied with the same manacles as the one outside. They also spotted dozens of Shadow Chaser's trademark calling cards—gold charms. Chan met Somerville upon his arrival.

"He was busy tonight," Somerville said while the rest of the officers entered the room and found the entire shipment intact.

"We found one more, sir," Chan replied. "He was on the rooftop of the next building." And pointed at the other warehouse. "The caller's tip lead us right to him."

"I take it he was cuffed as well," Somerville said.

"Yes, sir," Chan replied.

"Thanks, Chan."

"Anytime, inspector," Chan said, and returned to his investigation. A thug in cuffs yelled while the police escorted him to the squad car.

"I tell ya, this guy is like the Devil. We killed him. We killed him I tell ya. And he came back and brought the roof down on us." The cop smiled at the suspect as he placed him in the back seat.

"The roof appears to be in good shape to me, fella. He must have brought in a contracting crew to fix it after knocking out the lot of you."

"Go ahead and laugh. I tell ya the freak is a monster. God forgive me," he begged as the officer slammed the back door.

"Yeah, yeah, we'll call ya a priest. Stupid crook. Must be too busy using what he's been selling," the officer said, and continued with his duties. The team inside the building found crates containing uranium, anthrax, and labeled vials of the smallpox virus, all of the vials remained sealed.

"Thank God, they didn't get their hands on this. It could have been disastrous," one of the bio-terrorism team members said. The officers began to take away the prisoners, and Flynn looked on with anger in his eyes.

"The freak got the best of us again!"

"Well, for once I'm glad he did. A lot of lives were saved," Somerville said.

"We will get him for meddling in our affairs."

"Flynn, he saved us from another terrorist attack. I know what he is doing is wrong, but I can't condemn him for this one. The coast guard caught the ship and the ambassador. I have to admit he saved us a lot of grief tonight anyway."

"Yes, he did good, but next time he won't get away. Believe me," he vowed before storming out of the warehouse. Somerville followed Flynn outside and noticed Johnnie Eyes on his knees with his hands cuffed behind his back with a number of his other associates.

"Well, well. It looks like we caught the biggest fish in the lake tonight." Somerville grinned. A young constable dashed towards the two senior officers.

"I think we found something, sir."

"Lead the way, constable." Flynn and Somerville followed the young officer towards the crime scene investigators.

"What have you got?" Flynn asked. The forensic expert showed him a transparent bag marked evidence.

"It's a hunter's knife covered in blood. But notice the black fabric that's around it," the expert said. "We found a few more pieces in close proximity to the knife. The fabric feels like some sort of synthetic skin."

"His costume perhaps?" Somerville queried.

"Even better, we have his DNA," Flynn said.

"Now all we have to do is find out if we have a match on file," Somerville said. Flynn stared daggers at him.

"We do. In 1986, a year before he disappeared, the FBI and the RCMP were closing in on him on the Thousand Islands Bridge. He was fighting some other costumed nut and got hurt. He bled quite a bit, but he escaped us both. Anyway, we took some samples and we have them on file. So let's match the blood to see if it's the same guy—or if we have a copycat on our hands," Flynn said.

"I'll make a few calls when we get back to the station. In the meantime, let's just keep this quiet," Somerville cautioned.

"Agreed. Okay, tag it and bring it to the lab, Terry," Flynn said.

"Yes, sir." The forensic expert nodded and continued searching the scene. Both men vacated the warehouse when they noticed Mike Smith arriving with his tape recorder and note pad.

"I hate that bloodhound," Flynn said. "You deal with him." Flynn brushed right past the reporter without any acknowledgement. Somerville was about to follow Flynn, but Smith hopped in front of him.

"Inspector, don't walk away yet. I heard Shadow Chaser was here. I understand he stopped terrorists from importing uranium?" he asked.

"I'm not commenting on it yet, Smith. See you at the press conference in the morning," Somerville said, and tossed Smith a charm. "Here, this is all I have to say. I have to go."

"Hey this is a gold charm, the scales of justice. It's from the Shadow Chaser, isn't?" he probed with the usual enthusiasm in his voice.

Somerville replied, "Good night, Mike." The inspector walked towards his car, stepped in, and sped away.

Chapter 34

*B*rown had spent the previous half hour tending to Kevin's battle wounds. Despite the apparent failure of the Mark II suit, the advanced garment still allowed him to survive a beating that would have killed an unprotected man. Suit or not, the harbour came close to putting an end to the teen's career and his life. Patrick entered the room to find Taylor at the controls.

"How's our boy?" Patrick asked.

"He's getting his wounds checked out by Doc," Taylor said as the profanity escalated and amplified from the medlab next door. "As you can tell, there appears to be somewhat of a difference in opinion. Two stubborn fools if you ask me."

"Mr. Taylor, the lad did fine. He saved the lives of thousands by stopping those terrorists from utilizing that uranium," Patrick explained. "We can all sleep better tonight."

"I know you're right, Patrick. But we have to be more careful in the future," Taylor said, his voice returned to a more docile tone.

"Did NIGHT find out what caused the suit to go nuts?"

"No. Doc's got it doing a massive search on all possibilities," Taylor said, and tilted the chair slightly. "In all honesty, we may never know." The medlab door opened and Brown stormed into the command centre.

"You got sloppy and it almost killed you!"

"Hey, your suit decided to take a vacation! I was doing all right." Kevin followed.

"You are an expert in the Shadow Art. Master Tanaka and myself saw to it that you could take advantage of your training, so you're not always relying on the suits, weapons, and gadgets."

"Well, I couldn't rely on the suit tonight that's for sure."

"This is not a game, kid. Next time stay focused, or you're dead. And our entire mission is compromised. We're a team. Remember your priorities."

"Are we done here?" Kevin said.

"Yes we are," Brown said and turned his attention to the computer.

"Great. I've taped your few lines, so I can upload them into my iPod. I can repeat them as a source of inspiration during my next go-around." Kevin stormed towards the door that led to the tunnel and exited the command centre.

"I'm going to follow him," Taylor said before he stood from his chair and followed the teen. Patrick remained silent until Brown sat on his chair.

"A little hard on the kid weren't ya?"

"He made rookie mistakes out there. Next time it may kill him."

"You could have at least said thanks for stopping a possible nuclear threat. The fact of the matter is he's still a rookie."

"I don't need to be lectured by you, Patrick."

"I'm not five years old anymore, Art. You know I am right."

Brown hesitated, but replied, "I just don't want him to suffer my fate."

NIGHT in his usual habit of interrupting a conversation stated, "I have just downloaded the police files, doctor. And I have come up with some significant new information."

"Don't keep us in suspense, NIGHT. Let it out, this isn't a drama contest," Brown said.

"It appears the police have some torn fragments of the Night Fabric and blood samples that likely belong to Kevin."

"Great, more good news!" Brown said in anger. "Keep us posted on any other news coming from the police network."

"Acknowledged, doctor." NIGHT ceased to communicate, leaving Patrick and Taylor alone with their thoughts.

"So what now?" Patrick asked.

"We need to get that DNA back before the results are stored into the national database."

"You mean break into the evidence room at the police station?"

"An evidence room, a lab, whatever. If we can infiltrate a room full of mobsters and terrorists, then a few cops and few locked doors should be a breeze," Brown said, and prepared his next move.

In the outskirts of the city, the One occupied a Victorian-style mansion that housed the secret sanctum of the Scorpio Syndicate. The powerful boss had just returned to the country after a long stay in Switzerland. During his stay, the Thirteen held an ancient ritual to officially knight him into the order. With his recent successes for the Group of 13, the Overlord supplemented his organization with additional resources to use at his discretion. After recently becoming a member of the select Thirteen, the One now felt he had garnered the necessary fear and respect he had earned. With his new rank, the group honoured him the mask of the brotherhood, a mask reserved for the council members of the Thirteen. The half-black, half-white gothic mask displayed the Roman numeral thirteen just above the eyes. A tradition the Thirteen followed since the early days of the sect. Each member wore the mask when they represented the group's interests or when they sat in council. The One now had an additional veneer to conceal his already mysterious identity. His anticipation outweighed his patience as he awaited word on how the deal had transpired, so he could provide the Overlord with an account of his most recent success and acquire his cut of the forty million dollars in royalties. Sitting in the shadows of his private study, two of his men entered the lighter part of the room to give him a report on tonight's endeavours.

"Franky, so good to see you again. How did it go tonight?" Franky looked at the lieutenant next to him and said with fearful hesitation.

"Sorry, boss. It blew up in our faces."

"I'm sorry to hear that," he offered in a deadpan tone. "What happened, may I ask? Did those Middle Easterners screw us?"

"It wasn't the Arabs, boss. This guy busted us. He was unstoppable. All of the guys are in jail, even the Arabs. Somehow, the guy was even able to freeze our bank account," the other thug said. "Kenny said that for a brief moment, our guys thought they had killed him, but he came back at full force. The cops got everything."

"Who took the lead in tonight's debacle?" the One yelled.

"Johnnie, sir. He's in jail, too," Franky replied.

"Have him killed. Get one of our guys inside to do it," the One ordered.

The thug replied, "Johnnie, you want Johnnie iced?" The One turned his head towards the thug. "Right, boss."

"So, who was this guy who disrupted our transaction?"

"It was him, boss," Franky said.

"Him? Who is 'him'?" he asked.

"The Shadow Chaser," Franky said.

"The Shadow Chaser," the One screamed like devil. "He's back." And he knocked over his desk, crashing lamps, cocktails, and documents onto the floor.

"Don't worry, boss, we almost killed him this time. We will get him. He is only one man," the thug said.

"One man," he growled like a mad dog. "The refuge of all darkness can be dispelled by just one shed of light." The One reached into the top drawer in his overturned desk, took out his gun, and fired at the goon. The thug collapsed onto the floor, stone dead. The stench of gunpowder permeated the room. "I don't wish to hear any more excuses. Almost killed, almost killed." The One grinded his teeth in anger. "Franky, leave me now. And take this lump with you. I gotta make a call." Franky grabbed the thug, the warm blood still oozing like a fountain from the bullets lodged in his abdomen, and walked out of the room. The One grabbed the phone from the floor and dialed the Overlord.

"Honoured one, we have a problem. The Shadow Chaser has returned, and he has obstructed this evening's shipment," the One said. "We lost everything." A man known for invoking dread in his men and his enemies, the One now became fearful of subjecting his master to that same level of disappointment and awaited the Overlord's response.

"I am already aware, Member Thirteen. It's unfortunate this has happened this evening. May I ask what you've done with your man responsible?"

"He will be put to death, I have already seen to that."

"Well done. As for Shadow Chaser, we will meet in forty-eight hours to discuss this problem. He has ruined our plans in the past, and we can't allow him to run amok in our operations."

"Then, I will return to Switzerland immediately."

"No need, I've already dispatched six members of the group to visit you at your residence. We will discuss our plan there. I'll join you via video conference. Until then, Member Thirteen."

"Until then, Honoured one," he said, and hung up the phone with a trembling hand.

"Shadow Chaser, do you want to come back and fight? Very well, I look forward to a face to face confrontation. I swear you will not survive our next encounter," the One vowed, "our next meeting shall be your last." And then he stared into the darkness that consumed both the room and his soul.

At this moment, both the hero and the villain knew the war between them had just begun.

Check out some of the best writers, artists, and creators in independent publishing.

From the creative mind of Dan Barnes comes a new hero. In Studd City, he spreads hope as Father Gabriel by day, and by night, he fights the crime as Vatican: The Angel of Justice! http://www.vaticancomic.webs.com. Visit Tree Frogs Comics: http://www.facebook.com/pages/TREE-FROG-COMICS/293165938174?ref=mf.

Enter the universe of writer/artist Jade Arcade. He is the creator of the Circus Arcane™ series. http://www.jadearcade.com.

Check out the best-kept secret of the comic world. Author and illustrator Jay Piscopo is the mastermind behind The Undersea Adventures of Capt'n Eli all-ages graphic novel series. Check out the adventures here: http://www.captneli.com.

A new mage has arrived in the fantasy world of comics. His pencil will mystify you. Check out the works of Danny Kelly. http://www.facebook.com/pages/The-Art-Of-Danny-Kelly/312132716954.

Canadian sensation Patrick E. Charette is an up-and-coming artist who brings his own style to the art world. His work is available at http://www.charettesartgallery.webs.com.

Thank you all for supporting independent publishers, writers, and artists.

www.ingramcontent.com/pod-product-compliance
Lightning Source LLC
Chambersburg PA
CBHW050501260626
47157CB00004B/1140